D1012845

VINDICATION

Also by H. Terrell Griffin

Matt Royal Mysteries

Mortal Dilemma
Chasing Justice
Found
Fatal Decree
Collateral Damage
Bitter Legacy
Wyatt's Revenge
Blood Island
Murder Key
Longboat Blues

Ethan Fitzgerald Novels

The Assassin's Game

Nonfiction

Thrillers: 100 Must-Reads (contributing essayist)

VINDICATION

A MATT ROYAL MYSTERY

WITHDRAWN

H. TERRELL GRIFFIN

Copyright © 2018 H. Terrell Griffin

All rights reserved. No part of this book may be reproduced in any form or by any electronic or mechanical means, including information storage and retrieval systems, without permission in writing from the publisher, except by a reviewer who may quote brief passages in a review.

This book is a work of fiction. Names, characters, businesses, organizations, places, and incidents either are the products of the author's imagination or are used fictitiously. Any resemblance to actual events, businesses, locales, or persons living or dead, is entirely coincidental.

ISBN 978-1-60809-276-5

Published in the United States of America by Oceanview Publishing
Longboat Key, Florida
www.oceanviewpub.com

10 9 8 7 6 5 4 3 2 1

PRINTED IN THE UNITED STATES OF AMERICA

Jean
Always and until the end of time

ACKNOWLEDGMENTS

MY FRIEND PEGGY Kendall has been involved in my books from the beginning. The year was 2003, the place, a little bar called Tiny's that squatted in the corner of the parking lot of a small shopping center on the north end of Longboat Key, Florida. I had decided that my wife, Jean, was right, and it was time for me to tie myself to a chair and write the book I'd been talking about since she'd first become my sweetheart way back in my college days.

With a lot of trepidation, I announced to my friends in the bar one night that I was going to write a mystery novel. That drew much laughter, but it quickly dissolved into a semi-sober discussion that primarily involved the naming of the characters. Peggy and her husband, Dave, were part of that group. Most of the regular characters who have populated the ensuing eleven Matt Royal mysteries are based on people who were in the bar that night, and I might add, many subsequent nights.

Peggy and Jean formed what I think of as the dynamic duo who listen to my ramblings, add intelligent thought, read my scribbles as they exit the computer, edit my words, encourage me with love and laughter and sharp-edged comments, and generally treat me as they once did their teenaged sons. I couldn't do this without them. They have been an invaluable asset to me during the writing of each of the Matt Royal novels.

After Peggy's husband, Dave, died in 2009, she moved to The Villages. It was she who came up with the idea of placing this story in her new hometown, that pleasant community of retirees in North Central Florida. Peggy, along with her neighbors Patty and Bob Geoghegan, shared their time and knowledge of the area with Jean and me during the month we lived in The Villages when I was just beginning the writing of this book.

Tim Harding, a real estate agent without peer, shared his encyclopedic knowledge of The Villages with me and was always ready to take my calls to answer any questions as they arose. If there are mistakes in this book regarding The Villages, they are mine, not Tim's. He knows his community.

Then, there is my Starbucks cabal, my good buddies Lloyd Deming, Mark Bailey, and David Gilbert. They also listen to me and give me advice on plots and often ground me so that I don't get off on tangents that won't work. Envision, if you will, four old guys in the corner of a coffee shop, milling about, scissors in hand, trying to work out how to best kill someone with a pair of left-handed scissors. It was vivid enough that I decided to change the murder weapon in this book to a pistol.

David has served the Miss Florida Pageant as a board member for decades and it was his idea that started me on the plot of this novel. He shared his vast knowledge and resources of pageant life as it is now and as it was forty years ago. He saves everything and stores most of it, I think, in his car. Again, if there are mistakes in my writing about the pageant, they are mine, not David's.

The eleven baristas of the Maitland Starbucks, where I do much of my writing, always take care of us. They are unfailingly polite to all their customers in what has become a friendly small-town gathering place. They represent the best of our young people, many of them working diligently on college degrees as they concoct every coffee drink known to modern man and some that are unknowable. With their permission, I have used each of their names as characters in this book.

Finally, big thanks go to my readers, my family, and the men and women of Oceanview Publishing, particularly Bob and Pat Gussin, Lee Randall, and Emily Baar. None of this would be possible without you.

PROLOGUE

THE WOMAN'S BODY lay facedown on the concrete dance floor of Paddock Square. The bullet had punched a small hole in her blouse and burrowed deep into her back. The thin garment was stained by the trickle of blood that had seeped out in the brief moment that had elapsed between the bullet's entry and the instant of her death. A young man was bent over the woman, his fingers probing in vain for a pulse in her neck.

Except for the body and the man, the square was empty. Soon, the solitude would give way to the joggers, walkers, and cyclists; retirees getting their exercise in hopes of extending the lives they enjoyed in this unique place. A few hours later, the stores and restaurants that defined the square would open for business.

The March sun was beginning its quotidian climb into the Florida sky, its rays reaching silently for the roofs of the buildings that composed the eastern boundary of the town square known as Brownwood. The air was clean and a little chilled and carried the strident calls of unhappy crows that had settled on the roof of a nearby structure.

The young man stood, his face drawn by the sadness that penetrated to his bones. He had once been a soldier and had seen more death than most people see in a lifetime. Most of the dead were young, and this woman wasn't old. Early sixties maybe, perhaps younger. A waste. Each body was one more straw on the proverbial camel's back, and someday the final straw would find its way into his psyche. Then what? He shook off the feeling of dread and used his cell phone to call 911.

CHAPTER 1

MACON, GEORGIA – LATE 1960S

FILTERED SEARCHLIGHT BEAMS painted the building in soft pastels as they roamed across its face. Other beacons were pointed at the sky, their light dissipating high in the darkness of a summer evening. The Doric columns that lined the front and sides of the classical revival building added a touch of dignity to the evening's events.

Men dressed in suits and ties and women in long dresses were streaming through the front doors. The discordant sounds of an orchestra tuning up slipped from the building and created a pleasant din as they conflated with the murmur of conversation among those waiting on the sidewalk. Saturday evening at the City Auditorium in Macon, Georgia, the night of the final round in the annual Miss Georgia Pageant. A sense of excitement and anticipation permeated the air and infused the guests with a sense of well-being.

Backstage, fifty young women from all over Georgia were preparing for the big night, the night the winner would be chosen. It had been a grueling few days that started on Monday when they began the process of interviewing privately with the judges. The contestants would receive scores from one to ten in each of the events, and the women knew the interview would count for 25 percent of the total score for the week. It was important that each made a good impression, and they dressed and conducted themselves in a manner that would hopefully propel them toward the finals. Every little bit counted.

Tuesday had been the talent contest that counted for 50 percent of the scoring for the pageant. It was by far the most important event of the week. Miss Berrien County, Sarah Kyle, had won that competition hands down. She had sung Gilda's aria from *Rigoletto* and nailed it. One judge was heard to mumble that even Giuseppe Verdi would have given her a standing ovation.

There was no surprise when Sarah was announced as the winner of the talent competition. Because that one event counted for 50 percent of the total points, the money was on Sarah to win the whole thing and be crowned Miss Georgia.

Sarah's mother had died when she was twelve, and she and her two older brothers had been raised by her dad, a man who farmed a small acreage near the Berrien County seat of Nashville, deep in South Georgia, some fifty miles north of the Florida state line. There was not much spare money, and as the boys graduated from high school, they went to work on the larger farms that dotted the area.

Sarah had shown a talent for singing as a young girl and would often sing solos at the small church the family attended. One day, when Sarah was in her early teens, the organist from the church stopped by the family's small farmhouse to speak with Sarah's father. This gentle man taught music at nearby Valdosta State College and donated his services as organist to the church. He'd watched Sarah grow into a young teenager and recognized a raw talent that he thought could be coached into greatness with the right voice teacher.

The organist had a colleague in the music department at Valdosta State who taught voice, and he offered to arrange a meeting, an audition really, for Sarah. If the teacher accepted her, there would be a cost for the lessons, not much, but an amount that would stretch the budget of Sarah's father. Over the years that followed, her dad had given up any luxuries he might have enjoyed in order to provide Sarah with money for the voice lessons. When she passed her sixteenth birthday, she found part-time work as a waitress in a café across the street from the courthouse in Nashville and helped her dad pay for the lessons.

Sarah began to toy with the idea that she wanted to go to college. Nobody in her family had ever done that or even contemplated it, but she wanted something better than the future she saw for herself. If she stayed in South Georgia, her destiny was pretty much limited to marrying a farmer or factory worker and spending the rest of her life within a few miles of her birthplace.

Money was the problem. College was expensive and even with a part-time job Sarah didn't see how she could afford it. Then her voice coach told her about the Miss Georgia Pageant and the scholarship money the winner would receive and the personal appearance fees she could earn during her reign as Miss Georgia. It would be enough to pay her college expenses for a year or two and she would have a shot at the Miss America title and enough scholarship money to finish a degree.

The coach assured Sarah that she had come so far with her music, she would have a good chance of becoming Miss Georgia, since half the points needed to win were based on the talent competition. The coach was certain that no other young woman in Georgia had the vocal range and control that Sarah did.

First, Sarah had to win a local contest, so she entered the Miss Berrien County Pageant sponsored by the local Jaycees. Given that hers was a talent not ever seen before in South Georgia and the fact that she had grown into an eighteen-year-old beauty, she walked away with the title.

Her next stop was Macon and the Miss Georgia contest. One of the Jaycees, a local lawyer and banker named Bill Perry, offered to pay the wardrobe and other incidental expenses that Sarah would incur in Macon. Her hotel room and meals would be paid by the pageant.

Bill Perry paid for Sarah to go to Bradenton, Florida, to sit for David Bartley, a well-known photographer specializing in pageant headshots. Sarah would need a number of those for the official Miss Georgia program book and maybe for the press, especially if she won.

It was important that Sarah have a St. John knit suit for the interview process, preferably royal blue, and a white Ada Duckett swimsuit. Nobody ever accused these young women of being original, but everyone was afraid to deviate from the norm set by the powers that be, whoever they were.

Female chaperones chosen from a roster kept by the pageant staff were assigned to small groups of contestants. On the day of her arrival in Macon, Sarah was introduced to her group's chaperone and her hotel roommate, a young woman named Polly Norris, who reigned as Miss Atlanta Northside. At twenty-two, Polly was four years older than Sarah and was participating in her second Miss Georgia Pageant. The year before, she had not placed in the final ten, but had gained some valuable experience in both the competitions and the politics that played out just under the surface of the pageant

Polly told Sarah that she was from a wealthy family who lived in Buckhead, a very upscale neighborhood in Atlanta. She'd gone to the best private schools and had graduated from Agnes Scott College a month before the pageant. Sarah was taken with Polly's sophistication and impressed that her parents had given her a tour of Europe the summer before as a consolation prize for not winning Miss Georgia in her first try.

As the final competition got under way, all fifty of the women, dressed in their evening gowns, were on the stage. They came one by one to the microphone at center stage and introduced themselves. They all knew that the top ten had already been chosen and would be announced in a few minutes. Each was holding out hope that she would be among the select group. Nerves were stretched thin, but each one knew the process. She'd do her best, smile, and show some personality at the microphone. And if she didn't win, she'd congratulate the fortunate ten and go back to her real life, carrying with her a memory of a glorious week in a gracious city on the edge of the Georgia Piedmont.

As the contestants left the microphone, they returned to the back of the stage and formed a semicircle. The mistress of ceremonies, a local television personality who hosted an afternoon show devoted to women's issues, walked onto the stage, told a couple of corny jokes, congratulated all the participants, and announced the ten semifinalists, each of whom stepped forward amid applause from the audience and the other contestants. The curtain closed and the audience took an intermission while the semifinalists, which included both Sarah Kyle and Polly Norris, left to change into swimsuits for the next competition, which would be followed by another talent show.

This year, Polly's talent had been baton twirling, and no one thought she had placed very high in that part of the competition. She had been announced as the winner of the swimsuit contest, and most of the girls thought Polly must have done very well in the interviews in order to make the semifinals. After all, the swimsuit only counted for 10 percent of the overall score. The other events, evening gown on Wednesday and Monday's interview, together counted for 40 percent of the overall score. The winners of those events weren't announced, but if Polly had done well in the interview and been awarded the full 25 percent and had won the evening gown event for 15 percent, added to her swimsuit win, she would have 50 percent of the score, equal to the 50 percent that Sarah had won in the talent contest. Of course, this calculation didn't take into account that points would have been awarded to several contestants in each event, even though they didn't win. And some of the others might have won either or both of the evening gown and interview events. That must have been the case in order for the eight who were not announced as winners of the other two events to end up as semifinalists. It was impossible to figure, even for the math major from Georgia Tech who was one of the semifinalists. Just too many unknowns.

Now, the contestants would appear in the swimsuit competition, followed by a repeat of the talent they'd performed on Tuesday night, and concluding with the evening gown event. The top five would then be selected and out of that small group, the new Miss Georgia would finally emerge. Even in face of the math that led some to believe that this was now a contest between Sarah Kyle and Polly Norris, each of the semifinalists still had hope of making the final five. If they survived, they would be interviewed again, this time in front of the entire audience, and then each judge would score the contestants on the events, and the winner would be announced.

* * *

Sarah Kyle did not make the final five. Polly Norris, the twirler, did. Sarah smiled and hugged each of the remaining five and walked off the stage. She went to the dressing room where many of the original fifty contestants were changing into their street clothes and getting ready to board the bus back to the hotel. Some were in tears.

Several of the women came over to commiserate with Sarah. "I can't believe you didn't at least make the finals," Miss Ware County said. "You won the talent event, for God's sake. How can they not put you in the top five?"

Sarah shook her head. "I guess I got my hopes up too high. Maybe I didn't do as well with the aria tonight. We'll never know, but I've had the experience of my life."

"You can try again next year," Miss Savannah said.

"No. I'm done," Sarah said. "I needed the scholarship money for college. I didn't get it, so I won't be going to college. I guess I'll see about full-time work at the diner in Nashville."

"Who do you think will win?" asked Miss University of Georgia.

"We'll know in a few minutes," another woman said. "I'm betting on Miss Carrollton. I heard she was runner-up in the talent event."

"Polly Norris," Miss Atlanta said.

"Not a chance," Miss Augusta said. "I don't know how she even won the swimsuit event. She's kind of chunky, if you ask me."

Sarah laughed. "Come on, ladies. We have to be good losers. If Polly wins, it'll be because the judges thought she was the best person to represent our state in the Miss America pageant."

"That, and the fact that her dad's a big deal in Georgia politics," Miss Atlanta said. "I bet he knows the judges."

"Maybe so," Sarah said, "but what's done is done. It's out of our control."

* * *

Miss Atlanta had been right. Polly Norris won the crown and would spend the next year as Miss Georgia. Sarah went back to Berrien County and resumed her life. She wasn't too unhappy, although there were days when her feet hurt and her back ached from waiting tables, and her thoughts would turn briefly to what might have been. How would her life be different if she'd gone to college, studied voice, made it big in the entertainment field? She'd daydream a bit before snapping back to reality and laughing at herself. She might have worked hard and earned her degree but never made it as a singer. What then? She'd have ended up in Nashville waitressing in a diner and singing in church on Sundays.

Maybe the degree would have given her entrée to the business world where a good education and inquiring mind could have propelled her to great success. But she had come to understand that sometimes life comes at you hard and you just have to adjust. Maybe she had made wrong choices along the way, choices she didn't even know she had, and had thereby doomed herself to waiting tables. Maybe one's life is preordained and nothing you can do will change the trajectory. Maybe pipe dreams are just that. Pipe dreams.

Sarah had not seen Polly after the pageant. She spent the night in the hotel room alone and assumed that Polly was with her family. The next morning, Bill Perry drove Sarah and her father home to Nashville, and Sarah eased back into the rhythms of life in a small town in South Georgia.

It wasn't all bad, she told herself. She was surrounded by friends and family, people she'd known her entire life, and a majority of the customers in the diner were locals, most of whom she knew.

The local library was full of books about the larger world, and Sarah devoured them with a rapaciousness found only in the hungriest of minds. Over the years, her reading provided her with an education that would be the envy of most college graduates. Her knowledge of current events, literature, philosophy, history, and other liberal arts was wide and deep.

Sarah Kyle was a happy woman, but still, over the years, the "what ifs" would pop unbidden into her consciousness. What if she'd won? What if she'd become Miss Georgia, maybe even Miss America? What if her singing career had taken off? How would a college degree have changed her life? And she would shrug and tuck those thoughts carefully back into the recesses of her mind, because all the comparisons did was demean the only life she had.

CHAPTER 2

NASHVILLE, GEORGIA – JUNE 1985

SARAH KYLE WAS in her late thirties, but could have passed for fifty. She was waiting tables in the diner where she had worked since she was a teenager. A stranger, a man whom Sarah judged to be in his early sixties, was sitting in a booth next to the plate glass window that overlooked the street. He wore an expensive suit and silk tie. Carefully cut gray hair covered his head and his fingernails looked as if he had a manicurist on permanent retainer. He had finished his breakfast and was dawdling over coffee.

It was nearing nine o'clock and the place had emptied out. The people who lived in this rural part of Georgia were early risers who ate their breakfast and went to work. There was no time for lingering. The owner stood behind the cash register at the end of the counter, reading the morning newspaper. Sarah took a fresh pot of coffee to the man in the booth. "Refill?" she asked.

"Yes, thank you. You're Sarah Kyle, aren't you?" His voice was tinged with the distinct accent, recognizable to most Georgians as that of a person who'd lived his whole life in Atlanta.

Sarah was surprised, but nodded. "I used to be."

"Can you sit and talk for a few minutes?"

"I'm on the clock," she said, a bit wary now.

"I know. But I wanted to meet with you and I didn't know any other way to go about it."

"I don't understand. Why would you want to meet with me?"

"Are you still singing?"

She laughed. "God, no. Who are you?"

"My name's John Peters. I own a string of auto dealerships in Atlanta."

"And what brings you all the way down to Berrien County, Mr. Peters?"

"I came to see you."

"Okay. I'll bite. Why did you come all the way down here to see me?"

"To apologize."

"For what?"

"Ask your boss if you can take a fifteen-minute break to talk to me. I think it'll be worth your while."

"How so?"

"I was a judge in the Miss Georgia pageant years ago. The one you should have won."

That hit her like a jolt of electricity. She stepped back and stood stock still, staring at the man. "I don't understand," she finally said.

"Come talk to me."

Intrigued by the man and his mission, Sarah asked her boss if he'd mind if she sat with the guest for a few minutes. He didn't.

"Tell me what this is all about," Sarah said as she slid into the booth across from the stranger.

"I've lived a good life," he said. "I've built a large and lucrative business and I did it by hard work and honest dealings. I've raised my children to be men and women of integrity and I'm very proud of the way they've turned out. I was recently diagnosed with a rare and untreatable lung disease. It's terminal and I need to make right the only unethical thing I've ever done in my life."

"What does this have to do with me?"

"As I said, I was one of the five judges at the Miss Georgia Pageant. I was responsible for your not winning that year."

"I'm confused," Sarah said.

"I put out the word to the other judges that you were pregnant and we couldn't have a pregnant Miss Georgia."

Sarah was stunned. "That's absurd. I was still a virgin when I went up to Macon that year."

"Well, obviously, I didn't know about that, but it wouldn't have mattered. You were headed for the win, and I couldn't let that happen."

Sarah was confused. It had never crossed her mind that the pageant could have been fixed. She knew, of course, that she'd won the talent event, but she'd always assumed that she just didn't do well enough in the other areas to even make the final five.

Her mind was churning. She'd accepted her loss and was thankful for the opportunity to compete. She knew there was life after the pageant, and even if she'd gone on to the Miss America contest, the time for her to enjoy the fame was fleeting. As it was, she had left Macon disappointed that she would not be able to go to college, but still happy enough with her life. She came back to the diner and met a young man that had been four years ahead of her in high school and, after a year of dating, she married him.

It was a good marriage and in quick succession produced two boys, who were now in their teens. Her husband worked on a ground maintenance crew at the nearby Moody Air Force Base. His work was steady even if it didn't pay well. Her income from the diner supplemented his salary to the extent that they could live in a small house with a big mortgage, but there was little left over for luxuries.

Sarah had often wondered how her life could have been different if she'd been able to go to college, if she'd won the pageant and gotten the scholarship money, but it wasn't in her nature to dwell on disappointments or thoughts of what might have been. She was reasonably happy with her lot in life, loved her two boys, and liked her husband well enough.

Sarah came out of her reverie. "What are you talking about?" she asked. "Why would you do something like that?"

"I was having an affair with Polly Norris," he said, "and she and I cooked up a way for her to win."

"You were having an affair with Polly? She must have been half your age."

"I don't think you'd call it an affair, really. We were having sex during the pageant. It started a week before when I met her at a cocktail party put on by the organization that sponsored the Miss Atlanta Northside contest. She came on to me, and God forgive me, I responded."

"How did you pull it off?" Sarah asked.

"The affair?"

"I don't care about the affair. I mean how did you fix the pageant?"

"You did very well in the interviews on Monday. I thought you were the best and gave you a high score. So did the other judges. But, when I saw you sing in the event on Tuesday night, I knew nobody could compete with that. Polly's twirling certainly wouldn't come close. You were beautiful and I thought you'd do well in both the evening dress and swimsuit competition. I had to undo some of the interview scoring and make sure that you didn't win anything else. I couldn't touch the talent scores. You were that good."

"How did you fix that?"

"Easy enough. I told the other judges that I'd heard from a medical source in your hometown that you were pregnant. I'd known the rest of the judges for a long time and they trusted my word. Three of them have died, and I've fessed up to the one survivor. He agreed with me that I should talk to you."

"I don't know what to say, Mr. Peters," Sarah said, her anger rising. "It's too late to change anything, so I'm not sure why you came all the way down here to tell me this. Maybe it makes you feel better, but it just makes me think about what might have been, the opportunities I might have had, if you hadn't been so morally corrupt. Was your affair worth it?"

"The affair, if you can call it that, ended when the pageant ended. I think the last night was a kind of thank-you from Polly. The next morning, she told me that we were finished."

"What'd you do?"

"I went home to my wife and children."

"Did you tell your wife what you'd done?"

"No. It would have broken her heart."

"Did it occur to you that telling me this would break my heart?" The anger was subsiding now and morphing into a sad acceptance that even decent people sometimes do bad things to good people and walk away from the disasters they leave in the lives of those they have wronged. "Knowing that I didn't win has never been a big deal to me. I just got on with my life. Now, knowing that I should have won and my life would probably have been very different, I have to live with the fact that I got screwed out of a better life. Literally."

"I've thought about that. I've learned a lot about you, your family, and your life since the pageant. I may have robbed you of your best chance for a better life."

"Are you going to tell your wife now that you seem to need to make apologies to people you've wronged?"

"My wife died last year. She never knew."

"I'm sorry for your loss, but what do you want from me? Forgiveness?"

"No. I think that'd be too much to ask of you."

"Maybe. I don't know. If I'd won that pageant, I'd probably never have married the man I did, and I wouldn't have the two boys I love better than life itself. We have to work hard and scrimp to get by, but we live and work among friends. I've known most of them for my entire life. It's not a bad life when you think about it. So, if it'll make you feel better, I'll forgive you. I don't think I'll be able to forgive Polly. I thought she was my friend."

"I'd like to give you some money. Enough to make your life easier."

Sarah shook her head. "That's not necessary, Mr. Peters. I won't take your money. Certainly not just to assuage your guilt. Maybe that's your punishment. To end your life knowing you couldn't fully make amends. Thank you for coming." She stood, left the booth, and walked into the kitchen.

John Peters paid his check for breakfast and left the diner. He did not leave a tip.

* * *

Six months later, Bill Perry, the man who had paid for Sarah's extras at the pageant, came into the diner at midmorning. He stopped at the front and spoke quietly to the owner behind the counter. He walked over to Sarah and said, "Your boss said we could talk for a minute. Can you get us some coffee and sit with me?"

Sarah came back with two cups of coffee. "What's up?" she asked.

"I know you met with John Peters a few months back."

Sarah was surprised. She'd never told anyone about that meeting. She didn't want to hear a lot of commiseration. What was done was done and she couldn't change anything, even if she'd wanted to. "How did you hear that?" she asked.

"John came to see me right after he talked to you. He hired me to represent him as his lawyer and told me what he'd told you. He said it was privileged information and he was depending on the attorney-client privilege to keep me from ever speaking of it to another soul. Ever. He made one exception. He told me he wanted me to talk to you after he died."

"Is he dead?"

"Yes. His son just called me. John left written instructions to notify me upon his death."

"There's a part of me, that bitter part I try to keep tamped down, that wants to be happy he's dead, but I'm doing my best not to think like that. Did he tell you what happened at the Miss Georgia contest?"

"He did. It was despicable. Nobody can ever make that right for you."

"I'm okay, Bill. I was shocked when he first told me about the situation, but I'm not that disappointed about it. My life would have been different, but it might not have been as good. Knowing that if I'd won I probably wouldn't have my two boys makes me glad I didn't win. Those boys are my life. It all worked out. Still, that little kernel of bitterness doesn't go away. I just try not to dwell on what might have been."

"John told me he'd offered you money to help make up for what he did. You refused to take it."

"Yeah. It wouldn't have changed a thing, and I thought the only reason he offered me the money was to make himself feel better." She chuckled. "I guess I didn't want to let him off. He ought to feel guilty."

"He was a very rich man, Sarah, but he told me he would not insult you further by leaving you anything when he died."

"Good for him."

"However, he did say that he didn't think it would insult you if he left your children something."

"Crap. What did he do?"

"He had me set up a trust for each of your boys. Enough to pay for a college education for each of them to include room, board, tuition, books, and a generous stipend for spending money. It's enough to send them to the finest schools in the country."

Sarah was stunned. She sat back in her chair. "He was a smart bastard, wasn't he? He knew I couldn't turn down something like that for my boys. He knew we'd never be able to afford to send them to college. I can't turn him down, can I?"

"I don't see how, Sarah. It was very generous. I think he was genuinely remorseful about what he did to you. Take the money and give your boys the chances to do what you couldn't because of his chicanery."

"You know what, Bill? In the end, it's probably a fair trade. Who knows where that other road, the one that would have stretched before me if I'd won, might have taken me?"

"We'll never know, Sarah. Take care of those boys."

THE INVESTIGATION

CHAPTER 3

Conway Twitty was singing "Hello Darling," the mellow tones burrowing into my sleeping brain, goading me awake, and interrupting a pleasant dream that was dissipating even as I shook off the bonds of Morpheus. As awareness displaced the dream, I realized I was in my own bed in my cottage on the north end of Longboat Key, Florida. I'd once paid a buck twenty-five for the ringtone that was issuing from my cell phone. Jennifer Diane Duncan, the police detective known as J.D., the woman whom I loved, thought it a waste of good money, even though I had assigned the ring to her incoming calls.

The light of a March morning was peeking through the window blinds, the high angle of the sun glaring at me with disdain for sleeping so late on a Friday. I glanced at the clock on my bedside table. Nine a.m. Most mornings I had already finished my daily jog on the beach.

I fumbled for the phone, almost dropping it. "Were you afraid I was sleeping too late?" I asked.

"No. I've got a problem," J.D. said. "Aunt Esther is in the Sumter County jail."

"What?"

"She's charged with murder."

"That's absurd. What's going on?"

"I don't know. I just got a call from Sue Rapp, her next-door neighbor. She said the deputies took her away about fifteen minutes ago. One of them told Sue that Esther was being charged with murder. Apparently, Esther's house is crawling with cops. They're searching the place."

"There's got to be some mistake."

"Must be. I'm going to call the sheriff's office up there and see what's going on."

"No, don't do that. Let me handle it."

"She's *my* aunt, Matt."

"I know, but I'm her lawyer. Or I will be as soon as I can get to Bushnell. Let's not interject you into this just yet. If the authorities know you're a police detective, they might close ranks. They won't want there to be even a whiff of favoritism to come back and bite them. The sheriff has to face election, you know."

"You might be right."

"I'll make a call to the jail and get ready to go up there. Why don't you come on over. I'll put the coffee on."

I booted up my computer and found the number for the Sumter County Detention Center and called, identified myself as a lawyer, and asked to speak to the supervisor. I explained to him that I had been retained to represent Esther Higgins and that I would be arriving at the jail in a few hours. I insisted that he make a notation in the file that Esther was represented and that there would be no interrogation until I could meet with her.

The supervisor, who identified himself as Lieutenant Chris Ricks, told me that he expected Esther to arrive at the detention center momentarily. I asked for his email address and he gave it to me. I hung up and emailed him, confirming our conversation. I didn't want anyone at the jail to conveniently forget that I had called and invoked Esther's right to silence. And if they did forget, I'd use that email to suppress all the evidence they found as a result of any conversation they had with my client.

I was already thinking like a lawyer. I'd hoped I was over that, but I guess not. Three years of law school and a number of years in a courtroom tend to engraft a certain way of thinking onto one's brain. I've found that what works well in a trial does not lend itself to interpersonal relationships. Both the women I have loved were sensitive to my almost irrepressible need to cross-examine them when we were having what I thought of as discussions and they assured me were arguments. Either way, I lost more of them than I won and I assuaged my bruised ego with the thought that they were simply bereft of logic and therefore not worthy foils for my incisive, legally trained mind. I actually have better sense than to burden them with my thinking on that issue.

My name is Matt Royal and I live on a little slice of paradise known as Longboat Key, an island that lies off the southwest coast of Florida, sixty miles south of Tampa and about halfway down the peninsula. The key, a barrier island separated from the small cities of Sarasota and Bradenton by the broad sweep of Sarasota Bay, is ten miles long and a half-mile wide at its broadest point. It is a small community that each winter swells to a rather large community with the arrival of the snowbirds, our friends from the north who seek refuge from the colder zip codes. Most of them leave by Easter, and we find ourselves nestling down and preparing for the heat and somnolence that summer brings.

Easter came in late March this year, and at the end of the second week of March, our little slice of paradise was a mixed bag of year-round residents and snowbirds who never left before Easter, regardless of when it arrived. The weather was at its most pleasant and would remain so until mid-May when the sun seemed to focus on us, bringing the heat and humidity that kept all but the hardiest souls cowering in our air-conditioned homes.

I was once an officer in the United States Army, saw some combat, got some medals, came home and graduated from law school. I practiced law in Orlando for a number of years, worked too hard, drank too much, and spent too many hours chasing what had become the holy grail of too many lawyers—the almighty dollar. I lost the wife I loved to divorce, quit the practice in disgust, directed mostly at myself, cashed out all my assets and my interest in the law firm, and moved to Longboat Key. If I were frugal, the money would last me for the rest of my life.

I worked diligently and successfully at becoming a beach bum, in the process garnering a lot of support from my new friends on the island, good people who were masters of idleness. During the course of my transformation, I met Detective Jennifer Diane Duncan, J.D. to the islanders, and fell in love for the second time. The great surprise to me, as well as to my island friends, was that she loved me back. Life was good on Longboat Key, but no matter how hard I tried, I could not seem to get the lawyer out of the beach bum.

* * *

I heard J.D. come in the front door of my cottage as I stepped out of the shower. She had spent the night alone in her condo, catching up with the endless paperwork her job required. There wasn't much crime on our small island, but even the most mundane misdemeanor required pages of documentation. It was the part of the job that J.D. disliked the most, and sometimes it backed up so much that she had to hunker down alone and spend hours typing endless drivel into useless forms. Her words, not mine.

I shaved and dressed in shorts and an old Army t-shirt and walked into the living room. My cottage perched on the edge of Sarasota Bay, and the sliding glass doors that opened from my living room onto the patio provided a spectacular view east across the usually calm water. Today was no different. The bay was resplendent in its springtime mantle of turquoise, with not even a ripple to mar its flat surface.

J.D. was sitting at my computer, sipping from a mug of coffee. I leaned over and kissed her on the cheek. The computer screen was filled with the online edition of *The Villages Daily Sun,* the newspaper of The Villages, the sprawling community that covered much of Sumter County and parts of two others in North Central Florida.

"Good morning, sweetheart," I said. "What're you looking for?"

"Hi, sweetie," she said. Her soft voice carried a hint of the Old South, acquired during her childhood years in Atlanta. "I was trying to find out if anybody had been murdered in The Villages lately. I found it on the *Daily Sun*'s website. There's not a whole lot to the story in today's paper. I don't think they know anything yet. Somebody found the body of a woman named Olivia Lathom in the middle of Paddock Square in Brownwood at dawn yesterday. She was apparently killed and left there Wednesday night or early yesterday morning. The medical examiner ruled it a homicide, but there are no suspects, at least none that the cops are releasing to the press."

"Where's Brownwood and what's Paddock Square?"

"Brownwood is the town square not far from where Aunt Esther lives in the Village of Collier. Paddock Square is the outdoors entertainment venue in the middle of the town. She drove us there in her golf cart when we visited just before Christmas."

"I remember that. Scariest ride I ever took. I've had five near-death experiences in my life. Two of them were in the war and the other three were between Esther's house and Brownwood."

"Hush. That was a fun day."

"It was," I said. "Who is Olivia Lathom?"

"I Googled her. She is, or was, a mystery writer in Atlanta. She's written a couple of books that were released only as eBooks. They did okay, but her latest one came out in hard cover and has taken off. It's a top ten *New York Times* best seller."

"What was she doing in The Villages?"

"The paper said she had a book signing at the Barnes & Noble store in Lake Sumter Landing on Wednesday. It apparently drew a big crowd."

"What does Esther have to do with Lathom?"

"I don't know. Esther spent most of her life in Atlanta. Maybe she knew some writers. She was a high school English teacher for thirty years. Maybe Lathom was a former student."

"I'll know more when I get to Bushnell. Does it say how she was killed?"

"She was shot."

"Anything else? Like the caliber of the gun, location of the wound, that sort of thing?"

"No. Just some stuff about Lathom's background and career. The story doesn't have a lot of information. This was probably posted yesterday. Maybe we can find out more when they get around to posting this morning's paper."

"Did you get much sleep?"

She shook her head. "I turned out my lights around three and the phone rang just before I called you. I didn't sleep well. Had a lot of crap running through my head from those cases I was doing the paperwork on."

You hungry?" I asked.

"As a bear."

"I'll whip us up some breakfast."

I'm not much of a cook, but I can scramble eggs, fry bacon, toast bread, and make coffee. I put it on the table and we dug in. "Tell me about Aunt Esther," I said. "I know she's your mother's sister and the only family you have left, and that she lived in Atlanta her whole life and taught school. That's about it."

"She lived next door to us in Atlanta and was kind of a second mom to me. When I was twelve and we moved to Miami, she decided to stay in Atlanta. We were the only family she had and she and my mom were just a couple of years apart in age. They were very close and she spent the summers with us in Miami. She got about three months off every year and would head south when school ended in early June. My dad liked her a lot and encouraged her to stay with us."

"She never married?"

J.D. smiled. "No, but she had several torrid affairs over the years. When I got older, she'd tell me about the men. I think she fell in love every couple of years, got that out of her system after a few months, and endured what she called her 'doing without' periods until the next right man came along."

"Doesn't sound at all like the spinster schoolmarm."

J.D. laughed. "I think she was the exact opposite. Probably still is. There are a lot of single men in The Villages and she's only sixty-two."

I'd first met Esther about a year before when she had spent a few days with J.D. on Longboat. She had just bought a new house in The Villages and was waiting for it to be completed. Shortly before Christmas, after she'd had several months to get settled, J.D. and I spent a couple of nights with Esther at her new home. She was a gracious hostess, and I found her to be a delightfully funny and often ribald conversationalist. I liked her a lot.

"You don't have to do this, you know," J.D. said.

"Do what?"

"Mount your great white steed and ride off to do battle for Aunt Esther."

"Actually, I do. She's family."

"Not your family."

"She's your family, and that makes her my family, too."

She put her hand on top of mine, looked closely at me, smiled, and nodded. "Yes, it does."

CHAPTER 4

I CHANGED CLOTHES and put on a navy-blue suit, white dress shirt, and a red patterned silk tie, what we lawyers used to call our trial suit. Always look good for the jurors. That bit of wisdom also applied to the first contact with law enforcement. When the lawyer is jumping into the battle against all the forces of the state, the police, the prosecutors, the medical examiners, each with his or her own agenda, he wants to look his best. I'd saved a couple of expensive suits and wore them on the rare occasions that I found myself in a court of law. To be honest, I hadn't planned on any more trials, but I always thought it important to look good at funerals.

The opening draw on the Cortez Bridge brought me to a stop three cars behind the barricade that controlled the eastbound traffic. A slight shudder ran the length of the bridge, a reaction to the rumbling of the machinery that operated the draw. I waited, enjoying the view of sailboats moored just south of the bridge in the lee of Anna Maria Island. They stood as still as a painting, their reflections etched lightly on the surface of the aquamarine water. God, I loved this place and I was always sad to leave it, even for only a few hours.

I opened my sunroof and savored the gentle sun and slight breeze and thought of my girl, Jennifer Diane Duncan. A couple of years before, she had slipped onto my island and into my life. I was initially intrigued by this woman who, after graduating from Miami's Florida International University with a degree in criminal justice, had spent twelve years on the Miami-Dade police force, rising to assistant homicide commander. She was in her midthirties and had come to the conclusion that life in the fast lane that was Miami-Dade was burning her out. Her mother, the widow of a career police officer, lived in a condo on Longboat Key, and when she died of pancreatic cancer, her home devolved to her only child. J.D. decided to leave Miami and move to Longboat Key, and my friend Bill Lester, the island police chief, jumped at the chance to hire her to replace his retiring detective.

Jennifer Diane had been born in Atlanta, and in the way of the South, had been named for her two grandmothers. She was called by both names until her dad, an Atlanta cop, shortened that mouthful to J.D. It stuck and that was the name she preferred. She had grown into a beautiful woman, with shoulder-length dark hair and a trim body that she kept in shape by regular exercise. She had green eyes that flashed in anger or amusement, thankfully mostly the latter, but I was smart enough not to cross her. I think when it comes to the women we love, we men are essentially chickens. We're not proud of that, but we accept it as the way of the world. I was perfectly happy with that state of affairs.

In due time, J.D. became part of that small circle of friends, the year-round residents of our little community, and we were thrown together regularly. Soon, my infatuation with her turned into love. I was the smuggest man on the island when I figured out that she felt the same way about me.

The draw span closed, the barricade rose, and I drove on toward I-75. It was a two-hour drive north to Bushnell, the seat of Sumter County, a small town of about twenty-five hundred residents. The county has a little more than one hundred thousand residents, with the majority of them living in The Villages, a planned retirement community that sprawls across parts of three counties and has more people than all of the rest of Sumter County.

Years before, back in my other life when I was more lawyer than human being, I had tried a case in the old county courthouse, a beautiful Beaux Arts edifice completed in the early twentieth century. Unfortunately, that graceful old building had been replaced by a new judicial center, a place with no soul. The old building still stood, and I suspected the county fathers had found a use for it that was far below the dignity it had enjoyed as the seat of justice in Sumter County.

My case had been tried in a grand old courtroom that boasted trappings serious enough for the murder trial that was taking place. My client was a local physician charged with euthanizing an eighty-nine-year-old woman with terminal cancer that was causing excruciating and unremitting pain. The old courtroom made me feel a bit like Atticus Finch, Harper Lee's wonderful character in 1930's Alabama. It had been a tough week, but in the end, the jury acquitted my client.

The sheriff's deputy, who became the lead investigator on the case, had responded to the 911 call placed by my client. He found the doctor, a man in his late thirties named Jeff Carpenter, sitting in a chair next to the bed of the elderly woman's body, holding her lifeless hand. He didn't deny his actions, but he refused to talk to the law enforcement officers. The deputy, a deeply religious man, seemed to think it was his moral obligation to see that Dr. Carpenter was convicted and sentenced to death. He once told me that God had guided him in his efforts to wipe my client from the face of the earth.

I pretty much destroyed the deputy on cross-examination, making the case that his religious zealotry had gotten in the way of good police work. And then I turned the religious aspect around, arguing to the jury that this good doctor had a moral obligation to end the woman's pain, an obligation that transcended the dictates of the

Hippocratic oath and even the law. Her life could not be saved, but she would have lived for another three or four weeks in pain that was beyond the understanding of most people. What purpose would be served by prolonging a life that had been lived well and was ending terribly? None of us can define the wishes of God, I argued, so we have to stumble through life, trying to live it in the most moral way possible. My client had been trained to preserve life, but that training also taught him to know when he had been defeated by that awful disease that in some manner touched us all. So even if the overdose of morphine he'd given her had not been accidental, he had acted in the best interest of his patient, who had long ago signed documents instructing her caregivers to refrain from extending her life when it was obvious that she was terminal. I never knew whether the jury bought my argument that the state had not proved that my client had purposely injected a lethal dose of morphine or the argument that, under the circumstances, the death was justifiable homicide.

As I drove along musing about the case, I came to the conclusion that the good news was that I had won the case. The bad news was that the deputy who had been the lead investigator on the case was now the sheriff of Sumter County.

CHAPTER 5

THE SUMTER COUNTY Detention Center's supervisor came to the reception area to greet me shortly before noon. "Good morning, Mr. Royal. We've got your client settled in her cell and nobody talked to her. I told her you were on your way. She seemed a little taken aback, like she didn't expect you."

"I'm not surprised. I haven't talked to her. The first I heard about this situation was when your department arrested her earlier this morning."

"Have you represented her before?"

I looked at his name tag. "Good try, Lieutenant Ricks, but no. She's a family friend."

He laughed. "Can't blame a guy for trying."

"Not at all. Look, I just want to meet with her and let her know I'm going to handle matters for her. That is, unless she'd rather me not. Assuming she's okay with me representing her, I want to meet with the sheriff before I spend too much time going over things with her. And I guess we'll have the first appearance sometime this afternoon."

"The first appearance will be before a County Judge, Jim Mattox, at four thirty this afternoon. We'll use closed-circuit TV. The judge will be in his chambers, and we'll be here at the jail."

"That sounds like a plan, Lieutenant."

"The sheriff is in his office downtown. He wants to see you when you're finished here."

"How did he know I was coming?"

"I called him after you called me this morning."

"Is that standard procedure?"

The lieutenant laughed. "No, sir. But I was a road deputy back when you tried Dr. Carpenter's case. I watched you take the sheriff apart on the witness stand. I thought I ought to let him know you were going to represent Ms. Higgins."

"Would you have any objection to my meeting with my client later this afternoon before the video appearance?"

"Not at all, Counselor. We have an open-door policy for lawyers. Come anytime you want. I'm going off shift, but the supervisor who comes on will be glad to help you. Follow me on back. We've got Ms. Higgins in an attorney's conference room."

Aunt Esther was sitting at a table in a small, windowless room. I knew she was sixty-two years old, but even in this drab and joyless place, she looked fifteen years younger. Her short blond hair was a bit disheveled and she wasn't wearing makeup. The dark-blue jumpsuit the jail provided did nothing to add to the image. Still, as I entered the room, she smiled.

"Thanks for coming, Matt. I'm sorry to be such a bother."

I kissed her on the cheek. "J.D. wanted to come, but I asked her to stay out of this until I figured out what's going on. What can you tell me?"

"Not much. I heard a knock on my front door around eight o'clock this morning. It was a deputy sheriff telling me that they had a warrant for my arrest for the murder of Olivia Lathom and that they were going to search my home. I let them in, and one of the deputies handcuffed me and put me in the back of a patrol car and brought me here. Lord knows what they've done to my house."

"Did you know Ms. Lathom?"

"I've heard of her, but never met her."

"How did you hear about her?"

"She was a writer. I'd read one of her books. It wasn't very good, but a friend of hers is in our book club, and she had asked us to use it for one of our monthly meetings."

"Tell me about your book club."

"It's just a bunch of women who get together every week or so in a meeting room over at the Eisenhower Center. A friend of mine owns a bookstore in the shopping center over where the Publix is on Highway 44, and she invited me to join the club. We read one mystery novel a month and then talk about it. Most of us like to write mysteries, mostly short stories, you know, so we get together once a week and present some of our writings to the group for critiques. None of us are real serious writers, but it's kind of fun to hear what the others think of your stories. Nobody gets mean or anything. The criticisms are usually low key and always constructive."

"What's the lady bookstore owner's name?"

"Judy Ferguson."

"Does she live in The Villages?"

"Yes."

"I'll have to talk to her at some point. Do you know her address?"

"I know where she lives, but I don't remember the address."

"I'll get that later. You said the bookstore is on Highway 44?"

"Yes. In the Grand Traverse Plaza. Her store is right next to the large Publix Market."

"Okay. I'll find her. You said that a friend of Lathom's was in your book club. Have you seen her lately?"

"No. I dropped out of the book club a couple of weeks ago. I haven't seen her since."

"Why did you drop out?"

"The bitch who was the friend of the dead woman. Her name's Ruth Bergstrom. She was the club president and seemed to know a lot of people in the publishing industry. Or at least she let on that she did. A little over a year ago, I showed her one of my stories, actually a novel I'd been working on for years. She gave it back to me a couple of weeks later. She said she didn't think it was ready for a publisher and wasn't sure I could ever get it to the point that a publisher would be interested in it. She was nice enough, but said the plot was weak and the characters weren't well drawn.

"It turns out Ruth had sent my manuscript to that Lathom woman in Atlanta. Two weeks ago her publisher released Lathom's newest book and it debuted as number six on the *New York Times* best-seller list. It was my book."

"How did you find that out?"

"I read the damn book and compared it to my manuscript. It's identical, right down to most of the commas."

"What did you do about it?"

"Nothing. I hadn't copyrighted the manuscript, so how could I prove I wrote it? Besides, I can't afford a lawyer to sue Lathom or her publisher."

"There's a way around that, but we'll think about it when we get you out of this mess. Do you still have the manuscript?"

"Of course. I put it in my safe deposit box at the bank and I'm sure most of it will be on my laptop."

"The sheriff will have your laptop, I guess."

"Probably not. I was at my next-door neighbor's last night showing her some old pictures I'd taken of my yard in Atlanta. I ran off and left the thing on her coffee table."

"Have you told anybody about the book theft?"

"No. I was afraid I'd sound like some kind of nutcase taking credit for a book I didn't have the talent to write."

"I'm going to see the sheriff and find out what they've got on you. I'll come back to see you later today, and we'll talk some more. The sheriff must have something to cause him to arrest you. Do you know Ruth's address?"

"Are you going to see her?"

"I think so. She's the only lead we have right now."

"Lead? That sounds like one of those detective programs on TV."

"Remember, Esther. This is real life. I think it best if you don't talk to any of the other inmates. They'll sell you out for a ham sandwich. You get the least bit close to some of these characters, and they'll be happy to testify that you told them that you killed Lathom, or even Abe Lincoln, if necessary. Maybe I can get you into some sort of isolation. Away from the general population."

"If you think that's best."

"What about Ruth's address?" I asked.

She gave directions to the Bergstrom home.

"Do you need anything?" I asked.

"Well, I could use a ride home."

I smiled. "I'll see about that as soon as I can get you before a judge. See if we can get bail. I don't think the county judge who will handle first appearance will set bail, so you'll probably spend the weekend here."

"What are the chances of bail?"

I was quiet for a moment, shrugged, and said, "Esther, to be perfectly candid with you, the chances of getting bail on a murder charge are slim to none, and I'm afraid Slim just left town."

She didn't react. She sat there for a few seconds, and said, "Matt, do you know how Olivia Lathom was killed?"

"She was shot."

"In Paddock Square?"

"I don't know. She could have been killed somewhere else and dumped there. I'll know more when I talk to the prosecutor."

We chatted for a few more minutes, and I left for my meeting with the sheriff. I was saddened by the forlorn look on Esther's face, but she was tough and, according to J.D., would be able to handle whatever came her way.

CHAPTER 6

SHERIFF BRIAN CORNETT hadn't changed much since I'd last seen him. He was a tall, raw-boned guy with a shock of copper hair that was going to gray. He met me in the reception area, holding his big paw out for a shake. I reciprocated.

"Good to see you, Matt. I heard you were coming up to see Ms. Higgins."

"Bad news travels fast."

"I didn't think it was bad. I thought it was a good thing that she was going to have good representation."

"I'm glad you see it that way, Sheriff. I was afraid our last encounter might have left some hard feelings."

"We had a good case, Matt. There're not half a dozen lawyers in the state who could have gotten an acquittal. You did your job. I did mine."

"How's the doc?"

"He's still practicing medicine. I see him regularly. You haven't kept in touch?"

"No. I think I'm sort of a bad recollection for my criminal defense clients. Even if they were acquitted, I tend to bring back the memories of the worst time in their lives."

"I heard you were retired. Living down on Longboat Key."

"Yep. Living the dream."

"You're kind of young for that, aren't you?"

"Probably, but I just wore out earlier than most."

"What brings you up here? I'm surprised you'd be suiting up again. I'd think the beach beats the courtroom every time. May I ask how you got involved in this?"

"Esther Higgins is a friend of the family."

"Close enough friend to get you out of retirement?"

"Afraid so. What can you tell me about the evidence you've got?"

"Nothing, I'm afraid. I wish I could, but I'd better leave that to the state attorney."

That wasn't unexpected. The state attorney always controls the action leading to trial. I was entitled to all the evidence the state had, but it would have to come to me through the discovery process. Sometimes the prosecutor just hands it over without any argument. We'd see. "Can you at least tell me whether the victim was killed in Paddock Square or somewhere else?" I asked.

"I don't see why not. We're pretty sure she was not killed in the square. We think it was a body dump."

"And no idea where she might have been killed?"

"Not yet. We're working on that."

"Has a judge been assigned?" I asked.

"Ms. Higgins will have a first appearance this afternoon. The county judge will hear the bail motion and bind it over to the circuit court. The only circuit judge who sits regularly in Bushnell is Bill Gallagher. I'm sure he'll get the assignment."

"I remember him well."

The sheriff laughed. "Me, too."

"Isn't Brownwood actually in the city limits of Wildwood?"

He nodded.

"I was a little surprised to hear that your department was handling this rather that Wildwood PD."

"We usually take over on big cases. We have a lot more resources than the city does."

"Makes sense," I said. We shook hands and I left.

* * *

I drove two miles out of downtown Bushnell and stopped at a McDonald's drive-thru for a Big Mac and a Diet Coke. I eschewed the fries and congratulated myself for my healthy approach to eating. I merged onto I-75 for the twenty-five-minute drive to The Villages, my thoughts meandering through my brain, jumping from one subject to another. I knew we wouldn't get much out of the county judge in the way of bail. On a case this serious, the first appearance judge would usually leave it to the circuit judge to whom the case had been assigned to set bail. I'd try for a bail hearing as soon as possible, but I didn't hold out much hope that we'd be successful.

I was a bit confused by Sheriff Cornett's friendliness. I knew he hadn't been happy with me when he left the witness stand in the doctor's trial, and it had been my experience that self-righteous pricks like the sheriff carried grudges for a long time. Was he trying to sandbag me in some way? I'd have to be careful.

I wondered which prosecutor would be assigned to the case. The fifth judicial circuit of Florida was comprised of five counties including Sumter. Generally, the prosecutors who were assigned to the county where the case was to be tried would represent the state. But that rule wasn't written in stone, and the state attorney could assign any of his assistants to try a case anywhere in the circuit. I was pretty sure that only the most experienced prosecutors would be assigned to a murder case. I would not find out who it was at the first appearance hearing since the youngest prosecutors were sent to court for those kinds of pro forma hearings. The judge would read the charging documents to the accused and make sure she understood them. If the accused had a private lawyer representing him or her, that part of the process would likely be waived. If the accused did not have a lawyer and could not afford one, a public defender, who would be present in the courtroom, would be appointed. Like a lot of things in the court system, it seemed to me that it was a waste of resources, but there were good reasons for doing it this way. The American justice system is creaky and slow and often frustrating, but it usually cranked out justice, and in truth, was the envy of the civilized world. And rightly so.

The Villages is divided into ninety-one neighborhoods called villages, spelled with a lower case "v," I guess to distinguish it from The Villages, spelled with two upper case letters, which denoted the overall development. With a lot of help from the map on my GPS system and the directions Esther had given me, I found Ruth Bergstrom's house in the Village of Hillsborough. I took Highway 44A into The Villages, turned left onto Buena Vista Boulevard, and at the fourth roundabout, turned onto Hillsborough Trail. As I entered the neighborhood, I came to an unmanned gatehouse with a bar that blocked the road. There was a lane for residents and one marked for visitors. Residents had a device similar to an electric garage door opener that raised the barrier and gave them access. A non-resident had to pull up to a post on which sat an apparatus that housed a camera, a button that would raise the swing-arm guarding the street entrance, and a speaker that connected directly to a security post somewhere in the vastness of The Villages. I pushed the button and the bar went up and the camera probably took a picture of me. I didn't need the speaker, but I figured it had some function that was beyond my simple understanding of security matters.

As I went through the gate, I noticed another camera facing inward and at about the height to get a good picture of the license plate of any car entering the neighborhood. It was a fairly sophisticated security system and there would be no reason for it unless the security people kept a record of everyone who entered and left each of the villages.

The Bergstrom home sat on a small cul-de-sac, one of four similar houses placed close to each other on small lots. The houses were only three or four years old, each one sporting stucco and fresh paint. They all had garages that would hold two cars and a golf cart. It was a pleasant neighborhood with manicured landscaping and a generous number of streetlights. A small sign in the front yard assured me I was at the home of James McNeil and Ruth Bergstrom.

I parked on the street and walked to the front door and rang the bell. No answer. I gave it a beat or two and knocked. Still no answer. I was walking back to my car when a woman who appeared to be in her sixties pulled up in a golf cart, turned into the driveway, and stopped. "Can I help you?" she asked.

"I hope so. Are you Ruth Bergstrom?"

"I am."

"Ms. Bergstrom, my name is Matt Royal. I wonder if I could talk to you for a few minutes."

"About what?"

"You may know that Esther Higgins was arrested this morning. I'm her lawyer and would like to ask you a few questions, if you don't mind."

"About what?" Her tone was confrontational.

"I'd like to find out who killed Olivia Lathom. I understand you were friends."

"I'll tell you who killed Liv. Esther Higgins did it."

"What makes you think that?"

"Esther told me she was going to kill her."

"When did she tell you that?"

"A couple of weeks ago."

"Was that after she found out that you had given her manuscript to Ms. Lathom and Lathom published it as her own work?"

"That's a foul lie."

This wasn't going too well, but this lady was lying to me. She had stiffened herself into a defensive posture, her hands still gripping the cart's steering wheel so hard that her knuckles were turning white.

"What's a lie?" I asked. "That you gave Ms. Lathom the manuscript or that she sent it to her publisher claiming it was her own work?"

"You'd better leave now."

"Which was it, Ms. Bergstrom? I know you gave her the manuscript. Where else would she have gotten it?"

She climbed out of the cart without another word and walked toward her front door. I called to her. "I'll be back with a subpoena and you can answer my questions under oath."

"You do what you have to do, but you'll still get the same answer."

She stepped into the house and slammed the door shut.

CHAPTER 7

I LEFT HER house and drove the several blocks to Brownwood. The Villages include three town squares, each one holding a variety of shops and restaurants surrounding a square in the middle that was the entertainment venue. Brownwood was the newest of the three and was built to resemble a small nineteenth-century town on the Florida frontier. Golf carts were parked everywhere. It was the preferred mode of travel throughout The Villages, and almost everyone who lived there owned one.

There were 115,000 residents living in 70,000 homes and driving an estimated 60 to 80,000 golf carts. Eve Fletcher, one of Esther's neighbors, had explained to me that The Villages, like Longboat Key and many other places in Florida, explode in the winter with the influx of Northerners. The residents were divided into three classes: the snowflakes who drifted in and out of the area, spending a few days or weeks in their houses; the snowbirds who came in December and stayed until April; and the frogs who planned to live in The Villages until they croaked.

There were cart lanes on either side of the residential roads, but the carts did not share the major thoroughfares with automobiles. The developer had built paved tracks, called multi-modal paths, parallel to the four-lane divided boulevards. Tunnels under the main intersections gave the golf carts a safe transit from one point to another. People in cars tended to give them the right of way, and collisions between carts and automobiles were rare. There were 43 golf courses comprising 630 holes within The Villages, and many of the carts had golf bags strapped to the rear cargo carrier.

By two thirty, I was parked at Paddock Square, located in the middle of Brownwood, surrounded by shops, restaurants, and a movie theater. Tiered rows of bleacher-style seats took up one side of the square with a stage on the opposite side, separated by a large concrete area that in the evening would be filled with senior citizens dancing to whatever music was coming from the stage. There was entertainment every night in each of the three town squares and the crowds always came. The music stopped at nine p.m., so everybody could get home early. I understood that some of the revelers actually went home, but there were plenty of bars and restaurants in the town squares and the country clubs where people could go and drink and dance the night away.

I stood on the edge of the concrete area of Paddock Square, wondering just where Lathom's body had been discovered. Was she killed here or had she been killed somewhere else and brought here? Sheriff Cornett had seemed pretty certain that Olivia had been killed somewhere else and the square was just the body dump. I didn't trust the sheriff, but surely, he knew that I would soon figure out the truth about whether this was a murder on the square or somewhere else.

If the body had been moved, I doubted that Esther could have done so. She wasn't a big woman and she was sixty-two years old, a little long in the tooth for lifting and transporting dead people. I was sure that the forensics people who had examined the scene would have a better idea of whether Lathom had been killed at Paddock Square or somewhere else.

There was a timeline question, too. The newspaper piece J.D. had found online told us that the body was discovered at dawn. That wasn't very precise. The medical examiner could come up with a pretty good estimate of when the woman had been killed. If I knew that she hadn't been killed where she was found, and knew the approximate time of death, I would have some parameters to start with. I didn't expect the investigators to find the place where she had been killed, if it wasn't in fact in Paddock Square, but at least if it was determined that she hadn't died where she was found, I could begin to fashion an argument against the idea of my client killing the victim and then transporting her body to the square.

There was no indication of who found the body. That would be in the police reports, which would come to me in due course through the discovery process. I didn't want to wait, though. I needed to get ahead of the police on this if possible.

I was standing idly, letting the thoughts run through my brain. The trial lawyer starts plotting his strategy at the moment he's retained on a case. At least the good ones do. I don't think there's a waking moment between the time he's retained and the time the jury returns a verdict that, at least on some level, the case isn't percolating through his head. When he's asleep, the dreams come, always about the cases, always whispering that the lawyer hasn't done all he could for his client. Or her client, I should add. There are many top-notch women trial lawyers and they are plagued by the same self-doubts as we macho men. It's an occupational failing that affects anyone egotistical enough to take on the rigors of the courtroom and the possibility of losing an innocent client to the not-so-gentle embrace of what we euphemistically call the Department of Corrections.

Most lawyers have a lot more than one case going at a time, so the process is complex and convoluted. I only had one case, Esther's, but I knew in my gut that I would suffer the same doubts and uncertainty that had driven me to drink in my former life. I wouldn't sleep well until the jury came back with a verdict. If it was guilty, I'd start worrying about the appeal. No wonder lawyers with a heavy caseload drink too much. The stress never ends. One case after another, too many trials, too many losses, too many clients who are going to spend much of the rest of their lives in prison.

And if a lawyer tells you he's never lost a trial, ask him how many he's tried. Those of us who, like Roman gladiators, regularly go into the arena that is the courtroom have lost cases. Some of those losses sting more than others, but it has been my experience that while the memories of the wins fade, the lawyer never forgets the losses.

Why do we do it? It becomes a way of life, and God help us, we love the fight, the intellectual battles, the courtroom jousting. We lie to ourselves that our families understand, that the drinking is just a little relaxation after a hard day at work. And then one day, you wake up and find that the woman you loved has left you and filed for divorce. The life you worked so hard to create for yourself and for her, the money, the win-loss record, the reputation you built one case at a time, was merely a chimera. That's when you chuck it all, move to an island, and become a beach bum. Or at least that's what I did.

I saw a young man picking up trash in the bleachers. He wore a shirt that identified him as an employee of The Villages. I walked over and introduced myself. "Do you work here in Paddock Square every day?"

"Not every day. I alternate with another guy, so I'm usually here two out of three days. I handle all three of the outdoor theaters."

"Do you know about the body that was found here yesterday morning?"

"Yes, sir. I found her."

"You were working that early?"

"Yes, sir. I'm finishing up my day now, but yesterday I started here and then went on to the other places. Some days, like today, I do it differently."

"What time did you find the body?"

"Why are you so interested in this?"

"I'm a lawyer and I'm representing the lady who has been charged with killing the woman you found."

"Oh. Are you sure it's okay for me to talk to you?"

"Yes. You'll be a witness in the trial, so at some point I'll be taking your deposition."

"If you're sure. It must have been a little after seven when I arrived. I saw her when I first got here. The sun was just coming up. I start every morning as soon as it's light enough to see what I'm picking up."

"You have a lot to pick up?"

"Nah. These old people are pretty good about picking up after themselves. I'm usually finished by about ten, but we had a departmental employee meeting this morning, so I'm running late."

"When you found the body, did you see much blood?"

"No. She was lying facedown, and I could see a gunshot wound in her upper back. There was some blood on her clothes around what looked to be the entrance. I partially turned her but couldn't find an exit wound. She was in full rigor, and given the temperature, I'd guess she'd been dead for maybe ten to twelve hours."

"That sounds pretty professional. How do you know about entrance wounds as opposed to exit wounds and rigor mortis?"

"My other job is a paramedic with The Villages fire department. Before that, I was an Army medic. I've seen a lot of gunshot wounds and dead bodies."

"I was infantry," I said. "There was no soldier we respected more than the medics."

"I was assigned to an infantry platoon in Iraq."

"Welcome home, Doc," I said.

"You, too, sir. How can I help you?"

That was it. An instant bond formed between two warriors, a bond that lasts a lifetime and encompasses anyone who ever wore the uniform. It's almost mystical, a shared past even with those who never saw combat, a time when you had almost no control over your own life. You went where your superiors sent you, you did what they told you to do, you killed enemy soldiers when you were ordered to, you put your life on the line at the direction of people you never knew or even saw.

You often lived in circumstances that the Supreme Court has determined to be cruel and unusual punishment when applied to convicted felons serving time in prisons. And when you finished your tour of duty, you went home, to America, the States, the land of the big PX, and you put your uniform away, and resumed life as a civilian.

But the military never left you. You carried it within, because you knew you weren't the same person who had first walked onto the military reservation and started the process of learning to be a soldier, a Marine, an airman, a sailor, or a Coastie. You retained the pride, the discipline, the sense of having served a cause worthy of the years you put in. And when one veteran identifies himself or herself to another, regardless of service or rank, the bond is recognized, perhaps because only the veteran can understand the military life.

No matter how hard one tries to explain that lifestyle to the non-vet, it will fall on ears that cannot fully comprehend the pride that earning the right to wear the uniform engenders. And for all the years left in the vet's life after he takes off the uniform for the last time, that enduring tie binds him to every other person who ever served.

And when that life is over, many of them will be buried in a military cemetery among their buddies who also served. And so it was on that sunny day in Paddock Square between two former soldiers separated by time and circumstances.

"Do you think she was killed here or somewhere else?" I asked.

"Hard to tell. The wound looks like it came from a small-caliber slug. I turned her over to make sure there wasn't anything I could do for her and I didn't see an exit wound. There might not have been much blood to begin with."

"What's your name?"

"Kevin Cook."

"I'm Matt Royal. Did you notice anything out of the ordinary? Like disheveled or missing clothing, anything like that."

"No, sir."

"Did you see any bruising or anything that might indicate she'd put up a fight?"

Kevin stood quietly for a moment, thinking. "I didn't notice anything, but since she was shot in the back, she may not have realized she was in danger."

"Can you tell me exactly where in her back you found the entrance wound?"

"Pretty much in the middle, between the shoulder blades. If I had to guess, I'd say that the bullet likely hit her spinal cord. She was probably dead before she hit the ground."

"Any bruising on her face?"

"Not that I saw. Of course, I wasn't looking for anything like that, so it might have been there, and I didn't see it."

"If she was shot in the back and killed instantly, wouldn't you expect her to fall forward and be unable to catch herself?"

"I would," Kevin said, "and if she'd fallen onto the concrete face-first, I'd expect her to have some cuts or bruising."

"So, it'd be a pretty safe guess that she was probably killed somewhere else and dumped here."

"I think you're right, Mr. Royal."

"Can you show me exactly where you found the body?"

"Sure." He led me to a spot near the stage that was built to look like a frontier cabin. To the right of the stage, there was a life-sized bronze statue of a cowboy sitting on a fence. "That's Mr. Morse who was one of the founders of The Villages," he said, pointing to the statue. "The body was right about here."

He was pointing to a spot a few feet in front of the statue. I noticed a driveway of sorts that ran from a curb cut on the street corner into the concrete area that became a dance floor during the evening entertainment. If you stood on that corner you would look across Brownwood Boulevard to the World of Beer restaurant and across the intersecting street, West Torch Lake Drive, to the City Fire restaurant.

"Is this a driveway?" I asked. I was pointing to a corridor paved in brick and concrete that lay between two parallel fences and ended in a curb cut at the corner of the square.

"I don't know. There're curb cuts on all four corners of the Paddock. I don't really know what they're used for. Maybe the performers bring their equipment in that way."

"Thanks, Kevin. You've been very helpful. Do you work out of the same fire station all the time?"

"I'm usually at Station Forty-Five, right across from the Eisenhower Recreation Center on Buena Vista. We've got six other stations and sometimes I might be at one of the others. I'm on duty twenty-four hours and then I'm off for forty-eight hours. It'll be a hit or miss proposition as to where you'll find me."

"Can I get your address and phone number?"

"Not a problem." I handed him a ballpoint pen and a sheet of paper from the little pad I kept in my pocket. He scrawled the information on the paper and gave it back to me. We shook hands, and I walked across the street to the World of Beer restaurant.

* * *

The place was virtually empty. I took a stool at the bar and ordered a Diet Coke. The bartender was an attractive brunette whom I judged to be in her late twenties or early thirties. Her slender body reflected what must have been a rigorous workout schedule and her big smile lit up the room. She brought me a glass of Diet Coke, smiled, and asked how my day was going. "Don't see a lot of suits around here," she said. "Almost everybody wears cargo shorts."

"Alas," I said. "I'm a workingman. What can I say?"

"What do you do?"

"I'm a lawyer."

She grinned. "I might have guessed. My name is Amber Marris."

"I'm Matt Royal."

"What brings you to this sleepy town, Matt?"

"I'm representing the lady who is accused of killing the woman they found across the street yesterday."

"You mean Esther Higgins?"

"I do. You know her?"

"Yes. She comes in fairly regularly. Usually with a gaggle of women who play golf several times a week."

"I didn't know Esther was a golfer," I said.

"I don't think she is. Her friends are her neighbors, and she usually joins them for lunch or happy hour."

"I don't guess you work nights."

"Actually, I do. I'll be working tonight. I just came in."

"What about Wednesday night?"

"I was here. Why?"

"I understand the body was probably left in Paddock Square late that night or early Thursday morning." I didn't know that, but it was a pretty good guess. "Did you see anything suspicious that evening?" This was a shot in the dark, but sometimes you get a hit.

"No. Nothing out of the ordinary. There's usually a good crowd of people in the square on warm nights because of the music. But that stops at nine o'clock so we get a lot of the crowd in here. This week has been bigger than usual on account of Rocky and the Rollers playing in Paddock Square. They always draw a big crowd."

"What time did you get off?"

"We close at midnight, but we have people drinking their last drinks, and the staff stays until we get things cleaned up. I probably left between one and one thirty, maybe a little after."

"Did you go by Paddock Square on your way home?"

"No. I park in the lot behind the restaurant, so I would have gone out the back door. Wait a minute. I almost got hit by a van as I was turning onto Brownwood Boulevard."

"Tell me about that."

"I left the parking lot and turned right onto West Torch Lake Avenue and was making an almost immediate left onto Brownwood Boulevard. This van came out of nowhere and cut right in front of me. I had to slam on my brakes to miss him."

"I want you to think very carefully about the answer to my next question. Sometimes if you take a minute to empty your brain, you can remember things with a bit more clarity. Okay?"

"Shoot."

"Did you see where the van came from?" I could have asked if it came out of the square on the curb cut nearest where the body was found, but that's what we lawyers call a leading question. It tends to put ideas in the head of the person answering the question.

She stood quietly for a long moment, chewing gently on her lower lip. I could almost hear the gears grinding. "He came out of Paddock Square," she said, quietly. "I remember seeing him coming off that curb cut. I thought he'd stop, so I continued my turn, but he floored it and almost ran over me."

"Which way did he go?"

"Straight out Brownwood Boulevard. He'd have a straight shot to Buena Vista Boulevard and a few blocks to Highway 44. It's the quickest way out of town."

"Do you have any idea who the driver was?"

"No. I didn't even get a glimpse of him. The van was a white Dodge Promaster City van."

"You seem pretty sure about that."

"My husband is an electrician. He has his own business and he's thinking about buying a new work vehicle. I went with him last weekend to look at one just like the one that madman was driving Wednesday night. Or Thursday morning, I guess."

"I don't suppose you got a license plate number."

"No. Sorry. I assumed he was part of the Rocky and the Rollers crew and was just picking up equipment."

"Can you narrow down the time any better than the one o'clock period?"

"I can. Hold on." She pulled her phone out of her pocket and scrolled down a list. "Here it is. I called my husband to let him know I was on my way home. He wants me to do that so that he knows I'm safe. I called him from the parking lot at exactly one forty-two."

"Your guess was pretty good."

"Pretty close. Do you think the people in that van had something to do with the murder?"

"Maybe. That van may be what the killer or killers used to transport the body. It's a good start to finding out what is going on here. Have any law enforcement officers talked to you?"

"No. Should I call somebody about what I saw?"

A man in his seventies, sporting a deep tan and wearing a golf shirt and cargo shorts, came in and sat at the other end of the bar. The bartender called out, "The usual, Frank?"

"That'll do, Amber. Make it a cold one."

"Be right back," Amber said to me. I watched her draw a draft out of a tap with the logo of a local craft beer and deliver it to Frank. She returned.

"I can't tell you whether you should call the law with what you know," I said. "That's entirely up to you. Even if you don't, I may have to call you as a witness at the trial and I'll have to disclose your name to the state attorney's office. This is the kind of information they need to have and maybe the earlier they get it, the better."

"So, you think I should call them?"

"Let me put it this way. I wouldn't be upset if you did. If you decide to call, you might want to call the assistant state attorney prosecuting this case. I don't know who that will be, but I'll find out on Monday and let you know, or you can call the office in Bushnell, and they'll give you his name."

"I'll think about it."

"I have a big favor to ask of you. Would you mind going over the almost-collision again with me and let me record it? I'll bring you a typed transcript and you can sign it. I'll give you a copy."

"Sure. Let me check on Frank." She poured another beer, took it to Frank, and came back down the bar. I turned on the recorder on my phone and we were off to the races.

CHAPTER 8

I DROVE BACK to the detention center and met Esther in the same little conference room we'd used that morning. "How're you doing?" I asked.

She smiled. She was in good spirits considering the circumstances. "Pretty good," she said. "They even gave me a private cell."

The jail supervisor I'd spoken to that morning had done as I asked and segregated her from the general population. I told Esther what I'd been told by Kevin Cook and what had transpired with Ruth Bergstrom. "Did you really tell her you were going to kill Ms. Lathom?"

"No. I might have said something like 'somebody should kill the bitch,' but I would never have threatened the woman. If truth be known, I wouldn't mind a whole lot if somebody killed Ruth, too. But I wouldn't do it."

"Would anybody else have heard your comment other than Ruth?"

"No. We were standing in her front yard. I'd gone over there to confront her about giving the manuscript to Lathom. She denied it, of course. Said that my book was a piece of crap and Lathom had written a book for the ages. For the frigging ages. Can you believe that?"

"Did you go to the book signing at Barnes & Noble?"

"No. I was afraid my temper might get the best of me and I'd create a scene."

"And you're sure you've never met the woman?"

"Positive," she said.

"Have you ever noticed one of those little commercial vans we see around sometimes? They're usually marked up pretty good with company logos, that sort of thing, but I'm looking for a plain white one with no markings."

"I can't recall ever seeing one. I probably have, but it just didn't register. Why?"

I told her about my conversation with Amber Marris, the bartender at World of Beer. "That may have been the vehicle somebody used to transport the body. I'd sure like to find it."

"Did the bartender get a tag number?"

"No."

"There're cameras all over the place. I know they have them at all the gates to the various villages. Maybe one of them got a plate number."

"I've thought about that, but I don't think the people who run The Villages security are going to let me look at their videos or still pictures." I looked at my watch. "Okay. We're not going to accomplish anything else today, but we have the first appearance hearing in about thirty minutes, and then I've got a long drive back to Longboat. Do you have any questions?"

"When do you think we'll get to trial?"

"I don't know. I've got to get a better handle on what evidence the state has. I'll know more when we get past the hearing today and I have a chance to talk to the prosecutor. Then we can make a decision about filing a motion for speedy trial and asking for bail."

"So, I might be here for a while."

"Maybe. I'll try to get bail, but don't hold your breath on that."

"Thanks, Matt. I appreciate what you're doing for me."

A deputy knocked on the door and stuck his head in. "Mr. Royal, we're setting up for the first appearance. I need to take Ms. Higgins to the video area. It's just down the hall. You're welcome to come with us."

The hearing was short, only about five minutes. I told Judge Mattox that I would be representing Ms. Higgins and pleaded her not guilty. I waived the reading of the charges, and the judge asked me if I was going to apply for bail. I told him that I would file a motion in the next few days.

After the hearing, I told Esther that I'd see her on Monday, kissed her on the cheek, and headed to Longboat Key. I had called J.D. while driving to The Villages and again as soon as I left the detention center to drive home. I told her about my conversations with Amber Marris, Ruth Bergstrom, and Kevin Cook, the firefighter, and we discussed Esther's state of mind. By the time we broke the connection, J.D. knew everything I knew. Maybe we could talk about something more uplifting than murder when I got home. I needed a little downtime and would use the next two days, Saturday and Sunday, to get ready for Monday morning. I'd have to prepare a notice of appearance and some other documents to file with the clerk of court.

I told myself to stop thinking about it. I wanted to put the case aside for at least a short time so that I could have a beer or two and relax with my girl. There I was, thinking like a lawyer again, planning to drown the stress in alcohol. Except that now, with the exception of a few times that had nothing to do with the law, I limited myself to just two or three beers for the evening.

The day was dying as I crossed the Cortez Bridge. An onshore breeze, ripe with the smell of the sea, disturbed the bay's surface, sending ripples under the moored sailboats and causing them to tug gently at their lines. The sun was sinking into the Gulf, its upper half lingering briefly on the edge of the horizon, giving the appearance of the top half of an orange that somehow had been set afire. I turned south onto Gulf Drive and crossed the Longboat Pass Bridge, marveling at the brilliance of colors the sun was spreading across the darkening water, a pastiche of nature's splendor.

I could feel the tension of the day leaving my body. I was home and a wonderful woman was waiting in my cottage. I parked and walked in the front door, bellowing, "Home is the hunter." No response. I checked the rooms. She wasn't there. I was about to call her cell when I found a note attached to the refrigerator door with one of those little magnets, this one bearing a generic police badge. The note said, "Come to Tiny's. I've got a surprise for you."

I walked the four blocks to Tiny's, enveloped in the soft spring air and the glow of the fading light left by the receding sun. My little world was circumscribed by bay and Gulf and laid-back friends. We reveled in the peacefulness of our tiny dot of land on the edge of a great sea, and perhaps understood that we were merely taking up time and space until our lives came to their inevitable ends and others moved into the void left by our passing. Many of my friends, people in middle age, had first seen the island when they were children visiting grandparents who lived here. As the old ones died out, their children, and in their turn, the grandchildren, moved to the key and would live here until it was time to go to whatever lay beyond our earthly horizon. I guess it's the way of nature, and none of us knew when the end would come. So the prime directive of Longboat Key was simple. Enjoy it while you can.

Lights were coming on in the houses that lined the short and narrow street called Broadway. I often wondered about the person, now long gone, who must have enjoyed a sense of humor to come up with the name because it was so obviously too grand for this little street.

As I neared Tiny's, I could hear the din emanating from the little bar that took up the corner of a small strip-shopping center near the bridge that connected Longboat Key to its neighbor, Anna Maria Island. It was a place that tourists seldom ventured into, leaving it as a dive bar hangout for the locals who lived on the northern end of the island. One of my friends had once described it as the north end clubhouse. And she was right.

I walked in and saw J.D. sitting at the bar, her back to me. A man sat next to her, a bottle of nonalcoholic beer in front of him. I smiled. Jock Algren was my lifelong best friend, a man I'd grown up with in a small town in the middle of the Florida peninsula. He lived in Houston now, but visited regularly. He was an agent of the US government's most secretive intelligence agency, one that was so buried in the bureaucracy that it didn't even have a name.

"Is this man bothering you?" I asked J.D. as I walked to the bar.

"Yes. And I'm enjoying it immensely."

Jock turned and said, "Buzz off, podna. I got here first."

Susie Vaught, the owner of the place, put a glass of Miller Lite on the bar for me. Jock stood and gave me a bear hug. "You doing okay, podna?" he asked.

"Great, Jock. Glad to see you."

"I should have given you some warning that I was on my way, but my boss called early this morning and told me to go to Tampa and meet him. He had a new assignment. Turned out, by the time we got through with the meeting, the operation was called off. Apparently, they had handled it with a drone and a well-placed air-to-ground missile. I decided to just show up here for a few days."

"Glad to have you, buddy. Any time. You know that. Your room is always ready."

"J.D. was just telling me about her aunt. Sounds like you're ready to suit up again. I thought you were finished with all that."

"Me, too. But Esther is family. And besides that, I think I need something to juice up my life a bit. A trial will certainly do that."

"Getting a little tired of J.D.?"

"A little."

"Hey," J.D. said. "You guys knock it off. You're not nearly as funny as you think you are."

I took a stool at the bar and the three of us spent a comfortable evening doing what friends do. We drank a little, told and retold stories, laughed a lot, and talked to friends who wandered in.

We walked home, the quiet of the evening disturbed only by the feeble noise of traffic on Gulf of Mexico Drive and the occasional otherworldly squawk of the peacocks that made their homes in our neighborhood. Jock had never met Esther, but he knew her relationship to J.D. and that she was the only blood family J.D. had left. "I need to run some facts by you two," I said. "I need all the insight I can get on this case."

"I thought you might want the night off," J.D. said.

"I thought I did, too, but it's not working. It keeps running through my mind." I told them the facts as I knew them. "I don't think she was killed in the square," I said. "Somebody would have heard the shot. I bet the van was used to drop the body in the square. It'll be interesting to see what the medical examiner arrives at concerning the time of death."

"If the cops turn up that van, maybe they'll find some evidence that will lead us to the bad guys," J.D. said.

"I wouldn't bet on that," I said. "That van could have hit the turnpike within ten minutes of leaving Brownwood and could have been on I-75 within fifteen minutes. It could be anywhere by now."

J.D. shrugged. "The sheriff's detectives will be trying to figure out where Lathom was from the time she left the bookstore," she said. "Maybe we ought to do the same thing."

"Ruth Bergstrom would be a good person to start with," I said. "She must have spent time with her friend, both before and after the signing."

"Don't the publishers usually send an aide on the tours with those big-time writers?" Jock asked.

"I don't know," I said. "Maybe the publisher is the place for us to start. If an aide was with Lathom, he or she would be able to tell us her schedule that day. We'll have to wait until Monday to contact the publisher."

"Maybe not," J.D. said. "After you left this morning, an update of today's edition of *The Villages Daily Sun* was posted on the Internet. It didn't say anything about an aide, but the reporter mentioned somebody by name who gave her a lot of information. Maybe that was the aide. I think it'd be worth giving the reporter a call and see what we can find out."

"Will you give it a try on Monday?" I asked.

"Sure," J.D. said. "I don't guess you have any idea as to what kind of gun killed the lady."

"I don't know. The paramedic who found the body told me the entrance wound was probably from a small-caliber slug. It might have been a twenty-two."

"Geez," J.D. said, using what for her was an expletive. "Aunt Esther has a twenty-two-caliber revolver. A Smith and Wesson that my dad gave her twenty years ago. She wanted to learn to shoot. He took her to the police range several times."

"Does she still have the pistol?" I asked.

"Probably. I haven't seen it or even thought about it in years. But she's kind of a pack rat, and I don't think she'd throw away something my dad gave her. They were real close. Like a brother and sister."

"If that pistol was in Esther's house, the cops will have it by now. I'm sure they've run ballistics on it to determine if it is the one that killed Lathom."

"If they did," J.D. said, "that should be good for Aunt Esther. Even if it's the right caliber, the ballistics will show that it didn't fire the bullet that killed the victim."

"I'll have to ask her about that on Monday," I said. "I don't think it's a big deal. There are a lot of twenty-twos out there."

Turns out that I was dead wrong.

CHAPTER 9

On Monday morning, I sat on my patio sipping coffee as the night slipped away. The world was slowly revealing itself as feeble light from an invisible sun lurking just below the eastern horizon leaked onto my small island. During the night, sea fog had drifted in from the Gulf, thick and opaque. I was isolated in a bubble of air, surrounded by a cloud so dense that I could not see the edge of the bay less than fifty feet away. It was dead quiet, as if no sound could penetrate the walls of mist the early morning had built around me.

This kind of fog was rare in our latitudes, but not unheard of as we transitioned from winter into spring. The murk that sometimes enveloped the barrier islands along this coast rarely drifted inland. It would clear as I drove onto the mainland, but Longboat might be socked in all day.

Our weekend had been uneventful. Jock had played golf with my buddy Logan on both Saturday and Sunday, probably leaving divots all over the manicured course at the Longboat Key Club. On Saturday, J.D. and I had taken my boat, *Recess,* south on the bay to downtown Sarasota for lunch at the Marina Jack Restaurant. We picked at our salads and talked at length about Esther and about how sad it was that she was sitting in the Sumter County Jail while we were enjoying a beautiful day on the water. "We are a long way from sorting all this out," I said. "I wonder if I could convince a jury that Lathom committed suicide."

J.D. laughed. "Not a chance, buckaroo. Nobody in the history of the world ever committed suicide by shooting themselves in the back with a revolver. A person just can't reach that far."

"Good point."

"We do know one thing," J.D. said.

"What's that?"

"Aunt Esther didn't do it."

"I agree. Can you come up with anything else we might know?"

"I know you'll get her off."

"What if I don't?"

"Then I'll know you did your very best. That's all Esther, or I, for that matter, can ask for."

"I love you."

"I know. How could you not? That's why I trust you with my only living relative's life."

"You are indeed a bumptious woman."

She grinned. "I love you, too. It makes me hot when you go all lawyer."

"Time to go home," I said. I dropped some bills on the table and we set sail. Or cranked the big Yamahas, to be precise.

* * *

Sunday was a day for lying around doing mostly nothing. I perused the newspapers from Sarasota and Bradenton and fired up my computer and read up on the law in case I'd missed anything since the last time I'd done any legal research. J.D. and I walked to Mar Vista for lunch under the trees on the edge of the bay, went home, took a nap, and met Jock and Logan for drinks at Tiny's. As I said, it was an uneventful weekend.

* * *

The fog was not dissipating. I finished my coffee, looked at my watch. Six thirty. I decided I had time for one more cup before I started the trip to Bushnell. Monday morning was when the world woke from its weekend torpor and went back to work. Retirement changes that metric. Monday becomes just another weekend day when I could sleep in, jog the beach, fish, or just sit. Not today. I was back in the grind.

The sliding glass door behind me opened, and I felt a pair of arms snake around my neck, a kiss on the top of my head, the warm breath of J. D. Duncan caressing the back of my neck. "Good morning, Counselor."

"Don't start," I said.

"What?"

"I was just thinking about all the things I'd like to be doing today. Going to the Sumter County courthouse is not one of them."

"Want me to go with you? I don't have anything going on today that somebody else can't handle."

"I've been thinking about that. Do you think you could take some time off? Say a couple of weeks or so?"

"I don't think it'd be a problem. I've got a lot of comp time and vacation built up. Why?"

"What would you say to an undercover operation in The Villages?"

"Let me get a cup of coffee."

J.D. returned to the patio and sat in the chair next to me. "What have you got in mind?"

"I'm worried that I won't be able to get close enough to some of the people I'll need to talk to up there. And I don't think an investigator will either. These folks are retired and don't want to be bothered with a lot of what they might perceive as legal nonsense. If we had you up there, becoming part of the community with nobody knowing you're Esther's niece or a cop, you might dig up something."

"You've got to be fifty-five to live in The Villages. Are you suggesting that I could pass for that age?"

I laughed. "Not a chance, sugarplum. But I think I read somewhere that only one person in a household has to be over fifty-five."

"Okay."

"Do you know the lady who owns the bookstore up there who is a friend of Aunt Esther's?"

"Judy Ferguson. Yes. I've met her a time or two. Don't know her well. You met her when we visited at Christmas. She came to the Thursday-night driveway party at Aunt Esther's."

It had become a tradition. Many of the villages that formed the neighborhoods set aside a couple of hours on Thursday evenings for a driveway party. The person hosting that evening would put some sort of sign on their front yard, a plastic flamingo perhaps, and at five in the afternoon the neighbors would show up with a bottle of whatever they were drinking and an outdoor cocktail party would ensue. The host might provide light snacks from the grocery store and perhaps some mixers for the liquor drinkers, but no host was expected to spend more than a few bucks. By seven, everybody was gone. It was a chance for the neighbors to get to know each other, to chat about unimportant things, and enjoy the company of other retirees from all over the nation.

"I don't remember her specifically," I said, "but she and Esther are pretty close, aren't they?"

"Best friends, I think."

"Suppose we could get you up there to live with Judy, maybe as her niece, and put you to work part-time in her bookstore. You could join the book club that seems to be at the center of this whole mess and get to know some of the ladies. You might be able to come up with some information I'd never find."

She sat quietly for a moment, thinking. She took a sip of her coffee. "Matt, run this by Aunt Esther. If she thinks it'll help, I'll talk to the chief about taking a month off. I can probably use built-up time for that, and if I don't have enough accrued, I can take a short leave of absence. If I'm going to stumble over anything, I think a month might be more productive than a couple of weeks."

"I'll talk to Esther today, and if she likes the idea, I'll go see Judy. Is Jock still in bed?"

"Far as I know. Want me to get him up?"

"No. Let him sleep. I've got to get on the road."

"Be careful with that fog."

"It'll clear by the time I get to the fire station on Cortez Road."

She walked me to the front door and hugged me for a long moment. "Thanks for doing this, Matt."

That hug was all the compensation I needed to send me happily back into the legal jungle.

CHAPTER 10

I WALKED INTO the Clerk of Court's office in the Sumter County courthouse at nine o'clock on the dot. I filed a notice of appearance on behalf of Aunt Esther, a motion for her release on her own recognizance or, in the alternative, for the court to set bail, a motion to dismiss the second-degree murder charge, and a number of discovery motions. I doubted that the motions would do any good, but I wanted them on the record.

The charge against Esther was second-degree murder. The difference between that and first-degree murder was substantial in that a death sentence was possible only if the accused were convicted of murder in the first degree. However, that charge had to be brought by indictment by a grand jury and the prosecutor would have to convince a trial jury that the killing had been premeditated. I didn't think that would fly with Esther's case, but prosecutors often went for the indictment so they could use the death penalty as a bargaining chip with the defense team. "Plead guilty and we'll take the death penalty off the table." It could be an effective tool and it put tremendous pressure on the poor sap trying to defend his client and keep him or her out of the death chamber. Both charges, first- or second-degree murder, carried the possibility of a sentence of life without parole. Once I took the measure of the prosecutor, I'd be in a better position to gauge his intent about the indictment.

I left the Clerk's office and walked down the hall to the state attorney's suite. I went in and introduced myself to the receptionist and told her I would be representing Esther Higgins. I wondered if the case had been assigned to a prosecutor yet. She asked me to take a seat and she'd find out. "Can I get you a cup of coffee while I'm in the back?"

"Thank you. Black would be just fine."

She was back in a few minutes and handed me a Styrofoam cup of coffee. "Meredith Evans will be prosecuting the case, Mr. Royal, but I'm afraid she's tied up in court in Ocala this morning. She should be back before noon. Her secretary said she could see you then. I'd be happy to call you when she gets in."

"That'll work for me. Thank you." I gave her my cell number and left for the Detention Center, sipping the surprisingly good coffee.

* * *

Esther was in the same small conference room where I'd met her on Friday. "How are you holding up?" I asked.

"Piece of cake."

"Are all the women in your family as tough as you and J.D.?"

"She and I are the last of many generations of southern women."

"*Steel Magnolias*," I said.

She grinned. "Bet your ass, sonny boy."

I laughed. In this dismal, windowless, and sunless room, wearing a jailhouse jumpsuit, facing life in prison, or worse, and being fully aware of her plight, this delightful woman displayed a girlish insouciance that made me laugh. She and J.D. had certainly been crafted from the same gene pool. *My God*, I thought, *I can't lose this woman to the Florida Department of Corrections.*

"Esther," I said. "Do you own a twenty-two-caliber pistol?"

"I do. J.D.'s dad gave it to me years ago."

"Where is it?"

"In my closet at home. Why?"

"The bullet that killed Olivia was apparently a small caliber. Maybe a twenty-two. I'm sure the police would have found it when they searched your house. Do I have anything to worry about with the gun?"

"What do you mean?" Her voice was quiet, flat.

"Did you lend it to a friend? Anything like that?"

"No."

"I don't think it's anything to worry about, but I'm just trying to cover all the bases. I'm sure the police will have run ballistics on it by now and figured out that yours wasn't the gun used to kill Olivia."

We talked for an hour. I explained what I was doing procedurally, what I hoped to gain by doing it, and what I thought about our chances of getting her out of jail. I cautioned her that we might be facing an indictment for first-degree murder and told her how that differed from second-degree murder and what it might mean in any plea bargaining.

"Matt," she said, "there won't be any plea bargaining. I didn't kill that woman. If I'm going to prison for something I didn't do, the prosecutor is going to have go through a jury to put me there. I've got complete faith in your ability to get me acquitted."

"I appreciate your confidence, Esther, but I didn't win all my cases. No lawyer does. Not if he tries many."

She smiled and patted my hand. "You'll win this one. When do you think we'll get to trial?"

"The speedy trial rule requires us to start within one hundred seventy days of your arrest. That is almost six months. That could put us as late as the end of August."

"What are my chances of bail?"

"Not good. But I've filed a motion for bail, and I'll take a hard swing at it. If we don't get it, I'll push the prosecutor to get to trial a lot quicker than six months."

"How quickly do you think we can get to trial?"

"We'll just have to wait and see. If I can't get you bailed out of here, the prosecutor will want to drag things out as long as possible. The idea is that if you're sitting in the county jail, you're more amenable to agreeing to a plea deal."

"Years ago, the school system I worked for got in a jam and had to assign me to an all-boys junior high school to teach eighth-grade English. There is nothing in the world worse than spending all day cooped up in a room with thirty hormone-crazed, potty-mouthed thirteen-year-olds who can't think of anything but sex. You tell that prosecutor that if I could handle that for nine months, I can damn sure handle a jail cell for six months. No deals. Tell him not to even bother offering one."

"It's a her."

"What?"

"The prosecutor is a woman."

"You're kidding."

"Nope. We actually have women lawyers these days."

"I know that, you Neanderthal. I'm sure she didn't get to the point where she's prosecuting murder cases unless she's very good and paid a lot of dues. Worked her butt off."

"I'm sure you're right."

"I'm proud of her. Don't tell her I said that. She'll think I'm pandering, but I like to see a woman make her way in this world. Maybe if I'd come along a few years later, I'd have been a lawyer, or a cop like J.D. In my day, educated women usually became teachers or nurses. Not anymore. The floodgates have opened. Long past due. What do you know about her?"

"Nothing, yet. I just got her name this morning. Meredith Evans. I'll know more after I meet her and read up on her background. I'm sure she's pretty good if she handles murder cases. This won't be her first one."

We talked some more. I told her what J.D. and I were thinking about J.D.'s role in an undercover investigation. "What do you think?"

"I like it," she said. "Judy's a good friend, and I'm sure she'll help. She came to see me yesterday during visiting hours and said if I needed anything to let her know."

"I'll go see her today."

"She'll be at her bookstore. She works there all day."

We talked a few more minutes, and I got up to leave. I leaned over and kissed her on the cheek. "You make me proud to be an honorary member of your family," I said.

"Then don't screw up this case." She grinned, and in that moment, I saw J.D. twenty-five years in the future. I was staring into the face that J.D. would someday wear. The thought of our growing old together made me happy because it promised that we would be with each other even after the inexorable march of time took first our youth and then our middle age. And it made me a little sad, because the reality is that old age portends the end of life, and perhaps the end of togetherness.

CHAPTER 11

I CALLED THE state attorney's office and spoke again to the receptionist. She had not heard from the prosecutor yet and assumed she was still in court. I talked to Ms. Evans' secretary, and we set an appointment for us to meet in her office at three that afternoon. I drove to The Villages to talk to Judy Ferguson.

I found her bookstore in the Grand Traverse Plaza at the corner of Powell Road and Highway 44. Like most everything in The Villages, the place looked new. A variety of trees shaded the parking lot and the trill of tiny sparrows filled the air with songs that gave the world a reason to smile. Golf carts were parked two to a space, side by side with cars and trucks.

I found the bookstore several doors down from the Publix Market, sandwiched between a Chinese restaurant and a dental office. I walked into a pleasant space that was bigger than it had seemed from outside.

Casually dressed people were browsing the bookshelves that lined either side of the shop. Upholstered chairs were grouped in the middle of the room and tables stacked with best sellers were placed comfortably about the area. I saw a vaguely familiar woman, whom I assumed to be Judy, standing behind a counter on one side of the store finishing a conversation with a customer. The customer left, and Judy watched me walking toward her, a quizzical look on her face.

"Hi, Judy," I said as I reached the counter. "I'm Matt Royal. We met at Esther Higgins' driveway party back at Christmastime."

Her face broke into a smile. She was a pretty woman who wore her sixty-five years with grace and self-assurance. Her strawberry-blond hair was trimmed and shot with gray. "Matt. Of course. I couldn't quite place the handsome man I saw walking across my little store. How are you? And how is J.D.?"

"We're both fine, thank you. It's good to see you again."

"I suspect you're not here for a social visit. Esther told me you were going to represent her."

"I wanted to talk to you about Esther. I've got a pretty big favor to ask and I'd like to lay it out over lunch. Can you get away?"

She looked at the clock on the wall behind the counter. "It's almost noon now. Let me get one of the girls to look after things, and we can leave right away. Do you have any place in mind for lunch?"

"It's your town. You choose."

"There's a World of Beer over in Brownwood. They've got a giant Bavarian soft pretzel that'll melt in your mouth. And the dipping sauce is out of this world. How's that sound?"

I laughed. "Count me in. Actually, I was there Friday."

We took her golf cart with me riding shotgun. Our short drive was over asphalt tracks crowded with people in carts of all descriptions, smiling and waving. A friend of mine had once described the place as a large support group for old people. I suppose that was true in many respects, but if it seemed to be a bit frenetic, it was also a very happy place. Too happy for murder to intrude so rudely.

Judy found a parking space among a horde of other golf carts about half a block from our destination. The shops and restaurants and other establishments of Brownwood lined streets that formed the area that was the entertainment venue known as Paddock Square. It reminded me of the old southern towns with the courthouse square in the middle of their small business districts. It was in this pleasant place that Kevin Cook had found the body of Olivia Lathom.

We found a table just inside the restaurant near the doors that opened onto the outdoor seating area. Judy ordered an iced tea and I asked for water. I wanted to try one of the craft beers they had on tap, but I didn't want to meet the state prosecutor with alcohol on my breath. Not a very good first impression. Judy suggested that we split one of the pretzels.

"Okay, Matt. How can I help my friend?"

"I'd like you to adopt J.D. as your niece, change her name, move her into your house, and put her to work in your store. For about a month."

"Not a problem."

"That was easy. But you'd better let me tell you why. Esther said this was a lot to ask of you, and if you had any hesitancy at all, you shouldn't agree to it. She'll understand and not think any less of you or your friendship."

"What are friends for? I'll do it, but I would like to hear what you've got up your sleeve."

I thought about that for a moment. I realized I hadn't fully figured out a plan. My idea of J.D. as an undercover operative was more an amorphous concept than a plan. I decided to think it through as we talked. Maybe Judy could round off any hard edges that might not fit in a plan for The Villages.

Every community is alike in some ways, and so different in others. The demographics of this area were different from most. It was a retirement community of over a hundred thousand people, mostly well educated and still young enough to enjoy all the amenities offered by this unique place.

"This is a bit of a closed society you have here," I said. "All groups are like that to some extent. There is a kind of wariness, probably unconscious, among a lot of people. They're more careful about talking to strangers. They hold back information. And if a lawyer shows up, or an investigator, asking sharp questions, they close down completely."

"So your idea is that J.D. can become a spy."

"Sort of. She's a trained homicide investigator, so she'll know what to look for, what questions to ask. But if everybody knows she's a cop, the information starts drying up. If she's just the new girl in town, and your niece to boot, I think people who know something will be more forthcoming. Does that bother you? The spy part?"

"Good Lord, no. I think it's brilliant. I can put her to work in the bookstore and get her introduced around town."

"I'd like to get her into your book club as soon as possible."

"That's easy. We meet every other week over at the Eisenhower Center. But what if somebody recognizes her? She met some of the neighbors at Esther's driveway party back during Christmas."

"I doubt anybody paid a whole lot of attention. I think a new hairdo, a dye job, maybe a pair of glasses, and she'll look like a different person."

"This is going to be exciting."

"It could also be dangerous, Judy," I said. "We have to keep J.D.'s real identity very quiet."

"My lips are sealed. When will she be moving in with me?"

"I'm not sure. She has to get her time off work set up and have a couple of days to change her appearance. I don't think there will be a problem at work and she can get her hair done in a day or two. Today's Monday, so maybe by Wednesday or Thursday, if that works for you."

"That'll work. Are you going to be hanging around?"

"I'll be here a lot, but I need to stay away from J.D. I don't want to compromise her in any way."

"That's probably a good idea. Do you have a name for her?"

"I haven't thought about that. We ought to try to make it a name similar to her own. People get used to responding to their names, so I don't think Paulette or Vanessa would work. You have any ideas?"

"I have a sister named Beryl, which is a mineral, and she has a daughter named Jade, which is a rock. A little too much for me, but Jade is about the same age as J.D. and both names sound similar."

"Where does Jade live?" I asked.

"She's an Army Intelligence officer. She's stationed somewhere in Europe."

"Has she ever visited you here? Would anybody know her?"

"No. My sister and I had a falling out when we were in college and we've hardly ever spoken to each other since. I only met Jade once. That was at my mother's funeral. Jade was just a little girl then. I get a long family note from Beryl every Christmas, so that's how I know Jade is in Europe. Or was at Christmas, anyway."

"That might be a good cover. If anybody got nervous and was able to do some background checking, they'd find out that you really do have a niece named Jade. What's Jade's last name?"

"Conway. Jade Elizabeth Conway."

"Married?"

"Was," Judy said. "Divorced. No children."

"What if we set up some background for J.D. as a recently divorced woman who needed to get away from her old life and came here for an extended visit with a favorite aunt."

"Wouldn't J.D. have to come from somewhere that Jade lived? I mean if anybody was doing background checks."

"I don't know how we can cover for that. If somebody digs deeply enough, they'll be able to figure out that J.D. isn't Jade. If we tell people that J.D. lived in Miami, she could answer any questions since she lived there most of her life. She only came to Longboat Key about three years ago."

"And Jade's last duty station before Europe was an Army command down in Miami. This might work better than we thought."

"And," I said," on the off-chance that somebody finds out that Jade is in the Army and asks J.D. about it, she can claim she can't talk about it because of national security concerns. Not much chance of getting tripped up if you don't talk. This just keeps getting better."

"Sounds like a plan. Matt, I think you have a devious side."

"Occupational failing. All lawyers are afflicted with it."

We each ordered sandwiches, ate them, and finished our pretzel. It was nearing two p.m., and I noticed that my bartender buddy Amber Marris had come in and was helping the day shift tidy up behind the bar. I excused myself from the table and took the transcript of the recording I'd made on Friday and handed it to Amber. "Would you read this over and make sure it's correct?" I asked.

She smiled. "Sure." When she finished, she said, "Looks right. Do you want me to sign it?"

I handed her a pen and copy of the transcript. "Thanks. You've been a big help. I've got the name of the assistant state attorney who'll be prosecuting the case. She's Meredith Evans and you can reach her at the state attorney's office in Bushnell. I'm sure you'll be hearing more from both of us as this case moves toward trial."

Judy drove me back to the plaza and I headed toward Bushnell and my appointment with the woman I would be butting heads with for the next few months, Assistant State Attorney Meredith Evans.

CHAPTER 12

MY FIRST IMPRESSION of Meredith Evans was, well, average. She was an average-looking woman, wearing average-looking clothes, and had an average-looking smile. Her hair was average-looking, brownish and cut short enough that she didn't have to spend much time taking care of it. Her handshake was of average pressure, not too tight, not too loose, and her greeting was average for the lawyer she was. That is, it was average until she said the magic words. "So, you're the great Matt Royal."

Now that kind of greeting sent tremors of delight up and down my ego and made me think that this was a very perceptive woman. I mentally kicked myself for the fool I am and thought about what a hoot J.D. would have at my expense if she were here and could read my mind. Which, I'm pretty sure she's able to do.

"Great?" I asked.

"I watched most of that trial where you defended Dr. Carpenter several years ago."

"Sometimes you get lucky."

"That wasn't luck. Come on back to my office. Let's talk about Esther Higgins. Want some coffee?"

"No, thanks. I'm about coffeed out for the day."

We sat in her office, a bare place with institutional gray paint on the walls and a diploma that told me she had graduated from the University of Florida College of Law ten years before. A window looked out over a parking lot, with a side street beyond. She waved me to a chair and took her seat behind a cheap desk. "I heard you'd retired to the Keys," she said.

"Common mistake," I said. "Actually, I retired to Longboat Key near Sarasota. People hear the word key and they think Florida Keys."

"What brings you out of retirement for a case in Sumter County?"

"Esther is a relative of a friend of mine, and I was asked to help."

"You sure you want to get back into this mess?"

I laughed. "I'm pretty sure I don't, but duty calls."

"Do you want to talk about a plea?"

"Not even if you reduced it to a misdemeanor. Esther is innocent."

She smiled. "You guys always say that."

"Show me your cards," I said.

"Not yet."

"Why not? You'll have to give them to me sooner or later."

"I will, but I haven't even seen them yet. I was out of town this weekend and I've been up in Ocala all morning. I'll get it to you timely, though. I promise."

"I checked you out, you know," I said.

"Hah. I'm not surprised. Who did you talk to?"

"An old drinking buddy down in Tavares. Billy Ray Johnson."

"You know Billy Ray? That man could drink an alligator into a stupor. He's got to be pushing seventy now, and I don't see any sign of his slowing down."

"Yep. He and I go way back. I figured if anybody in this circuit could tell me about you, it'd be him."

"What did he say?"

"He said you kicked his butt last year in Ocala."

"Barely. And I had a cop for an eyewitness who saw the perp shoot the victim. What else did the old bastard have to say?"

"He said you were tough as nails, honest as the day is long, and always prepared. You've probably noticed he likes clichés. He has a very high opinion of you, and Billy Ray is not lavish with his praise of prosecutors."

"When did you talk to him?" she asked. "He sounds like he's mellowing some."

"I called him about an hour ago."

"My boss thinks you're the best lawyer he ever faced in a courtroom. You beat him on a case he didn't think he could lose and he says you did it fair and square."

"I hope he doesn't hold a grudge."

"Not at all. The doctor you sprung is a model citizen and helps out a lot of folks that don't have insurance and can't pay for medical care. I think you did the community a favor."

"I doubt the sheriff feels the same way."

"You might be surprised," she said, with a small smile. "Look, Matt, I understand your client is an upstanding citizen who taught school for most of her life."

"Not exactly the profile of a killer."

"People surprise us. It wouldn't be the first time I've prosecuted someone I never would have thought had it in them to commit a crime."

"I've met those people, too, but I don't think Esther is one of them."

"I guess we'll see. I should have the investigative material coming in over the next couple of weeks, probably starting with the first reports tomorrow. Why don't you file a motion, and we'll get the judge to enter an open order so that I have to provide the discovery to you as it comes in. Say, with ten days' grace time from the day I get it."

"I appreciate that, Meredith. I filed the motion first thing this morning." I reached into my briefcase and pulled out a copy and gave it to her. "Are you going to get any pushback from your boss?"

"No. He lets me run my cases the way I want."

"How about bail?"

"Sorry. I can't agree to that. I don't want to push my luck. My boss has to run for reelection this year, and he has an ironclad rule about not agreeing to bail in murder cases."

I stood. "I'll look forward to working with you, Counselor. Time for me to head for the beach. I'll be in touch." I gave her my business card and told her to call me anytime.

I stopped by the detention center and spent another hour with Esther, telling her about my day and my conversations with Judy and the prosecutor. "We're going to have a hard time getting bail set. Evans is going to argue against it. You might be here until trial."

"Do what you can, Matt. If you can't get bail, I'll understand. Are you going to be spending a lot of time up here?"

"Yes. I've got a lot of people to talk to, and we'll probably have a lot of hearings between now and the trial."

"Why don't you move into my place for the duration? No sense in your driving back and forth to Longboat Key every day."

"What if we get bail?"

She laughed. "You stay in the guest bedroom. J.D. will understand and the neighbors will think I've scored with a younger man. My next-door neighbor Sue has a spare key. Make yourself at home."

"That's probably a good idea. I'll let you know." I told her I'd see her in a couple of days and kissed her cheek good-bye.

I left the jail, connected my iPod to the Explorer's sound system, turned on some classic country music, and started the two-hour drive to Longboat Key. I have to admit that I sang along with all those good old boys who were mostly dead now. Except for Willie Nelson, of course.

CHAPTER 13

J.D. WAS WEARING shorts and a halter-top, sitting in a lounger on the patio. I walked in the front door of my cottage, threw my coat and tie over the back of the sofa, grabbed a beer from the refrigerator, and joined her. She looked up from a book and said, "Jock's playing golf with Logan Hamilton, Sam Lastinger, and Tom Stout."

"Where are they playing?" I asked.

"Don't know. Sammy called and gave me the directions to give to Jock. He said to tell him to take Bee Ridge Road east until he runs into the dump. Turn right and when Jock thinks he's gone too far, keep going."

"Great directions."

"Well, it *is* Sammy. Did you talk to Judy Ferguson?"

"She's your new aunt." I told her about my day and all of the ideas Judy and I had discussed about J.D.'s undercover operation.

"I think that sounds like a plan. Maybe I'll become a blond. What do you think?"

"Well, they do say that blonds have more fun. Might be good for you."

"Are you suggesting I'm no fun?"

"No, ma'am. You are loads of fun." I'm constantly amazed at how easily I can find myself on thin ice simply by muttering something stupid.

She laughed, the tinkling one that always made me feel like a big shot, and reached for my hand. "Then you don't really think my being blond is going to make any difference?"

"Not at all," I said, and adroitly changed the subject. "Have you talked to the chief about some time off?"

"I did. He has no problem with it. He's going to make Steve Carey the acting detective, and I can be gone for a month."

"Maybe I haven't given this idea the attention it deserves. A month apart is going to really disrupt our lives."

"Maybe not too much. We'll see each other up there."

"Only in passing," I said. "We can't let on that we know each other."

"I'll get out of there every few days and meet you here. Nobody will figure it out. If anybody asks, Judy can tell them that I have to go to Miami now and then because of the divorce proceedings."

"When do you want to move in with Judy?"

"I need to do something about my hair, pack some things. I'll see if Gary Winters can squeeze me into his salon tomorrow and, if he can, I should be ready to go on Wednesday morning. When do you have to be back up there?"

"Not until later this week. I think the prosecutor is going to send me some initial stuff in the next couple of days—police reports, that sort of thing. I'll need to get back up there and talk to some of the witnesses again."

"Are you going to hire an investigator to do some of that?"

"Maybe. Right now, I'd like to talk to these folks on my own. Maybe I can get some leads that I can pass on to you for follow-up."

"I talked to that *Daily Sun* reporter today," J.D. said. "Told her I was your assistant and was trying to follow up on some stuff for you. She gave me the name of the aide the publisher sent along with Lathom on the book-signing trip. She's a freelancer based in Cincinnati and does this kind of thing for several of the major publishers. She babysits authors around the Southeast and Midwest. Her name is Peggy Keefe." She handed me a piece of notepaper with the aide's name and a cell phone number.

"I'll give her a call tomorrow. Either that or go to Cincinnati and talk to her in person. Did the reporter have anything else to tell you?"

"Not much. She said that Ms. Keefe was very cooperative and anxious to get home. She spent quite a bit of time with the sheriff's detectives and then left on Friday morning. What do you hope to find out from her?"

"I'd like to re-create Lathom's last hours. When I get the autopsy report I'll have an approximate time of death, and we know about what time she finished the signing at Barnes & Noble. I hope Ms. Keefe can tighten that timeline up a bit. She'll know what time she and Lathom separated, so then we only have to fill in the time between when Keefe saw her last and the time of death."

"And how do you plan to do that?"

"Good question. I noticed that when a visitor enters one of the villages, they're staring into a camera as they push the button to raise the bar at the gatehouse to let them in. I can't believe The Villages security people wouldn't have some way to identify the guests. They'll have a picture of the driver and probably a license plate number. If we can narrow the time down, maybe we can get a look at the pictures from those cameras. We might be able to tell where Lathom went and when she went there. If she was killed in one of the villages, somebody took her body to Brownwood. We may be able to find out which neighborhood she entered last by determining that she didn't go into another."

"What about her car?" J.D. asked.

"Another good question. If she was traveling alone, she had to have a car. Where did she get the car? Peggy Keefe might know something about that. If we can narrow that down, it'll save us a lot of time looking through pictures of drivers. I'll bet the security people can search their database by license plate numbers. If we can get a plate number to give the security people, that should help us find when the car went through the security gates."

"And why is that so important?"

"Right now, only because it may help us pinpoint the location where she was killed. That'll be a starting place to find the killer."

She smiled. "You'd have made a pretty good detective."

"Only pretty good?"

"We'll see how this plays out. Want some dinner?"

"I'm feeling expensive. Let's go to Euphemia Haye. Chef Ray has the best steak au poivre in the state."

"What about Jock?"

"Those guys will be drinking and eating in the clubhouse wherever they're playing. Besides, I want to get a little dressed up and spend some quality time with my honey."

"Your honey?"

I grinned. "Yep. My honey."

CHAPTER 14

My Tuesday morning jog on the beach cleared my head of the extra beers I'd drunk at the Haye Loft bar the night before. J.D. and I had enjoyed a comfortable evening with great food and a quiet togetherness that we seemed to seldom find for ourselves. After dinner, we climbed the stairs to the Haye Loft bar and sat quietly listening to the jazz pianist Michael Markaverich.

I'd been wrong about the golfers staying in the clubhouse at the course they'd played. They nosily arrived in the Haye Loft about twenty minutes after we sat down. Given the warmth of the day and the eighteen holes they'd played, they didn't smell as rank as I would have expected.

We joined them and probably enjoyed the evening too much. None of them were great golfers, but Tom Stout had been to golf school, whatever that is, in Orlando for a few days, and had apparently learned enough to beat the other three. The lies they all told were mildly humorous, but as the bartender Eric Bell pointed out, the same stories were told several times and the retelling ran the gamut from a little bit funny to hilarious. Eric figured that was a direct result of the amount of alcohol consumed by the participants. Including yours truly.

Tuesday was shaping up to be one of those glorious days we often get in March. I'd slept in a bit and gotten a late start on my daily jog. At a little after ten in the morning, the humidity was low and the thermometer hovered at seventy degrees. People were on the beach taking advantage of the weather. Many were lounging on beach chairs reading books, some were walking along the water's edge, and a few were surf-fishing.

The Gulf was calm, its turquoise waters flat and as reflective as a freshly burnished mirror. Cumulus clouds floated high above, their whiteness stark against the rich blue of the sky. Pelicans were diving for their breakfast, splashing into the surface and gulping down the hapless fish they'd spotted. Sandpipers skittered out of the way of the walkers and nearby a colony of seagulls was squawking loudly as they fought over the remains of a fish that had washed in with the tide. Far out on the horizon, a sailboat was moving on a northerly course, its sails billowing in the breeze that barely touched the shore.

Endorphins were flooding my system, the exercise and the beauty of my surroundings conflating to send my spirits into paroxysms of joie de vivre. God, I loved this island. And here I was, about to exchange days like this for days in a courtroom. I decided I must be nuts. There isn't a trial lawyer in the world who would have disagreed with me.

J.D. had stayed the night at my cottage and left early for a trip to see her hairdresser on the mainland. I planned to call Peggy Keefe when I got home and see if she could tell me anything that might be of use in defending Esther. I didn't hold out much hope of finding the proverbial smoking gun, but she might be able to add a few details that over time would merge with other facts from other witnesses, and like the pieces of a jigsaw puzzle, begin to merge into a recognizable pattern.

Building a defense is a process. Different witnesses know different things. They are often only aware of a fact or two, and do not initially see how what they know might fit into the narrative that the trial lawyer must assemble in defense of his client.

When the lawyer starts to put together the pieces of the puzzle, everything is hazy. But over time, as the investigation proceeds and more facts surface, the picture starts to form. When the puzzle is nearly finished, and only a few crucial pieces are missing, that moment of clarity strikes, and the lawyer begins to see his way to an acquittal.

A case, civil or criminal, is a mind game. The lawyer never entirely stops thinking about it. Little tendrils of ideas constantly play across his brain, one hypothesis forming only to be replaced by another when new facts emerge and new theories are formed. The process is mentally exhausting and not nearly as much fun as fishing. But sometimes, one does what one has to do, and Aunt Esther's freedom was certainly worth my giving up a few months of indolence.

I jogged the beach for the better part of an hour and was walking as I neared the North Shore Road boardwalk that spanned the dunes. My phone rang. I answered.

"Good morning, Matt. This is Meredith Evans."

"Good morning to you, Counselor. How are you?"

"For being stuck in an office, not bad. How about you?"

"Just finishing a jog on the beach."

"You're a mean person, Matt Royal."

I laughed. "Why don't you drop the charges against Esther Higgins and get out of the office for a few days? We'll both feel better."

"Right. Look, I've got a question for you."

"Shoot."

"Are we going to get along on this case?"

"I hope so," I said. "Billy Ray Johnson says you're a straight shooter, and maybe a little bit of a hard-ass."

"That's very strange. He said the same thing about you."

"Ah, you checked me out."

"Yep. Billy Ray said he thought you and I could work together and maybe get this case handled with as little grief as possible."

"I hope we can do that, Meredith. Are you planning to go for an indictment?"

"Probably not. I think first degree would be overkill. And at this point, I don't think I can prove premeditation. At least not with what I've seen so far."

"It would give you some bargaining room. Lots of prosecutors do that."

"Billy Ray said all that would do is piss you off and that a pissed-off Matt Royal is not a pretty sight. Besides, I'm very conscious of the fact that, while I represent the state and need to go for the conviction, I also have an affirmative duty as an officer of the court to seek justice."

"That would sound a little sanctimonious coming from a lot of prosecutors, but Billy Ray said you really believe in what you're doing and how you do it."

"Do you believe him? Do you believe me?"

"I believe both of you."

"Okay, Matt. Look, we're going to be exchanging a lot of information and ideas over the next few months. I got the autopsy report this morning and I want to fax it to you."

"You're not going to wait for the formal discovery process?"

"No, but I took a look at your discovery motions. I'll respond in a timely manner so you'll eventually get the same documents that I'll be voluntarily sending you. You can compare them and assure yourself that I'm not playing loose with the documents."

"Meredith, you know there are going to be some things I can't and won't share with you. Not voluntarily, anyway."

"I won't be offended. I might try to force your hand if I think you're off-base with what you're withholding, but I'm comfortable letting the judge decide those disputes."

"What about bail?" I asked.

"I can't agree to that. Not yet, anyway. As I told you, my boss is not big on bail, and I don't want to get kicked off this case."

"Do you have the police report yet?"

"No, but I'll send it to you as soon as I get it."

"Scrubbed?"

"No, sir. I'll send you exactly what I get."

"Why are you doing this?"

"I'm told that there is enough evidence tying your client to the crime, that she has to be involved. I'm going for a conviction. But, she's got no record, and by all accounts I've heard, she's an upstanding citizen and much beloved by a couple of generations of students up in Atlanta. I want her to have a fair shot. I'm glad she's got a good lawyer, and I'm going to do my best to beat your sorry ass and put her in jail. But when it's all over, and you go back to Longboat Key with your tail between your legs, I want to look old Billy Ray in the face and tell him I beat you fair and square. And then you and I will need to drink some whiskey together."

"Then I guess we'd better suit up. I'm looking forward to working with you, Meredith. I think Billy Ray was right on the money."

"What do you mean?"

"He said I'd like you, and that I could trust you, but the first time I let my guard down, you'd punch me in the nose."

She laughed. "Billy Ray is a very perceptive man. I'll fax the autopsy report to you in the next few minutes. Thanks for having Amber Marris call me." She hung up before I could answer.

I thought about that somewhat strange phone call as I walked down Broadway toward my house. I'd had those kinds of cooperative relationships with opposing counsel in the past, but they were always in civil lawsuits. I had never seen this kind of approach from a prosecutor. I wondered if there was something other than professional ethics behind Meredith's offer to work closely together and her decision not to seek a first-degree murder indictment. No telling what that might be.

On the other hand, maybe she was just an honest person doing a tough and often thankless job and trying to do it in a manner that comported with her sense of justice. It has often been said that justice, like beauty, is in the eye of the beholder. The result is that justice is generally an ephemeral concept at best.

I was still worried about the sheriff's reaction to my being involved in this case. I had expected him to treat me like a pariah, and yet he was respectful and even cordial. And now Meredith Evans was being overly cooperative and perhaps giving me an advantage that prosecutors almost never provide defense lawyers.

I mentally shrugged it off and decided I'd know more as I became better acquainted with the political and legal landscape of Sumter County. I walked on toward home and a hot shower.

I opened the front door of my cottage and saw a blond woman sitting at my computer. Her hair was cut short and she was wearing black horn-rimmed glasses. "I want to tell you up front," I said. "I'm in love with a woman named J.D., so if you have any designs on my body, you'd best stifle them right now."

J.D. turned to look at me through the clear glass of her new spectacles. "Jock's out playing golf again with Mike Nink. Are you interested in finding out if blonds really do have more fun?"

"Right now?"

"I think I can stifle my designs until you take a shower."

"Give me a minute."

She wrinkled her nose. "It's going to take more than a minute, lover. You're sweating like a hog and you stink."

"God, I love it when you talk mean to me," I said, and ran for the shower.

CHAPTER 15

THE VOICE ON the other end of the telephone connection was pleasant. After I'd showered, assured myself that blonds did in fact have loads of fun, and shared a lunch on the patio with J.D., I called Peggy Keefe, the victim's traveling aide. I identified myself and explained my interest in the case. She was cordial and happy to help. I asked about her job and how she came to be working with Ms. Lathom.

"I'm kind of a freelancer," she said. "Publishers keep a list of people like me who take on their minor authors. I think the major authors get somebody who works for the publisher full-time. I take the traveling aide job if the author is going to someplace I've wanted to visit. If the author is pleasant and not too full of herself, it's usually a lot of fun."

"I thought Ms. Lathom was a *New York Times* best seller," I said.

"She is. But this is her first book to hit the best-seller list. I think before the publishers spend too much money, they want to make sure that the author in question is going to become a regular best seller. Until then, they get the freelancers, like me."

"How did you come to be Ms. Lathom's aide?" I asked.

"The usual thing. I got a call from somebody at the publisher who schedules authors at bookstores. She asked if I would be interested in working with an author who would be touring Florida. I was told that Olivia was easy to get along with and the trip would only be for a week. All in Florida."

"Where did you start?" I asked.

"The Villages was our first stop. We flew into Orlando, rented a car, and drove up to The Villages."

"What kind of car?"

"Chevrolet, I think."

"Do you have the paperwork on the rental?"

"Yes."

"I'd like some information off the paperwork. Do you mind?"

"Of course not. Give me a minute to dig it up." She was back in a couple of minutes. "What do you need?"

"Make, model, color, tag number, rental contract number, name of rental company, time out and time in."

"I've got a scanner. Would it be easier for me to email it to you?"

I laughed. "Welcome to the twenty-first century, Royal."

"I know the feeling," she said. "Give me you email address and I'll have it on the way as soon as we hang up."

"Great, but I've got a few more questions if you've got time."

"Sure."

"What time did you get to The Villages?"

"Just about noon. We went right to the hotel and checked in. The publisher had taken care of the reservation."

"Which hotel did you stay in?"

"The Waterfront Inn in Lake Sumter Landing. It's within walking distance of the Barnes & Noble store. We had lunch in the hotel and walked over to the bookstore."

"How long did the signing last?"

"It was scheduled for two hours but it ran over a little. We had a lot of people there, and Olivia didn't want to leave until everybody got a signed book."

"What did you do then?"

"We went back to the hotel, and I told Olivia I wanted to take a nap before dinner. I'd started out in Cincinnati before dawn and met her at the airport in Atlanta. She asked if I minded spending the evening alone if she took the car to visit a friend. She was planning on having dinner with her. That suited me. I wanted a quick nap, then dinner, and an early evening."

"Where did you have dinner?"

"I walked over to RJ Gators, had something quick, and came back and read for awhile."

"When did you see Olivia next?"

"I didn't. The detectives came to my room on Thursday morning around ten. I hadn't been able to reach Olivia by phone. Her cell went right to voice mail, so I thought she might have decided to spend the night with her friend. I called room service for breakfast and had just finished eating when the detectives knocked on my door."

"Do you know how they found you so quickly?"

"They told me Olivia had her room key and driver's license in her pocket and when they checked with the hotel desk, the clerk told them we were traveling together."

"Do you know if Olivia had any family or someone to get in touch with in case of an emergency?"

"I don't. She was a widow and didn't have any children. She talked about that while we were passing the time of day on the flight down. I don't know about anyone else."

"What was your schedule for Thursday?"

"We were supposed to go to Orlando in the afternoon and then on to Tampa for a library fund-raiser that evening. As it turned out, I stuck around Thursday in case the police needed anything else from me. I left for Cincinnati on Friday morning."

"Did you turn in your rental car?"

"Nobody could find it. The detective talked to Avis and told me not to worry about it. I took a shuttle down to Orlando and flew home."

"What time did Olivia leave the hotel to go meet her friend?"

"I'm not sure. We separated about four thirty, so I assume she probably left sometime shortly after that."

"I don't suppose she told you the friend's name."

"No. And I didn't ask."

"Do you know whether it was a man or a woman?"

"Not really, although I thought it was a woman. That was probably just my assumption."

"Did you think her friend lived in The Villages?"

She was quiet for a moment. "I think so, but that may have just been another assumption on my part."

"Did you see Olivia spend more time than usual with any one person at the signing?"

"No. It all went smoothly. She only took a few seconds with each fan."

"Can you think of anything else that might be pertinent?"

"No. Not off the top of my head, anyway. I did see Olivia talking to a man before the event started. We walked into the store, and he came up to her. They chatted for a few minutes and the man left the store. It probably doesn't mean anything."

"You're probably right, but can you describe the man?"

"I'm sorry. I didn't pay that much attention to him."

"Did you get a sense of his age?"

"I think he was probably about her age, but I don't have any recollection of what he looked like. He was dressed like most of the people. Very casual."

"You've been a big help, and I appreciate your time. I hope it won't be necessary for you to come down for the trial."

"I hope so, too, Mr. Royal. But if you need me, let me know. Can I call you if something else comes to mind?"

"Please do." I gave her my number and terminated the call.

A few minutes later, my computer pinged, announcing the receipt of an email. It was the car rental agreement sent by Peggy Keefe. I also found an email from Meredith Evans attaching the autopsy report on Olivia Lathom. I copied the automobile information into my notebook in the hopes that I could use it in some manner as the investigation proceeded.

The autopsy report didn't have anything I didn't already know, except the estimated time of death. The medical examiner thought she'd probably died about eight o'clock on Wednesday evening. Olivia's death was caused by a twenty-two-caliber bullet that entered her back, pierced her heart, and its energy almost expended, exited her chest and came to a stop in her clothing. I wondered briefly if Olivia's dying brain had any coherent thoughts in the short time between the shooting and the instant of death.

The big anomaly was the notation that when the medical examiner sent the victim's fingerprints to the state, there were no matches. Olivia was a ghost, but somebody had decided to kill her. I wish I knew the name of the friend she'd had dinner with on the night of her death. I was pretty sure that somewhere in the seventy thousand homes sprawled among The Villages, there was a house where the shooting had taken place. I'd be very surprised if we ever found it.

* * *

When I finished my work for the day, I went to J.D.'s condo to help her pack. I kissed her good-bye and watched as she drove off into her new life as the niece of a bookstore owner in The Villages. The afternoon was drawing to a close and I was already a bit lonely. Every time

J.D. went out of town, I was thrown a bit off my feed. It wasn't like we were together twenty-four hours a day, but when I knew I wouldn't see her for a while, a kind of dolefulness settled around me, barely felt, but noticeable, like a minor temblor shaking my very ordered little world. Oh, well, I had a bail hearing in Bushnell the next morning. I'd try to figure a way to see her without blowing her cover.

I called Jock. He and Mike Nink were enjoying a beer after finishing their round of golf. They would join me at Tiny's for another round or two. Beer, not golf. Over the years, I'd found that it's nearly impossible to be lonely for very long on our little island. Friends will always come to the rescue and jolly you out of your dark mood.

CHAPTER 16

I WAS SITTING in the hallway outside Judge Bill Gallagher's hearing room at a few minutes before ten on Wednesday morning when Meredith Evans slipped into the chair next to me. "Ready to give up?" she asked, grinning.

"Hurrumph," I mumbled.

"You hurrumph like an old man," she said.

"Go away, girl, before I have the bailiffs remove you."

"They like to be called court deputies."

"Yeah. How was your weekend?"

"Good. How was yours?"

"I live in paradise. Do you have to ask?"

"Bastard. I talked to my boss about some kind of agreement on bail. He nixed it. He thinks we have a pretty good case."

"He's wrong," I said.

"I'll pass that along."

"Are we going to have any trouble with a speedy trial?"

"No. You've got a right to that. We might even be amenable to moving it up a bit if we can get all the discovery out of the way."

"Let's see how that goes."

Two men in suits, each carrying a bulging file folder, came out of the hearing room. A couple of minutes later, the court deputy stuck his head out of the same door and said, "He's ready."

Judge Gallagher sat at one end of a conference table and Meredith and I took seats on either side. "Good morning, Meredith," the judge said and then nodded at me. "It's been a while, Matt. Glad to see you."

"Thank you, Your Honor. I understand I'm in for a rough ride with Meredith on the other side."

"Probably so," the judge said.

"We have a mutual friend," Meredith said. "Billy Ray Johnson."

The judge laughed. "Well, you're both in good hands. Are you going to agree to bail, Meredith?"

"No, sir."

"No surprise there. Matt, why do you think this defendant is entitled to bail?"

"She's a retired schoolteacher, Your Honor. No criminal record of any kind. Owns a house in The Villages. I can't see her as a flight risk."

"I'd like to know a little more about her," the judge said. "I'm going to continue this hearing. I'm going to order something along the line of a pre-sentence investigation from the state attorney's office, and, Matt, you can provide me whatever you want me to consider. Meredith, I want the report from you by next Monday. Tell me all the reasons Ms. Higgins shouldn't get bail, and, Matt, you do the opposite by Wednesday. Meredith, fax a copy of your report to Matt and he can respond to it. We'll set a hearing for Thursday of next week. How does ten in the morning work for you?"

Meredith and I both nodded. The judge made a note on his calendar and said, "If you two haven't worked this out by then, I'll rule. Meredith, please draw the order. Anything else?"

"No, Your Honor," we said in unison. He rose and left the room.

"I'll email you a copy of the order later this afternoon," Meredith said. "Let me know if it's okay, and I'll get it to the judge for a signature."

* * *

I drove out to the detention center to meet with Esther. She was in good spirits, as always. "Why're you looking so glum?" she asked.

"We didn't get bail."

"Neither one of us thought we would."

"We're going to get another bite of the apple," I said, and told her about the judge's ruling. "I think we'll actually have a pretty good chance next week. Maybe we can get you out of here."

"That'd be great, but I won't hold my breath."

I told her about my conversation with Peggy Keefe and what I had learned from the autopsy report, which wasn't much. "J.D. moved in with Judy Ferguson yesterday," I said. "Went to work in the bookstore today."

"Are you going to see her?"

"I'm not sure. I'll call her when we're finished and check on how she's settling in. I don't want to blow her cover. If anybody sees us together, they might make the connection. I don't want that to happen."

"Are you going to move into my house?"

"Not yet. But soon. Maybe later this week."

"I've been thinking about the van that the bartender at the World of Beer told you she saw. With the information you have on the rental car, you may be able to use the security cameras at the gates to track both of them. You need to talk to Hole-in-One Patty."

"Interesting name. Who's she?"

"A neighbor of mine. Patty Geoghegan. She and her husband, Bob, live behind me on Kelvington Road."

"How in the world did she get that name?"

"Right after she and Bob moved down here from Maryland, Patty decided to go with some of her friends to one of the golf courses. She'd never played before but didn't think it looked too difficult, so she asked to borrow a driver. She hit one off the first tee and it went right into the hole on the first green. She got a lot of press on that one, and hence the new nickname."

"I'll be damned. How can she help me with the security system?"

"Her nephew works for the security group run by The Villages developer. I know the boy's job has something to do with computers. He's majoring in computer science at the university in Gainesville. He's a little weird."

"What's his name?"

"Willingham Hall. He goes by Will."

"Does he live in Gainesville?"

"No. He was in the freshman dorm up there, but didn't like the name of the building. Said it was bad karma, or something. So he moved in with Patty and Bob for the semester and commutes. Like I said, he's weird, but he may be able to help find that van."

"I'll check it out. I'm not sure if I'll get back up here in the next couple of days, but if you need me, the jailers will let you use a phone. Just keep in mind that those phone calls are recorded. You don't want to say anything other than that you need me to come. I'll be on my way."

We chatted for a few more minutes and I left. Even the better jails are not conducive to idle conversation.

* * *

I sat in my car parked in front of the detention center and called J.D.'s cell phone. When she answered, I could hear the low hum of voices in the background. "You at work?"

"Yep."

"Wanna take some time off and fool around?"

"Can't do it. I'm a workingwoman. Get off at six."

"I'll be at Tiny's by then."

"Ugh. I don't know why I put up with you. I haven't had lunch yet. We could get something to eat, but that's all. I think my boss might frown upon my disheveled look if I fooled around and came back to work."

I looked at my watch. Almost noon. "I'm not sure I want to waste my time on lunch if there's no fooling around involved."

"Suit yourself. I've already been asked to dinner by a healthy looking elderly man. He even offered to paint my name on his golf cart, right in front of the passenger seat. I can always fool around after dinner if I'm in need."

"Perish the thought. Can you meet me at the Olive Garden up on Wedgewood?"

"You think that'll be okay? What if we see somebody we know? That might blow my cover."

"We'll be okay. The restaurant is pretty far from Brownwood, and we can get a booth in the back."

"How do I find it?"

"GPS," I said.

"You're a big help. See you there in half an hour."

* * *

"How's the undercover operation going?" I asked over our linguini.

"I met two of the book club ladies this morning in the store," J.D. said.

"Was either one Ruth Bergstrom?"

"Afraid not. She's your best suspect, isn't she?"

"So far, my only suspect. When's the next book club meeting scheduled?"

"There's one tonight. Do you have any other leads yet?"

"We might have gotten lucky with the van," I said, and told her about Will Hall. "I'll get in touch with him later in the week and see if he's willing to help us."

"I wouldn't think he could do that legally."

"You're right. And the evidence wouldn't be admissible if he did give it to us."

"Then how do you get what you need?"

"I'll ask Will if the security technicians have a program that can isolate the kind of information I want. If so, I'll serve a deposition subpoena on whoever runs that section. I'll describe the van in detail and require him to bring all recordings and pictures relating to it that were taken of the van and driver by the gate cameras. I can do the same with Lathom's rental car. Maybe we can put both vehicles in the same village at the same time."

"Do you think knowing the vehicles were both there at the same time would be useful? There're a lot of houses in each one of those villages."

"Yeah, too many to be of much use to us, but maybe we can at least tie the van to the rental."

"Your subpoena will telegraph your interest in the van and the car to the prosecution."

"Can't be helped," I said.

"Wouldn't it be easier to ask the prosecutor to get a warrant for the information and share it with you?"

"Yes, but then I wouldn't be in control of the process. I think Meredith Evans is a very ethical prosecutor and will follow the rules and disclose all information she gathers. But I could be wrong, and who knows what kind of pressure she might get from above. This way I'll know I have the information I need."

"You're a cynic."

"All trial lawyers are cynics. We live by the creed that if anything can go wrong, it will. If I leave it to the prosecutor to get it for me, I might not get everything I need. Or I might end up with hours of recordings from every gate in The Villages. It'd take me a year to go through all that. This way, I can specify only recordings of the van and its driver, and the security people can use their filters to isolate just the footage or pictures I want."

"Then you'll have to depend on them instead of the prosecutor."

"I'll get the information from the security people under oath."

"You think they wouldn't lie if it was in their best interest?"

"It's been my experience that if you tell the witness up front about perjury and the penalties, including jail, for lying under oath, they're more likely to tell you the truth."

"And that works?"

"It does if I put on my mean face when I'm telling them about the consequences if they don't tell the truth."

"I didn't know you had a mean face."

"You've never seen it, sugar, and you won't, unless I see your name painted on some old guy's golf cart."

She laughed, the little tinkly one that makes me shiver with the delight that comes from just being in her presence.

"Okay. I'll be good," she said.

"Can you do something else for me?"

"I'll try."

"Check with the Barnes & Noble store and see if you can get a look at their surveillance tape from Lathom's book signing. I'd like to get a still of the man she was talking to just before the signing started."

"They might not give it up that easily. Can I tell them I'm an investigator working for the defense counsel?"

"I don't see why not. It's the truth."

"What if I have to flash my badge?"

"I'd be a little more careful about that. It could get you in trouble and might bite me in the ass at the trial if it comes out."

"You've got a point. Two points, actually. I'll see what I can do. Are you going home this afternoon?"

"Yes. The island's kind of lonely without you."

"You've got Jock."

"There's that."

"And I heard that Tom Jones will be in town and there's Logan, Sammy, Les, Cracker, leftover snowbirds . . ."

I interrupted. "I get it."

"While you're at Tiny's with our friends, I'll be spending the evening watching TV with Judy."

"Okay, okay."

"I'll miss you, too. Unless there's something good on the tube."

"You need something to keep you busy. And I'm not talking about some dandy old dude in a souped-up golf cart."

"Why don't I talk to Will Hall. If he knows I'm Esther's niece, he might be more amenable to cooperating with me than he would with you."

"That's not a bad idea," I said. "Do you think it's okay to tell him who you really are?"

"I don't see why not. Will doesn't socialize much, and we probably won't casually run into each other. I know his aunt Patty, and she knows who I am. I don't think we need an elaborate story for her. She doesn't belong to the book club, and I try to stay away from the south end of The Villages when I'm out and about. If anybody hears that J. D. Duncan came to visit Patty's nephew to talk about her aunt, they won't think anything of it."

"Can you do that tomorrow?"

"I sure can."

I watched her drive out of the restaurant's parking lot with a sense of loss. I'd see her in a couple of days, but the very thought of being separated stirred up feelings of loneliness, something I hadn't felt since I first met her.

It was time to head home. Twenty minutes later, I was on I-75, sucking on a mammoth cup of Diet Coke, my Explorer headed south to paradise.

I was thinking about Jock. I had suggested that J.D. ask him to stir up his agency computers and see what they could find out about Olivia Lathom and Ruth Bergstrom. I didn't really want to bother him with the security computers in The Villages, although I suspected it would be a piece of cake for his agency to breach their firewalls.

The agency would have plenty of background on Bergstrom and Lathom, just as they did on almost everybody. While Jock could get anything he wanted, I felt that a request to breach the security of a legitimate business network would be much more onerous than asking the agency to divulge information that would already be in their possession. Not much of a moral distinction, but certainly a practical one.

If Will Hall could get the information, I'd have a start on tracking the van. If it was stolen, the information he could glean from the security section's computers would be worthless. Still, it was worth a try.

CHAPTER 17

J.D. LEFT THE Olive Garden and drove back to the bookstore, taking Buena Vista Boulevard. She had not spent much time in The Villages before this trip and she had been surprised at the flowers that bloomed in the middle and the edges of the large roundabouts that controlled traffic on the major thoroughfares. She identified salvias, begonias, zinnias, marigolds, and petunias, but there were a number of others she didn't recognize. Judy had told her that the flowerbeds were replanted at the beginning of each season so that there would be blooms all year round.

The road was flanked at regular intervals by well-manicured golf courses, providing a view across the fairways and watercourses to homes that backed up to the courses. Golf cart lanes paralleled the road, occasionally crossing to the other side via tunnels.

She already missed Matt, but she'd left him in good hands. He was surrounded by friends who would make sure that he didn't get too lonely. She knew she had a lot to do in a short time. She was a bit hamstrung in that she couldn't use the police resources that were usually available to her. She'd have to rely on old-fashioned digging, but she did have an ace in the hole for uncovering information that was not readily available. Jock.

She smiled at the thought of her friend. She and Matt were his sister and brother, his only family. It had taken J.D. some time to come to terms with what Jock did for a living and how he went about it. His job was in direct contravention to the life she led as a law enforcement officer. She lived by rules and laws and regulations that Jock flaunted with impunity.

She had, over time, come to understand the necessity of what he had to do for his country and how much the job took out of him. Every mission Jock undertook diminished him, snatched a little bit of his humanity and dumped it into a bottomless pit, never to be retrieved. Matt was afraid that one day Jock would just disappear, his conscience at a breaking point. When things got so bad that Jock stood on the edge of the abyss, the healing times, the days of drunkenness and self-pity and the slow recovery pulled him back, but never completely. He always left a piece of himself on the rim of the precipice, the part of him that stared into oblivion and saw the pit as his escape. Jock had recently come dangerously close to making that leap, and J.D. and Matt had pulled him back. Barely. She worried about him, but all she could do was love him like a brother and be there when he stumbled.

The bookstore was busy, men and women milling about, checking out the shelves of new books, some sitting on the couches and chairs reading the first few chapters of the newest releases. J.D. stood behind the cash register, taking care of those who had made their decisions and were on the way home. Some of the customers introduced themselves and seemed interested in the new employee. J.D. told each of them that her name was Jade Conway, that she was Judy Ferguson's niece, and that she would be visiting for a while.

Two more women who were members of the book club introduced themselves and encouraged J.D. to come to their meetings at the Eisenhower Center. She assured them that she would do so.

By midafternoon, the crowd had thinned out. J.D. noticed an attractive sixty-something woman dressed in slacks and blouse standing by one of the tables looking through some of the books that were on sale. As the last of the customers standing in line in front of the register paid for their purchases and left, the woman walked over to J.D. "I understand you're Judy's niece," she said.

"I am," J.D. said. "I'm Jade Conway."

The woman stuck out her hand. "I'm Ruth Bergstrom," she said. "I'm a member of our book club. I hope we can count on you to join us. We need some younger perspective."

The name sent a small jolt of electricity down J.D.'s spine. This woman was her target. J.D. shook the proffered hand and said, "I'm looking forward to it. My aunt said you do mostly mystery novels. Do you ever do other genres?"

"We pretty much limit it to mysteries. You interested?"

"Sure."

"We're meeting tonight at the Eisenhower Center. Why don't you get Judy to bring you?"

"I'll do that. Sounds like fun."

"Hi, Ruth." Judy Ferguson had walked up. "How're you holding up?"

"As well as can be expected," Ruth said. "It's hard losing a friend."

"I see you've met my niece, Jade."

"I have. I was just inviting her to our book club meeting tonight."

"I'm sorry for your loss," J.D. said. "Were you close?"

"Very. We'd been friends for many years. We used to work together in Atlanta."

"I'm sorry to hear that. It must be a great loss. May I ask what kind of work you did?"

"We worked in a library. Liv grew up in Buckhead where all the rich people live and had inherited a lot of money. She didn't need to work, but she did it to keep busy, I think. We became very close. She became a best-selling writer, you know."

"Wow," J.D. said. "That's great. Maybe I've read one of her books. What's her name?"

"Olivia Lathom. She was murdered last week. Right here in The Villages. Killed by one of our book club members."

"Accused," Judy said.

"She did it," Ruth said.

"We'll see," Judy said. "I don't think Esther did it."

"Any way you look at it," J.D. said, "it's tragic."

"Yes," Ruth said. "We'll be talking about Liv's book tonight. It's going to be hard."

"What's the name of the book?" J.D. asked.

"*Beholden,*" Ruth said.

"You know, Ruth," Judy said, "we don't have to do that book tonight. We can do it later when your loss isn't so raw."

"I don't think Liv would want us to change our plans. And, it might make me feel better to talk about her."

Ruth turned back to J.D. "It's been nice meeting you, Jade. Where are you from?"

"Miami. How about you?"

"I lived just outside Atlanta most of my life. My husband and I moved down here when he retired. I'm afraid I've become a golf widow. Are you married?"

"Yes," J.D. said, "but I'm in the process of getting divorced."

"I hope it's not too unpleasant."

"I wish it weren't."

"Bad, huh?"

"Pretty bad."

"Do you have any children, Jade?"

"No. I guess that's a good thing, given the circumstances. Do you have children?"

"Yes. Three. They're spread all over the country. We see them on holidays sometimes and that's about it. Gotta go. Get Judy to bring you to the meeting tonight."

"Count on it, Ruth. Nice to meet you."

That was kind of a bust, J.D. thought. She didn't really learn anything. She thought about it for a moment, called over one of the part-time girls who worked in the store, and asked her to cover the register while she used the restroom. She went to the back of the store, past the small sign that said, "staff only," and entered the ladies restroom. She shut the door and called Jock.

CHAPTER 18

JOCK ALGREN HAD spent the day lounging on Matt's patio, his nose buried in a new Arabic language book about Jordanian politics. He knew he could be sent into the Middle Eastern cauldron at any moment and he tried to stay current. His world was one of violence and death and it had been that way since he had graduated from college more than twenty years before. He'd been recruited into America's most secretive clandestine agency, undergone a year of intensive training, and was then sent into the field as a spy and sometime assassin. During his training, he had discovered that he had an affinity for languages and had become fluent in Arabic, and over the years, acquired fluency in several other languages. The Arabic insured that he would spend a lot of time in the Middle East.

Longboat Key served as his respite from the wars. He was always welcome in Matt's house and he had developed a lot of friends on the island. It was his place to decompress and live a normal life, at least for a while. Sometimes, when he'd had a particularly rough time on an assignment, when he had survived by killing the enemy, when he felt so dirtied by his actions that he could not face another day, he would come to Longboat and drink himself into a stupor. Matt would watch over him and after four or five days of what they called the healing time, help him sober up and regain enough of himself to once again join the fight against his country's enemies.

This was not one of those bad times. He'd had an opportunity to visit his best friend and relax in the March sun, and he took it. Soon enough, he'd be sent back into the muck that was his life as an assassin, and he'd carry the memory of this quiet time with him. He hoped it would sustain him during the battles to come.

Jock had risen in the ranks of the agency and was known as perhaps the best agent in America's intelligence community. He had a direct phone line to the President, and although he'd only used it once, it was a mark of how he was valued in the clandestine services. Within his own agency, he reported only to the director, and everyone knew that when Jock made a request, it was to be acted on immediately.

His phone rang. The caller ID told him it was J.D. "Is Matt still bothering you?" he asked by way of answering.

She laughed. "He keeps trying. I just sent him back to Longboat. Take care of him tonight. I have a big favor to ask."

"Granted."

"You don't even know what I want."

"Doesn't matter. You know that."

"I'd like to get some background information on the victim and also on one of the women in the book club. I can't use my usual police resources or I wouldn't ask you. Can you ask some of your people to look into them? Don't do it if it makes you uncomfortable."

"No problem at all. Whom are you interested in?"

"A woman named Ruth Bergstrom. She lives in The Villages and is probably in her early sixties." J.D. gave him Bergstrom's address that she'd retrieved from the bookstore's database. "And the murder victim, Olivia Lathom. She lived in Atlanta, but that's about all I know. She's about the same age as Bergstrom. The police usually have a lot of background on the victim in their reports, but this time the victim's fingerprints didn't match any in the usual databases."

"I'll have you something by this evening, tomorrow morning at the latest. Want me to email it to you?"

"Yes. Thank you, Jock."

"Does Matt know about this?"

"It was his idea. He said you were a pushover."

"He's right, of course. At least when it comes to you."

"Pshaw. Now you're making me blush."

Jock laughed. "Talk to you tomorrow."

Jock called one of the computer techs at the agency headquarters outside of Washington, DC, and gave him Ruth Bergstrom's name and address and asked for anything he could find on her and on Olivia Lathom. "She apparently lived in Atlanta or somewhere close by," Jock said.

"I'll get right on it," the tech said. "The boss is standing next to me. Wants to talk to you."

"Put him on."

"He says if you're secure, he'll call you in two minutes."

Jock hung up and sat watching the white pelicans on the far edge of the lagoon that separated Matt's cottage from Jewfish Key. These birds flew down from the upper reaches of Canada each fall and stayed through the winter. They were quite a bit bigger than the brown pelicans that were native to this coast, and they fished by gathering in a circle and herding the fish into the middle of an ever-tightening gyre.

Jock's phone rang. His boss. "Hello, Dave. I hope it's not time for me to get back to work."

"What are you doing?"

"Sitting on Matt's patio watching a bunch of white pelicans hunt their dinner. What's up?"

"We have a situation brewing in Tampa, and I wanted to give you a heads-up. I may need you to look into it."

"What's going on?"

"We've been getting rumblings of jihadist activity directed at Tampa. We don't know what it is or who is behind it, but the director of national intelligence wants us to look into it."

"Why doesn't the DNI give it to the CIA?"

"Well, you know they're not supposed to operate in this country."

"I know that, but I'm not sure the CIA knows that."

"Probably not, but we may have to take some interest in this. Do you have any weapons with you?"

"I've got my Sig Sauer. I probably won't need anything else."

"Okay. I'll keep you updated."

"You sure know how to ruin a guy's vacation."

"Maybe nothing will come of it. Tell Matt and J.D. hello for me." The line went dead.

Dave Kendall was the director of Jock's agency and the man who had recruited him when he was a senior in college. Dave knew that Matt and J.D. were the only family Jock had and he was comfortable with Jock sharing everything with them. Both had been thoroughly vetted by the agency and given what amounted to high security clearances. It was an unusual arrangement, but then Jock was an unusual agent, and it was in the government's interest to keep him happy.

CHAPTER 19

As I APPROACHED the Cortez Bridge to Anna Maria Island, I was sorely tempted to pull into Tyler's Ice Cream Shop. They make the best ice cream I've ever put in my mouth, but like the binge drinker or the potato chip lover, I can't eat just one. Scoop, that is. If I stopped in, I wouldn't be able to waddle back to my car until I'd eaten myself sick. J.D. would not be pleased. And somehow, she'd know.

I drove on, feeling very virtuous, enough so that I decided I deserved a pizza from Ciao's tonight. I called Jock to see if he agreed. He did, and I ordered the large with everything on it. Well, I left off the black olives.

I swung by Ciao's, and was greeted in the kitchen by my old buddy Bill, another Tiny's habitué. "Your pie will be ready in about five minutes, Matt. I hope J.D.'s going to help you eat this thing."

"She's out of town, but Jock's got dibs on half. You about ready for the season to end?"

"Oh, yeah. Don't get me wrong. I like the busy season and I'll miss the tips, but it'll be nice to take a breather."

"I gotcha." We chatted about absent friends, which, on our island, peopled with so many older retirees, usually meant someone who had left us for the great beyond.

A large pizza box was set on the counter by one of the cooks. Bill looked at the little label and handed it to me. "Tell Jock I said hello," he said. I assured him I would, and drove the two miles to my house.

Jock was on the patio, his nose in a book. He must have heard me come in. He joined me in the kitchen. "Smells good."

I put the pizza in the middle of the table and opened a beer for myself and an O'Doul's for Jock. "So how have you wasted your day?" I asked him.

"Doing some work J.D. sent my way. Looking into Olivia Lathom and Ruth Bergstrom. I'm afraid I crapped out on one of the jobs," he said. "Olivia Lathom is a cipher."

"I didn't know J.D. had given you marching orders. I told her to call on you if she needed help. I didn't think you'd mind."

"Not at all. You know that."

"J.D.'s going to be disappointed. She thinks you walk on water."

"I do, sometimes. We found out a lot on the other woman."

"Other woman?"

"Yeah. Ruth Bergstrom."

"Boy, she's a hard case. Tell me about her."

"She was born Ruth Donnelly in a little burg outside Montgomery, Alabama. She grew up there, graduated from high school, moved to Atlanta, and got a job as a secretary in a law firm. Two years later, she married one of their clients, a man named Jake Bergstrom, who was almost twenty years her senior. They had three children in quick succession and when she was thirty, her husband divorced her and got custody of the children.

"Apparently, Mrs. Bergstrom had developed a bad problem with prescription drugs. Her husband put her in rehab twice, once out at the Betty Ford Clinic in California, but nothing took. She wound up doing some time in the Georgia women's prison that used to be located in Milledgeville.

"It looks like she almost stayed straight after she got out. She went back to Atlanta and took some waitressing jobs. There was one incident where the police were called because the restaurant manager suspected her of stealing money from the till, but they couldn't prove it, so the case was dropped. Somewhere along the line she met and married a man named James McNeil. She kept the Bergstrom name for some reason and got a job as an assistant in a public library. She stayed there until she retired with a small pension.

"McNeil had done an Army tour at the tail end of Vietnam and then stayed in the National Guard. He retired as a master sergeant and started getting his pension when he turned sixty. His civilian job was as a meat market manager at one of those big warehouse stores. He ended up with a pension from them and took his social security when he turned sixty-two. So did Ruth.

"They sold their house in Marietta and used the proceeds to buy a house in The Villages. He plays a lot of golf, and she seems to be the neighborhood busybody. Like a lot of the people in The Villages, they're not rich, probably not even well-off, but they're getting by."

"What happened to Ruth's children?"

"They stayed with their dad until they were grown. They seem to be doing well, and we don't think they ever had much contact with Ruth after the divorce."

"But now you're telling me that you can't find my murder victim?"

"Actually, we found her. I mean, she *is* famous, a national best-selling author and all, but we can't get anything on her. We don't even have fingerprints, except for the ones the Sumter County medical examiner sent to the state."

"That didn't get any hits," I said.

"Yeah. I know. J.D. said she had grown up wealthy in a high-dollar zip code in Atlanta. The Fulton County property records did show us that a Lathom family lived in Buckhead during the time that Olivia would have been a child, but the family moved out of that house thirty years ago."

"Where did they go?"

"Some people with the same name showed up at about that time in a small town in South Georgia. Douglas. They moved into an assisted living facility and died some years later. The records show they were survived by two sons, but not a daughter."

"Do you think Olivia Lathom might be in the witness protection program or something like that? It seems odd that she just pops up in her early forties."

"She's not in any of the protection programs. We checked. And we'd know if she was part of that."

"Did you get anything on her?" I asked.

"Not much. She worked in the Fulton County public library system for part of her adult life. There's nothing on her before she went to work there about twenty years ago. We believe that's where she and Ruth Bergstrom met. As far as we can tell, she never got married, never worked anywhere but the library, or traveled very much. She did have income from some pretty savvy stock market investments but she didn't live too high on the hog. The stocks produced enough to pay her living expenses and make the mortgage payments on a small house she's lived in for the past twenty years, but her principle was diminishing."

"Ruth Bergstrom said she was a widow."

"If she was married, we missed it."

"Okay, what else?"

"Lathom started writing mystery novels a few years back. She self-published two of them and developed a respectable following around Atlanta. Then, recently, out of the blue, her latest book debuted on the *New York Times* best-seller list and took off."

"That's the one we think she stole from Esther," I said. "Where the hell did she spend the first forty years of her life?"

"Is that important to the case?"

"I don't know, but if I don't find out, especially now that I know she was off the grid for about two-thirds of her life, it's going to drive me nuts. Maybe there's some connection in her early life that brought about her murder all these years later."

"Our nerds only had time to do a cursory search. We'll stay on it, but it's a puzzle. So far. Our guys are the best in the world, Matt. They'll turn up something."

But, as it turns out, they didn't.

CHAPTER 20

The Eisenhower Center is a place of homage, not so much to Ike as it is to the men and women who served in the military during World War II. The Villages' residents who fought in the war had donated many of the pictures and memorabilia that were prominently displayed. It was a place, J.D. thought, that would make veterans feel at home.

Judy had driven them over in her golf cart, and they were directed to a room near the front door that could accommodate the dozen or so women who usually showed up for the meetings. J.D. was introduced to several of the women who welcomed her to the club. They were interested in why she was in The Villages and if she planned to move there permanently.

J.D. told them the shortened version of the story of her life in the Army and in Miami and the woes of her divorce. It seemed to satisfy everyone's curiosity. Ruth made her way through the crowd and welcomed J.D. "Glad you could make it," she said. "Let's find a seat."

The women were gathered in a small seating area that consisted of two sofas and several chairs. J.D. and Ruth took an empty sofa and another woman joined them, with J.D. sitting in the middle. Ruth introduced the newcomer as Kelly Gilbert.

"Nice to meet you, Jade," Kelly said. "Where're you from?" Like in much of Florida, that was an icebreaker question. The state is a place for newcomers. In 1980, the population was something over nine million people. Today, it tops twenty-one million. Everybody is from somewhere else and the ritual inquiry into a person's antecedents is not considered rude.

"I grew up in Miami, but I'm an Army officer and have lived all over the world. Most recently, in Miami again. I've been stationed there for the past three years."

"That sounds exciting. What brings you to The Villages?"

"Judy Ferguson is my aunt and I needed to get out of Miami for a while. She invited me to come stay with her. I had some leave time built up, so I took her up on her offer."

"And how are you enjoying our little community?"

J.D. laughed. "Love it, but I wouldn't call it little anymore. Have you been here long?"

"My husband died, and I moved here about three years ago."

"Oh, I'm sorry to hear that."

"Thank you. The loss gets easier, and I've found a new life. My first husband died years ago. He was killed when a dump truck blew a stop sign and killed him. I got a settlement from the accident and a couple of years later married a lawyer from home. He'd never been married before and it turned out to be a really good marriage. Better than my first one. He sold everything and we moved to Orlando to live out our lives in the sun. Two years later, he had a heart attack and died. He left me everything he owned, which, as it turned out, wasn't a lot. But it was enough to take care of me for the rest of my life. I sold out, moved here, bought a pink golf cart, and settled in with my dog, Mugsy."

"Did you know Ruth's friend, the author?"

"No. I've heard Ruth talk about her, but I never had the pleasure of meeting her. She wrote a great book, though."

The woman who'd been introduced earlier to J.D. as the president of the club stood and said, "Okay, ladies. Let's talk about this book. Who's first?"

* * *

After the book discussion, punch and cookies were served. J.D. had enjoyed hearing the women's different observations about the story. They were all positive. J.D. had bought and read *Beholden* as soon as she learned that her aunt Esther had written it. It was a good book, intricately plotted and sprinkled with sharp dialogue and bits of humor. She also found a digital copy of one of Lathom's earlier books and thought it was awful. A little digging turned up the fact that both books Lathom had previously written were self-published. She wasn't surprised that no self-respecting publisher would put them on the market. A lot of self-published books were wonderful pieces of work, and some even became best sellers. Lathom's was definitely not one of those.

J.D. had restrained herself and did not take part in the discussion of *Beholden*. She was afraid she might slip up and reveal a deeper interest in the book than her assumed personality, Jade Conway, would have. She'd also told some of the women she'd met in the store earlier that day that she hadn't read the book. She sat quietly, her cop's eye trained on the women of the club, one of whom might be the killer.

J.D. was sipping her punch and nibbling at an oatmeal raison cookie as she talked with Ruth. "I enjoyed the discussion," she said. "I'm going to read the book this week."

"I think you'll like it," Ruth said.

"Tell me some more about the author. I've never met one."

Ruth laughed. "I've met a number of them over the years, but trust me when I say they're nothing special. Except for Liv. I met her when we worked at a library and we became friends. Over the last few years, after my husband and I moved here, I saw a lot less of her, but we stayed in contact with phone calls, emails, and regular visits. I knew she was working on a book, but she'd never talk about it other than to say it was a mystery. She sent me an advance reader's copy, what they call an ARC, several months before it was published, and I was blown away at how good it was."

"She never shared the manuscript with you?"

"No. She kept that all to herself."

"I did know one author," J.D. said, "but he wasn't very good, and I never think of him as a writer. As far as I know, he never published anything. He was an intelligence officer I served with in Germany. Very bright, but couldn't write worth a flip. He inundated me with his manuscripts though." She laughed. "He'd write a couple of pages and bring them to me at the office. I never screwed up the courage to tell him he needed to pursue another hobby."

"Liv never did that. She kept it all to herself until the book was ready to be published. She'd written two other books before this one. The books weren't very successful, but she had fun writing them and she found an agent who proved to be worthwhile when Liv wrote *Beholden.* He got it to the right publisher and negotiated a top-dollar deal for her."

"Do you write, Ruth?"

"Not really. Like a lot of our ladies, I scribble, but I don't think anybody will ever publish my work." She laughed. "I certainly wouldn't."

"Judy told me that a lot of you write and share your work with the others. Sort of a critique group."

"Yes, but my writing is so bad I don't even share it with my friends. The members usually write short stories of about three or four pages. They bring it in and we talk about it. Some of the work is pretty good, but some is just horrible. We all try to be kind in our criticisms."

"Is anybody working on a book?"

"If they are, I've never seen it. I've got to run. Are you coming to our next meetng?"

"I hope so. Thanks for inviting me tonight."

J.D. had noted Ruth's quick exit when she had asked her if anyone was working on a novel. She hoped she hadn't spooked the woman. Sometimes a fairly innocuous question bites too close to the bone and puts the person to whom it's directed on guard. She'd have to be careful with this lady.

Judy Ferguson was standing across the room chatting with Kelly Gilbert. J.D. joined them. "Did you enjoy the discussion, Jade?" Kelly asked.

"I did. I can't wait to read the book."

"Have you read it, Judy?" Kelly asked.

"Yes. It's a first-rate book."

"Kelly," J.D. said. "Do you know Ruth well?"

Kelly frowned. "Not well, and I don't really trust her."

"Why not?"

"She has a way of talking about people behind their backs, if you know what I mean. She gossips a lot."

"What about her husband?"

"Never met him. I think he plays a lot of golf."

"Keeps him away from her, I guess," Judy said.

"You don't like her either," J.D. said.

"She's all right, I guess," Judy said. "I need to learn to keep my mouth shut. I'm going for more punch. I'll be ready to leave whenever you are, Jade."

"Kelly, do you know if anyone in the club is writing a book?"

"No. That doesn't mean nobody's working on one, but I've never heard anything about it."

"It was nice meeting you, Kelly. Guess I better catch up with Judy. She's my ride tonight."

In the cart on the way home, Judy said, "Sorry for that slip about Ruth. Knowing what you told me about her just makes me want to rip her eyes out."

"No harm, Judy. I doubt Kelly even paid attention to your comments."

"Yeah, but if they get back to Ruth, she might begin to wonder if I know something I shouldn't. I'll be careful. Promise."

CHAPTER 21

I DROVE SLOWLY along a street lined with elegant mansions set well back from the road. Well-kept lawns were shaded from the early afternoon sun by ancient oaks that partially obscured the houses. This was Buckhead, the very affluent neighborhood of Atlanta, the one where the old families lived with their fading glory and diminishing assets. They were the gentry, the remnants of the old aristocracy that grew out of the plantation culture of the antebellum South. They'd all be gone in a few years, their wealth dissipated into nothing by the birth rate of each succeeding generation, the money spent frivolously by descendants who did not earn it. The old English notion of primogeniture had its advantages.

Thursday morning had brought no better information on Olivia Lathom from Jock's agency. Jock made the call at six a.m. as we drank our coffee and ate a breakfast of eggs, bacon, and toast. "Sorry, podna," he said as he hung up the phone. "They can't find anything in the databases. They asked if I wanted to send field agents out to see what we could dig up, but I didn't think that was a workable proposition."

"It's not. I shouldn't be calling on your agency to help with my investigation at all, and certainly not asking you to send agents out to help. There's probably a limit to what your boss will put up with."

"Probably."

"I think I'll get my tired old butt to Atlanta and see what I can turn up. Can you get me hard copies of what your geeks did find on Olivia?"

"It's on my computer. I'll print it out for you."

I called my trusty travel agent, a guy I'd gone to high school with who had just retired from the Florida Highway Patrol as a major and set up a travel agency. He got me on a plane out of Tampa at ten o'clock. That would give me time to get a rental car and drive to Buckhead by a little after noon.

Everything ran on time. I had a pleasant flight, a drive that wasn't too bad by Atlanta standards, and a leisurely lunch in a chain restaurant in a Buckhead shopping area. I ate and went over my notes and the printouts Jock had provided. I left the restaurant and began my search for Olivia Lathom's trail among the luxurious mansions that were the heart of Buckhead.

This was the neighborhood where, according to what Ruth Bergstrom had told J.D., Olivia Lathom was born and where she had lived until she left for college. It was a place that cossetted its young from the world at large, protected them from the daily travails visited upon the middle class, and sent them out into a world for which they were woefully unprepared. I suspected that the only middle-class man living in any of the mansions of this sprawling oasis was the Georgia governor, whose official mansion graced West Paces Ferry Road on the periphery of Buckhead.

As a young Army officer stationed briefly at Ft. McPherson on the southwestern edge of Atlanta, I had visited the Buckhead home of a friend, another young officer who, like me, was awaiting shipment to the war zone. His family had lived in the same house for several generations, and he, in turn, would inherit the name and the house and live out his life ensconced in luxury.

They were gracious people who welcomed me as if I were one of them. I felt like an imposter. I was a self-conscious young man who had worked his way through college with the help of an Army ROTC scholarship, which I would repay by leading a group of other young men in combat. I was shipping out the next day to take command of a Special Forces team, a unit of the storied Green Berets that was heavily engaged in combat. I knew the statistics. The death rate among new lieutenants in combat was astronomically high. Yet, my memory of that evening was not the fear of the coming war, but the fear of using the wrong fork and embarrassing myself and, probably, my friend and his family.

I was completely out of my depth that evening but, as far as I know, I didn't pick up the wrong piece of silverware or slurp my soup. I had watched closely to see what they did before I reached for a fork or spoon. If any of them noticed my subterfuge, they were too well bred to mention it.

After that night, I never saw those pleasant people again. Their son left for the war zone soon after I did, and on his third day in combat, he was shot through the head by a sniper and died instantly. I wrote his parents a letter of condolence, but never heard back from them. I survived and their son didn't. The war had exacted a heavier price from those genteel Southerners than it had from me. I came home with some bad memories and a gut full of shrapnel. They lost their only child. Their family line ended in an uninhabitable desert on the far side of the world.

I found the address I was looking for. The house was antebellum in its architecture and was probably built in the 1930s. It had obviously been updated. There was nothing of the decaying look that so many of the truly pre–Civil War homes sprinkled around the South wore with such despair.

Olivia's family had apparently gone the way of many of the gentry who had lived here. Their money slowly faded away and they were left only with a name that opened a lot of doors. But an old name didn't pay for the upkeep of the house or vacations in Europe with their friends. The Fulton County property records told me that the Lathoms had sold the house thirty years before and that the buyers still lived there.

I pulled into the wide circular drive and parked in front of the house. An older black woman wearing a black uniform dress with a white collar answered the door. "May I help you, sir?" she asked.

"My name is Matt Royal. I'm a lawyer down in Longboat Key, Florida." I handed her a business card to prove it. "I was in the neighborhood and I was hoping that either Mr. or Mrs. Halstead might be available for a short conversation."

"May I tell Mrs. Halstead what this is about?"

I was beginning to wonder if maybe I should have appeared hat in hand and knocked on the door to the servant's entrance. "As I said, I'm a lawyer . . ."

"I understand that, sir." Her voice was steely and practiced, as if she had to deal with uncouth interlopers on a daily basis. "What I need to know is why you need to see Mrs. Halstead."

"It has to do with a murder and a claim against the property, which would probably end up with this house being owned by someone else, and more importantly with the end of your employment. If she can't see me, I'll just go on down to the Fulton County courthouse and get things started." I lied a little. Well, maybe more than a little, but I can't stand officious people.

"Wait here, please." She shut the door in my face and left. Officious people always make dramatic exits.

After several minutes, a pleasant lady who was probably in her early seventies appeared. "Good afternoon, Mr. Royal. I'm Beth Halstead. Won't you come in? I hope Sadie didn't give you a hard time." Her accent was one developed while growing up in the wealthier precincts of Atlanta. I wouldn't be surprised it she was born and raised in Buckhead.

"No, ma'am," I said. "She was very nice."

Mrs. Halstead grinned. "I'm sure she was. She's worked for us for a long time, since before we bought this house, and sometimes she's a bit protective. Overly so, on occasion."

She led me into a pleasant room at the back of the house. "I apologize for taking so long to get to the door. My husband, Steve, is a lawyer and I called him to see what I should do about talking to a Florida lawyer I'd never heard of, and who says we may have a problem with a murder and with ownership of our house."

"I may have overstated the problem I'm here about. I just sort of added a property dispute to the conversation to focus Sadie's attention. Actually, it's only a murder I wanted to discuss with you."

"That sounds more interesting than a property dispute. Anyway, my husband, the always cautious lawyer, put me on hold and called a colleague of his in Sarasota who told him you were the real thing, highly ethical, and that you were working on a murder case. He said you wouldn't be here unless it was important."

"I appreciate that, Mrs. Halstead," I said, smiling. "But the question remains, can you trust the lawyer in Sarasota?"

She laughed. "I'll take a chance. Would you like some iced tea?"

"No, thank you."

"Well then, how can I help you?"

I told her about the murder of Olivia Lathom, that I represented the accused, Esther Higgins, and that I was trying to get some background information on the victim. "I don't think my client killed her. If I can understand who Ms. Lathom was and what she did with her life, I may be able to figure out who killed her and why."

"I don't know how I can help you, Mr. Royal. I never met the woman."

"The only connection I can see is that, according to the Fulton County property records, you and your husband bought this house from her parents."

"We did buy it from the Lathoms. It was kind of sad. They were an old Atlanta family who had fallen on hard times. They had to get out from under the mortgage they carried on this house. They had let it fall into disrepair, so we got a good deal on it. But, I'm quite confident that they only had two children, and both of them were boys. Well, young men, really. They were both in their early thirties and one of them had a family of his own by then. The Lathoms were in their early seventies and were moving into a retirement community down in South Georgia somewhere. It was really sad."

"Are you sure they didn't have a daughter?"

"Positive. We got to know them pretty well, and met both their boys. They never mentioned a daughter."

"Would you remember the boys' names?"

"I don't," she said. "But I remember that they spelled their name with an 'o' instead of an 'a.' L-a-t-h-o-m. There used to be a radio executive here in Atlanta who spelled his name with an 'o', but there were very few others who spelled it the way they did. I wish I could be of more help."

"Does the name Olivia Lathom mean anything at all to you?"

"It rings a vague bell, but I'm not sure from where."

"She's a mystery writer who lived here in Atlanta. She recently released a book that hit the *New York Times* best-seller list. I know she was written up in the *Atlanta Constitution* about four weeks ago."

"Yes. That's where I read that name. I remember she said she'd been raised in Buckhead and I wondered if she were related to the Lathoms who used to live in this house. Not a daughter, but maybe some other kind of relative."

"I've done a lot of research on Olivia, and the Lathoms who lived in this house are the only ones who called Buckhead home during the years that she would have been growing up."

"I wish I could help, Mr. Royal, but I can't explain that unless she was living with someone with a different name. Maybe it was a coincidence that she had the same last name as the people who lived here and she was actually living somewhere else in the neighborhood."

"You have been very helpful, Mrs. Halstead. You've also deepened the mystery. I got the impression she came from a wealthy family and the only Lathom I could find in the property records used to own this house. Maybe you're right. Maybe someone else adopted her or took her to raise. But, without their names, I'm not likely to find Olivia's trail."

"I'm sure the Lathom couple we bought it from are dead by now. They'd be over a hundred years old if they were still alive. The boys must be at least in their sixties."

I stood. "Thank you for your hospitality, Mrs. Halstead. I apologize for barging in on you like this, but I don't have a lot of time before Esther's trial starts."

She walked me to the door. We passed the maid on the way out. "He didn't look too savory to me, Miz Halstead," she said, nodding at me. "I hope he didn't bother you too much."

"Not too much," Mrs. Halstead said, smiling.

It's been my experience that officious people often get the last word.

I had barely cleared the long driveway when my phone rang. I answered. It was Beth Halstead. "Mr. Royal, I mentioned your problem to Sadie and she remembered the boys' names. Danny and Charles. Her mind is like a steel trap."

I laughed. "So is her mouth, but please thank her for me."

"I'll do that."

CHAPTER 22

THURSDAY MORNING IN The Villages was like most other days, except that in many neighborhoods, one of the house's front yards was graced with plastic pink flamingos. J.D. and Judy traveled through several neighborhoods in Judy's golf cart on their way to breakfast at the Evans Prairie Country Club and had seen a small flock of flamingos planted in yards in each village. Judy pointed out that a grouping of the birds was called a pat for some reason. The notice of the party had gone out overnight by email and the gaudy flamingos marked the location of the evening's festivities in case anybody missed the memo. It was part ritual, part event, and mostly just a good time. The neighbors would gather and talk about things of little or no importance, but it was the ritual of friendships, new and old, that made it work. New neighbors did not stay strangers past their first driveway party.

After breakfast, J.D. called Sue Rapp, Esther's next-door neighbor, and got a phone number for Patty Geoghegan. She called and identified herself and said, "I hope I'm not disturbing you, Patty."

"Not at all, J.D. It's wonderful hearing from you. I've been so worried about Esther."

"Thank you. I'm sure she's not guilty. You've met my friend Matt. He's defending her."

"I heard that. I understand he's got a big reputation."

"He's pretty good, Patty. Actually, I'm calling on an issue that may be of some assistance to Esther. She suggested that your nephew Will might be able to help her."

"Will's at home. Come on over now, if you like."

Twenty minutes later, J.D. pulled into Patty's driveway and knocked on the door. Patty greeted her and escorted her to the back of the house and introduced J.D. to her nephew Will, who was seated at a computer staring fixedly at the monitor. He was a gangly young man with a shock of dark hair that looked as if it hadn't been combed since he graduated from junior high school. He wore a pair of ragged jeans, flip-flops, and a t-shirt advertising a computer store in Gainesville.

"I'll leave you two alone," Patty said. "Can I get you something to drink?"

"No, thank you, Patty," J.D. said. "I just finished breakfast."

Will smiled at his aunt and shook his head. "How can I help you?" he asked after they were seated in the living room.

"I guess your aunt told you why I'm here."

"She told me that you're Ms. Higgins' niece and a cop down in Longboat Key. I love that lady."

J.D. was a little surprised at that announcement, but let it go. "It sounds as if you know her pretty well," she said.

"Yeah, she and Aunt Patty belong to the Civitan club and work on projects together. I help them out some. I've gotten to know Ms. Higgins pretty well."

"I understand that you work with computers in The Villages security department."

He nodded.

"Can you explain to me how the cameras at the gates at all the entrances to the different neighborhoods work?"

"We call them villages."

"What?"

"We don't call them neighborhoods. They're villages, and there are ninety-one of them. A lot of them are named after Florida counties. For example, this house is in the Village of Pinellas."

"I got it," I said. "Can you tell me about the cameras?"

"Sure, but what's this got to do with Ms. Higgins' predicament?"

"She doesn't exactly have a predicament, Will. She's in jail charged with murder and facing a life sentence."

"Sorry. Didn't mean to denigrate her situation."

J.D. smiled to herself. She supposed he'd learned "denigrate" at the university and liked to use it when he could. For a moment, she almost remembered her college days but mentally shrugged them off. She said, "We have a witness who saw a white van leaving the area where the body was found. I want to find out if that van entered or left any of the villages and hopefully get a license plate number. If I can get that, we can find out who the van belonged to."

"There's got to be a million white vans around here."

"Yes, but the one I'm looking for is one of those little Dodge Promaster City vans. And it was plain, no graphics or signs on it. There aren't too many of those around." She showed him a picture of one of the vans she'd taken from a Dodge dealer's website.

"It's pretty distinctive," Will said, "but the cameras don't really show the vehicle. The one at the entrance, just above the red button that visitors use to activate the gate, takes a picture of the driver. The one on that low post just past the gate only gets a shot of the license plate. Same with the cameras pointing at the cars leaving the villages."

"Can you give it a try?"

"I can try, but I wouldn't hold out much hope that we can find the van."

"I'd also like to check on whether a rental car entered and exited any of the villages. I've got the tag number."

"That'll be a piece of cake," Will said.

J.D. knew from the autopsy report that Lathom had been killed at about eight o'clock on Wednesday evening. According to Amber, the bartender at World of Beer, the van that almost ran into her as she left work had come screaming out of Paddock Square at shortly after 1:42 on Thursday morning. Assuming that the killer called somebody with a van to pick up the body, it would have entered the gate that controlled the particular village at some time after eight p.m. On the other hand, the van could have been owned by the killer and parked in his or her garage for days. Either way, the van had to have left one of the villages at sometime between eight o'clock and the time that Amber almost had a collision with it at about 1:45 a.m. Of course, this scenario assumed that Lathom had been killed somewhere in The Villages, and there was no evidence that the friend she was going to visit lived there. J.D. and Matt had decided that, until proven wrong, they were going with the hypothesis that Lathom had been killed somewhere in the forty-two square miles that comprised The Villages.

"Okay," she said. "And you said there are cameras that record vehicles leaving the neighborhoods?"

"The gates open automatically for cars leaving the villages, so there are no pictures of the driver. But there are cameras that again record the license plate as the vehicle drives out of the gate. We'd be able to tell if somebody came in and didn't leave."

"Are your computers programed to track tag numbers?"

"Sure. We can plug in the number and the computers will tell us when the vehicles came and went and what gates they passed through."

"Could you have the computers show you pictures of the license plates of every vehicle that came and went through any of the gates during a particular time period?"

"They could, but there are ninety-one villages here and at least two hundred gates. That's a lot of cars."

"Suppose we narrowed that down to a thirty-minute period, say, around one in the morning."

"That shouldn't be too hard. Most of the folks around here are in bed asleep at that time of the morning. Traffic would be very light."

"Can you do that for me?"

"Probably, but why don't you just go through channels? I'm sure the bosses would be glad to help."

"They'll want a search warrant, Will. Or at least, a subpoena. I'm just a moonlighting cop digging around in a jurisdiction where I have no authority. If the lawyer were to go that route, he'd have to let the prosecutor know where he's headed with this line of investigation. We don't want to alert the law enforcement people to what we're doing. At least, not yet." A little cloud was forming in the back of her mind obscuring that part of her moral compass that included Matt's view of legal ethics. She mentally whisked it away. Now was not the time to get technical.

"I could get in a lot of trouble if I'm caught monkeying with the computers."

"Can you hack them? Not leave a trace?"

"Maybe."

"Will you try? To help Ms. Higgins?"

Will sat quietly for a few moments, chewing at a fingernail. Finally, he ran his hand through his hair and said, "Give me a couple of days. Let me test the system and see what happens. I'll let you know."

"Thanks, Will." J.D. gave him her business card with her personal cell phone scrawled on the back, said good-bye to Patty, and left. She drove to Lake Sumter Landing and found the Barnes & Noble store and asked to speak to the manager.

A woman who appeared to be in her midthirties came to the front of the store and introduced herself to J.D. as the general manager. "How can I help you?"

"I'm J.D. Duncan. I guess you know about the murder of Olivia Lathom right after she had her signing in this store."

"I get asked about that by at least twenty people a day."

"I'm an investigator working with the lawyer who is defending the woman accused of the murder. We've come across some information that Ms. Lathom spent a few minutes talking with a man just before she began the signing event. I'm sure you have surveillance cameras in the store."

"We do. They cover the entire area."

"I'm hoping I can get a look at your security tapes of that day to see if we can identify the man Ms. Lathom was talking to."

"I would gladly give them to you if you had a subpoena. Do you have one?"

"No. I'm sure we can get one, but it's a lot of effort, and we'll waste a lot of days getting the court to issue one."

"I'd like to help. Let me call my district manager and see what he has to say. Do you have any identification?"

"I do, but let me explain something. I'm a detective with the Longboat Key Police Department, but I've taken a leave of absence to work with the defense lawyer on this case. I don't have any jurisdiction here, or anywhere else for that matter while I'm on a leave of absence. I'm working completely in a private capacity, but the badge and ID I'm about to show you are my official LBKPD credentials."

"I understand, Detective." She looked for a moment at the ID card and badge and handed them back to J.D. "I'll call my boss and explain this to him. I'll make it clear that you're here in a private capacity. Give me a few minutes. There's a Starbucks over in the corner of the store. Make yourself comfortable."

The manager was back in ten minutes. “My manager was sold on the fact that you’re a real detective. I made sure he knew that you were working in a private capacity and not officially and he said he understood. He told me to go through the security recordings and find the one with Ms. Lathom talking to an unidentified man.”

“If that’ll take a while, I can come back.”

“Shouldn’t take long. We can narrow down the time because we know when she started the signing. Relax and I’ll be back in a few minutes.”

“Would it be too much to ask for a still picture of the man? The best shot you can get of his face?”

“Not a problem.”

“Can you email it to me?”

“Sure.”

J.D. gave the manager her email address and went back to her coffee.

Ten minutes later, J.D.’s phone pinged, alerting her to an incoming email. It was from the store manager and had two pictures attached, the first, a picture of a man talking to Olivia Lathom and a second one of just a head shot of the man.

“Did you get the pictures?” the manager asked as she walked up. She handed J.D. two pictures that she had printed on photographic paper. They were the same as the emailed photos.

“I did. Thank you very much.”

“It’d probably be better if you kept this to yourself.”

J.D. smiled. “Mum’s the word.”

CHAPTER 23

BACK AT MY hotel in Atlanta, I fired up my computer and ran a search for Danny Lathom. I found an obituary from some twenty years before with his name, a short little bio telling me nothing about his life other than the bare facts of birth, death, and survivors. He had died young, but the obit didn't say of what. His place of death was Douglas, a town in South Georgia. The date and place of his birth seemed to match the man I was looking for, and he was survived by a brother named Charles. There was no reference to a sister or any other siblings, children or wife.

A Charles Lathom showed up with office and home addresses in Vinings, a trendy community of upscale homes and high-rise office buildings not far from Buckhead. He was a financial advisor and would be in his sixties by now. It was getting late in the afternoon, but Vinings was only about five miles from my hotel. I drove to Charles Lathom's office and gave the receptionist my card and asked if I could speak with Mr. Lathom on a confidential matter.

"I'll see if he's in," she said. It was a small office that probably didn't have a back door, so I guessed she was trying to decide if my unexpected presence warranted an audience with the big kahuna. It was my day for officious people. She disappeared into the back of the office and returned a few minutes later. "Mr. Lathom will see you now," she said, and led me back into a sumptuous office with an expansive view all the way south to the skyscrapers of downtown Atlanta.

Charles Lathom had come around his desk to shake my hand. He was a large man with a head full of white hair and a red face. He was well into his sixties now, and what had once been an athletic frame was going to fat. "Welcome, Mr. Royal. I wonder what I can do for a lawyer from Longboat Key. I do love that island." The accent rolling off his tongue was pure Atlanta upper class. I could smell liquor on his breath, but if he'd been drinking a lot, he didn't show it.

"Sounds like you're familiar with the island," I said.

"My wife and I used to spend a little time at the Colony before they closed it. We'd go down every year for some tennis and the beach. What brings you up our way?"

"A delicate matter, I'm afraid. It may have to do with your family, and I wouldn't intrude if it weren't important." I told him about Esther and the charges against her and what I knew about the victim. "I spoke with Mrs. Halstead, who bought your parents' home, and she said she remembered you and your brother, but didn't know anything about a sister. Yet, Olivia was from Atlanta and Lathom, the way you spell it, is not a common name. The victim's friend down in The Villages told me that Olivia came from a wealthy family and had grown up in Buckhead. Olivia also told that to a *Constitution* reporter."

I noticed Lathom's face turning a darker red as I spoke. He looked as if he were straining at lifting weights. I was beginning to think he was having a stroke, when two words, surrounded by a fine spray of spittle, exploded from his mouth. "That bitch!"

"You know her?" I asked.

Lathom nodded his head. "A long time ago, she was my sister-in-law for about a month. Then my brother died."

"I'm sorry about that. I found his obituary online when I was looking for you. He was a young man when he died."

"Yes, he was. Forty-two. Just a little over a year younger than me. That's what made it so tragic."

"What happened to Olivia after your brother's death?"

"I have no idea. I never heard from her again and I sure as hell didn't try to find her."

"May I ask why?"

"The sun is over the yardarm and it's five o'clock somewhere or whatever excuse the alkies use for taking a drink. You want one?"

"If you're having one, I'll join you."

"I'm having Scotch. What do you drink, Mr. Royal?"

"Beer, if you've got one."

"I think we can manage that." He picked up his phone, pressed a couple of buttons, and ordered our drinks. "Now what was your question?"

"It sounds like you and Olivia didn't get along. May I ask why?"

"Well, for starters, she was a foursquare bitch. She took over my poor brother's brain. Reminded me of one of those movies where the dead take over the bodies of live people. Only this time, it was like she took over his brain."

"Can you be more specific?"

"It's a long story."

"I've got time," I said.

"Right after the Civil War, my second great-grandfather started a construction business and was part of the reconstruction of Atlanta. He also bought up property on the edges of the city, which was then very small. Over the years, he and his son, my great-grandfather, made a large fortune in construction and real estate. In his time, my grandfather took over the business and bought out his two sisters who had each inherited a third. Five years later, he sold the business and the remaining real estate and spent the rest of his life spending the money. When he died, my dad, an only child, inherited what was left, which still amounted to a medium-sized fortune.

"My mother came from old money, older than ours, but by the time my brother and I came along, it had dwindled to nothing but a small trust fund that was administered by a bank. Her family had owned a massive plantation down near Douglas in South Georgia. When the slaves were freed, the cotton plantation became a lot less profitable because they had to pay wages to get the infernal stuff picked.

"The family turned to the timber business. They had bought up a lot of wooded acreage before the war that they'd planned to clear and plant with cotton. But the war happened and life as they knew it came to a rather abrupt and bitter end.

"Mother's family made a lot of money selling timber, but the recession that followed World War I pretty much broke them. Nobody needed lumber. Her dad, my maternal grandfather, had the good sense to cash out before we got into the war in France, and he put his money into industries that became part of what President Eisenhower later called the Military-Industrial Complex. He made a lot of money and after the war, reinvested the majority of it in other stocks. When the depression hit, he lost most of it."

He paused, jabbed at the buttons on the phone, and said, "Bring us another one." He looked at me and I nodded. "Bring another beer, too. Might as well bring the whole Scotch bottle and a bucket of ice. And the rest of that six-pack in the refrigerator."

"Just one more for me," I said. "I've got some more work to do tonight."

"Forget the six-pack," he said into the phone and hung up. "Now, where was I?"

"Your maternal grandfather just survived the depression." I had the uncharitable thought that this tale was going to be a lot longer than I had anticipated, but I didn't want to stop him while he was on a roll. I suspected that the more Scotch he drank, the more involved his story would be. I'd learned a long time ago that there were often kernels of substance in the disjointed stories of the inebriated.

"Oh yeah. Grandpa had had the foresight, or luck maybe, to put some of the money that was left into buying gold and other precious metals. Those survived the depression, and the family lived pretty well during the bad years, and he set up a trust fund for my grandmother, my mom, and her sister. Grandpa died in 1940 when my mother was twelve.

"When Mom finished high school, she came up here to Agnes Scott College. My dad was finishing at Emory and the two got married. My dad went off to fight in Korea and right after he came home, both his parents died within a couple of months of each other. My parents inherited the Buckhead house and moved in. When the will was read, my dad was surprised to learn that there was not a lot of money left, and what there was, he squandered over the next twenty years. By the time they sold the house, they were living off my mother's trust fund."

"You seem to be doing okay," I said.

"My brother and I were given good educations. I got a degree in finance and have made that work for me."

"What about your brother?"

"He graduated from Georgia Tech with a degree in civil engineering and went to work for a large homebuilder in this area. He was doing well, but when my parents sold the house and moved to Douglas, Mom's hometown, he moved, too. Mom and Dad settled in a retirement community just outside Douglas. It was one of those places that was ahead of its time. You bought into the assisted living part and had an apartment that you could live in the rest of your life. Depending on how frail you become, they'll increase the level of care until you need the nursing home part of it. Danny was pretty close to them, and he wanted to live near them, and I had already married and started a family here in Atlanta."

He finished his glass of whiskey, shook the ice cubes, and was reaching for the phone when his receptionist came through the door carrying an ornate silver-plated ice bucket and stand and an unopened bottle of Scotch clamped under the arm. She placed the ice bucket in its holder and the bottle on the desk. "I'll be leaving now," she said, "if you don't need anything else."

Charles waved his hand absentmindedly. "See you tomorrow, Patrice." He poured himself another drink.

I could tell by the light coming through the big south-facing windows that the sun was getting lower in the western sky. I had finished my second beer, but kept the bottle in my hand in a pretense of still drinking from it. I didn't want Charles to offer me another one. I might have accepted, and I still had to drive back to the hotel. No sense in taking a chance on a drunk driving charge.

"So, what did Danny do in Douglas?" I asked.

"He started his own construction company. Going back to the roots of the family fortune, I guess." He chuckled, but it sounded a little bitter.

"Did it work for him?"

"He did well. The company grew and he was making good money. My mom's trust fund took care of her and Dad and Danny didn't have a wife and kids. He actually lived pretty simply. He sent me a fair amount of money to invest for him. We got a great return, and he actually ended up pretty wealthy."

"What about your parents?"

"Danny took good care of them. He visited regularly and I went down when I could. When they got older and ended up in the nursing facility, Danny was there every day. The trust fund that was supporting our parents would terminate with their deaths. My dad died first, and a year later, my mom followed him. Twenty-two years ago this month. There was a provision in the trust documents, something to do with tax law, that provided that at the death of the last of my parents, the trust's principle would be distributed to their heirs, namely Danny and me."

"A substantial sum?" I was pushing a little, but since the ice and Scotch bottle had arrived, Charles was making its contents disappear at an ever more rapid pace. I thought it was worth the try.

"Not a lot. About two hundred grand. The principle wasn't very large to begin with, and in their final years, they'd eaten into it. The trust was set up so that they could invade the principle if they needed the money for medical purposes. I also found out that Danny was putting a lot of his money into their care. I asked him why he didn't let me know, and he said he had enough money to last him a lifetime and I had a family to support. I waived my share of the trust so that he got all the money. He tried to talk me out of it, but I didn't need the dough and he certainly deserved it."

"Danny sounds like a good guy."

"He was. Probably the best person this family has produced in ten generations. And then the bitch showed up."

"Tell me about Olivia."

"Wow, where to start?" He paused, took a long breath, and sat quietly. He seemed to be thinking.

"The beginning?" I asked, interrupting.

"As good a place as any, I guess. She just sort of appeared one day. I was sitting in my office downtown when Danny walked in and introduced her to me."

"When was this?"

"About a month before he died." He was quiet again, remembering, I guess. He took a big swallow of Scotch and reached into the ice bucket, retrieved two cubes, put them carefully into his glass, and poured more whiskey over the ice

I interrupted again. "You said she just appeared. Where did she come from?"

"Keep in mind that Danny was not very sophisticated when it came to women. He was very shy and he'd hardly ever dated. After my parents died, he stayed in Douglas and kept busy, but I never heard him mention a woman.

"Apparently, he drove up here the afternoon before he brought Olivia to my office. He was staying in a hotel. He always did that. Said he didn't want to intrude on my family. I didn't even know he was in town. The evening before he showed up in my office, he checked into the hotel late in the afternoon when the front desk shift was changing. Olivia was a clerk there and was about to get off work. Somehow, they ended up going out for a drink. That was the same place Danny always stayed when he was in town. Maybe he knew her from before, but I can't imagine him asking her out for a drink. Maybe she asked him. Anyway, they went to a bar when she got off and then back to the hotel where she spent the night with him."

"Pretty quick for a couple their age," I said.

"I thought so. Danny was in his early forties and she looked to be the same age."

"Did he take her back to Douglas?"

"Yeah. But first they drove over to South Carolina and got married. He called that afternoon to tell me they had gone to Anderson, just over the state line, and said their I dos. That day in my office was the last time I saw my brother. Thirty days later, Danny was dead."

"Of what?"

"The death certificate said it was a heart attack."

"But you don't believe it."

"Not for a minute. We have no history of heart problems in our family, and Danny never smoked and almost never took a drink. He jogged every day, took good care of himself."

"Was an autopsy done?"

"No. The authorities said there were no suspicious circumstances, and Olivia had the body cremated the same afternoon that he died. She didn't even notify me. I only became aware of his death because she told the funeral home to send me the bill for the cremation. They sent it a few days later and even added the cost of the obituary in the local paper."

"That was the first notification you got of your brother's death?"

"Yes."

"I read that obituary. I noticed that there was no mention of a surviving wife."

"I asked the funeral home about that when I called about the bill. They told me that the woman who arranged for the cremation told them she was a friend and that Danny's only living relative, me, was traveling in Europe and couldn't be reached. Of course, that was a lie."

"The funeral home went for that?"

"I guess so."

"That still seems pretty thin. Did you follow up with the authorities down there?"

"Yes. I called the sheriff's office and also talked to the medical examiner, who's a family doc and moonlights as the ME. Neither of them found anything suspicious."

"What about the money?" I asked.

"Gone. In those days, I was with one of the large brokerage firms. Danny had cleaned out his account the day after he got married."

"Wouldn't he have had to go through you to do that?"

"No. He could go to any staff member and get it done. Normally, I would have been notified when someone requested something like that, but not this time. Nobody told me about it because Danny had specifically instructed the person he'd talked to not to let me know about his closing his account. Said it was a family matter. He had the cash transferred to his account at a bank in Douglas. When I found out about his death, I looked at his account with my firm and found it closed. That was quite a shock. And then I found out that on the same day that he closed the brokerage account, he had added Olivia's name to his bank account, making it a joint account. By the time I discovered all this, she had already cleaned all the bank accounts out and disappeared."

"How much money was involved?" I asked.

"Something north of a million and a half bucks. It turns out he'd sold his company to his chief assistant for a ridiculously small amount and put the cash in the same bank. He refinanced his house with a different bank and put all that money into the same joint account."

"Olivia cleaned out the accounts."

"Bet your ass. She did it the same day he died."

"And disappeared?"

"Yes."

"And you never heard from her?"

"Not directly. I did see a piece in the newspaper recently about a woman named Olivia Lathom who had become a best-selling author. I guess it might be the same woman, but who knows?"

"Did you follow up on it? Try to find out if it was the same person?"

"No. It wouldn't change anything, and I wasn't interested in putting myself through another emotional hurricane."

"After Olivia and the money disappeared, did you tell the law enforcement people about it?"

"Sure, but they thought she might have left out of grief. After all, she'd only lived in Douglas for a month and had no ties there. She hadn't even developed any friends to speak of. I figured they just didn't want to deal with any of it, so I gave up."

"What do you know about her background?"

"Nothing. I met her that once for about ten minutes, and never even had a conversation with her."

"Do you remember her last name?"

"I've racked my brain trying to remember that, but I think Danny just introduced her as Olivia. I'm pretty sure he didn't mention her last name. If she'd had a name from one of the old families, if she'd really grown up in Buckhead during the fifties and sixties like that newspaper article said, I think he would have mentioned it. We have a bad habit in Georgia of pegging people into the social order based on who their fathers were. We're big on last names that mean something, or maybe just used to mean something. There are a lot of those ghosts around. Third- and fourth-generation descendants of prominent men who made a lot of money. The money's gone, but the ghosts hang on."

Charles finished another glass of Scotch. "I've talked too long and said too much, Counselor."

"I appreciate your help, Charles. I know this can't be fun to talk about."

"Actually, it's kind of cathartic, talking about it. Well, with a little help from the Scotch to loosen my tongue." He looked at the bottle, now substantially diminished, and smiled ruefully. "Maybe more than a little Scotch, huh?"

He looked a bit confused, the mien of the truly inebriated. "Did I tell you about Danny's son?" he asked.

"No, you didn't. I thought Danny had never been married until he met Olivia."

"He hadn't, but you don't have to get married to knock somebody up. Back when Danny was sowing his wild oats, which wasn't until about a year or two before he met Olivia, he met a woman who worked behind the counter of one of those sex shops you see advertised on the interstate. This place was down near Valdosta, right at one of the off-ramps. God only knows what he was doing in a place like that. It was a one-night stand right after our folks died. Maybe their death set him off in some way I don't understand, but he got her pregnant that night."

"Do you know anything about the child?"

"Only that it was a boy and Danny took care of him. Sent money to his mother every month and visited the boy regularly."

"Are you sure it was his son? Not somebody else's whom the mother might have been sleeping with?"

"He was sure. He had some tests run and he showed me a picture of the boy one time when he was up here on business. The boy was the spitting image of Danny at the same age."

"What happened to the boy's mother?"

"I don't know."

"Did you ever try to make contact with her or with your nephew?"

"No. I knew the boy was taken care of and I had my own family to worry about. I figured I'd just leave well enough alone."

"How was the boy taken care of?"

"Danny set up a trust for him. Funded it with monthly donations and set up a life insurance policy that in the event of his death would be paid to the trust. The big hit came when Danny died. Two million bucks in life insurance money poured into that trust. As I said, the boy was well taken care of."

"Do you have a name for the boy or his mom?"

"I don't, but it'll be in my records. I set up the trust, but I'll have to dig for the files. They're in storage somewhere."

"Will you do that for me?"

"Yeah. First thing tomorrow. Is the number on your business card your cell?"

"Yes."

"I'll text you the information."

The Scotch was taking hold. He was slurring his words more and couldn't seem to focus his eyes. He kept blinking, trying to stay awake. I was ready to leave. If he forgot to text me the information about the boy and his mother, I'd call him. I picked up one of his business cards from the little holder sitting on the edge of his desk.

"Can I give you a ride home?" I asked.

"No, thanks," he said, holding up his glass. "I think I'll have a few more of these and call Uber. I haven't talked about my brother's death in a long time, Matt. Maybe it'll help. I truly loved him and then he was ripped out of my life without even a chance to say good-bye. I think the bitch killed him, but I couldn't prove it. That's where the story ends, I guess. If your victim is the same woman as the one who married my brother, I hope she suffered before she died."

"Maybe she did, Charles. Maybe she did."

CHAPTER 24

IT WAS A little after seven the next morning when I drove the rental out of the hotel parking lot. I stopped at a McDonald's and ordered an Egg McMuffin and coffee to go. I found my way to I-85 North and started the two-hour trip to Anderson, South Carolina, just over the Georgia state line. Traffic was heavy, a typical morning in Atlanta. I drove out of it eventually and found myself tripping along an open road at seventy-five miles per hour.

I crossed a bridge over a narrow arm of Lake Hartwell, turned off I-85, and was soon driving down Main Street in Anderson. I found the Anderson County courthouse, parked, and went to the Judge of Probate's office. A middle-aged woman with coiffed hair and a deep southern drawl greeted me with a smile. "May I help you?"

"I'd like to find a marriage license that was issued here, probably about twenty years ago."

"Certainly. Do you have the couple's names?"

"One of them."

"That'll probably do."

"The groom's name was Danny Lathom. I'm not sure about the bride's name."

She turned to a computer, typed on the keyboard, and said, "Here it is. May 16th, twenty years ago. He married a woman named Olivia Travers."

"You mean I could have done this online without bothering you?"

She smiled. "No, sir. We're not online and we've only digitized the index. If you want a copy of the marriage license, we'll have to get it off microfiche. It'll cost you five dollars."

"Would that take long?"

"No. Since I have the date, I can get it for you in a jiffy. Well, maybe two or three jiffies, but it's pretty quick."

"Would you mind?"

"No, sir. Give me a minute." She disappeared into the back of the office. I pulled a five-dollar bill from my wallet and waited, wondering who Olivia Travers really was. At least I had a last name. But, what if it wasn't the name she'd been born with? She'd been in her forties when she met Danny and the chances were good that she'd been married before. Oh well, this was a start. The clerk returned, handed me the document, and I handed her the five.

"I've got a question for you," I said. "What kind of IDs do you require from people trying to get a marriage license?"

"A birth certificate, if possible, but you'd be surprised at how many people don't have one. Twenty years ago, a driver's license would have sufficed. The clerks back then weren't too particular, especially if the applicants were from out of state. We used to get a lot of people from Georgia coming up here because we didn't have a waiting period between the issuance of the license and the wedding. The clerks would issue the license and perform the ceremony, all in about ten minutes."

I looked at the license the clerk handed me. I couldn't see anything that looked out of the ordinary. It was a fairly uncomplicated document, simply showing the names of the bride and groom and the date of the issuance of the license. I stuck it in my pocket, thanked the lady, and left.

I sat in my car for a few moments and fired up my laptop. I hooked it to my phone so that I could access the Internet, and pulled up the website for Coffee County, Georgia, of which Douglas was the county seat. I found that the probate court was the repository of death certificates, but the bureaucracy had been working overtime to frustrate the average taxpaying citizen. I would have to appear personally and pay a twenty-five-dollar fee before I could get a look at Danny Lathom's death certificate.

I searched some more and found that it was impossible to fly commercially into Douglas or anywhere closer than Atlanta. I also discovered that I was looking at a five-hour drive. It was not even ten o'clock yet. If I left immediately and stopped somewhere south of Atlanta to grab a fast-food burger and ate in the car, I could get to Douglas before closing time at the courthouse.

I was scheduled to fly out of Atlanta late that afternoon. I was planning to go to Tampa and then drive on home to Longboat. But I needed that certificate. The wife's maiden name was usually listed on the document, and maybe that would give me a clue that would lead me to the mysterious lady who'd married poor old Danny Lathom a month before his death.

I pulled up Google Maps and plotted a course to Douglas. I called Hertz and arranged to keep the car for another couple of days while I drove south, stopped in Douglas, before going back to the Tampa airport to retrieve my Explorer.

The drive was brutal. I took I-85 South, enjoying sparse traffic until I neared the Atlanta bypass. Even at midday the cars and trucks were stacked up like so many ants swarming a donut morsel. I crawled through the bottlenecks and finally exited onto I-75. I stopped in

Barnesville for a chicken sandwich and a Diet Coke and ate lunch while I drove southward. I passed Cordele and after a few more miles, turned off the interstate for the fifty-mile drive to Douglas.

The Coffee County courthouse was a modern building, like most of those in the small towns throughout the South. The communities had outgrown the aging buildings with their antiquated amenities that had served as courthouses for decades. These gracious old edifices had been replaced by buildings that looked more like a Walmart than a palace of justice. They had new wiring, new plumbing, furniture, and courtrooms that looked like every other one in the state. The old courtrooms, the dignified places where lawyers had plied their trade for generations, were at best consigned to the museums that the old courthouses had become. It was a pity.

The clerk who waited on me was polite, helpful, smiling, and called me sir. A typical Southerner, not unlike the woman who'd helped me in Anderson a few hours before. I missed that. Florida was a southern state only in a geographical sense. The influx of Midwesterners over the past thirty years had edged out the southern influences that had once been endemic to Florida. That wasn't all bad, because the newcomers were for the most part gracious people who had brought with them their innate amiability. Still, it was different, and being back in the state of my birth brought a sense of belonging that was often missing in a place peopled largely by untethered snowbirds whose knowledge of Florida was restricted to beaches and Disney World.

I gave the nice lady a twenty and a five from my wallet and took the proffered death certificate. I sat in a chair in the waiting area and looked it over. It showed that Danny Lathom had died of cardiac arrest. Interesting. I think in the final analysis everybody dies of cardiac arrest, whether it is brought on by a bullet to the heart, a disease process, or some other calamity. That didn't tell me much.

The box for the name, including the last name before marriage, of the surviving spouse simply said, "Olivia Travers." There was a name typed in the box for the medical examiner. I went back to the clerk and showed her the name. "Is the medical examiner still working for the county?" I asked.

"No, sir. He died five or six years back." Dead end.

"Can you point me to the sheriff's office?" She smiled and gave me directions.

CHAPTER 25

I WALKED INTO another modern building and asked the desk clerk if it was possible to see the sheriff. "Sure," he said. "Name?"

"Matthew Royal. I'm a lawyer from Longboat Key, Florida." I handed him my business card. He walked through a door to the back of the building and returned almost immediately. "The sheriff will be right with you," he said. I marveled at the fact that in small counties one does not have to go through layers of bureaucracy to see the top man in any department. It turned out that I was not going to see the top man after all.

A uniformed woman came through the door the clerk had used a few moments before. She appeared to be in her midforties and was almost as tall as my six feet. She had a trim body, blond hair tied in a tight bun, and an engaging smile that brightened the room. Her uniform was devoid of any rank insignia. Probably another clerk, I thought. "Mr. Royal," she said, approaching me with her hand extended. "I'm Sheriff Phyllis Black."

I was surprised. I guess there is some expectation in many of us that the person in charge will always be a man. I don't think it's a prejudice, just something that's been a part of our culture for so long that we're slow to accept the change when seen in a microcosm. I wouldn't be surprised to see a woman governor on TV, but I guess when you're in the small-town South, even if you were born in a similar place, you expect the sheriff to be some big-bellied good old boy with a backwoods drawl.

We shook hands, and I followed her into the bowels of the office. "Would you like some coffee?" she asked.

I nodded. "Black." We stopped in a kitchen, poured a couple of cups from a pot that had probably already boiled the taste out of the brew, and went to her office, a compact affair mostly consumed by a desk and chairs.

"How can I help you?" she asked after we were seated.

"I'm representing a woman down in Sumter County, Florida, who is accused of murdering a woman who used to live here. Her husband died about twenty years ago and left her a sizeable amount of money. They'd only been married for a month or so when he died."

"Danny Lathom," she interrupted.

I guess my surprise showed. She laughed. "We're a small county, Mr. Royal."

"I guess so," I said, smiling. "Did you know the couple?"

"I knew Danny pretty well. He and my dad were hunting buddies, so he was around our house a lot. I never met his wife. I was in college when he married her. It was kind of a scandal around town. Danny was well liked and everybody knew they'd eloped and gotten married a day or two after he met her. Then he died at the end of May. I graduated from Mercer University the same day. My parents were in Macon for my graduation, and Daddy got a call about Danny's death. I rode home with them that afternoon. I met his wife briefly at the service the day after he died. She left town the very next morning, and I don't think anybody's seen her since."

I handed her the death certificate. "Have you ever seen this?"

She looked at it. "Yes. My dad was suspicious of Danny's death and asked me to look into it."

"You looked into it?"

"Yes. After I finished at Mercer, I enrolled in the police academy up in Macon. When I graduated, I was hired on in this department as a deputy. Been here ever since. My investigation of Danny's death was what I like to call quasi-legal. I didn't burden the old sheriff with what I was doing in my off-hours."

"Did you come up with anything? Like who the widow really was?"

"Nada. I did find out that Danny had a little over two million dollars in his accounts at the bank. Danny had recently turned all his accounts into joint accounts with his new wife. The day he died, she stopped by the bank and told them she would like the entire amount of all the deposits put into a cashier's check payable to her. She picked up the check the next day, right after the funeral, and left town the next morning. The house keys were on the kitchen counter with a note saying that she wouldn't be back and that the county should sell the house and furnishings and give the proceeds to charity. The problem was that after the mortgage note—the one Danny had put on the house a week before his death—was paid off, there was no money left. In fact, the bank had to eat most of that mortgage."

"You seem to know a lot about Danny's finances. How did you swing a warrant working under the radar?"

She winked at me. "I was sleeping with the man who had all the information." She paused, smiled, waited for my reaction. I sat stone-faced wondering at the things that go on in small towns. She laughed, "Jack, my husband at the time, owned the bank. In fact, he still does and he's still my husband."

"Poor Jack," I said. "I pretty much live with a cop myself."

Sheriff Black laughed again. "Then you understand the tough position my poor husband was in."

"I surely do. Were you suspicious about the cause of death the ME put on his report?"

"Sure. He died at home and a doctor who lived next door pronounced him dead. Natural causes, he said. The medical examiner, who never was great shakes at determining cause of death, went along with it. He just put in the cause of death as cardiac arrest because his heart sure did stop. Olivia had called a funeral home to come get the body and ordered that he be cremated at once. The neighbor who pronounced him dead, the doctor, okayed the cremation."

"Was that normal procedure?"

"No, but it didn't break any law and it saved the ME some time. He didn't have to do an autopsy."

"Who was the doctor? The one next door."

"Fellow named Bunky Allen. He's dead now. Cardiac arrest."

I raised an eyebrow.

"Caused by a stab wound in the chest about five years ago," she said. "Severed his aorta and he died in seconds."

"Do you think Bunky's murder had anything to do with Danny's death?"

"It wouldn't appear to be connected. A man who'd lost his wife through some action on Bunky's part, or so the man claimed, stabbed him in the hospital corridor late one afternoon. Several people saw the attack. The perp is spending the rest of his life as a guest in one of Georgia's finer prisons."

"Was Bunky really responsible for the man's wife's death?"

"Maybe. Bunky wasn't much of a doctor."

"What did you do about finding Olivia?"

"Keep in mind that I didn't get involved in the case until a year or so after Danny's death. Our forensic people had dusted Danny's house for prints right after his death."

"Wasn't that a bit odd since the death was ruled natural?"

"The old sheriff didn't have a lot of faith in our ME and he thought something might pop up later about the death being suspicious. He treated the house as a crime scene for a few hours, got what information he could, filed it away, and forgot about it."

"Did the old sheriff run the prints?"

"No, but I did. There were some that were most likely hers and I ran them. There were no matches in any of the databases. That's not uncommon, you know. Unless somebody has to get an occupational license of some sort, or was in the military, or arrested, there might very well never have been a reason for her to be fingerprinted. I ran several other sets of prints I found in the house and got hits. They were all people who had reason to be there."

"How about other databases?"

"I checked everything. Births, marriages, high school and college graduations, welfare rolls, you name it. She wasn't listed. She was a ghost. The first record I could find that included Olivia was a marriage license issued in Anderson County, South Carolina, when she married Danny. The name on that license was Olivia Travers. I never found any other records of her under either Travers or Lathom."

"Yeah. I've got the marriage license. What about nicknames, like Liv? Did you run those?"

"I did. I used every variation of Olivia that my computer and I could come up with. Didn't find a thing. A month after that marriage, she was a rich widow who dropped off the earth."

"The Sumter County ME down in Florida didn't get a hit either. A source I trust said Olivia's prints weren't on any database in the world. Did you follow up on the cashier's check?"

"Yeah. She deposited it in a bank in Atlanta and immediately transferred money into several new accounts in other banks. The accounts were in different names, and those accounts were closed within a few days of the money transfer. All the accounts were opened with small deposits during the weeks before Danny's death."

"Sounds like evidence of premeditation," I said.

"You bet. But I couldn't prove murder without a confession from Olivia. I didn't have a body to exhume and no way to determine if Danny had been killed or actually died of natural causes. And Olivia was gone."

"What about the bank accounts and their dates of opening?"

The sheriff shrugged. "You're a criminal defense lawyer. How far do you think I'd get with only the bank accounts for evidence?"

"I can't even see you getting an indictment."

She nodded. "Neither can I."

"Were you ever able to find anything at all about Olivia?"

"No. I tried for several years. Every year or two, I'd run the prints through the databases again, but she had just dropped off the world. Are you sure your victim is the same Olivia Lathom Danny married?"

"I think so. Do you still have her prints on file?"

"I do."

"I'll send you a copy of the print card on our victim. The one the ME took. Just to make sure."

"I'll run it all again, once we verify that your dead woman is the one who was married to Danny Lathom—maybe we can pick up her trail."

"Did you know that Danny had a son?" I asked.

"Yes. Well, I knew he had a child. That was kind of common knowledge around here. I don't think anyone ever knew the baby's sex."

"Do you know where he or his mother live?"

"I don't. That was a great mystery that was never solved. I don't know how the word got out that Danny had a child, but he never denied it. He never told anybody where the woman and the baby lived or anything about them."

I grinned. "But you know something, don't you, Sheriff?"

"I found some records in his checking account where he had been sending the mother a check every month. At least I assumed it was the mother. It was a regular check in the same amount every month to a woman named Grace Hanna."

"Did you get an address?"

"No. There were just canceled checks."

"Did you find the name of the bank where she cashed or deposited the checks?"

"You think she might be able to help you find Olivia?"

"Probably not, but it's a loose end."

"I'm sure I have copies of the checks in my old file. Do you want to take a look?"

"That'd be great."

Sheriff Black left the room and returned in a few minutes. "More coffee?" she asked as she walked in the door, file in hand.

"No, thanks. Did you ever try to follow up on Grace?"

"No. I didn't see any connection between them. That child would have been a couple of years old before Danny even met Olivia."

"How did you get the child's age? Was there paperwork somewhere with that information?"

"Not that I ever saw. I didn't even know the child's gender until you mentioned that Danny had a son. How did you find that out?"

"Danny's brother, Charles, told me. How did you find out about the child?"

"Idle gossip, I guess. It was the talk of the county for a week or so, and then everybody forgot about it. It wasn't that unusual for a man to sow his oats, and sometimes those oats produced what we used to call yard children." She pronounced "children" as "chillun." "They were bastards that nobody cared much about or paid any attention to."

She passed a copy of a check across the desk to me. I examined it. It was in the amount of two thousand dollars, made payable to Grace Hanna. I whistled. "Were all the checks this big?"

"Same amount, from about the time the child would have been born until a couple of weeks before Danny died. There were also several checks made out to Valdosta State University over a two-year period. The little 'for' line on the checks said they were tuition checks for a certain number, which looked like a student ID number to me."

"Did you follow up on the tuition? Find out who it was for?"

She shook her head. "No. It didn't seem important."

"Yeah, I agree. I can't see how it would have anything to do with Danny's death."

I turned over the check payable to Grace Hanna. The stamp was faded, but I could read the name of the bank. Farmers Mutual Bank in Cordele, Georgia, another small town about an hour and a half's drive from where I sat.

We finished our coffee and wound down our conversation. She gave me her business card with a phone number scrawled on the back. "That's my personal cell. If you need anything, feel free to call."

It was getting late and I was tired. I sat in the parking lot and reviewed my day. I'd driven several hundred miles, kept my strength up with fast food and Diet Coke, and met some nice people in two counties in two states. I'd gotten some information, but it was as murky as a silt-filled tidal pool. I wondered if it had been worth the effort and the two days out of my life. Maybe the new facts would make more sense down the line when I'd learned more and the mosaic was coming together.

I checked for messages on my phone. Old Charles, drunk as he was, proved to be a man of his word. He'd texted me the names and last known address of Danny's son and his mother. The address was in Cordele. I drove a few blocks to another fast-food restaurant, got dinner to go, and found a Hampton Inn with an available room.

I called J.D. and told her what I'd found out during my day on the road. She told me that she was planning to go to Longboat for the weekend and wondered when I'd get home. "Probably late tomorrow," I said. "I'm beat and just checked into a hotel here. I've got to drive up to Cordele tomorrow morning and see what I can find out about Danny Lathom's illegitimate son and his mother."

"You think they might be involved somehow?"

"Not really, but it's a loose thread. Pull at enough of those, and you're bound to hit pay dirt."

"You're really not very good at metaphors," she said, "but I get your point. Guess that means I'll be sleeping alone tonight."

"You'd better be."

"What are you going to do?"

"I've got an old law school buddy who practices in Cordele. Tomorrow is Saturday, but I'll call him tonight. He can probably help me find the people I need to talk to. He's lived there all his life and knows everybody."

"When do you plan on getting back to the island?"

"As soon as I can get done what I need to do in Cordele, I'll head south. It'll take me about six hours to get home."

"Why don't you just stop off in The Villages? You can stay at Aunt Esther's place. I'll stop by for a visit. I can put off going to Longboat. The only reason I was going down there was because I thought you were heading home."

"I don't have the key yet."

"I'll get it from Sue tomorrow. She's in on my undercover operation. I told her what was going on because I was afraid I'd run into her somewhere and she'd recognize me and blow the cover. She lives with a ex-cop, so she knows the drill."

"Sounds like a plan. Maybe we can get to the island next weekend. I'll call you when I finish in Cordele."

CHAPTER 26

SATURDAY MORNING IN The Villages was like any other morning. Somebody once told J.D. that when you're retired, every day is Saturday. J.D. thought it was really the converse in The Villages; Saturday was like any weekday. The same things were happening. The multimodal paths were full of golf carts packed with clubs and couples on the way to tee off on one of the forty-three courses available to the residents. The sun was shining, the sky clear, and the sweet aroma of spring flowers suffused the air. Just like every other day.

J.D. was in Judy's cart on the way to meet Will Hall. He'd called late Friday to tell her he had a lot of data from the video surveillance at the gates of the ninety-one neighborhood villages. He assured her that he hadn't hacked anything or committed a crime to gather the information. He'd simply gotten permission from his boss to look into The Villages' servers to see if he could find two vehicles and chart their travel. He had the results on his laptop at his aunt's house.

Bob Geoghegan answered the door and invited J.D. in. "Want some coffee?"

"That'd be great. Black, please. Are you playing golf today?"

Bob laughed. "Tried it. Didn't like it."

"I don't blame you. Same thing happened to me."

"Patty's in the kitchen and Will's in the living room. Go on in. I'll have the coffee ready in a minute."

Will was at his computer. He stood when J.D. entered the room. "Have a seat on the sofa," he said. "We can look at my laptop together."

Patty came in with the coffee. "Hope you made some progress," she said. "I'll leave you two alone. Bob and I are off to the farmer's market in Brownwood."

When Bob and Patty had gone, J.D. asked Will, "Were you able to isolate the vehicles?"

"I think so, at least the rental car, but I'm not sure about the van."

"Tell me what you've got."

"I put the Chevy's tag number into the computer and it came up quickly. It only showed up one time—going into the gate at Hillsborough Village." He pulled up a picture. "This is the plate and you can see from the area around it and tell that it was an automobile as opposed to a van or a truck. Now look at the next picture. This was taken from the camera at the same gate."

The picture clearly showed Olivia Lathom leaning out of the window, presumably pushing the button to raise the bar. "That's her," J.D. said. "What time was this?"

"There's a time stamp in the lower right corner. The picture was taken at six thirty-two on Wednesday evening two weeks ago."

"She was driving to her death," J.D. said. "Did the car ever exit one of the gates?"

"No. At least, not with the same license plate on it. It could have been switched and we'd never find it in all the security footage."

"Did you find anything on the van?"

"That was a little easier to look for since I only had the gates to Hillsborough to look at, but on the other hand, I didn't have a plate number. I made some assumptions and then narrowed the search field. For example, if the victim was killed around eight o'clock on Wednesday evening, I figured it would take at least an hour to get somebody in a van to remove the body. If the van was seen in Brownwood a little before two on Thursday morning, I assumed it would take about twenty minutes or less to get from the Hillsborough gate at Buena Vista Boulevard to Brownwood where the van was seen. I then limited my search to the time between nine p.m. and one-thirty a.m. Given the different vehicle configuration in the area where the license plate would be mounted, I went through the pictures and isolated only the ones that appeared to be vans. From that angle you can't really tell the difference between a passenger van and a utility van. There weren't many vans though, and all but one had visible license plates. None of those left Hillsborough Village during the time frame I was using, so I assumed they were residents returning home for the night. Only one of the vans did not have a plate visible, and that van entered at twelve fifteen a.m. on Thursday and left through the same gate about an hour later at one ten."

"Do you mean that the van didn't have a plate at all?"

"When you look at the picture very closely, you can see that it looks like a metal plate covered the tag. There are devices that you can install in a vehicle that, with a push of a button by the driver, will let down a metal plate to cover the tag and then bring the metal plate back up when you don't need it anymore. They sell these things on the Internet for people who want to avoid paying tolls on toll roads."

"And you're sure this was a van?"

"Pretty sure. Look at the area surrounding the license plate. It's straight up and down. Most cars would have some curvature in the area. We can't be certain, but given the lack of a license plate, and the fact that it went in the same gate that the victim's rental car used, I'd think it's a pretty good guess."

"What about the picture of the driver?"

Will touched a couple of keys on his laptop and a picture of a man with short-cropped dark hair appeared. "Do you recognize him?" Will asked.

J.D. shook her head. "I've never seen him before."

"Well, that's the end of my magic show."

"Can you email me the pictures of the car and van and the people driving them?" She gave him her email address.

Will tapped a few more keys on his laptop. "They should be in your inbox now."

CHAPTER 27

I MET JAMES Hurt in his office on Saturday morning. He hadn't changed much since our law school days and we sat and drank coffee and caught up with each other. I'd called him the evening before and told him that I was looking for Grace Hanna and wondered if he could help.

"Drive on over here tomorrow," he'd said. "I think I know who you're looking for. Besides, I want to hear all about your beach bum life."

James' office was pleasant and quiet on a day when the staff didn't come into work. We drank more coffee, laughed at some of the antics of our fellow law students, told stories of our lives since, and enjoyed each other's company. When we finished our small talk, James changed the subject. "May I ask why you're looking for Grace Hanna?"

"I'm hoping she can tie up a loose end in a murder case I'm working on down in Sumter County, Florida."

"I thought you'd retired."

"I have, but the accused is my girlfriend's aunt."

"You must be serious about this girlfriend to take on a murder case."

"She'd be my wife if she weren't so picky."

James laughed. "Smart girl."

"Do you know Grace?"

"As a matter of fact, I do. I represented her son about four years back."

"How many sons does she have?"

"Just the one. His name's Josh Hanna. About twenty-two now, I guess. He'd just turned eighteen when he was arrested."

"What was the charge?"

"Assault and battery. The boy beat the pure hell out of one of our more marginal citizens. Kid's got a real temper on him."

"What made him do that?"

"The victim called the boy's mama a whore."

"Did you try him?"

"Yep. Not guilty. I think our jury thought he had good reason to beat on a guy who called his mama a whore."

I laughed. "God, I do love small-town Georgia."

"That's the reason I've lived here my whole life. We still believe in civility. It's part of the code, our ethos if you want to sound high falutin'."

"Is Josh still around?"

"He's back. After the trial, he joined the Army. Ended up in intelligence. Did a couple of tours in Afghanistan, got out and came home."

"What's he doing now?"

"Don't know. Probably just relaxing. He only got home a couple of weeks ago."

"What can you tell me about Grace?"

"A real sweetheart. She's a teacher over at Crisp County High School."

"Husband?"

"No. Never married."

"Unwed mother?"

"Seems so. She never talks about it, but she went off to college and came back with a degree and a little boy whose last name is the same as her maiden name."

"She grew up here?"

"Sure did."

"Where did she go to college?"

"Valdosta State."

"Did her family send her there?"

"No. Her dad was killed in an accident out on the interstate when she was in high school. Her mom worked in the office at the local Pontiac dealer. Grace worked at various jobs all through high school and then college. She's a pretty determined woman."

"Where can I find her?"

"I can take you out there and introduce you to her, if you like."

"That might put her at ease. I'd appreciate it."

"Let me call her."

* * *

Grace Hanna was in her midforties, blond, petite, and a bit nervous. James had assured her that we were only looking for information and that nothing had happened to her son, Josh. Grace's concern about an adult child gave me pause, but I decided it was probably nothing more than a mother's constant worry about her chicks, even the grown ones. She and James didn't run in the same social circles, so his call may have disconcerted her a bit. After all, the only other connection she'd had to James was her son's run-in with the law.

If the old Confederacy has a national drink, it is iced tea. I don't think I'd ever been in a Southern home that I hadn't been offered a glass of tea. And that meant iced tea. Few Southerners drank what we called "hot tea." This home, a small well-kept bungalow, was no exception. We accepted.

After we were seated, our glasses on coasters provided by our hostess, introductions made, and pleasantries exchanged, James asked Grace if Josh was home. "No," she said, "he's been gone for about a week. He went down to Florida somewhere to get some beach-time. He's still decompressing from his last tour in Afghanistan. I gather it was pretty bad."

"As I told you on the phone, Matt and I were law school classmates. He has some questions to ask you and they might be a little personal. If you want me to leave at any time, just say so, but understand that anything said in this room today will remain absolutely confidential."

"No worry, Mr. Hurt. After what you did for Josh, I trust you totally, and you know how grateful I am."

"Ms. Hanna," I said, "I practice law down in Florida and I'm representing a woman, a retired schoolteacher as a matter of fact, down in The Villages. She is accused of killing a woman named Olivia Lathom." I saw something cross her face, a fleeting little flinch perhaps, a small acknowledgment of the name. "Did you know her?"

"I knew of her, but I never met her."

"Ms. Hanna," I said, "I've done a lot of investigation on this case, and I know things that aren't any of my business. I hope you'll understand that I wouldn't be asking you these questions if a woman, whom I am convinced is innocent of the charges, wasn't facing life in prison."

"I understand, Mr. Royal. If Mr. Hurt hadn't taken my son's case, he'd probably be in prison now. I know he had to ask some hard questions of people, but he did it to protect my son. I'll answer anything you need to ask."

"Was Danny Lathom Josh's father?" That was blunt and quick, like a question in a courtroom that comes out of left field and is meant to shake the witness, to let him know that I know a lot more than he might think and that I wouldn't accept anything but the truth. I was sorry to use the tactic on this kind woman, but it didn't seem to rattle her.

She bowed her head and said quietly, "Yes."

"But you never married?"

"No."

"May I ask why not?"

"We weren't in love, or anything like that. I met him when he was visiting a client on some business matter, and we ended up sleeping together. It was what you call a one-night stand. I'm not proud of it, and that's the only time in my life it happened. Danny was almost old enough to be my daddy, and that may have had something to do with the attraction. He was very shy, just like my father had been. I can't really explain the whole thing."

"You said he was visiting a client. What was that all about?"

"I worked in a care facility, an old folks home. They weren't really patients because they weren't sick. Just old and feeble. We called them clients."

"Where was this?"

"Valdosta. I was a student at the college there."

"Did you ever work in a sex shop out near the Interstate?"

She seemed shocked by the question, then laughed. "No. My Lord, where would you hear such a thing?"

"Obviously, from a poor source. I apologize for the question. Did you let Danny know you were pregnant?"

"No. But about a year later, Danny showed up at the care facility again. I didn't work there any longer, but he asked about me. One of the other caregivers told him I'd had a baby three months before and was here in Cordele living with my mother. He called and came for a visit."

"Did he have any suspicion that the baby was his?"

"Not really. I think he did the math and figured out that he might be the father. I didn't plan on telling him, but when he showed up here and saw Josh's head of red hair, I think he knew."

"Knew that Josh was his?"

"Yes. Josh's hair was the same color as Danny's."

"Danny had red hair?" I asked.

"Yes. You didn't know?"

"That never came up," I said. "What was Danny's reaction?"

"He asked if he was Josh's father. I told him he had to be since I hadn't had sex with anyone else in almost a year before that night in Valdosta and with nobody between that night and when I learned I was pregnant. He offered to support Josh, and I told him that wasn't necessary. He said he wanted to pay child support and be Josh's daddy. He wanted to visit regularly and for Josh to know who he was. He said it was a trade-off. He would help support Josh in return for being able to be a real daddy to him."

"And you agreed?"

"After we came to terms on some guidelines."

"Like what?" I asked.

"He would have the right to visit at any time, and as often as he wanted, but he had to call ahead and arrange the visit. I would have complete authority to raise Josh. Danny would have no control over that."

"Danny accepted those terms?"

"Yes. He told me he would send me a check for two thousand dollars each month, and he wanted me to go back to school and get my degree. He'd pay tuition at Valdosta State, and if the money he sent wasn't enough to take care of day care for Josh, he'd pay more."

"Was there a court order implementing the agreement?"

"No. It was a handshake deal. And Danny never missed a payment."

"He sounds like a very generous man," I said. "Did he insist on a DNA test?"

She smiled. "No. I did."

"You did? Why?"

"I wanted him to be absolutely sure Josh was his son. I didn't ever want him to have second thoughts."

"You were afraid he'd change his mind about the money?"

She frowned, as if the question was distasteful. "No. I was afraid he might have second thoughts about being Josh's daddy and I couldn't stand the thought of him getting to know the boy and then abandoning him."

"I'm sorry, Ms. Hanna," I said. "That was a stupid and unnecessary question."

"Not really, Mr. Royal. You don't know me. I can see how it was a reasonable question."

"So Danny had the tests run?"

"Yes. By some lab up in Atlanta."

"How did the relationship go with Josh?"

"Wonderful. As I said, Danny never missed a check, and he usually delivered it himself. He'd come over several times a month to see us. We kind of fell into a pattern. I was working again, waitressing at a restaurant here in the evenings, and Mama was keeping Josh. We'd go to lunch somewhere, the three of us, and he always got some playtime with Josh. When I moved back to Valdosta, he helped us move and put the security deposit on the apartment I rented. The visits continued, and as Josh got older, he developed a close attachment to Danny. Called him 'Daddy.'" She wiped at her left eye, brushing a single tear away. "Then he died, and it may have been my fault."

"How was it your fault?"

"I graduated from Valdosta State when Josh was two and was offered a job teaching at the high school here. I took it and was planning to move back when Danny came to visit one evening. I hadn't worked since going back to school. Danny made sure we didn't need anything.

"Up until that time, Danny had shown no romantic inclination toward me at all. I told you he was very shy and there always seemed to be some distance between us. But a few days before I left Valdosta,

Danny came for dinner. After we put Josh down for the night, Danny told me he had to ask me something. Then, out of the blue, he asked me to marry him. I certainly didn't see that coming and I tried to tell him that, while I thought the world of him, I wasn't in love with him and I couldn't marry him. I explained that we would always be family of sorts, that Josh would always be our son, and that I had so enjoyed our times together over the past couple of years that I hoped they would continue."

"How did he take that?"

"I could see that he was hurt, but he seemed to accept it. He left, telling me that he had to go to Atlanta on business and that he would see me the next week."

"Did he show up?"

"No. He called and told me he would have to put off his visit. Josh and I moved back to Cordele, and Danny came to see us a couple of weeks later, I think it was. He told me he'd met a woman, fallen in love, and gotten married, and that he'd made a terrible mistake. He told me that he didn't really love the woman and he was going to file for divorce. He was very sad. He didn't seem to want to talk about it, so I didn't push. I didn't understand it, but I thought maybe he just wanted to get married and found somebody. He was in his forties by then, and maybe his biological clock was running. He apparently jumped into something he didn't think through. He thought it was now or never, and when I turned him down, he went to his backup plan. A week later, he was dead."

"How did you find out about his death?"

"His brother called me. I didn't even know Danny had a brother, but Charles told me he'd just found out about Danny's death and he wanted me to know that Danny had taken out a life insurance policy payable upon his death to a trust he had set up with Josh as the beneficiary. My name was on the policy because Josh was a minor and I was named as trustee. Danny had changed our address with the insurance company the week before he died. Changed it from the Valdosta apartment to here in Cordele. I think it was right after his last visit."

"Did he say anything about being sick or thinking about death when he was here that last time?"

"No. He was depressed about his marital situation, but certainly not suicidal. If he was sick, he didn't mention it to me."

"So why do you think you're responsible for his death?"

"If I'd agreed to marry him, he wouldn't have met that woman he married. I think she killed him."

"Why do you think that?"

"From what Charles told me, Danny had sold all his assets and mortgaged his home and put all the money in joint accounts that his wife cleared out the day after he died. They cremated his body without ever doing an autopsy or finding out what caused his death. The wife left town with all his money the day after she cleared out the bank accounts. It just seems suspicious to me."

"Did you ever follow up on your suspicions?"

"No. I wasn't his wife and I had no standing to do that. I didn't have a clue as to how to proceed even if I thought we could prove anything."

"Does Josh have any memory of his father?"

"Some. He was almost two and a half when Danny died. At first he would ask about his daddy, but that finally stopped. He tells me that he has snatches of memory of him and Danny playing out in the yard. He took a copy of that picture with him when he went off to the Army." She pointed to a small bookcase on which sat two eight-by-ten photographs, one of a younger Grace with a man and a small boy, both of whom had red hair. They were grouped in front of a bush overflowing with bright red roses. The other picture was of a handsome young man with red hair wearing Army camouflage, standing on a dusty plain with mountains in the background. Afghanistan, I thought. "That was taken on Danny's last visit," she said, pointing to the photo with the little boy. "We were out in the backyard and my mom snapped the picture." She pointed to the rear of the house.

"Is this your mom's house?"

"Yes. She left it to me when she died about ten years ago. It's the house I grew up in."

"Did you ever share your suspicions about Olivia with Josh?"

"No. He was too young at the time of Danny's death and by the time he was old enough to discuss it, I didn't want to burden him with my suspicions that his father might have been murdered. Better to let him think Danny died of natural causes. Which he might have, for all I know."

"What did you do with the money from the life insurance policy?"

"I put it in an interest-bearing account and used the money to help support Josh and me. The principal is still in the bank, all two million dollars, plus some more now that the interest is still running and Josh didn't need anything while he was in the Army. As soon as he figures out what he wants to do with his life, I'm going to give it all to him. That's what his daddy would have wanted."

She noticed that my glass was empty. "Let me get you some more tea," she said.

"Thank you." She left the room, and I quickly used my phone to snap a picture of the photos on the bookcase.

Grace returned with a pitcher, filled our glasses, and asked, "Now. Where were we?"

"You never married?" I asked and took a sip of the tea.

"No," she said, smiling. "The right man just never came along. I suspect I compared them all to Danny, and they came up wanting. That wasn't fair to them. I've thought for a long time that I should have married Danny when he asked me to. I would probably have learned to love him and I would never have had to think about other men. Josh would have had a daddy, which he really needed when he got a little older. And Danny might still be alive. As it turned out, Danny's dead, Josh grew up without a father, and I'm what we used to call an old maid schoolmarm."

"You seemed a little worried about your son when James first contacted you this morning. Why was that?"

"Just the mom coming out in me, I guess. I worried every day when he was in Afghanistan and when Mr. Hurt called this morning, I was afraid Josh had gotten in trouble again."

"Does Josh have a car?"

"Yes. He bought a van just before he left for Florida."

"What kind of van?"

"I don't know one from the other. It was just a van to me. A used one. He said he got a bargain."

"Was it like a passenger van or more like a work van? One without side windows."

"A work van, I guess. He was going to fix it up with a mattress and portable potty so he could live in it down in Florida and not have to spend money on hotels."

"What color is the van?"

"White."

"Any markings on it? Graphics, that sort of thing?"

"No. Just plain white. Why?"

"No particular reason. Just my lawyer brain trying to be thorough. Have you told Josh he's about to come into two million dollars?"

"No. He doesn't even know about the money. I wanted to surprise him with it. Now that he's an adult, there're probably legal requirements that I turn it over to him, but I planned to do that anyway."

I had no more questions. We drank our tea and talked about life in Cordele for a few minutes and then took our leave. James drove us back to his office and offered to take me to lunch. I explained that I needed to get on the road, thanked him for his help, and headed south on I-75.

CHAPTER 28

I SLEPT LATE on Sunday, enjoying the soft bed in Esther's guest room and the languor stirred by the memories of an evening spent with my lover. It was nearing nine, and the sun slanting through the east-facing windows of my bedroom was struggling to overcome the air-conditioning. I was coming awake slowly and reached across the bed for J.D. Then I remembered the kiss on the forehead and the soft closing of the door as she left early that morning. Time to get up.

It was nearing sundown when I had arrived at Esther's house the day before. J.D. had borrowed Judy's car and parked it in Esther's garage out of sight of any nosy neighbors or The Villages security patrols who might want to know whose car was parked in the driveway while Esther was in jail.

J.D. opened the front door to my knock, and I was engulfed by the aroma of frying chicken. She hugged me, gave me a kiss, and said, "Dinner's about ready. Sit down on the sofa and relax. We'll be ready to eat in fifteen minutes."

I took a deep breath and said, "I was hoping for sex, but fried chicken is better."

She made a face. "I'll remember that. I don't mind frying chicken, you know."

"That sounds like you'd rather toil over a hot stove than roll around in the hay with me."

"You are one perceptive man."

"I was kidding," I said.

"I wasn't."

If she hadn't been smiling when she said that, I would have thought I'd stepped in it again. My big mouth, which she once told me wasn't nearly as funny as I thought, is apt to get me in trouble. I'd have to work on that some.

Over dinner, I filled J.D. in on the details of my trip and what I'd discovered. "It's still a jumble," I said. "I can't see a picture taking shape."

"What's bothering you?"

"Josh Hanna, for one. He's Danny Lathom's son, and even though he was very young when his dad died, he does have some vague memories of good times. Over the years, he may have built Danny up into a hero, an icon. And if he had any indication that Olivia killed his dad, he might have come down here and taken care of her."

"That might not be a bad hypothesis," she said.

"Yes, but how would Josh have found out anything about Olivia? I didn't think his mother shared any of that with him. She said she didn't and I believe her. She spent the last twenty-two years living for that boy. She never spent any of the life insurance money on herself. She just used the interest to make life a little easier for her son than she could provide on a teacher's pay."

"Are you sure about that? Is the principle of the life insurance still in the bank?"

"James Hurt is going to check on that. Discreetly. He said he could probably find out if she had a large sum in the bank even if he couldn't get the exact amount."

"How?"

"I asked. His answer was, 'It's a small town.'"

"And the van?"

"Grace couldn't tell me a lot about that, but it's troubling. The bartender at World of Beer saw a white van and we know the make and model. What we don't know is whether the van Josh bought is even close to the one that almost ran over the bartender. I'd like to know more about that."

"If his mother didn't tell him about her suspicions concerning Olivia, would Josh have any way of knowing anything about the circumstances of Danny's death?"

"I don't see how."

"When did he get home from Afghanistan?"

"A couple of weeks before Olivia was killed."

"So if he knew something and was out for revenge, he could have found her schedule and come to The Villages."

"I guess," I said, "but that seems to be a pretty good stretch."

"Her speaking schedule was posted on her website and on her publisher's website as well. I checked."

"That would presuppose that Josh would have known that Olivia had become a semi-famous writer."

"Yeah, you're right. It's probably a stretch. Want some dessert?"

"I saw that lemon meringue pie cooling on the counter."

She smiled. "Just for you. And I've got something else for you." She put a slice of pie in front of me and handed me four photos. "Will Hall gave me these on Thursday. You can clearly see the rental car coming into Hillsborough Village and here's the picture of the driver."

"Olivia Lathom."

"Exactly. Here's the van, we think." She explained to me how the device worked to hide the license plate. "You can see that it came into the Hillsborough gate at twelve fifteen Thursday morning and left at one twenty. Just about enough time to make it to Brownwood, drop the body, and almost run over Amber Marris at one forty-five."

"That's probably the van Amber saw. I wonder if it could be Josh Hanna's?"

"But if it is Josh's, wouldn't he have been in the Hillsborough Village earlier if he'd killed Olivia?"

"Good point," I said, "but maybe he was in another car, one that Will wasn't looking for, and he left after the murder to go get his van to transport the body."

"If he had a car, why wouldn't he just have put the body in the trunk?"

"Maybe he was driving a golf cart."

She showed me the picture of the man driving the van. "Is this Josh?"

"No. This guy looks a lot bigger than Josh and Josh has red hair."

"Do you have any idea who this guy is?"

"No. I've never seen him before."

"How about these?" She put two photographs on the table.

"What's this?" I asked.

"The one is Olivia Lathom and the man she was talking to at Barnes & Noble just before the book signing. The other is a headshot of the guy. Look familiar?"

"No. I've never seen him. Have you shown those to anybody else?"

"No."

"Let's keep them to ourselves for now. He might be important or he might just be a fan. Let's let this thing develop a bit before we start showing the pictures around."

We finished the evening on the sofa watching an old war movie starring a young John Wayne, and to tell you the truth, we may have snuggled a bit. We made an early night of it since J.D. had to leave before dawn. "It wouldn't do for the new bookstore chick to be seen leaving the house of the prominent defense lawyer," she said.

I finally rolled out of bed, showered, and used Esther's golf cart to drive to Darrell's Diner in the Pinellas Plaza. I found a table near the door. I ate a big breakfast, lingered over my coffee, and read the morning paper. There was a follow-up story about Olivia Lathom's murder, but it pretty much admitted that the writer didn't know any more than he had a week ago. Not much help.

I sat and mulled over my day. I needed to type up some affidavits that I would send to two of Esther's teaching colleagues in Atlanta that would attest to her good character. I had talked to the women and they were happy to help. I'd email the affidavits, have the women sign them on Monday morning before a notary, and email them back to me. I would also need a couple from Esther's neighbors, but I would take those by their houses and notarize them myself. Once I got the prosecutor's paperwork on Monday, I'd fashion a response and file it by Wednesday in time for the hearing set for Thursday.

The affidavits would be very similar and, thanks to the copy and paste function on my computer, it wouldn't take me long to draft them up. I couldn't risk spending the day with J.D. lest we manage to blow her cover. For better or worse, I had the day all to myself.

I was finishing my coffee when I noticed a large man come through the diner's front door. He appeared to be in his twenties and wore a ball cap, dark sunglasses, and a full beard. He walked straight to my table and sat down facing me. He looked vaguely familiar, and I was wondering if I knew him when he said, "Listen up, asshole. You need to get out of town. Now. Go back down to the Keys and stay there." His accent was southern and country.

"Why?"

"Why what?"

"Why should I leave?"

"If you know what's good for you, you'll be on your way before the sun goes down."

"What? Did you think we're in Dodge City? Get out of town before sundown? Are you a friend of Logan Hamilton?"

"Who the hell is Logan Hamilton?"

"He's the only friend I have who's dumb enough to set up a stunt like this."

"I don't know nobody named Logan."

"Then I have to assume you're just some dumb peckerwood who showed up to interrupt my breakfast."

"Are you calling me dumb?"

"Yeah. If the shoe fits and all that."

"I could wipe up this restaurant with you, asshole."

"I doubt that. Who sent you?"

"Nobody sent me."

"Then why are you here?"

"You're messing in something you don't know nothing about. Big mistake."

"And what would I be messing in that causes you to object?"

"The case you're working on."

"Ah," I said. "Murder most foul."

"What?"

"A quote from the Bard. Don't tax your brain. It might make you constipated."

"I don't know nobody named Bard, but I know you're going to be in a heap of trouble if you don't walk away from this thing."

"I'll give it some thought. In the meantime, don't ever interrupt my breakfast again."

He slammed his left palm on the table and started to rise. As his hand came off the table, I grabbed his thumb with my thumb, my fingers wrapping up his wrist. I used all my strength to push his thumb back against his wrist. It's a quick maneuver and causes almost unbearable pain. His first instinct was to withdraw his hand, but I had a solid grip that he couldn't loosen. He raised his right arm, his hand balling into a fist. I pressed harder on his thumb. He yelled. "Put your fist down," I said quietly. He did as ordered. Pain constricted his face. I stood, looked him in the eye, and said, "You scream like a girl. You ever bother me again, you won't be able to use that hand for the rest of your life. Are we clear?"

He nodded.

"One more thing. Longboat Key is not down at the end of the state. It's off the coast of Sarasota. You got that?"

He nodded again. The whole fiasco hadn't taken more than a minute. The diner was about half-full and the murmur of conversation had stilled abruptly when the bearded man screamed.

A harried-looking man wearing a short-sleeve dress shirt and a knit tie came from behind the counter. "Is there a problem, sir?"

"No. This man was just leaving. Do you know him?"

"No, sir."

I looked at the bearded man. "You're leaving quietly, right?"

He nodded.

"Okay." I let go and he left the restaurant holding his left hand with his right.

I turned to the man whom I assumed was the manager. "I'm sorry for the disturbance."

"Not your fault. I saw him come in and just sit down. I could tell he was acting ugly. Your breakfast is on the house. I'm sorry for the intrusion."

"Thank you, but it wasn't your fault either."

"Still on the house. We don't tolerate that kind of stuff in here."

As we talked, I was watching through the plate-glass windows that fronted the diner, trying to see what kind of car the bearded man was driving. It turned out to be a motorcycle, a big Harley with a very loud engine and inadequate muffler. The license plate was too small for me to see from my vantage point.

I put a ten-dollar bill on the table for the waitress and left. I had noticed that the man's beard was attached to his face by spirit gum. When I was standing face-to-face with him, I could see the remnants of the adhesive, and up close the beard's color didn't quite match the hair on his head. It was a disguise, and a pretty good one. About all I could see was his nose. His eyes were hidden by the sunglasses and the rest of his face by the fake beard, his head by the ball cap. I wished I'd tried to pull the beard off his face, but the manager was trying to defuse the situation, and I didn't want to raise the ruckus any higher.

The weather was so pleasant I decided to drive the cart up to Lake Sumter Landing for a latté at Starbucks. I still had a bit of the newspaper to read, and sitting at an outside table with a latté was a good way to finish the morning. After that, I'd decide how to spend the rest of the day in a place where I knew almost nobody. Too bad I wasn't a golfer.

I drove along one of the multi-modal paths that bordered golf courses, small lakes that were really carefully disguised retention ponds, and past the entrance gates to several of the villages. People waved and smiled, and cars exiting the neighborhoods stopped to let the golf carts pass. The air was filled with a sense of happiness, or goodwill, or maybe just well-being. I could understand why Aunt Esther had found her home here.

The warm weather, the blossoms on the shrubs that lined the path, the flowers at the roundabouts, and the friendly people made for a pleasant ride. But dark thoughts intruded. I had been a bit shaken by the confrontation at Darrell's Diner. Who was the bearded man and how did he know I would be having breakfast there that morning? What was his stake in all this? Why would he think getting rid of me would change anything? I would have made certain that Esther had a good lawyer if for any reason I couldn't continue to represent her. Who was he working for, or did he have some direct part in the murder? Did I have to be on my guard, watch out for him? Were there others who might want to do me harm? Musings of a paranoiac? Maybe. But as the old saying goes, even paranoiacs have enemies.

Lake Sumter Landing is one of the three town squares in The Villages. It was fashioned after a New England village with buildings that looked like they'd been there for a century. There were even plaques attached to many of them that gave a history of the buildings, what they'd been in the nineteenth century, or which historical person had lived there. It was all fantasy. The buildings were only a few years old and the bits of history displayed on the plaques were nothing more than little stories made up by the developer's advertising agency. It all worked to provide an agreeable setting that was often described as a Disney World for retirees. I liked the place.

Starbucks was located on a street named Old Mill Run and squeezed between a breezeway and a men's clothing store. Market Square, the entertainment venue, was directly across the street. I ordered my latté and found a seat at a table on the sidewalk. I sat and sipped and watched the parade of people ambling by, a collection of couples and individuals clad in a variety of dress. Most of them were of retirement age, but there were a few younger couples accompanying them, some with children, all part of the families of the villagers. Many of the men, veterans who had fought the war in Vietnam or manned the line to ensure peace during the Cold War, sported ball caps bearing the logos of a military service or the name of a Navy ship or an Army or Marine regiment or division. It was a justifiable emblem of pride, a testament to a part of their youth that had been consumed by duty. Only about 7 percent of the American people have ever worn the uniform, served in the armed forces, and dedicated a part of their lives to the nation that sustained them. These aging men had well earned the right to wear those hats.

My thoughts drifted back to the altercation at Darrell's Diner. How had the bearded man found me? I thought it would be simple enough for somebody to park near Esther's house and follow me. But who knew I was staying at Esther's? My car had been parked in her driveway overnight, but finding my car there would be like locating the proverbial needle in a field of haystacks. Even if he knew my car and tag number, he wouldn't have found my car since the one I was driving was the one I'd rented at the Atlanta airport on Thursday.

It was not outside the realm of possibility that he just happened to see me in Esther's cart, recognized me, and followed me to the diner. That seemed a little far-fetched.

There were three questions that had to be answered to solve the riddle of the bearded man. First, how did he know I was in Darrell's Diner on a Sunday at midmorning? Secondly, who was he? Thirdly, why threaten me? There was no order to the questions, but once I had the answers to all three, I'd be able to respond and neutralize the threat. And I was pretty sure it was an ongoing threat, not a onetime thing.

I called Jock. "What're you doing?" I asked when he answered.

"Sitting on your patio, drinking your coffee, and enjoying your view. You miss me?"

"No. I wanted to run something by you."

"Shoot."

I told him about my encounter at the diner. "Do you have any thoughts?"

"I'll be there in a couple of hours. Does Esther have an extra bunk?"

"No need for you to come up here. I can handle this. I just thought you might have some suggestions."

"My suggestion is that I'm on my way."

"I'm fine, Jock. I don't need your help."

"Yeah, but J.D. might. I'll see you in a couple of hours." He hung up.

I started to call him back and tell him to stay put, but if there was anything I'd learned about Jock Algren over all the years I'd known him, it was that he was single-minded. If he thought either J.D. or I might be in the slightest bit of danger, he'd be on his way to help. And of all the men in the world, the one I'd most want in my corner in the event of trouble was Jock. I really hadn't meant for him to come rushing up, but to be honest, I already felt better. I also felt a little like a wuss. For God's sake, I was once an Army ranger and a Green Beret. I knew how to take care of myself. But I was glad Jock was on his way.

CHAPTER 29

I CALLED J.D. and told her about my run-in with the bearded man and that Jock was on his way to The Villages. "I'm glad he's coming," she said. "He can help us figure out who that guy was this morning. Do you think he might be trying to protect the real murderer?"

"That crossed my mind. I can't think of any other reason somebody would want to interfere with Esther's trial."

"We have to figure out who he's protecting."

"I agree. If we do that, we'll know who the real killer is."

"Where is Jock going to stay?"

"I guess with me at Aunt Esther's."

"I don't think that's a good idea."

"Why?"

"Let's keep him undercover. He can be my boyfriend visiting from Miami. If he's living with you, he won't be much good at finding the bearded man."

"As much as I love you both, I'm not going to have him sharing a bed with you."

"Judy's got three bedrooms."

"He can stay in one of the hotels. He can still be your boyfriend, but it won't crowd Judy, and you won't be tempted."

"Maybe."

"Maybe what?"

"Maybe I won't be tempted."

"Right. I'll tell him he's going to be stuck in a hotel for a few days." I looked at my watch. "It's not quite eleven yet. Maybe the three of us can get together for lunch."

"Where? We have to be very careful, you know."

"I'll think of something and get back to you."

I called Jock and told him to meet us in the parking lot of the truck stop on I-75 at the Highway 44 exit at Wildwood. "J.D. and I want to have lunch with you. We're going to have to put you in a hotel, but the good news is that you get to be J.D.'s boyfriend for a few days."

"With privileges?"

I laughed. "It's okay by me, but I wouldn't set my heart on it if I were you." I hung up.

* * *

The parking lot at the TA truck stop was crowded with eighteen-wheelers bearing logos of companies from all over North America. It was a huge place, offering every service that a long-haul driver could want. It was a little after one o'clock in the afternoon and many of the professional drivers were finishing their lunches and mounting up, pointing their rigs north or south, moving out to deliver their loads to some distant terminal. They were prepared for hours of boredom and moments of terror as unwitting amateurs drove their cars maniacally in hopes of shaving a couple of minutes off their trips. And later, in another truck stop not unlike this one, they would find time to rest, perhaps sleep, have a warm meal and a bit of camaraderie with other members of their fraternity.

The drivers, mostly men and a few women, were dressed in blue-collar fashion, jeans, boots, and button-up shirts topped by the ubiquitous ball caps with a million different logos. They carried to-go cups of steaming coffee, the elixir meant to heighten their alertness. Among the crowd leaving the restaurant, I spotted a nattily dressed man with a runner's wiry physique, wearing black trousers, a black silk shirt, tasseled Italian loafers made of expensive leather, and a plain black ball cap. No logo to mar the monochromatic look. He walked with one shoulder lower than the other, eyes alert, a man completely aware of his surroundings. Jock had arrived and he was carrying his own Styrofoam cup of coffee, a grin spreading over his face. "Hey, podna," he said. "Glad you could make it."

"You're looking very monochromatic today," I said.

"Not really. Black is not considered chromatic, mono or otherwise. Actually, I'm achromatic."

"Then I must say you're looking very achromatic today. For an asshole."

"Good to see you, too. I can't say that I've missed you while I've been enjoying your hospitality on Longboat Key. It's better when you're not there."

I saw him coming out of the corner of my eye, a short stump of a man, maybe five-six and two hundred pounds of solid gristle. He was moving at a fast walk and carrying an athletic sock in his left hand, the toe filled with weight, rolls of quarters probably. "You bastard," he said in a low growl. "You broke my brother's thumb."

His left arm was moving up and over his head in preparation for beaning me with whatever was in the sock. I was turning toward the man, readying myself to meet his onslaught and disarm him. About five feet separated us when I saw Jock step between us and with a quick underhanded movement, threw his hot coffee, cup and all, into the man's face. The squat assailant let out a howl and dropped the sock, putting both hands to his face in a futile attempt to stop the pain triggered by hot coffee meeting facial skin. His momentum was carrying him straight toward Jock, whose right hand was just completing the movement that had loosed the coffee when he swiveled on his left foot and brought his right foot forcibly into the outside of the left knee of the oncoming creep. The chunky man fell to the pavement, one hand grabbing for his knee and the other still trying to wipe the coffee from his face.

The action took only a second, certainly no more than two or three. Jock's quickness was legendary and had been a part of his physical repertoire since he quarterbacked our high school football team to a conference championship. "I was handling this," I said, deadpanning.

"Sorry I interrupted," he said, "but I saw J.D. drive in and thought you might be distracted." He pointed to J.D.'s red Camry just driving into the parking lot.

I pulled out my cell phone and hit the J.D. speed-dial button. She picked up. "Keep driving," I said. "Park on the other side of the lot and wait in the restaurant."

"Okay." She didn't quibble. She knew I wouldn't have used a certain tone of voice and ordered her to do something if it weren't important.

"She's driving her own car," Jock said. "Aren't you afraid somebody will check up on her tag number?"

"She borrowed a plate from the LBKPD. They jiggered the Department of Motor Vehicle's database to show that tag belonging to a woman named Jade Conway at a nonexistent address in Miami. It'd take some real digging to get past that."

"What're we going to do with this jerk?" Jock asked.

The man was lying on the pavement, groaning. Usually a small crowd would have gathered after somebody got the crap beat out of him, but these truck drivers had schedules to meet and didn't have time to hang around talking to cops. The air was full of cranking diesels as Jock and I stood over the poor guy curled into a fetal position.

"Should we call an ambulance?" I asked.

Jock bent down and pulled the man's hand from his face, took a quick look, and moved to his knee. He wiggled it, drawing a moan from its owner. Jock stood. "He's okay. I pulled the kick so it didn't destroy the knee. He'll be limping for a few days, but nothing serious. His face looks like he got a pretty good sunburn. No big deal. I think we ought to kill him."

"Here?"

"You never know who's looking out a window. Let's put him in my trunk and find some woods. You got your pistol?"

"In the car," I said.

"Is it traceable?"

"Nah. I took it off that cop we killed last month."

"Hold it, man," the man on the ground said. "I didn't mean no harm. Why you want to kill me?"

"You tried to hit me with that sock," I said.

"Just a little tap. That's all." The man sat up, a pleading look on his face. "It wasn't nothing personal. You hurt my brother, that's all."

"Why was your brother bothering me this morning?"

"That's a secret, man. I can't talk about that."

"Let's kill him," Jock said.

"If you kill me, you won't find out why my brother came to see you this morning."

"Man has a point," Jock said.

"We could torture him some before we kill him," I said. "That'd probably get him in the mood to tell us what we want to know."

Jock looked down at the man. "I think my buddy's right. Let's get you in my trunk. Can you walk?"

"Hold on now. There's an old lady involved here. You don't wanna be causing her any harm."

"Wouldn't be my first old lady," Jock said. "What about you, buddy?"

"Nah," I said. "Wouldn't bother me a bit. She probably hasn't got long, anyway. We'd be doing her a favor."

"That's my grandma," the man on the ground said. "You shouldn't be talking about her that way."

"I have a suggestion," I said. "If we take you to the woods, you'll tell us her name and where she lives. Sooner or later, you'll be wanting to tell us everything you know. Probably about the time we get the branding iron heated up. But maybe we can compromise."

"I don't see why not," the man said. "What's the deal?"

"Tell us what's going on, why you and your brother are bothering the hell out of me, and we'll just have a little talk with your grandma. Warn her, you know. We won't hurt her."

"What about me?"

"Oh," I said. "We're still going to kill you."

"Why?"

"Because you're a pusillanimous pissant."

"I don't know what that is. Is it an insult?"

"Can the truth be considered an insult?"

"What?"

"Never mind."

"Okay," he said. "No offense taken. Look, I got a little farm up in Georgia I could give you if you let me go."

"Where in Georgia?"

"Up near Homerville. Can I stand up?"

I nodded. He rose and we looked like three guys standing on a parking lot passing the time of day. "Homerville's in wiregrass country," I said.

"Yessir. You'd like that farm. Enough room for you and your friend here."

"If we let you go, where will you go?"

"Home, man."

"I'd have to have your contact information in case I need to find you."

"Why would you need to find me?"

"If anything you tell me proves not to be true, I'll have to come find you. Or if you or any other member of your annoying family ever bothers me or my friend again, you and I'll have to have a discussion."

"Just talk?"

"Yep. Then I'll kill you."

"And I can go home today?"

"Yep."

"Can I take my brother?"

"Sure."

"And if I never talk about nothing again, we'll be okay?"

"Sure."

"Then we have a deal?"

"We have a deal," I said. "What's your name?"

"Lionel Steerman. People call me Chunk."

"And your brother?"

"Nope. Just me. We call him Biggun."

"What's his real name?"

"Buford Steerman."

"And where does he live?"

"Kinda next door to me. He has a hog farm down the road."

"What's your grandmother's name?"

"Sally Steerman."

"Where does she live?"

"In The Villages."

"What's her address?"

"I don't know, man. I could show you her place, but I can't tell you how to get there."

"We'll find her."

"You're not going to hurt her, are you?"

"Not if you cooperate."

"I'll cooperate. I *am* cooperating, ain't I?"

"You got a phone up there at your hog farm?"

"Well, I don't have a hog farm. I raise chickens."

"Phone?"

"Yep." He gave me the number. "You going to call me?"

"Maybe."

"How will I know it's you I'm talking to?"

"I'll remind you of where we met."

"That's good, 'cause I ain't never met nobody else here."

"How did your brother find me this morning?"

"He followed you in that woman's golf cart."

"How did he know that I'd be in that house?"

"The man on the phone."

"Who was that?" I asked.

"I don't know. It was just a man who called yesterday and told us that our grandma would be arrested for the murder of that writer woman if your client didn't get convicted. He wanted us to help get rid of you."

"Kill me?"

"No, sir." He spoke emphatically, as if he wanted to make sure I believed him. "He just said to run you off."

"And he told your brother I'd be in that house?"

"Yeah."

"Biggun didn't get his name?"

"No, sir."

"And you were going to run me off on his say-so?"

"Well, yeah. I didn't want my grandma to get in trouble."

"Did you ever think the man on the phone might be lying to you?"

He looked at me like I was the idiot. "Yeah, but so what? Even if he was lying, you'd be gone, and Grandma wouldn't be any worse off."

"How did you find me here?"

"I went back to the house where you're staying and parked down the street and saw you come back in the cart and get your car. I just followed you here. No big deal."

A Sumter County sheriff's cruiser sped into the parking lot, siren and lights screaming urgency. It screeched to a stop near where we stood and a uniformed deputy climbed out of the car. He was young, probably early twenties, and most likely fairly new to law enforcement. "You guys okay?" he asked as he approached us.

"Sure, Deputy," I said. "No problems here."

"We got a call that there was a fight involving three men."

Chunk piped up. "These guys assaulted me," he said. "Sucker-punched me."

"Okay, gentlemen, I'd better see some ID."

Each of us gave him our driver's licenses. "You from Georgia?" he asked Chunk.

"Yes, sir."

"Where the hell is Camilla, Mr. Steerman?" the deputy asked.

"Uh, near Albany," Chunk said.

"That's not anywhere near Homerville," I said.

Chunk glanced at me, a sheepish look on his face, and shrugged, as if saying, "Can't blame me for trying."

The deputy looked at Jock. "You're Jonathon Simpson?" He apparently had a Texas license in the name of one of his many aliases.

"I am."

"From Houston?"

"Yes."

"What brings you to Florida?"

"Just visiting my friend here, Matt Royal."

The deputy looked at my license. "Are you the lawyer, Mr. Royal?"

"Yes."

"You're the one representing the woman accused of killing that writer in The Villages?"

"I am."

"May I speak to you privately?" the deputy asked.

I nodded and we walked off a few yards. *Here it comes,* I thought. The word had probably been put out quietly by the sheriff that his deputies were to harass me every chance they had. A night in jail for engaging in fisticuffs in a public parking lot would be more than harassment, but I wouldn't put anything past this sheriff.

The deputy stopped walking and turned to me. "Mr. Royal, all the deputies who patrol this part of the county have verbal orders directly from the sheriff to lend you any assistance necessary if you ever needed anything. Are you sure everything's okay here?"

I was shocked, even more so than I'd been when I'd first met with the sheriff in his office on the day of Esther's arrest. I couldn't figure out his game, but I thought it wouldn't hurt anything to take advantage of whatever was going on. Chunk had lied to me about his home being near Homerville. Camilla was at least a hundred miles from there. I would have looked at that license before I'd have let him go home, and would not have honored our agreement once I'd seen that he lied to me. I wouldn't have even considered letting the little weasel loose if I'd had anyplace to keep him. Maybe I did have a place now.

"To tell the truth, Deputy, Mr. Steerman attacked me with a sock full of quarters. My friend Jonathon Simpson intervened and took him to the ground and retrieved the sock. He'll vouch for my story, and I think he stuck the sock in his pocket."

"You want me to arrest this guy?"

"He told me his intent was to run me off so I couldn't represent Ms. Higgins. I think his intention was to bash me in the head with that homemade sap. Put all that together and you have a felony. I think you'd be within your rights to arrest him on that information."

The deputy grinned. "I think you're exactly right, Counselor."

"Is there any way some of your paperwork could get lost and you could keep him there for a few days?"

"I'll have to check with the sheriff, but I don't think it'll be a problem."

As we walked back toward Jock and Steerman, the deputy pulled his handcuffs from the holder on his equipment belt. "Turn around, Mr. Steerman. You're under arrest."

"What for? What did I do?"

"You're under arrest for assault. Now, turn around. Don't make me tase you."

Chunk turned around reluctantly and was handcuffed by the deputy.

"You have the right . . ." he began and read Steerman his rights. He walked Steerman to the cruiser and put him in the backseat and turned to me. "I'll have his truck towed to impoundment."

"Thanks, Deputy. Here's my business card. The phone number is my cell. Give me a call if you need anything. I'd also like a heads-up if you're going to release him, if that's not too much to ask."

"I'll see what I can do about that, Mr. Royal."

CHAPTER 30

JOCK AND I found J.D. in the restaurant and crowded into her booth. We filled her in on what had happened in the parking lot and what we'd learned. "He really thought you were going to kill him?" she asked. "I can't believe that."

"Look at Jock," I said. "He's certainly ugly enough to scare the bejesus out of a South Georgia chicken farmer."

"Hey," he said. "Watch out."

"I think Jock's kind of cute," J.D. said. "Of course, it's well known that I don't have very good taste in men."

"This is a rough crowd today," Jock said.

"She's kidding, I think," I said. "J.D., did you ever hear the name Sally Steerman?"

"No. Don't think I have. Who is she?"

"Supposedly the grandmother of the dirtbag Jock beat up in the parking lot. She lives in The Villages, and he said he was trying to get rid of me so he could protect her."

"And you're wondering if the grandmother might be involved," J.D. said.

"Right."

"I'll look into it. See if anybody knows her. I can check the property tax records in the three counties and see if she owns a house. She could be renting. What did you do with the grandson?"

I told her about the deputy and the sheriff's directive and that Mr. Steerman was on his way to jail. "What do you think is going on with the sheriff?" she asked.

"Beats me," I said, "but I thought I ought to take advantage of the situation."

"I don't trust him," J.D. said. "You made mincemeat out of him in a courtroom a few years back and now he's doing everything he can to help you out. That order to the deputies is over the top. I've never heard of a cop doing something like that."

"I understand. I'm keeping my distance from him, but I didn't know anything else to do with Steerman but take advantage of the sheriff's good nature."

"Be very careful," J.D. said. "I wonder if it might be worthwhile for me to go see the sheriff and introduce myself, my real self, a cop and the niece of the accused. See if I can give him some new avenues of investigation and maybe convince him that Esther is not guilty."

"Maybe. But I don't think you have enough evidence right now. Let's give ourselves a little more time."

The waitress came and took our orders. Hamburgers and fries all around. When she left, Jock asked, "Did you learn anything in Georgia, Matt?"

"A lot, I think. I don't know how much good it will do me." I related my trip to Georgia and South Carolina using all the detail that Jock thrived on. I knew if I didn't give it to him chapter and verse, he'd drive me crazy with questions.

When I had finished, Jock said, "Lots of avenues."

"Jock," I said, "can you run the name Olivia Travers through your system? That was the name she was using when she got married. The sheriff in Georgia couldn't find any trace of such a person, but you probably have a better system."

"I'll call my geeks when we get through here. We'll see, but I wonder if Josh Hanna might be the best shot."

"Why?" I asked.

"He's got a white van and he's been in Florida during the critical time."

"Yes," I said, "but according to his mother, he doesn't know anything about his father marrying Olivia. I don't see any connection between Josh and Lathom."

"Suppose he found out and thinks Olivia killed his father?"

"How would he have found out? That's a big stretch."

"You said he was in Army intelligence. Those guys have access to a lot of information and they're pretty much whizzes on computers. It'd be pretty easy for Josh to find out just about anything from the databases he had access to, and if necessary, hack into computers that he didn't have access to. Maybe he stumbled onto something about Olivia while trolling the Internet, something that was connected to his father."

"It'd be pretty tough growing up without a father," J.D. said. "Maybe when he figured out who Olivia was, he decided to kill her."

"But why?" I asked. "Danny's death was written off as being from natural causes. What would make him think his dad was murdered?"

"Suppose there was a data trail," Jock said. "It wouldn't have to be a big thing. Maybe just a note stuck away in a law enforcement computer somewhere. If Josh knew what he was looking for, he might have found it."

"Damn," I said. "Let me check on something." I pulled Sheriff Phyllis Black's card from my wallet and dialed her cell phone. She answered on the third ring. "Sheriff Black, this is Matt Royal. I apologize for calling you on a Sunday afternoon."

"It's not a problem, Mr. Royal. What can I do for you?"

"I know you told me you were working on the Danny Lathom matter off the books, as it were. I wonder if your office had a computer system back then."

"We did. We were pretty tech savvy, even in Coffee County."

"Would you have ever filed any reports or notes about your investigation in the computer system?"

"Sure. My investigation wasn't a big secret. Remember, we're a small town, after all. I didn't want to challenge the sheriff on his decision that the death was from natural causes, but I wasn't really hiding it from him. I think we had a kind of tacit agreement that I could undertake the investigation as long as I didn't bother him with it."

"Would those files still be in your system?"

"Yep. Once in, never out. Would you like a copy?"

"I sure would. Can you email it to me tomorrow?"

"I can do it now. I'm in the office working on my budget. The fiscal year starts on June first. Give me your email address, and I'll have it on the way in a few minutes."

"One more question, Sheriff. Do you have any way of knowing if your computer system has been hacked?"

"I don't know the answer to that question. I'd have to ask our information technology people tomorrow. Can I get back to you?"

I gave her my cell number, thanked her, and hung up. Our meals had been delivered while I talked, and we dug in. "Jock," I said, "you might be on to something. The sheriff I told you about who did some investigating into Danny's death did it off the books back when she was a young deputy, but she put all her notes and investigation files into the sheriff's computer system."

"And," Jock said, "I bet they don't have a great deal of security on that system."

"We're going to have to look into Josh Hanna," J.D. said.

"I know," I said. "I hope he's not involved. His mother doesn't need this. Jock, did you get a chance to look into the financials on Ruth Bergstrom?"

"Yes. I'm sure we got all the accounts she and her husband have. Remember, his name is James McNeil. I guess Ruth kept her first married name for some reason. There were no big deposits made in accounts held in either name over the past three years. The only money coming into the accounts was in amounts that matched her and her husband's pension and social security payments. They're not poverty stricken, but they're living near the edge."

"Any big purchases?" J.D. asked. "Something that they might have paid cash for. Money that never went into a bank."

"It doesn't look like it," Jock continued. "They're driving a seven-year-old Honda plus a golf cart they got as part of the deal they made on their house in The Villages. The money they used to pay for the house came from the sale of their home outside Atlanta. I don't think we're going to find anything useful there.

"They did buy some living room furniture last weekend, but it looks like they bought it at one of those places that sells whole rooms and you only have to make a small down payment and pay the rest off over two or three years, interest free."

"How about the financials on Olivia Lathom?" I asked

"Oh, yeah. She got a huge advance on the book. Low seven figures. She already had a couple hundred thousand dollars in the bank, apparently from her marriage to Danny Lathom. She's been spending it regularly, and the principal is getting low."

"That could be a motive for her stealing Esther's book," J.D. said.

"It could be," Jock said. "The amount of the advance was deposited into Olivia's account about a year ago. It was a wire transfer from the publisher."

"And Ruth didn't get any of it?" I asked.

"Nope," Jock said. "And revenge would be a pretty good motive for murder."

"What happens to the money now?" J.D. asked.

"The state of Georgia will probably move to probate the estate, and when they prove there is neither a will nor any natural heirs, the money will go to the state."

"That's kind of funny in a macabre way," J.D. said. "All the scheming to get the money and it ends up in the state coffers."

"And the government will figure out a way to waste it," I said.

"If Olivia knew Ruth was mad at her about the money," J.D. asked, "why would she agree to have dinner with her?"

"Maybe Ruth never expected to get anything out of the book deal," I said.

"I don't see it," J.D. said. "The financials show that Ruth and her husband could use the money. It doesn't make sense that Ruth would commit a felony including theft and fraud by stealing the book and not expect some payment."

"Do you think you can get close enough to Ruth to see if you can figure out if she's the bad guy here?"

"I'll give it a try, Matt, but I think I'd better talk to some of the other book club ladies about her first. They may have picked up on some gossip that might be helpful."

My phone dinged. An email from Sheriff Black with a rather large attachment. I'd wait until I got back to Esther's to download and print it. "It's the stuff from Sheriff Black. I'll print it when I get home. Do either of you want a copy?"

"Not me," said Jock. "Since I managed to pull your ass out of one more fire, I'm headed back to Longboat. I've got some more relaxing to do on your patio."

"My ass thanks you, old buddy. Sure you don't want to stick around a few days?"

"No, thanks. I've got a feeling my boss is going to put me back to work and I've got some more golf to play before he calls."

"Forward the email to me, Matt," J.D. said. "If I spot anything, I'll call."

CHAPTER 31

J.D. HAD SPENT the night with me again and left before daybreak on Monday. I slept in until almost seven, brushed my teeth, put on my jogging clothes, and left to get some exercise. The air was cool, bracing, and fresh. The scent of newly mown grass rode the slight breeze wafting over the Sweetgum golf course. The sun was up, but still low on the eastern horizon. The sky was clear, not a cloud to mar the canopy of deep blue. Other joggers and walkers were out enjoying the morning and golfers were already on the course teeing off.

I was jogging along the sidewalk that runs beside Hendry Drive. I had passed the Collier Neighborhood Recreation Center and was nearing the gate at Buena Vista Boulevard when my telephone pinged, alerting me to the receipt of an email. I looked at the tiny screen and saw that it was from Meredith Evans and included two attachments. Her email said, "Both reports were put on my desk on Friday while I was in court all day in Tavares. I saw them for the first time when I got in this morning. Sorry for the delay."

I hadn't heard from her in almost a week and I guessed that one of the attachments was the report on the bail issue the judge had ordered. The other was probably the police report.

I had only covered about a mile and my joints were a bit creaky. I tried to jog daily on the beach at Longboat Key, but the past week had been so busy I hadn't found time to engage in any of my usual routines. It was telling on my body. I was breathing harder than I should have been and my legs were tiring. That was my excuse anyway. Mostly, I wanted to see the documents and I'd rather print them from my laptop and read the hard copies. I know. I'm a Luddite. The printer and laptop were at Esther's house.

I turned onto McLin Lane and then onto Eisenhower Way and slowed to a walk as I approached Orista Court and Esther's house. The breeze had shifted and the tock-tock of pickle balls striking the paddles wielded by the players at the nearby Big Cypress Village Recreational Center tickled my ears. I stripped as I entered the bathroom, showered, and dressed in clean clothes. I didn't want to saturate Esther's furniture with smelly sweat.

The first attachment was the report on the bail issue. I printed it and began to read. The report was shorter than I'd expected, concise and to the point. On the first page, Meredith conceded that Esther had lived an upstanding life, taught a couple of generations of Atlanta's children, and had never been in trouble. On the second page, she began the litany of evidence that she argued would ensure a conviction.

She mentioned the book that Esther had supposedly authored, but there was no evidence that it existed. Meredith brought up the proposition that Esther might be delusional and that her murderous anger at the victim was fueled by the fantasy that she had written the book and Ms. Lathom had stolen the manuscript from her. If her fantasy persisted, she might very well be a danger to the community, particularly to those working for the victim's publisher.

The defendant had threatened to kill the victim for stealing her work, telling Ruth Bergstrom two days before the murder that she "would kill the bitch," referring to Lathom.

I read the first two pages of the report and stopped to mull over what was there and trying to figure out how to rebut it. Meredith didn't know about the laptop Esther had stashed with her neighbor or that it was in my possession, and I wasn't required to tell her about it. If she specifically asked for it in a discovery motion, I'd argue that most of what was there was not relevant to the murder and what might be relevant was protected by the work product privilege. The computer and its contents were part of my work product and thus privileged, that is not discoverable, unless I planned to offer it into evidence. I would argue that using the contents of the computer in rebuttal to show that the state's witness was lying was permissible. It was also part of the exception to the agreement I'd made with the prosecutor, that there might be evidence I couldn't—and wouldn't—turn over to her.

I could prove that Esther had written the book and probably that Ruth Bergstrom had provided it to Lathom, and that Lathom had sent it to her publisher claiming it to be her own work. That proof alone would be enough to eviscerate Meredith's argument about Esther having delusions, but I would hire a psychologist to examine Esther and be ready to testify that she was not delusional. The trial lawyer can never be too careful, but on the other hand, you didn't want to inundate the jury with evidence you didn't need. I'd have the shrink on standby in case I needed him.

I wanted to get Esther out of jail, but if I disclosed what I knew, it might not be enough to get the charges dropped, and yet, I would have laid out my trial plan. That could be a disaster because it would give the cops and the prosecutors months to find any evidence that could be used to completely disembowel my case. I wouldn't want to risk it, but I'd have to talk to Esther about it.

I turned to the third page, and the last bit of evidence Meredith presented hit me in the face like a sledgehammer. I brought up what I hoped was the police report. It was. And it appeared to be complete. I perused it quickly, looking for anything of importance. I'd seen a lot of similar documents and they were always full of police jargon and boilerplate used to fill in the answers to standard preprinted questions. What jumped out at me was the answer to a question that had been bugging me since I had gotten into this case. Why had the sheriff's department jumped so quickly to charge Esther with murder when all they had was the statement from Ruth Bergstrom that Esther had threatened to kill Olivia Lathom? And why had the state attorney moved forward with a case that seemed to rest upon such a thin reed of evidence?

Meredith must have read the police documents and appended them to her report. I had the answer to my question about the reason for the charges and it upended my whole game plan. It may have also sealed Esther's conviction.

CHAPTER 32

I CALLED J.D. "We've got a big problem."

"What?"

"The police found Esther's gun and ballistics tied it to the gun used to kill Olivia."

"No way. There's got to be a mistake."

"It was in the crime lab's report. Meredith attached it to the police report she emailed to me this morning."

"Aunt Esther didn't do this."

"I know, but this might be a tough one to get around."

"Tell me about the gun," she said.

"It's a twenty-two-caliber Smith and Wesson model 67 revolver. An older model. It was found on a shelf in Esther's bedroom closet."

"I bet that's the one my dad gave her years ago. He wanted her to have it for protection, but the gun scared her more than the thought of some criminal assaulting her. My dad insisted that she take a gun safety course and when she finished that, he took her to a police firing range to teach her how to shoot. She quit after the first session. I doubt she ever fired the gun again."

"Ballistics confirms that the slug that killed Olivia was fired from this gun. The gun had been fired recently and the cartridge was still in the cylinder along with five unfired rounds. The fired cartridge had Esther's fingerprints on it. So did the gun."

"It was her gun, so I'm not surprised that her prints were on it or on the cartridge. She would have loaded it so you could expect the cartridges to have her prints on them. Did they run prints on the other five bullets? The ones that hadn't been fired?"

"Hold on. Let me look at the report."

"While you're at it, see if the report has anything about how long the prints would have been on the cartridges."

The report did not mention the age of the prints that were on all the shell casings. I conveyed that to J.D. "I think the ballistics people have developed techniques that can now pull prints off the cartridges no matter how long they've been there."

"Yeah," J.D. said. "It's called Cartridge Electrostatic Recovery Analysis. It's scientific gobbledygook to me, but it works and the results have been admitted into evidence by the courts."

"The prints can be explained no matter how long they've been on the gun or the cartridges. But if somebody else used the gun to kill Olivia, what happened to his prints?"

"Good question. I'll have to think about that. Wouldn't the prosecutor have to prove a connection between the fingerprints and the murder? I mean, it was her gun and you'd expect her prints to be on it."

"Not necessarily," I said. "Meredith could simply prove that the gun was the murder weapon, that Esther owned it, had access to it, and only her prints were found on it. The jury would be allowed to draw the inference that, under the circumstances, Esther was the murderer."

"Gotta go. I'm at work, and I've got a customer waiting to check out. I'm going to try to meet with one of the book club women after work today. Call me after you meet with Aunt Esther."

* * *

I headed back to Bushnell, cogitating about my strategy in light of the new evidence. I'd called Meredith Evans and asked if the crime lab had taken any photographs of the pistol with the fingerprints outlined. They had, and she agreed to call the lab director and ask her to supply me with a copy of the photos. I stopped by and picked them up on the way to the jail. The only fingerprints on the pistol were wrapped around the grip in the same way they would have been if the pistol were held in the firing position.

When we were seated in the attorney conference room, I told Esther about the gun being found in her house with no fingerprints except hers and that the ballistics expert was confident that her gun was the murder weapon. "I know you didn't kill Olivia," I said, "so there's got to be an explanation."

"I honestly don't know, Matt. Unless somebody stole the gun and used it to kill Olivia."

"Did anybody know you had the gun?"

"Probably everybody. I had it out cleaning it one day, oiling it, that sort of thing and left it on the kitchen counter. Some of the book club people came over that afternoon for one of our critique meetings. We have these little groups within the book club that get together every week or so just to talk about what each other is writing. It's always a lot of fun and we rotate the meeting so that everyone in the group gets to host one. The girls saw the pistol and for a few days called me Annie Oakley. Then they forgot about it."

"Esther, the fact that you owned that gun and only your fingerprints are on it is probably going to sink any chance we have of getting bail. If I could show the possibility that someone stole the gun, we'd still have to make sense out of the fact that your fingerprints were the only ones on the pistol. And we'd need a lot more evidence than we have that one of the book club women, or somebody they might have told about the gun in your closet, stole it and killed Olivia."

"Do you want to throw in the towel?"

"Maybe on the bail hearing. We might get the prosecutor to agree to an early trial date in return for us withdrawing the bail motion."

"Then let's see if we can get an agreement to set the trial as early as possible. If we can't, so be it. I can handle this place for a couple more months. The only thing I really miss is the opportunity to teach my kids how to read."

"I didn't know you were still teaching," I said.

"I don't think of it as teaching like I did for so many years in Atlanta. I volunteer at the elementary school in Wildwood two mornings a week. I help with the younger kids who don't get much of what you might call intellectual stimulation at home. Some of those kids are as bright as a newly minted penny. They pick up on the reading very quickly, but some of them struggle. I like to think I'm making a little bit of difference in some of their lives."

"Do you do this at a set time every week?"

"Yep. Every Tuesday and Thursday morning from ten until eleven."

"Do any of your friends know about this?"

"Sure. All of them, I guess. I never made a secret of it."

"How long are you out of the house on those mornings?"

"Not long. The school is just up the street off Highway 44 A. It only takes me ten or fifteen minutes to get there, and I spend an hour with the kids and come home."

"I bet you don't lock your doors when you leave the house."

"Heavens, no. We don't have much crime in The Villages, you know."

"Did the ladies in the group who found out about your gun know where you kept it?"

She was quiet for a moment or two and said, "I'm not sure, but I might have told them that I keep it in on a shelf in the closet in my bedroom. I was dusting in there the morning of the meeting and I saw the gun and thought I ought to clean it since I hadn't touched it in years. J.D.'s dad tried to teach me to use it, but the damn thing scared me. The fact that I decided to clean it was a spur-of-the-moment thing. I probably explained that to the girls as the reason it was laying on my kitchen counter."

"Did you keep it loaded?"

"Sure. I can't imagine that a gun would be much use if it weren't loaded."

"But you were afraid of it."

"I kept the safety on," she said, with a smile. "Probably doesn't make much sense, but there you have it."

"So a number of people would have known that you're gone on those mornings that you teach and that you don't lock your door. Anyone could just have just walked in and taken the gun."

"I suppose, but so could anybody who found out about the gun second- or thirdhand. It wouldn't have to be one of my friends. But wouldn't the person who pulled the trigger have left fingerprints on the pistol?"

"They would have, but there were no other prints on the gun. If somebody had wiped it clean after using it, how would your prints have gotten on it?"

She thought about that for a beat and her face lit up. If this had been a comic book scene, a small glowing light bulb would have appeared above her head. "Matt," she said. "Kelly Gilbert came to visit me late on Thursday morning right after I got back from school. That was the day they found Olivia's body. Kelly brought over some cookies she'd baked and wanted to talk about Olivia's death. By then probably everybody in The Villages had heard about it. She said that she was upset and was thinking about getting a gun for self-protection. She asked if she could see mine. I got it out of the closet and showed her how to hold it in a shooting stance. I told her I was afraid of the thing, and except for the emotional attachment I had to it because it had been a gift from my late brother-in-law, I would have gotten rid of it a long time ago."

"Do you remember holding the gun in any other way than by the grip during your little demonstration?"

"No. J.D.'s dad insisted I take a gun safety course, and one thing I learned is to never hold a pistol except by the grip and never point it at anybody, loaded or unloaded."

"Did Kelly ever touch the gun?"

"No. I offered it to her, but she said she didn't know anything about guns and would wait to take some lessons."

"That would explain how your fingerprints ended up on the gun and the shooter's did not."

"Yes, but Kelly wouldn't do anything like that. She's a very sweet woman. I don't think she's capable of murder or even the kind of deceit it would take to get my prints on the gun. It would have been an innocent mistake on her part if that's what happened. I don't want to get her in any kind of trouble."

"My job is not to prove you innocent, but to show there is reasonable doubt as to whether you are guilty as charged. I wouldn't have to prove that Kelly was involved in any way, just that she was in your house and watched you handle the gun."

"Explain this all to me, Matt."

"You were at the school on Tuesday morning. Gone from home for an hour and a half or so. Your front door was not locked. Somebody comes in, takes your gun, and leaves. You don't notice that it's gone, because you don't usually pay attention to it. The somebody who took the gun uses it on Wednesday night to kill Olivia, wipes the gun clean of fingerprints, returns it to the closet while you're at school on Thursday morning. When you get back home, Kelly shows up with cookies and arranges for you to put your fingerprints back on the pistol. When the police search your home the next day, they find the gun that had been recently fired and your fingerprints are on the cartridges and the grip. That will be awfully good evidence that you were the shooter."

"What do you suggest?"

"The state can't take your deposition because of your Fifth Amendment right not to be compelled to incriminate yourself. I think we should keep this new information to ourselves for now. The prosecutor will no doubt make a big issue in her case about your gun being the murder weapon and the fact that only your fingerprints were found on it. Then we come along in our case and explain to the jury why the murder weapon only had your prints on it. That will take a lot of wind out of the state's sails."

"How are you going to prove that?"

"If Kelly Gilbert had nothing to do with the murder, she'll be happy to testify that on the day they found Olivia's body, she came over to your house and asked you to show her the gun. If she won't testify to that, I'll figure out why and be ready to impeach her."

"Impeach her?"

"Cross-examine her and show that she's lying. And either way, I'll put you on the stand."

"Wouldn't that information help in the bail hearing?"

"It would, but we'd be disclosing part of our trial strategy that I'd prefer to leave until the trial so that we can surprise the state. Look, I don't want you to have to sit in jail, but I also don't want to let this little nugget of information about the gun get to the prosecutor. Meredith might have already talked to Kelly and figured it out, but she won't know if we figured it out. If Kelly had nothing to hide and admits to asking you to handle the gun, it won't make any difference. But, if for some reason, Kelly didn't disclose that to the prosecution, we'll have a surprise waiting for the state when we go to trial.

"We may not win any points on this issue at trial, but if I use this one in my bail memo to the judge, it definitely won't be of much use to us at trial. The state will have had time to figure out a way to counter our evidence, like getting Kelly to lie about it."

"Do you think Ms. Evans would do something like that?"

"No. But I can't take the chance that she's not the ethical person I think she is."

"So, what happens if you don't use what we know in your bail hearing?"

"If I don't show it to the judge, he's never going to grant bail. The gun and the fingerprints, without anything to dispute the prosecution's position, will sink any chance we might have had at getting bail."

"What do you suggest, Matt?"

"We don't have a trial date. Maybe I can approach Ms. Evans with a deal. I'll withdraw the motion for bail if she'll agree to a trial date in, say, thirty days. That'll mean you'll be stuck here for the duration."

"What if she won't agree to the quicker trial?"

"Then I think we still need to withdraw our bail motion. I don't like the idea of making an argument I can't possibly win. It makes me look like an amateur and tends to make the judge testy for wasting his time."

"If we go to a hearing on the bail motion and lose, can we appeal it?"

"Yes. But that'll just delay the trial even further, probably by months, and I don't think the appellate court would overturn Judge Gallagher, given what the prosecutor will argue. Unless we divulge our strategy on the fingerprints and the computer, we're going to lose.

And we could lose even if we put it all in our response to the state's memorandum."

"Then let's see if we can get an agreement for a quicker trial. If we can't, so be it. I can handle this place for a couple more months."

"I want you to look at some pictures and see if you recognize anyone." I pulled the photos out of my briefcase and showed her the one of the man driving the van taken by the security camera at the village or Hillsborough gate.

"I've never seen him before. Who is he?"

"I don't know. We think he's probably the man who drove the body from wherever Olivia was killed to Paddock Square. How about this one?" I showed her the picture of the man talking to Olivia in the Barnes & Noble store.

"Sure, I know him."

CHAPTER 33

I LEFT THE detention center feeling like I'd failed my client. Some decisions are harder than others, and the decision to recommend to Esther that she stay in jail was gut wrenching. But I knew it was a better choice than telegraphing an important part of my trial strategy.

I called the prosecutor as I drove back to The Villages. "Meredith, what would you say to an agreement where I withdraw the bail motion and you agree to a trial no later than thirty days from now?"

"Ah, that fingerprints on the gun kind of grabbed you, huh?"

"Gloating is unbecoming in a valued sister at the bar of justice."

"Yeah, but it's fun."

I laughed. "I'll bet. What say you about a deal?"

"Can you be ready that quickly?"

"I don't see why not."

"If Judge Gallagher gives us a time certain for the trial, he's going to hold us to it."

"Will you agree to an earlier date?"

"Yes," she said. "Let me put you on hold and check with his judicial assistant about a time. Can we finish this in five days?"

"I don't want to promise you that, but at this point, I can't see any reason why we couldn't. How long do you think you'll take with your case?"

"I can probably do it in a day and a half after we seat the jury."

"That'll give me two days and go to the jury early on Friday afternoon. That should be enough time."

"Hold on. I'll get right back to you."

Two minutes later, Meredith came back on the line. "The judge can give us the number one slot on his docket for the trial period beginning on April 24th. That'll give us five weeks to get ready."

"Grab it," I said. "I'll electronically file the notice of withdrawal of the bail motion as soon as I get home."

I thought about turning around and going back to the jail to let Esther know what Meredith and I had agreed to. I decided to call the jailer and see if he could convey a message to her and if so save me a trip back to Bushnell. I talked to the supervisor, identified myself, and asked if he could do me a favor.

"Sure thing, Mr. Royal."

"I need to get a message to my client, Esther Higgins."

"Not a problem."

"Would you simply tell her that we have a trial date for April 24th?"

"I'll get it done in the next five minutes. The sheriff left standing instructions for us to do anything we could for you."

"Thank you."

There it was again. Sheriff Cornett doing me a favor that was not something I had expected. I was still worried about his change of heart. I knew he had not been happy with me when I'd tried Jeff Carpenter's case, so why was he going out of his way to be nice to me? It was a quandary. I appreciated his gestures, but I didn't trust him. What was he up to?

I decided to go home. To Longboat Key. I'd been away for only five days and I was surprised how much I missed the place. Besides, I needed to turn in my rental and get my Explorer out of long-term parking at Tampa International Airport. It was nearing three o'clock as I made my way to I-75. I called J.D. We had determined that since somebody had figured out that I was staying at Esther's house, we might be watched. We didn't want her cover to be blown, so we'd decided that she should lie low for a while. I'd be sleeping alone tonight and I figured I might as well do it on Longboat as in The Villages.

I called her cell. "I'm going to Longboat," I said when she answered. "Why don't you drive down and join me? You can stay tomorrow and tell everybody you had to go back to Miami on some legal matters about your divorce."

"I'd like to do it, Matt, but I've got a meeting with Kelly Gilbert tonight and I don't want to put it off. I could drive down in the morning and come back on Wednesday or Thursday."

"That'll work, but what am I supposed do tonight?"

"I'm sure Jock and Logan will have some ideas."

"I'll probably get in trouble if I listen to them."

"Try to be good. I'll call you when I start out in the morning. Unless you want me to call tonight about my meeting with Kelly."

"No. I'm going to Tiny's."

She laughed. "Now, there's a big surprise. How did it go with Aunt Esther?"

I told her about our meeting, what we'd decided, and about Kelly Gilbert's involvement in getting Esther's fingerprints on the pistol grip. "That sounds suspicious," I said. "Maybe you can get the conversation with Kelly turned in that direction."

"I don't know, Matt. This is our first meeting. I don't want to spook her, but I agree, that whole act of Kelly's on the day they found the body seems a bit hinkey. I'll play it by ear. Something might come up. What about bail?"

"Esther agreed with me that we should skip the bail hearing. I can't say she's happy with staying in jail, but she understands the situation. She's stoic as hell."

"She is that."

"I talked with the prosecutor and we've agreed to start the trial five weeks from today. If we win, Esther will be out within six weeks. If we lose, it won't matter because she'll be heading straight to prison."

"Don't even think like that," she said. "I'll talk to you tomorrow."

I was on the exit to I-275 when my phone rang. I answered. "Mr. Royal, this is Phyllis Black up in Douglas."

"How are you, Sheriff?"

"Not so good, actually. I just got a report from our computer guy. It's mostly technical jargon, but the gist of it is that we were hacked a couple of months ago. It was apparently a very sophisticated operation and our people couldn't identify anything about the hacker, who he was or where he came from. Our people think it was so state-of-the-art that it might have been a government operation. Lord knows why the government would be interested in our network. If they wanted information, all they have to do is ask."

"Could your people determine if the hacker was after any specific information?"

"Yeah. That's the interesting part. Whoever it was went looking for anything we had pertaining to Danny Lathom."

"So they would have gotten your file on his death."

"Without question."

"Were your people able to tell if the hacker might have been from a military unit, specifically an Army operation?"

"No. The report says that they were not able to identify any government or agency that made the intrusion. It just states that the hack was so sophisticated that it must have been a government operation. Would you like for me to send you the report?"

"That would be great, Sheriff. Can you email it to me?"

"I'll get it out in the next few minutes. I'm sorry about this, Matt."

"Don't be. This might be a break in my case. I'll let you know what comes of it. Did you get the copy of the print card I emailed you on our victim?"

"I did. No doubt about it. Your victim is the long-lost wife of the late Danny Lathom."

CHAPTER 34

J.D. MET KELLY Gilbert at the bar at Sonny's Barbeque Restaurant in Lake Sumter Landing. Kelly was sitting at a table on the wide veranda when J.D. arrived in Judy Ferguson's golf cart. "I hope you haven't been here long," J.D. said as she sat down.

"No. Just got here. I haven't ordered yet."

A long bar ran along one side of the veranda and was situated so that it opened into the restaurant on the other side. The stools on both the inside and outside of the bar were full of senior citizens enjoying a libation after their golf games. Some would stay longer than they should, and others would have one or two and be on their way home. Some couples were leaving to do some dancing. The country strains of the Steel Horse Band playing in the Market Square three blocks away washed faintly over the bar, drawing the dancing couples deeper into the evening.

It was nearing six o'clock, and the sun, low in the western sky, dappled the veranda with shadows. The aroma of barbeque titillated J.D.'s senses, urging her to stay for dinner. The light air was cool and the guests dining al fresco would need sweaters when the sun disappeared. J.D. had brought one to ward off the chill if she stayed long enough.

A waiter ambled over and took their orders, a white wine for J.D. and a Manhattan for Kelly. Pleasantries were exchanged and sips were taken from the drinks. Then, J.D. said, "Kelly, I hope you don't mind if I ask you some questions about some of the book club members. You know my aunt Judy is a good friend of Esther Higgins and she thinks Esther is innocent."

"I think Esther's innocent, too," Kelly said. "But that doesn't mean one of our book club members is the murderer. I can't imagine why anyone would want to do that."

"I agree with you, Kelly, but I need to get to know the members and then branch out from there if I'm going to help my aunt help her friend."

"Are you trying to investigate a murder?" Her voice telegraphed a certain incredulousness.

"Not really. But I thought I might be able to ask questions and turn over some rocks."

"Do you have any background in murder investigations?"

"No, but I'm an Army intelligence officer and I do a lot of investigations dealing with national security."

"Why don't you just let the police do their jobs?"

"I've talked to the investigating officer. He doesn't seem to be digging any further. He thinks he's got his killer and he's not inclined to spend any time looking for other suspects."

"I'm surprised he talked to you."

"He extended me that courtesy since I'm an active duty Army officer, but he wouldn't tell me much that hasn't already been in the newspaper."

"Did you have somebody specifically that you wanted to talk about?"

"Not really," J.D. said. "Can we keep this conversation confidential?"

"My lips are sealed." She made the gesture of sealing her lips, locking them, and throwing away the key. J.D. thought that people who did that usually were inveterate gossips and couldn't be trusted with a secret. She'd have to be careful.

"If you had to put the finger on any member of the book club who you think would be capable of murder, who would it be?"

"I can't believe any of the women in the club would be a murderer. They're all retirees. I haven't met a mean one in the bunch."

"Esther says Ruth Bergstrom gave her manuscript to Olivia Lathom and Olivia published it as her own."

"I'm sure Ruth's capable of that," Kelly said. "Especially if there was money involved. But that's a long way from murder. Was there money involved?"

"I don't know. I think Olivia made a lot of money on the book, but I don't know if she shared it with Ruth. Do you know a woman named Sally Steerman?"

A momentary shock seemed to twist Kelly's face, so quick that J.D. wasn't sure she had seen anything. It might have been some sort of natural tic, nothing of importance. "No, I don't think so," Kelly said. "The name doesn't sound familiar. Why? Who is she?"

"Just a name I heard who may have had a motive to kill Olivia. I think she lives here in The Villages."

"So do a hundred and fifteen thousand other people." Her voice had taken on a steely undertone, as if she hadn't liked the question.

"I know. I just thought that if she was connected to Olivia Lathom, she might have had some link to the book club."

"Do you have any evidence that the Steerman woman was the murderer?"

"No. It's just a name. Somebody heard she might have had a beef with Olivia. You know how gossip is."

Kelly just shook her head and signaled the waiter for another drink. J.D. declined another and decided not to continue the conversation about the murder. Kelly was obviously not comfortable discussing it.

"How long did you live in Orlando?" J.D. asked.

"Not quite two years before my husband died and I moved here."

"Do you have any children?"

"Two boys from my first marriage. Both grown men now. I don't hear much from them anymore."

"I'm sorry to hear that."

"Oh, well, you know how it is. Ungrateful bastards." Her voice dripped with bitterness. "I went through a lot to give them a better life. The older boy is the town drunk in a little burg just south of Atlanta. He never even finished high school and wasted all the money I'd saved for his college education. I doubt he even knows I'm still alive. The younger one is a well-to-do radiologist in Charlotte, but he didn't like my marrying my second husband. If you don't follow the doctor's orders, he gets pissed and cuts off contact."

"I'm sorry, Kelly. It must be difficult."

"Yeah," she said and ordered her third Manhattan.

"Any grandchildren?" J.D. asked.

"Not really. The older boy married some slut he'd met in a bar and for some reason adopted her teenage sons. She ran off with a long-haul truck driver and left my son with the boys. I guess they're my stepgrandchildren and I tried to help them out some when they were younger. They turned out to be as bad as their mother, so I don't have much contact with them either. They'll call sometimes when they need something. Usually money. My younger son, the doctor, is gay, so there's no hope of grandchildren there."

"Well, it looks like you landed on your feet."

"Yeah," she said, sarcasm tingeing her voice. "A miserable life with a semi-happy ending marooned in this cheerful paradise filled with golf-playing nutjobs. It could have been so much better."

"Would I be prying if I asked how it could have been better?"

"No, but there's no magic in the answer. When we're young, we all have dreams. Mine didn't come true. But I've read enough to know that sometimes those dreams do have happy endings. Maybe mine would have materialized if my life hadn't taken a wrong turn a long time ago."

"Do you want to talk about it?"

"No. Water under the bridge. I was just young and stupid. How about your dreams?"

J.D. chuckled. "Sure, I had dreams and they didn't include a career in the Army, but it's turned out to be a good life and I feel like I'm doing some small service for my country. No regrets."

"Your marriage?"

"Yeah. Well, there's a regret for sure, but I've fixed it. I think. I wish it had turned out better."

"Maybe next time," Kelly said, her words slurring now, the alcohol grabbing at her brain. "My one piece of advice is to stay the hell away from lawyers. They'll die on you when you're least expecting it." She laughed and signaled the waiter for another Manhattan.

A couple of Manhattans tend to loosen one's tongue. Three Manhattans is even better, so J.D. took another stab at gleaning some information from Kelly. "Have you heard anything else about the murder? Something that hasn't been in the newspaper?"

Kelly took a long drink from her cocktail, draining the glass, and leaned over the table, lowered her voice, and winked. Or tried to wink. It looked more like an errant facial tic than a wink. She exhaled a burst of bourbon-laden breath, strong enough that J.D. sat back in her chair. She looked at J.D., her eyes not quite focused, and used her index finger to gesture J.D. to lean in close. J.D. complied, and Kelly spoke just above a whisper. "You need to look at that fireman who found the body." She sat back, a crooked smile appearing, as if satisfied that she had imparted a message of great importance to J.D.

"Why him?" J.D. asked.

"He's the one who found the body."

"Yes, but wasn't he just doing his job cleaning up the square?"

"So he says."

"You don't believe him?" J.D. asked.

Kelly shrugged. "You never know." She favored J.D. with a crooked grin and raised her hand to order another drink.

J.D. decided to take a stab. "Did you know that Esther had a gun?"

"Yeah. She was waving it around one day when some of the girls from the book club were at her house."

"That might not be a bad thing to have for security purposes."

"You're probably right, but Esther said she was afraid of the gun and only kept it because her dead brother-in-law gave it to her."

"Do you keep a gun for security?"

"Nah, but I know a lot about guns. Used to use them on the farm to kill varmints. But I sure as hell wouldn't keep a twenty-two like the one Esther had. Not enough firepower. I'd want something that would kill with the first shot."

"Kelly," J.D. said. "Maybe you should hold up on the next drink. You've got to drive home."

"I'm in my cart and you can't get in much trouble in those things. Besides, I'm going dancing when I finish the next drink. I love country music. I've been taking a class in line dancing."

J.D. gave up. She'd had her share of encounters with drunks when she was a patrol cop in Miami. She knew the breed and knew there was no reasoning with them. "I need to get home," she said. "Are you sure you're okay?"

"Right as rain." The bitter half-smile again.

The waiter brought Kelly's fourth Manhattan to their table. J.D. asked for the check and gave the server her credit card. After the card was returned and the check paid, J.D. stood and said, "Kelly, I really enjoyed our evening. I hope to see you again soon."

"You too, darling. I'll see you."

As she walked toward her cart, J.D. turned off her recorder and looked back at the veranda. Kelly was sipping her drink and staring into space, a dejected look on her face. *There is the picture of loneliness*, J.D. thought. And of despair, and bitterness, and regret, and disappointment all rolled into one sad woman bereft of a future.

CHAPTER 35

IT WAS ALMOST eight by the time I got to Tiny's. I'd caught the rush hour on I-275 as I drove into Tampa. The traffic had been miserable all the way from Bushnell, and Malfunction Junction, where I-275 and I-4 merge, was enjoying its usual dysfunction. I never drove through there that I didn't think the death penalty would be appropriate for the traffic engineers who designed such an abomination. To be fair, a lot of these roads were designed before anyone could have reasonably foreseen Florida's population explosion, but I wasn't in a charitable mood. Off with their heads.

I left my rental at the Hertz lot, caught the shuttle to the terminal, boarded the monorail to the long-term parking garage, and recovered my Explorer. I-275 through St. Petersburg was like a parking lot, but finally cleared some as I approached the Skyway Bridge over Tampa Bay. By the time I finally got to the island, I was in dire need of a beer.

The bar was virtually empty. Les Fulcher and Cracker Dix were sipping wine at a high-top table in the corner. Another couple, whom I didn't know, were at the other table, holding hands, their drinks sweating on their coasters. Jock and Logan were taking up a couple of stools at the bar, and Susie, the owner of the place, was clicking at her computerized cash register running a tape of some sort that apparently gave her information she needed. She looked up when she heard the door open and moved quickly to the beer cooler. My bottle of Miller Lite was sitting on a coaster next to a cold glass by the time I got to the bar.

"Thanks, Susie," I said as I sat down. "I bet you're in the mood for a little intelligent conversation for a change."

"Yes. Finally," she said.

"Who're you?" Logan asked.

"Just a stranger in town looking for a little human contact. It doesn't look like I'll find it here."

"Go to hell, Counselor. I think you just insulted Susie, but you drink enough beer and she'll get over it. Glad you're back."

Logan was my best friend on the island. He was a native of Massachusetts and had come to Florida for college at the University of Tampa. He became an executive in a financial services company, made a lot of money, and bought a vacation condo on Longboat. I'd first met him during those days when he'd spent as much time as he could among us beach bums before he had to return to the buttoned-down world in which he prospered. He took to the key's lifestyle with an unrepressed ardor and became so much a part of it that he decided to retire at forty and move permanently to his vacation condo. His stated reason for his move to the key was that somebody had to take care of Matt Royal. He may have had a point, but once J.D. showed up, she relieved him of that duty. Mostly. He and I had become close and during Jock's regular visits, he and Logan had discovered a mutual love of playing bad golf. They became fast friends and golfing partners, and on any occasion they thought warranted it, drinking buddies.

"I didn't expect you back so soon," Jock said.

"There's not much I can do up there for the next week or so. J.D.'s coming down tomorrow for a couple of days, but she'll need to get back."

"I heard back from the geeks. There's nothing on a person named Olivia Travers in any database in the world."

"Another dead end."

"Are you going to win this case?" Logan asked.

"Hope so."

"Want to go fishing tomorrow?" Logan asked. "Do the bay at first light?" I laughed. Logan never got up in time for an early fishing trip. He'd suggest one, and the next morning, when I called to get him out of bed, he'd always say that the bay looked too rough for boating. That was Logan-speak for "Leave me alone. I'm too hungover to think about getting in a boat."

"I think I'll sleep in tomorrow," I said. "J.D. will be here by midmorning. If the weather's nice, you could get Marie and find Jock a woman who's not too proud to be seen with him, and we can take *Recess* up to Egmont for a late picnic lunch."

"Nobody's going to go with Jock," Logan said. "At least, nobody I'd want to be seen on a boat with."

"Watch it," Jock said. "I'm a walking aphrodisiac for the average woman."

The conversation meandered from boating to golf, politics to weather, and, of course, to women. In the end, we decided to provision at Harry's Deli, load *Recess*, and head for Egmont Key, a state park at the mouth of Tampa Bay, accessible only by boat.

Sometime, in the shank of the evening, an attractive Memphis native named Cindy, one of the servers at the Haye Loft, walked into Tiny's. Her southern accent and friendly nature made her a favorite with her customers. She was a regular among those whom Sam

Lastinger, the bartender at the Haye Loft, called the second shift, the servers and bartenders who came to Tiny's each evening when the island establishments where they worked closed for the night.

"Cindy," Logan said, as she took the stool next to him. "You want to go boating tomorrow? You can be Jock's date. He claims to be a walking, breathing aphrodisiac."

"Boats always do that to me," Cindy said, grinning.

"You're the woman I've been looking for all my life," Jock said.

"Ah, Jock," Cindy said with a laugh. "With you there, I won't even need the boat."

Sam came in with his latest girlfriend, a tourist from Minnesota whom he had met at his bar about an hour earlier. "Did I hear you say something about a boat ride?"

"A trip to Egmont for lunch tomorrow," I said. "You're welcome to join us."

Jock and I had one more beer and left for home and bed. Logan stayed for a few more with the second shift. I was tired and my bed was calling me. I lay down in my clothes, and the next thing I knew, sunshine was pouring through my bedroom windows and the aroma of frying bacon was teasing my olfactory receptors. Jock was cooking breakfast. Time to get up and shower.

"Jock," I said over breakfast, "I talked to the sheriff from Coffee County yesterday. It seems that her computers were hacked, but her IT guys can't determine much about the hack. They said it was so sophisticated it must have been a government agency that invaded the sheriff's network. However, the sheriff's people were able to determine that Danny Lathom was the target. Do you think your people could take a look at the sheriff's computers and figure out the identity of the hacker?"

"Maybe. I'll give them a call."

"I've got an email from the sheriff with a copy of her report attached. I'll forward it to you."

* * *

Tuesday was one of those days when everybody calls their relatives in the still-chilly North to rag them a little about the gorgeous days that a Florida spring produces. The ride to Egmont was smooth, the turquoise water crystal clear, the sun bright, and the sky cloudless. J.D.; Logan; his girlfriend, Marie; and I sat in the stern while Jock took the helm with Cindy in the seat next to him. Sam and the woman from Minnesota lounged on the bow cushions.

After lunch on the beach and a dip in the Gulf, still cool from the winter chill, we motored back to my dock, and cleaned up the boat. We agreed to meet later at the Lazy Lobster for dinner. It was a day of sunshine and easy living, a day that was not at all unusual in our subtropical paradise.

Sam had called the restaurant's owner, Michael Geary, and secured us a table. We dined on the patio under the trees, an evening with good friends, good food, and good conversation. A fine way to end what we referred to as JAPDIP—just another perfect day in paradise.

CHAPTER 36

J.D., Jock, and I went to the Blue Dolphin restaurant for breakfast on Wednesday morning. The island was slowing down, moving inexorably toward the summer doldrums. Those of us who lived on the key year-round reveled in the quiet of those months when we ventured out in the heat only when we were heading for the water. Even the beach sand would be so hot some days that we raced to the relative coolness of the Gulf. It was the season when J.D. and I spent a lot of time on *Recess* anchored on a sandbar in the bay or simply drifting in the Gulf. When we sweated too much, we just went overboard and cooled off.

Spring had officially arrived and the day was bright and cool, the humidity low, the thermometer hanging in the low seventies. "Sure you can't stick around, J.D.?" I asked. "*Recess* would be happy to see us, and a little sun would do your pasty complexion some good."

"Pasty?" she asked. "You're a sick person, Matt Royal."

"I've been telling him that for years," Jock said.

"Just a little joke, my sweets," I said.

"Well, to be truthful, I wish I didn't have to leave, but I'm meeting Ruth Bergstrom for lunch."

"Are you looking for anything specific?" I asked.

"You mean other than wanting to know why she's implicated my aunt in her friend's murder?"

"No. I guess that's enough."

"I want to try to get a sense of her. I've talked to several people, mostly ladies in the book club, who just don't like her. Some of them can't put a finger on just what it is they don't like, but somehow, Ruth puts off a bad vibe. I want to explore that some. Maybe I'll break the case."

"Maybe she's just got a congenital nasty disposition," Jock said.

"Yeah, but even taking that into consideration, I can't see any reason she'd try to make Aunt Esther the scapegoat in a murder."

"I'd think if she's trying to hide the theft of a book that made Olivia a lot of money, that'd be reason enough."

"Maybe Ruth shot Olivia," Jock said.

"That's my thinking," J.D. said. "Maybe I can get her to slip up over lunch."

"I'm going to miss you," I said.

"Yeah. Me and my pasty complexion," she said. "I'm sure you will."

"Matt, I'm not surprised that you act like an idiot," Jock said, "but I'm astonished at how often you do it."

"Okay," I said. "I'll get the check."

"Good," J.D. said. "I've got to hit the road."

* * *

J.D. was on the road by midmorning, navigating the thick traffic on I-75 on her way back to The Villages. She'd arranged to meet Ruth Bergstrom at the Glenview Country Club for lunch.

She drove through the gate and past the carefully manicured golf course to the clubhouse. She arrived a few minutes early and was greeted by a hostess who guided her through the barroom. Dark wooden booths lined one side of the room beneath a mural of a golf course set among rolling hills. A long bar ran the length of the opposite side, its chairs empty except for a lone man nursing a beer at the far end. A line of tables was placed between the booths and they were full of men in golf clothes discussing their games, not a plate of food in sight, only glasses glistening with beer and whiskey.

The hostess led J.D. to a table on the enclosed veranda overlooking the course. Minutes later, Ruth arrived. J.D. wondered if she was about to have lunch with a murderer. She had met a lot of them when she was climbing the ladder at the Miami-Dade County homicide unit, but to her knowledge, she'd never had lunch with one.

Ruth was escorted to the table by the hostess and took her seat. "I hope I didn't hold you up," she said.

"Not at all. You're right on time. I got here a little early. I wasn't sure how to find the place."

"My husband plays a lot of golf here. The course is twenty-seven holes and he usually plays every one of them. He says it's a tough course."

"Do you play?"

"Oh, Lord no. These guys get addicted. The main reason we moved here was so that he could play golf every day. The nine-hole courses are free, and I think that attracted him more than the courses themselves. You have to pay to play the championship courses like this one, and now he refuses to play the free ones. He just has a good time, regardless of whether we can afford it."

The waitress came and took their orders and returned quickly with their drinks. Iced tea for both. "Your sandwiches should be out shortly," she said.

"Are you getting settled in?" Ruth asked.

"I think so. I had to run down to Miami yesterday and just got back."

"I hope everything's all right."

"Yeah. Just some more legal nonsense about my divorce."

"Are you thinking about settling here permanently?"

"Afraid not. I'll be going back to Germany for a two-year tour when my leave is up."

"What do you do in the Army?"

"I'm an intelligence officer."

"Like chasing spies and that sort of thing?"

J.D. chuckled. "Not really. We mostly analyze data and advise our commanders."

"You must have an exciting life."

"Sometimes. But I'm afraid most of it is mundane work."

"I think I'd like to live in Germany," Ruth said, wistfully.

"Have you ever been there?"

"No. I've read a lot about places all over the world, but I've never been anywhere other than The Villages. Talk about boring. Now I'm just a golf widow."

"What would you like to do?"

"I don't know. We don't really have the money to do much of anything. We live on our pensions and Social Security, and that doesn't leave enough to do a lot."

"Suppose you came into some money. Say, a long-lost relative dies and leaves you a bundle. What would you do with it?"

Ruth laughed. "I'd divorce the hell out of James for one thing. He probably wouldn't even know I'm gone. He'd just shack up with one of his chippies."

"Oh. I'm sorry."

"He thinks I don't know," Ruth said. "Did your husband ever pull that on you?"

"That's the reason for the divorce."

"You poor thing. If we had the means I'd divorce James, but there just isn't enough money to take care of two of us living separately. As it is, when he's at home, I usually stay in my own bedroom."

J.D. smiled. "Okay. After you got a divorce lawyer, what would you do?"

"Off to Europe, I think. I'd visit all the great art museums, soak up the history, maybe learn French. Find one of those neat Parisian cafés and meet a rich Frenchman. But I'd save enough of the money to set me up for life. My greatest fantasy is to be in a situation where I don't have to worry about money."

"If you had all that money, where would you live?"

"I'm not sure. Some place warm. Maybe the Caribbean, but I've read that many of those islands have a lot of crime. South Florida? Who knows, but I'd be kissing this place good-bye."

"What about your kids?"

"What about them?" An edge had crept into her voice.

"Would you use some of the money on them?"

"God, no," she said. "Those people don't care if I'm alive or dead. I never hear from them."

"Are they in contact with James?"

"No. And he doesn't give a damn about them either." She looked at J.D. questionably, perhaps suspiciously.

J.D. changed the subject. "I read *Beholden,*" she said. "Your friend wrote a very good book."

"Lot of good it did her."

"Yeah, but hitting the *New York Times* best-seller list is a real big deal. Did she make a lot of money on the book?"

"I don't know. I never asked her about that."

"A shame to end her life just as it was about to take off. Do you have any idea why that woman from the book club would have killed her?"

"Esther Higgins is her name. I think she's mentally ill. She seemed to really believe that she'd written the book and that Olivia and I had conspired to steal it from her."

The waitress brought their sandwiches and asked, "Do you need anything else?"

Ruth shook her head and J.D. said, "Don't think so. Thank you."

When the server had gone, J.D. asked, "Did you actually see the manuscript?"

"I did. She gave it to me and asked me to read it and see if I thought it was worth trying to get an agent."

"What did you think?"

"I read the first few chapters and it was terrible. I just told Esther I didn't think it was ready for publication."

"After the murder, were you afraid Esther might come after you?"

"Oh, yeah. Her lawyer was bringing up what they call a bail motion before the judge tomorrow. I was going to testify that I feared for my life if they let her out of jail."

"Do you have to go to the hearing? I think that would be scary."

"No. They canceled it. The prosecutor told me the lawyer withdrew his motion or something like that. Esther has to stay in jail until the trial."

"I guess that was a relief."

"It sure was. No telling what that woman is capable of."

"Had you had any trouble with her before she killed your friend?"

"No. She seemed a little pushy, but it didn't bother me. I just didn't like her very much."

"I wonder how the Higgins woman got Olivia to meet her for dinner. I read in the paper that she told the traveling aide that she was going to dinner with a friend. That wasn't you?"

"No. I'd promised a neighbor I'd drive her to the Orlando airport that evening, and I couldn't back out on her. I didn't get home until late. I don't have any idea who she was supposed to meet. In fact, I didn't even know she was coming to The Villages until I saw it in the paper. I called her in Atlanta, and she told me it would be a really quick trip and that we'd get together after the book tours were over."

J.D. moved the conversation into more mundane matters about The Villages. When they'd finished their sandwiches, J.D. looked at her watch. "I've got to go, Ruth. I told Judy I'd be at the store by one thirty." She waved at the server and mimed signing a check. "I've really enjoyed the lunch."

"Let's split the check. I'm glad I had a chance to get to know you. How long before you have to leave?"

"Lunch is my treat. I've got three more weeks, then off to Germany."

"Thanks for lunch. I hope to see you again before you leave. If not, have a good life."

They left the restaurant together and walked to their cars. J.D. turned off her recorder as she drove out of the parking lot.

CHAPTER 37

J.D. LEFT THE Glenview Country Club on a road that wound between fairways, crossed the iconic stone bridge over Country Brook, and turned south on Buena Vista Boulevard. She called Matt.

"I hope you didn't go back to bed," she said when he picked up the phone.

"Absolutely not," he said. "I jogged on the beach, had lunch at the Longbeach Café, and am now at Mar Vista with Cracker, Jock, and a cold one."

"The life of a beach bum. And here I am working for no pay." She told him about her lunch with Ruth Bergstrom. "She's not a happy person. She needs money and wants to have a lot of it. I can see that as a motive to steal Aunt Esther's manuscript. If she expected money from Olivia and didn't get it, I would say she had a motive."

"But she said she drove a neighbor to the Orlando airport and didn't get back until after Olivia was killed."

"She could have been lying. I'd like to talk to the neighbor, but I was afraid to ask Ruth for a name. I didn't want her to think I was zeroing in on her as a suspect. I thought I'd ask around, see if anybody might know of someone who planned to travel. If that person was a member of the book club, one of the members would know who left town. Was Jock able to find out anything about the hackers?"

Matt had told her about Sheriff Black's problem with her computers and that he'd asked Jock to look into it. "Yes," he said. "They were able to find the links back to the hacker. They don't have a name, of course, but the hack was initiated from an Army intelligence unit in Afghanistan about two months ago."

"Josh Hanna?" J.D. asked.

"Most likely. Whoever the hacker was, he was in the same unit Josh was and at the same time."

"Had to be Josh."

"Exactly. Now we've got to find him. He owns a white van, he's probably the hacker, and he's supposedly in Florida."

"How would he have gotten Esther's gun?" J.D. asked. "It's pretty clear that her gun was the murder weapon."

"We'll have to work on that. I'm certainly not willing at this point to cross Kelly and Ruth off our list of possibilities. I'm also still interested in Sally Steerman. Who is she and how is she involved?"

"I checked the property appraiser's records for Sumter, Lake, and Marion Counties yesterday while you were out on the dock with your boat. There's no property in any of the three counties that make up The Villages listed as owned by Sally Steerman, or any other person named Steerman. Nothing in the phone listings, either. I even went into the Department of Motor Vehicles database, which I'm not supposed to do except for legitimate police business. No driver's license listing for anybody named Steerman in the three counties, and no Sally Steerman in the entire state."

"I'll have to make another run at those idiots who came after me," Matt sad. "Something will turn up."

"When are you coming back here?"

"Not sure. I'm wondering if this might be a good time for you to introduce yourself to the sheriff."

"Might be. We probably need to see if we can get him to keep Chunk Steerman in the clink for a bit longer. At least until you decide to get up here and talk to him."

"I know you can't use the LBKPD to put out a Be On The Lookout for Hanna's van, but maybe you could talk the sheriff into helping with that."

"Let me see how the meeting goes. If he's not willing to help, I'll talk to Chief Lester. Maybe he can come up with a reason to put out a BOLO even if it doesn't have anything to do with one of his cases."

"Can you meet with the sheriff this afternoon?"

"I'll try," she said.

J.D. called and identified herself as a detective with the LBKPD and asked for an appointment with the sheriff as soon as possible. She was told that the sheriff could see her that afternoon if she could get there by three thirty.

CHAPTER 38

SHERIFF BRIAN CORNETT strode into the waiting room of his office and walked over to J.D. He was in uniform, the four stars of his rank glinting on his collar points. He smiled. "You must be Detective Duncan," he said. "I'm Brian Cornett."

"Nice to meet you, Sheriff. I appreciate your seeing me so quickly. Do you need to see my credentials?"

"No. I've already talked with your chief. He vouched for you and told me that you and Matt are joined at the hip professionally. Come on back to my office. I'm always glad to help out. I have to admit that I was a little curious about what Matt Royal's connection was to Ms. Higgins. He said she was family, but didn't explain it."

"She's my family, and I guess you could say that Matt and I are family. We practically live together." She'd decided to get that out in the open. She didn't want there to be any blowback on her department and she didn't want to mislead the sheriff.

"I appreciate your telling me that, Detective, even though it's none of my business. I'm glad Matt's found somebody."

"Frankly, Sheriff, Matt and I were both a little worried about your reaction to him representing Esther. He said you and he locked horns a few years back and he was afraid you might be holding a grudge."

"May I call you J.D.?"

"Certainly."

"Do you know anything about that case, J.D.?"

"I only know that the case involved a local doctor being charged with murder because he apparently helped an elderly woman die. You were the lead officer on the case and were pretty much convinced that it was murder."

"I was a man of faith, J.D. I still am. I was pretty sure that God was using me as His instrument to make sure the doctor was punished for the sin of murder. A couple of years after Matt won that case, my eighteen-year-old daughter was involved in a horrible traffic accident way out on Highway 301. It was late on a rainy night and she was on her way home from Gainesville after a night class at the university. She slid off the highway and hit a tree. She was trapped in the car and terribly injured. Jeff Carpenter was coming back to town from a house call, something most doctors don't do anymore, and came across the accident right after it happened. He took care of my girl and saved her life. He called for an ambulance and the fire department because they had to cut her out of the car. He rode in the ambulance with her to the hospital up in Gainesville. If he hadn't been there, she'd be dead. As it is, she's now twenty-three, married, and pregnant with my first grandchild. She graduated from the University of Florida with a degree in nursing and works at The Villages Regional Hospital.

"We don't always understand where God is leading us, but I surely got my signals crossed when it comes to the doc. Now I believe that Matt was God's instrument and he beat me up pretty good in that trial so that the doc would be in the right place at the right time to save my daughter. I can't know for sure whether I'm right or wrong on this, but I do know that I owe Matt big-time. By the way, Jeff and I have become good friends. He's forgiven me for being such a self-righteous prick, if you'll excuse my language."

J.D. laughed. "I've heard it before, Sheriff."

"Please call me Brian. I didn't tell Matt about how all this worked out because I didn't want him to think I'm some kind of religious nutcase. I might have been that way back then, but I'm not nearly as rigid as I was."

"Thanks, Brian. I have some other things to talk to you about. Did Chief Lester tell you that I'm on a leave of absence?"

"That didn't come up."

"I've been here for a week staying with a friend of my aunt's. I've been doing some undercover work, unofficially. I realize I have no jurisdiction here, and in fact I don't have any authority anywhere as long as I'm on a leave of absence. I certainly would never step on the toes of your investigator. I'd like to discuss this with you on an absolutely confidential basis."

"Why so hush-hush?"

"Can I be candid?"

"Certainly."

"I'm not sure your investigator has looked into things very well. It's like he found a suspect in my aunt and just never followed up on any other evidence. I think this case is much more complicated than it appears. I've come across some evidence that I think should be looked at, but unfortunately, I can't let a lot of it out. Even to you. It's part of what the lawyers call work product, and since I've done it on behalf of the defense attorney, I can't disclose it until after the trial."

"J.D., excuse me for being blunt, but your aunt is charged with murder. We don't have a lot of that up here, but I suspect it's more than you ever have on Longboat Key."

J.D. chuckled. "That's true, Brian, but I'm conversant with murder cases. Before I joined Longboat Key PD, I was the assistant homicide commander at Miami-Dade PD."

"Sorry, Detective. I wasn't trying to be dismissive. I know your chief and I know he runs a very professional department. If you weren't a professional, you wouldn't be there."

"I didn't take it that way, Sheriff."

"I'll keep everything you tell me confidential. I'm sure you've had more experience investigating murders than all my people put together. So I'll take what you have to say very seriously. Have you considered that if you show me all you've got, the state attorney might be willing to drop the charges?"

"Matt and I've talked about that, but if the state attorney does not agree to dismiss, Esther would have shot her wad and the state attorney would be able to capitalize on it. And I think you'd be obligated to give the details to the state attorney, including the things I've turned up."

"You're probably right, come to think of it. Tell me what I can do for you."

"I think there's a chance that a man named Josh Hanna might be involved in some way. He owns a white van recently registered in Georgia. I'd like to talk to him. I wonder if you'd be amenable to putting out a BOLO on the van."

"I don't remember anybody named Hanna connected to this case."

"His name won't be in the reports. Matt came up with it during his investigation."

"And you can't give me even the context of how his name came to Matt's attention?"

"Sorry, Brian. I'm afraid not."

"Do you have a license plate number?"

"No. I couldn't get into Georgia's database without using police authority. I didn't want to do that. Since I'm not exactly a cop right now, it's against the law."

The sheriff smiled. "Well, it does have something to do with an active case in my office. I'll look into it and let you know."

"Thanks, Brian. I think it best not to arrest Hanna, but if an officer can pull him over on some pretense and find out where he's living, I'll go talk to him. This is my cell phone number." She handed him a piece of notepaper. "I really appreciate your time and your help. I know I'm asking you to buy a pig in a poke."

The sheriff laughed. "It wouldn't be the first time, J.D., but I've got to tell you, you're more persuasive than most hog salesmen."

"Oh," J.D. said. "I almost forgot. You're holding a man named Lionel Steerman."

"Yeah. Matt asked us to do that."

"I know. And I know he appreciates you helping out on this. I wonder if I could talk to him this afternoon."

"I don't see why not. We've held him longer than we should, and I've got to either charge him or cut him loose in the morning."

"I'd also like to meet privately with my aunt without going through all the rigmarole to be a visitor."

"I'll call Lieutenant Ricks and tell him to set you up for a visit with your aunt. You can use one of the attorney rooms so you'll be completely private. I'll tell him to let you have a visit with Steerman in the same room. Who do you want to see first?"

"Steerman. Thanks, Sheriff. I'll be on my way. If I can ever do anything for you in Southwest Florida, let me know."

"Count on it, Detective."

CHAPTER 39

CHUNK STEERMAN WAS not in a good mood. He was seated at a small table and manacled to a large U-joint buried in the concrete floor. "Who the hell are you?" he growled.

I'm Detective J. D. Duncan," she said, not bothering to burden him with any more information than he needed; like the fact that she was not a member of the Sumter County Sheriff's Office.

"I've got rights, you know. You can't just put me in jail and forget about me."

"Sorry about that, Mr. Steerman. There's been some kind of mix-up in the paperwork, but I can solve that little problem. We'll either charge you first thing in the morning and arrange for a bail hearing, or, and I hope this is the case, not charge you and get you out of here right after breakfast. I do have some questions, though."

"What am I supposed to be charged with?"

"Assault, but I've talked to Mr. Royal and he's agreeable to dropping the charges if you'll cooperate with his defense of Ms. Higgins."

"What kind of cooperation?"

"Well, for starters, tell me why you came after him with a sock full of quarters?"

"He's trying to get my grandma in trouble."

"Is that Sally Steerman?"

"Yeah."

"What makes you think that?"

"A man called the house and talked to me. He told me that Mr. Royal was going to accuse my grandma of a murder so that he could get his client off the rap."

"Who was the man who called you?"

"I don't know."

"Yet, you were ready to do great bodily harm to Mr. Royal on the word of somebody you didn't even know?"

"He sounded like he knew what he was talking about."

"I'll need your grandmother's address."

"What for?"

"I want to talk to her before I sign off on your release."

"I don't know the address."

"Can you tell me how to get to her house?"

"I guess." He reluctantly gave her directions from the Publix Market on Highway 44 A.

"Is your brother still there?" J.D. asked.

"No. When your people busted me, Biggun went home to Georgia."

"To Camilla?"

"Yeah."

"Why did you tell Mr. Royal you lived near Homerville?"

"He said he'd kill me if things didn't work out. It didn't seem like it was a good idea for him to know where to find me in case he got pissed off at me."

"Okay, Mr. Steerman. Here's the deal. I've got your home address in the jail booking records. I've got your truck in our impoundment lot just down the street. I'm going to arrange for you to get out of here first thing in the morning. We'll get your truck back to you and you can head for home. But, and this is a big but, you're going to have to wear an ankle monitor."

"What for?"

"You're not out of the woods, yet. We may still charge you with attempted murder."

"Murder? I wasn't going to kill nobody."

"That sock of quarters would have done a lot of damage to somebody's head. Whoever got hit with it could have died. If you want to go home, you'll have to agree to the monitor. Otherwise, I'll charge you and you'll stay in jail until we can get to trial."

"Okay," he said, sullenly. "I guess I don't have any choice."

"No, you don't. Now listen very carefully. You'll be able to move around if you want. The ankle monitor we're going to use communicates with a satellite so we'll know where you are at all times. If you go more than, say, twenty miles from your house, we'll know it and you'll be arrested and brought back here. If you even try to cut the anklet off, we'll know. Do you understand that?"

"Yeah."

"Okay. I'll arrange for you to be released tomorrow morning right after the ankle monitor is attached to your leg. Don't let me down, Mr. Steerman. You piss me off and you'll rot in jail. Do we understand each other?"

"Yes, ma'am."

"Now, one other thing. If you tell anybody about our arrangement, even your brother or your grandma, we'll know you've talked, and you'll be right back here before you can finish your conversation. The ankle monitor has a microphone hidden in it, and we'll hear everything you say."

"Everything?"

"Everything."

"Shit."

"Yep. Be careful."

J.D. opened the door and motioned to the nearby guard who came and got the prisoner. Now what? She had been playing it off the top of her head. She didn't know if she could get the ankle monitor installed, but she had a contact in the company that Sarasota County used. They had offices all over Florida and she wasn't aware of any prohibition against them doing private work. She'd make the call as soon as she saw Esther.

J.D. didn't think Steerman was smart enough to figure out that she didn't have the authority to do any of what she was doing, but she didn't want him to talk to anybody about the situation, because somebody else might figure it out. If she could get the monitor on him, they'd know right where he was at any time. Too bad there really wasn't a microphone in the device, but she was betting Chunk wouldn't figure that out.

She went to the booking desk at the front of the facility and talked with Lieutenant Ricks. He laughed as she related the story of what she'd told Steerman. "He's not the brightest bulb on the Christmas tree," Ricks said. He agreed to let somebody from the company, which happened to be the same one that Sumter County used for their monitors, come in and install the anklet on Steerman.

Ricks agreed to get Steersman's truck out of the impoundment lot and have it ready to go as soon as the prisoner was released. He had no objection to the man who would bring the ankle monitor attaching a GPS monitor to the truck.

J.D. next called the man she knew in Sarasota and arranged for the monitor to be installed and the tracker attached to Steerman's pickup at seven the next morning. She had done all she could do. If this thing fell apart, she'd be open to criticism and probably worse. She thought she might have committed a crime or two in the process, but Esther was her aunt and she was innocent.

J.D. was taking a page from Jock's book, doing what had to be done even if it violated the law. She wasn't comfortable with it, but the bigger travesty would be the conviction of an innocent woman.

J.D. went back to the little conference room to find Esther sitting unshackled in the chair that Steerman had recently vacated. "I'm so glad to see you, J.D.," Esther said. "Have you given up on your undercover operation?"

"No. I'm here in my own name. I've met with the sheriff and he seems like a pretty good guy."

They talked about things of little importance for half an hour or so, and J.D. left to drive back to The Villages. She called Matt and told him about her afternoon and what she'd done about Steerman. "If this ever hits the fan, I think I could be in big trouble," she said.

"Don't worry about it. I think we can make a good case that, since you weren't working in any official capacity, you didn't do anything wrong. So you lied to a dumbass, but it was for a good cause."

"Yeah, but it wasn't right."

CHAPTER 40

BREAKFAST ON THURSDAY was pancakes, sausage, and the morning paper at the Longbeach Café. I loved the early mornings in spring. The air was cool enough for a long-sleeve shirt, and the locals, who seemed to hunker in their homes during season, were reappearing a little early this year. Several came in and stopped at my booth to chat for a minute or two.

J.D. had called me before I left for breakfast to tell me that the ankle monitor had been put on Chunk and the GPS tracker attached to his truck. I knew the sheriff had to cut Chunk loose and I thought we'd have a pretty good idea of where he was because of J.D.'s ingenuity. I was at my dock cleaning off the little presents regularly left by the pelicans that liked to settle on my boat's bow rails between fishing trips, when my phone trilled the first bars of "Hello Darling." J.D. was calling.

"Sheriff Cornett just called me. Josh Hanna was spotted an hour or so ago in St. Pete."

"Did the cop find out where he's staying?"

"Apparently, he's checked into a small motel on Highway 19."

"I'm going to run up there and have a talk with Mr. Hanna."

"Matt, he was driving a van, but it doesn't look anything like the one Amber Marris described. His van is a four-year-old full-size Chevrolet."

"That may be good news. I was hoping he wasn't involved in this, but whoever hacked the Coffee County Sheriff's computer was in his unit in Afghanistan. I can't imagine that being a coincidence."

"Neither can I." She gave me the address of the motel. "The sheriff gave me Hanna's license plate number, and I've asked Will Hall to run it through his system to see if his van ever entered any of the neighborhoods. He said he'd do that this morning and get back to me. I'll let you know. What are you doing?"

"Cleaning *Recess*."

"Have fun." She was gone.

* * *

The motel was a 1950s vintage, concrete block building with peeling paint set back from Highway 19, a major thoroughfare. It looked shabby, as if nobody had bothered much with maintenance this century. Not the kind of place where a guy with two million bucks would stay. I guess his mom hadn't yet told him about his trust.

The motel was squeezed between a used-car lot and an ancient barbeque restaurant whose chimney was belching smoke carrying the aroma of meat cooking on an open fire. It was almost noon, and from the number of cars in the parking lot, I thought the food must be a lot better than I would have guessed, given the looks of the building.

The one-story motel was U-shaped with all the room doors opening into the parking lot nestled between the arms of the U. A sign identified the office located at the end of one of the arms. I spotted a white Chevrolet van with Georgia plates two doors from the office and pulled in beside it.

The desk clerk was as shabby as the building he inhabited. He was young, maybe not yet twenty, and sported a Mohawk haircut dyed a strange shade of orange. He wore a t-shirt that revealed skinny arms with tattoos covering them from the elbows to the wrists. "Need a room?" he asked, as I walked through the door.

"Not today," I said. "I've come to see Josh Hanna. Can you tell me which room he's in?"

"No, sir. I'm not allowed to do that."

I fished a twenty-dollar bill from my pocket and showed it to him.

"Try room four," he said. I handed him the bill and left the office.

The door to room four opened to my knock, and a tall, good-looking young man with red hair opened the door. "Yes?"

"Josh, my name's Matt Royal. I'm—"

"I know who you are. Come on in. I talked to my mom last night, and she said you were a friend of Mr. Hurt. I was going to call you this evening. I'm surprised you found me."

"Why don't we walk next door to the restaurant and talk over lunch?"

The inside of the restaurant was surprisingly clean and modern. We ordered our lunch, and Josh said, "What can I do for you, Mr. Royal?"

"I'd like to ask you some questions, Sergeant Hanna, but first let me tell you what I know."

"It sounds like you know I was in the Army."

I nodded. "I also know about the purple heart and the bronze star for valor. Very impressive. I used to be a soldier myself. I also know about your dad and that you hacked into the computer system of the Coffee County Sheriff looking for information on Olivia Lathom."

"What makes you think I hacked the sheriff?"

"I have a lot of resources. Whoever hacked that computer was in Afghanistan and was in your unit. I can't believe that any other person in such a small outfit would have an interest in Olivia Lathom. I'm not here to bust your balls. I don't care about the hack. I just need some information to properly defend the woman who's charged with Lathom's murder."

"That's what my mom said on the phone last night. Do you think I had something to do with the murder?"

"Did you?"

"No, sir. I think she probably killed my father, but I've seen a lot of dead people over the last few years, a lot of them the victims of revenge killings. I want no part in that sort of thing. I was just trying to satisfy my curiosity. I didn't have any intention of following up on anything."

"Have you ever been to The Villages?"

"No, sir."

"I think you can agree that I can find out a lot of things, including how to find you. I'll know today whether your van ever entered any of the neighborhoods in The Villages."

"You won't find anything like that."

Our meal arrived. The pulled pork tasted as good as it smelled coming through the chimney. We talked some more, about his growing up in Cordele, life in the Army, his deep appreciation of his mother, and the longing for his dead father. I told him I was confident that he had nothing to do with the murder and nobody would bother him with it again.

We finished and walked back to the motel and said our good-byes. He went into his room and I went to the back of his van, looked closely at the license plate, and could see no trace of a device that would obscure it with the flick of a button in the cab. I was about to pull out of the parking lot when my phone beeped, indicating an incoming text. It was from J.D. "Hanna's van did not go through any of the gates. Ever."

I called her. "You got my text?" she asked as she answered.

"Yeah, and Josh is in the clear. He's a war hero who wanted to know about the woman who may have killed his father. He hacked Sheriff Black, but that's where it ends. I'm thinking it's about time for you to come back home. I don't know that there's anything else we can do in The Villages right now."

"Are you sure?"

"Yes. I need some time on the island to recharge my batteries before we start the trial. And I need that time with you. I'm sure Chief Lester would be glad to have you back on the job."

"There's a meeting of the book club tonight. I can tell them I need to head back to duty and slip out first thing in the morning. Would that work out?"

"It does. I'll see you tomorrow."

THE TRIAL

CHAPTER 41

My alarm jangled me awake at four on Tuesday morning. I rolled out of bed, turned on the coffeepot on Esther's kitchen counter, took a quick shower, and dressed in a pair of shorts and a t-shirt. The air-conditioning system was in mortal combat with the unseasonably late April heat, and so far, cool seemed to be winning. Not by very much, but the temperature in the house was comfortable. I wouldn't count on it being that way all day and I didn't even want to think about August. On the other hand, by the time the dog days rolled around, I'd be back on Longboat Key.

I sat at the dining room table where my files were spread out in what could be described as organized chaos. I sipped my coffee and glanced over the transcripts of depositions that had been taken in the case. I wasn't sure who Meredith would put on the stand as her first witness. I had to be prepared to cross-examine any number of people who had shown up on the state's witness list, some of whom would never be called to testify. Still, I had to be ready if they were called. I had either talked to each of the people on the list or taken their depositions, but there were always surprises. Trying a case was a nerve-racking experience and the first day of testimony always stirred the butterflies in my stomach. I could only look forward to more of the same as the week wore on.

Monday had been spent picking a jury. Since the state had announced that it would not be pursuing the death penalty, we would only have six jurors and two alternates. If, for any reason during the course of the trial, one of the jurors could not continue to serve, the alternate would be substituted. Meredith and I both thought the trial could be finished in one week, so we felt safe with just two alternates. If we lost more than two jurors, the judge would have to declare a mistrial, and we'd start the trial all over. That was never a good outcome. For either side.

We'd taken all day to seat the jury, and in the end, we settled on three men and three women. Five of the members lived in The Villages and one man lived with his family in the small town of Coleman. The alternates, both retirees, lived near Bushnell. The man who lived in Coleman was a guard at the federal prison that stood on a patch of palmetto and scrub oak between Coleman and another little town called Sumterville. I'd taken a gamble on him. Typically, in a criminal trial, the defendant's lawyer doesn't want a law enforcement officer on the jury. Their jobs programed them to lean toward the idea that the defendant wouldn't have been arrested if she hadn't been guilty as charged.

Prison guards were often the most cynical of people. Every day, they watched the very worst people in our society go about their daily routines while locked up in the most brutal institutions in the nation. Of course, not all the prisoners were drawn from the most ruthless individuals that our society produced. Some were people who'd committed crimes of passion while in a rage, people who had never entertained a thought of hurting another human being. Yet, the crimes these otherwise upstanding citizens had committed were so egregious that they were sentenced to the same prisons that housed the worst people our tribe could spit out. The guards knew this and were able to differentiate between the worst ones and the ones who, except for a momentary lapse, might have lived out their lives in middle-class anonymity.

I decided that a prison guard would also be able to differentiate between a retired schoolteacher like Esther and a really bad guy, or even one who had slipped and found himself in a federal penitentiary. Maybe he'd give her a break.

Judge Gallagher swore in the jury and read them the charges describing their responsibilities, which included not watching TV or reading newspaper reports about the trial. He asked if the jurors had any questions, whether the lawyers had any issues to resolve, and recessed the court until nine the next morning.

Meredith and I walked out of the courtroom together and stood for a moment on the steps watching the traffic. We were both tired, our brains ready to quit for the day. The constant strain of the courtroom wears on the lawyers, and at the end of the day only a troubled sleep beckons. She looked up at me and said, "A prison guard, Matt? That's some kind of a gamble."

"He'll be the foreman," I said. "He'll carry a lot of weight in the deliberations. If he's with me, we walk."

"And if he's with me?"

"Then Esther's up shit creek and I'm in big trouble with my sweetie. I'll appeal immediately."

"Did you ever hear the story about the young Atlanta lawyer many years ago who'd been sent down to South Georgia to try a murder case that nobody thought he could win? After a week of trial, much to everybody's surprise, the jury acquitted the young lawyer's client. He sent his boss in Atlanta a telegram that said, 'Justice has prevailed.' The boss wired back, 'Appeal immediately.'"

I laughed. "We'll see, Counselor. You have a good evening."

"You, too, Matt. See you in the morning."

My practice during a trial is to get as good a night's sleep as possible. I don't work in the evening. I might watch a movie on TV or one of the inane programs that pass as entertainment these days. I want to empty my mind of any thoughts of the trial or what I had to do the next day. If it worked, it made me sleep better. I'd get up at four a.m. and get a fresh start with a clear mind, and prepare for the day in court.

But it was a hit-or-miss proposition, and sometimes, like the previous night, I tossed and turned, dreaming of disturbing things I could not remember the next morning. I'd wake up with a sense of dread enveloping me like a dark fog and the only thing I could do to alleviate the anxiety was to throw myself into preparations for another day in court.

I'd tried a lot of jury trials, both civil and criminal, everything from real estate disputes to murder cases. Yet, even in the most mundane trials, the fear never leaves. I worry that I've missed something that my opponent didn't, that there was some fact that would be sprung on me and ruin my carefully constructed trial plan. The nineteenth-century Prussian field marshal Helmuth von Moltke said something to the effect that no battle plan survives contact with the enemy. That is also true of a trial plan. Things change in an instant in the courtroom. Witnesses shade their testimony from what they said in pre-trial depositions, a witness you didn't depose decides not to honor a subpoena and fails to show up, your opponent knows something about one of your witnesses that you failed to ferret out, and she lays into him on cross-examination, leaving you to do your best to rehabilitate him.

It's a crapshoot, but I always tried to know everything about my case. I met with witnesses, took their depositions, spent the days just preceding the trial going over their testimony with them trying to make sure we were in sync when they got on the witness stand. The trial lawyer has to be nimble, ready for anything, prepared to fend off the surprise attack and in turn assault the witness in a calm demeanor that doesn't anger the jury but will destroy the witness, his testimony, his credibility, and render his evidence useless.

I was up against a seasoned prosecutor and that was good. I'd always found trials to be easier when my opponent was competent and honest. I was convinced that justice was more likely to be reached under those circumstances than when the opponent was either unethical or incompetent or both.

I looked at my watch. I'd been at it for a little over three hours and had actually gotten some work done while cogitating on my plight as a trial lawyer. When I get in these moods, I always recall a time long ago when a wise old judge, named Bernard Muszynski, and several tired lawyers were sitting around in his chambers on a Saturday night waiting for a jury to return a verdict in a case we'd tried all week. We lawyers were complaining about working so late and on a weekend to boot. The judge chuckled and said simply, "This ain't work, gentlemen. Hod carrying is work. And those boys do it outside in August." I thought the judge was right, although I never did figure out what a hod was.

I dressed, poured coffee into a travel cup, and drove toward Bushnell and the courthouse. I rolled all the windows down, opened the sunroof, and let the warm breeze and the black coffee wake me up.

CHAPTER 42

My workday started with Meredith Evans' opening statement. She did a professional job and didn't take up too much time. She laid out her case, but didn't argue the facts. She hammered on the proposition that the evidence would show that the defendant, Esther Higgins, had become obsessed with the victim who was the author of a national best-selling novel. Esther herself had also written a novel, and she suffered from the delusion that Olivia Lathom had stolen her book. The fact that Esther had shown her manuscript to a member of her book club, Ruth Bergstrom, who was a friend of the victim, was the only link between the victim and the defendant. Ms. Higgins had never met Olivia Lathom.

"You will hear from Ruth Bergstrom," Meredith said, her tone dropping a bit, her voice softer as she leaned in toward the jury. "She will tell you that she read part of Ms. Higgins' manuscript and thought it was so awful that she couldn't finish it. In fact, she gave it back to the defendant and, in an effort to spare Ms. Higgins' feelings, apologized for not having time to read it. It was from this thin thread that Esther Higgins decided that the book she wrote had been stolen by the victim who published it under her own name and made a bucket of money.

"Ms. Bergstrom will tell you," Meredith continued, "that she certainly did not and would never have sent something so amateurish to Olivia Lathom. Ms. Bergstrom will testify that when confronted by the defendant, she tried to explain all of this, but Ms. Higgins was adamant that it was her book that was published under Olivia's name. And it was at that point that Esther Higgins threatened to kill Olivia Lathom.

"Dr. Melissa Cooper, the director of this judicial circuit's crime lab, will testify that Olivia was killed by a single shot from a twenty-two-caliber pistol and that a similar gun was found in a closet of the home of the defendant sitting at counsel table with her lawyer. An expert in ballistics will testify that the bullet that killed Olivia Lathom was fired from that gun. The gun was owned by the defendant, and she had shown it to a group of friends from her book club shortly before the murder. The fingerprint expert from the crime lab will tell you that the only fingerprints found on the murder weapon belonged to the defendant. The defendant, Esther Higgins, sitting right there next to her lawyer." She pointed to our table.

"You'll see," Meredith said, "that the defendant had a motive, even if it was sheer delusion; the opportunity, since Olivia was in The Villages for a book signing; and the means, a pistol that she'd owned for many years and had been taught how to shoot it by a career police officer. I think you'll find it very interesting that the method of killing this fine writer was the same as she wrote about in her best-selling book. A shot in the back from a twenty-two-caliber pistol. Thank you." She took her seat.

"Mr. Royal?" the judge said.

I stood. "I'll postpone my opening until my case, Your Honor."

"Okay." He turned to the jury and gave the instruction that explained that it was my right to delay my opening statement until the beginning of my case. That's not always a good ploy, but in this case I knew things that I didn't think Meredith was aware of. If I mentioned them in an opening statement at the beginning of the trial, she'd have time to readjust her case to take some of the sting out of the evidence I would present.

I wanted to talk in my opening about all the evidence that pointed to someone else as the murderer. I wanted the jury to anticipate my witnesses and I wanted them to be thinking about who else might have killed Olivia Lathom. I thought I had some pretty strong evidence that pointed to someone else. If the jurors were looking for that person, thinking about who that someone might be, they might be more inclined to accept one of my theories as the truth. In fact, I didn't need truth. I just needed reasonable doubt. The jury would be charged that the law requires a finding of guilt beyond a reasonable doubt, and if I could establish in the jury's mind enough doubt of Esther's guilt, I would get an acquittal.

It is said that truth is the goal of any trial, but I have always been a little skeptical of that notion. What is truth? It is really just the opinion that one reaches after hearing all the facts. Some of the facts might not even be true, and the decider, in this case the jury, has to factor that in when reaching an opinion as to what is the truth. An expert's opinion of facts within his field of expertise may carry more weight with the decider, but every trial lawyer knows that somewhere there is another expert in the same field who will disagree with the first expert.

The job of the criminal defense lawyer is not to ferret out the truth, but rather to make the prosecutor prove the truth. Or at least prove the state's version of the truth. The defense lawyer just has to chip away at the prosecution's case until reasonable doubt springs up in the minds of the jurors. Then the acquittal comes and the defendant leaves the courtroom a free man or woman and the lawyers go home.

The lawyers always go home, but the defendants don't. Some of them go straight to jail. And that's what kept me up at night.

Meredith called her first witness, Kevin Cook, the young fire department paramedic who had found the body in Paddock Square. She took him through his training as a paramedic, his service in the Army, his part-time job of picking up trash, his discovery of the body, and his call to the emergency operator.

"How did you know she was dead?"

"I checked for a pulse in her neck."

"Was there any indication at the scene of what caused her death?"

"No, other than the small hole in her back. Probably from a small-caliber pistol."

An objectionable answer that I let go. A paramedic isn't qualified under the rules of evidence to give an opinion on the cause of death. On the other hand, it was a fact that would be borne out by the crime scene photographs, and I didn't want the jury to think I was trying to hide anything from them. And in any case, the medical examiner would later testify that Esther's pistol was the instrument of death.

"Where was the bullet hole? Low back, middle, high, where?"

"Right in the middle between her shoulder blades."

"Any other marks or bruises that you could see on the body?"

"Not that I saw."

"How was Ms. Lathom dressed when you found her?"

"Slacks, long-sleeve blouse, and flat-heeled shoes."

"So, about the only parts of her body you could see were her ankles, hands, neck, and head?"

"Yes, ma'am."

"Did you see any blood on the pavement around the body?"

"No, ma'am. It was obvious to me that she'd bled out somewhere else." Another objectionable answer because it gave an opinion, but one that the prosecutor knew I wouldn't object to. Or maybe she hoped I would. She was crowding the line, but I'd do the same thing. If you can trap your opponent into objecting to innocuous questions just because the evidence code said she could, she'd end up looking like a fool, or like she was trying to hide something. The lawyer never wants the jury to think badly of him because it may very well reflect poorly on his client.

"Did you draw any conclusions from that?"

Meredith had stepped over the line with that one. "Objection, Your Honor," I said, rising. "Mr. Cook is a very bright young man, but he hasn't been qualified as an expert. I'm sure Ms. Evans can get this evidence in through the medical examiner, whom I understand will be testifying today or tomorrow."

"Sustained," Judge Gallagher said. "You only have to state the grounds of your objection, Mr. Royal. We don't need a speech." He was a bit peeved at me, but he'd get over it. I wanted the jury to know that I wasn't trying to keep any evidence away from them, but I thought it might be time to rein Meredith in a little.

"Thank you, Your Honor," I said, and sat down.

"What time did you find the body?" Meredith asked.

"It was early. Just after sunrise."

"Was it light enough for you to see clearly?"

"Yes, ma'am."

"Did you see anybody else in Paddock Square at that time of the morning?"

"No, ma'am."

"Any vehicles moving about the area?"

"No, ma'am."

"So, it was just you and the body?"

"Yes. Until the police got there."

"Who arrived first? The ambulance or the police officer?"

"They got there about the same time."

"Which department was the officer with?"

"Wildwood PD."

"And the ambulance?"

"The Villages Fire Department. It came from my firehouse. The one across the street from the Eisenhower Center."

"So it didn't have far to come."

"No, ma'am."

"Did you disturb the body, move it in any way when you found it?"

"I turned her slightly to see if there was any blood on her torso and I left her in the exact same position she was in when I first saw her. She was obviously dead, so I used my cell to call 911."

"Did anybody on the ambulance crew disturb the body?"

"No, ma'am. They never touched it."

"So, when the police officer arrived, the body was exactly the way you found it."

"Correct."

"Let me show you some pictures that we'll have marked as state's Exhibits A through C and ask if you can identify them." She brought them first to my table and showed them to me.

"No objection, Your Honor," I said. "Ms. Evans previously provided those to me."

She put them on the rail of the witness stand. "Can you identify these three photographs?"

"Yes, ma'am. They're pictures of the body I found in Paddock Square in Brownwood."

"And these pictures correctly represent the scene as you found it on that morning?"

"Yes, ma'am."

She turned to the judge. "I'd like to offer Exhibits A through C for identification into evidence as Exhibits one, two, and three." Because all exhibits used in a trial have to be identified for the court reporter, the practice is to offer exhibits identified by letters of the alphabet. Once the court accepts the exhibits as evidence, the clerk marks them sequentially with numbers.

"Any objection, Mr. Royal?" the judge asked.

I rose from my chair. "No, sir. I'll stipulate that these pictures were taken by the Sumter County Sheriff's photographer," I said, and sat down. I was playing to the jury a bit with my stipulation, but it would add nothing to my case or to the prosecution's to require her to bring in the photographer to authenticate the pictures. Besides, it never hurt to let the jury know what an agreeable fellow I really was.

Judge Gallagher looked at the pictures and handed them to the clerk. "Please mark these into evidence as the state's Exhibits one, two, and three."

"I have nothing further, Your Honor," Meredith said.

"Your witness, Mr. Royal," the judge said.

I rose. "No questions, Your Honor." There is a lot of standing and sitting back down in a courtroom. I think lawyers should be on their feet when speaking, and most judges in Florida require it. Some don't. Courtrooms have gotten more and more informal, and that's a shame. These are formal proceedings, governed by an evidence code and procedural rules that have evolved over eight hundred years of Anglo-American jurisprudence. The formality of the lawyers and judges add dignity to the proceedings and give the whole process a verisimilitude that is appropriate for the dramas that unfold in any courtroom.

"May the witness be excused?" Judge Gallagher asked.

Meredith and I both stood and agreed.

"It's nearing midmorning," the judge said. "We'll take a fifteen-minute break." He stood and left the bench.

CHAPTER 43

FIFTEEN MINUTES LATER. Everybody was in their place in the courtroom and stood as the judge entered and called the court to order. The judge took his seat and looked toward Meredith. "Call your next witness, Ms. Evans."

Meredith called the Wildwood policeman who had been the first law enforcement officer on the scene.

"State your name for the record," she said.

"Matt Burns."

She took him through the scene of the crime, what he found when he arrived, what he did, and when he did it. He explained that he first called his dispatcher and told him he had a dead body in Paddock Square and to notify the Sumter County Sheriff's Office. "Why did you want the sheriff's office notified?" Meredith asked.

"It's protocol. Our department often gets the sheriff involved if we have something big on our hands, like a murder. They have more investigators trained to handle homicides. Particularly in The Villages."

"Do you have a lot of murders in The Villages?"

"No, ma'am. I can only think of one several years ago."

"Did you examine the body when you arrived?"

"Only cursorily."

"Describe to the jury what you saw."

"The body was lying facedown and there was a small bullet hole in the middle of her back."

"What did you do then?"

"I put up crime scene tape to keep everybody out until the sheriff's detective showed up."

"How long after you called did the detective arrive?"

"Not long. Less than half an hour."

"Who was the detective?"

"Deputy Ben Appelgate."

Meredith studied her notes for a moment and said, "I'll tender the witness, Your Honor."

"Mr. Royal?" the judge said.

"No questions, Your Honor."

"Call your next witness, Ms. Evans," the judge said.

The sheriff's detective who had investigated the murder took the stand. "State your name, please," Meredith said.

"Deputy Ben Appelgate."

"Occupation?"

"I'm a detective with the Sumter County Sheriff's Department."

"For how long?"

"I've been a deputy for fifteen years and a detective for five of those years."

"Did you investigate the death of Olivia Lathom?"

"I did."

"How did that come about?"

"I was the detective on duty when the Wildwood PD dispatcher called to tell me there was a body in Paddock Square in Brownwood. I responded immediately. Went to Brownwood. It took me about twenty minutes to get there, I think."

"What did you find when you got there?"

The detective walked her through the scene. It was identical to what the first two witnesses had described, except that by the time he got there, more people were milling about. Citizens had seen the commotion and drifted toward the knot of cops and the body lying in the square. He testified that the Wildwood police officer had strung yellow police tape around the whole square, so the crime scene would not be disturbed. The forensic techs arrived shortly after he did and went to work. When they released the body, The Villages fire department ambulance crew took the remains to the morgue.

"Did you talk to the witnesses?"

"Yes. Several."

"Did you talk to Esther Higgins?"

"No. She invoked her right to counsel."

"Who were the witnesses you talked to?"

"The first one was the Wildwood police officer Matt Burns who was the first law enforcement officer on the scene. I talked to Kevin Cook, the fire department paramedic who found the body, and I took a statement from Peggy Keefe who was the victim's traveling companion. Later in the day, I talked to the medical examiner and the chief of the crime lab. Finally, I took a statement from Ruth Bergstrom on Thursday afternoon."

"When did you talk to all these folks?"

"I talked to all of them on Thursday, the day we found the body, except for Ms. Higgins. I tried to talk to her on Friday."

"Tried?"

"Yes, as I said, she invoked her right to counsel and to silence."

"Nothing further, Your Honor," Meredith said and sat down.

"Your witness, Mr. Royal," the judge said.

The courtroom clock inched toward noon. I stood. "May we approach the bench, Your Honor?" I asked.

He waved us forward. "Your Honor," I said, "it's getting close to the noon hour and my cross is going to take a while. Could we recess for lunch a little early so there'll be no breaks in my cross?"

"I don't see why not," the judge said. He turned to the jury and told them we were breaking a little early and gave them a time to return to the courtroom. Meredith and I and the other court personnel stood as the jury filed out. It was another of the customs I found so appropriate for the serious business of a court of law.

Meredith and I stood in the well of the courtroom, trying to work out some time sequence for the afternoon. "Do you think your cross is going to take long?"

"It depends on what the deputy says, but it could take up a large part of the afternoon."

"I'll put my technical people on standby. They can get here quickly."

We separated for lunch. It wouldn't do for jurors to see us breaking bread together. Laymen never seem to understand that lawyers who compete in the courtroom are often friends outside the courtroom.

* * *

We were back in court and Deputy Appelgate was on the stand. The judge reminded him that he was still under oath and turned to me. "You may proceed, Mr. Royal."

I stood. "Detective, where did you arrest Ms. Higgins?"

"In her house."

"Where in her house?"

"The living room."

"Did you tell her what you were arresting her for?"

"Yes, sir."

"What exactly did you tell her was the reason for her arrest?"

"I don't remember the exact words, but I would have conveyed to her that she was under arrest for the murder of Olivia Lathom, the woman whose body was found in Paddock Square the morning before."

"Did you put handcuffs on her when you arrested her?"

"Yes, sir. Standard procedure."

"And did you read her your Miranda rights card?"

"Yes, sir."

"So you told her she was under arrest for murder, that she had a right to counsel, and that she had a right to remain silent."

"Yes, sir."

"And she took you up on your offer to keep her mouth shut until she talked to a lawyer."

"I guess. She refused to talk to me."

"You mean she refused to talk to you about the charges."

"Yes, sir."

"And you asked Ms. Higgins about the murder for the first time when she was handcuffed in the back of a patrol car on her way to jail."

"That's correct."

"She talked to you about other things, though, didn't she? Like the state of the weather, or how you were doing, or something like that, right? Pleasantries."

"Yes, sir."

"But she did take you up on your offer to remain silent on the charges until she talked to a lawyer."

"Yes, sir." His voice was getting a little tight. He didn't like the questions. He'd tried to slip into his testimony the idea that Esther wasn't cooperating, as if invoking her constitutional right not to speak was proof of guilt. I wanted to make him own up to the fact that she was only exercising her rights. None of this was really appropriate testimony, but everybody who'd ever watched a mystery or a police procedural on TV knew about the accused's rights, and I was certain that included every one of my jurors.

Then I went a question too far. A common mistake among trial lawyers. We get on a roll and our egos take over and we just can't stop ourselves. "Then you weren't surprised by her reticence, were you? Most people accused of murder do invoke their rights, don't they?"

"Not the innocent ones."

Damn. I should have quit while I was ahead. What now? My mind was whirling. If I just sat down, I'd leave that last answer hanging out there. The jury would be drawing the wrong inference. I could object, but I might not prevail. After all, I'd asked the question. I decided to attack, but I'd sneak up on him first. By the time he left the stand, I wanted the jury to think he was a prick. "What did Ms. Keefe have to say?" I asked calmly.

"She told me that the victim was going to dinner with a friend and took the rental car they were using." He looked down at his notes. "She didn't know the name of the friend the victim was having dinner with or where they were planning to eat. Ms. Keefe went out to eat and then to bed. She was getting ready to meet the victim when I arrived at her door Thursday morning."

"You keep referring to the victim. Wouldn't it be a little more respectful to call her by her Christian name? Olivia Lathom?"

"Okay."

"That was her name, wasn't it?"

"Yes, sir."

"How did you verify that?"

"What do you mean?"

"Did you do anything to make sure Olivia Lathom was, in fact, her real name?"

"We had her driver's license."

"Were you aware that the medical examiner could find no record of her fingerprints?"

"I was."

"That didn't pique your curiosity as to why there was no fingerprint record of Ms. Lathom?"

"No, sir. There are all kinds of reasons that somebody's prints might not be in the system."

"But you didn't do anything further to determine if the body in Paddock Square actually belonged to a woman named Olivia Lathom?"

"No, sir." The tightness was back in his voice.

I switched gears. "What did Ruth Bergstrom tell you?"

This finally got Meredith to her feet. "Hearsay, Your Honor. I let it go the first time, but I'm afraid it's getting a little out of hand."

I jumped in with a response before the judge had a chance to rule. "Ms. Evans is correct, Your Honor, but both Ms. Keefe and Ms. Bergstrom will testify here later this week, and if there is any discrepancy in what they say and the deputy's memory, we can clear it up. I'm getting to the probable cause for the arrest. I would like for the detective to explain to the jury why he arrested my client. Perhaps if I dropped back and laid a predicate."

"Lay your predicate, Mr. Royal. I'll withhold ruling on Ms. Evans' objection."

"Thank you, Your Honor. Detective, may I see your notes?"

"Which notes?"

"The ones in your lap that you keep referring to."

The detective looked toward Meredith who remained in her seat. He turned to Judge Gallagher who said, "He has a right to the notes, Detective. Give them to him."

"May I approach the witness, Your Honor?"

"Approach," the judge said.

I walked to the witness box and held out my hand. The detective handed me his notebook. I spent a minute or two looking at it and handed it back. "Were these notes made contemporaneously with your interviews of the witnesses?"

"Yes, sir."

"And you're using the notes to refresh your recollection today?"

"Yes, sir."

"And you wouldn't stray from your notes, would you?"

"No, sir."

"So what you would testify to now is exactly what the witness said to you back in March?"

"Yes, sir."

"How did you come to interview Ms. Bergstrom?"

"She called me."

"On Thursday?"

"Yes. In the early afternoon."

"Did you take the statement over the phone?"

"No, sir. She volunteered to come down to my office."

"In Bushnell?"

"Yes."

"I've got another question for you, Detective, but I'd ask you to give Ms. Evans a chance to object if she wants to." I am indeed an agreeable fellow.

He nodded.

"What did Ms. Bergstrom have to say to you?" I didn't think Meredith would object this time. She knew the testimony would come in through Ruth Bergstrom, and since the detective would be testifying from his notes, she'd look like a bit of a fool if she tried to stop me again. I was right. She held her seat.

He paused, stared at the prosecutor with a pleading look on his face. He got no response. He looked back at me. "She said that Ms. Higgins had told her she was going to kill Ms. Lathom because Ms. Lathom had stolen her book and made a lot of money from it." He stopped talking.

"Look at your notes, Detective. That's not all she said, is it?"

"Um, no, sir. She told me that Ms. Higgins had given her a manuscript to read and she read the first couple of chapters and told Ms. Higgins she didn't think it was publishable. She gave the manuscript back to Ms. Higgins and didn't hear anything else about it until Ms. Lathom published her book. Ms. Higgins read it and went to Ms. Bergstrom's house and said she would kill Ms. Lathom."

"So, she did tell you that she had read Ms. Higgins' manuscript?"

"No, sir, just a couple of chapters."

"Did she tell you when the conversation with Ms. Higgins took place?"

He looked down at his notes. "A few days before Ms. Lathom came to The Villages for her book signing."

"Did this conversation take place before Ms. Lathom's schedule had been released?"

"I don't know."

"So, it'd be fair to say that you don't know if Ms. Higgins would have been aware that Ms. Lathom was planning to be in The Villages?"

The detective looked perplexed. "I guess that's right. I don't know."

"What did you find out from the medical examiner?"

He checked his notes. "That Ms. Lathom died from a gunshot wound. The bullet perforated her heart and killed her instantly."

"Do your notes reflect when you talked to the medical examiner?"

"Yes. On Friday."

"The day after the body was found?"

"Yes."

"What time of day did you talk to the medical examiner?"

"I don't have the exact time, but it was in the afternoon."

"And did the crime scene techs tell you they'd found any evidence in Ms. Higgins' home that would appear relevant to a murder?"

"Yes, sir."

"What did they tell you?"

"They found the murder weapon."

"And did you talk to the crime scene techs?"

"I talked to Dr. Cooper, the director of the division."

"And when did that conversation take place?"

"On Friday afternoon."

"Did you talk to the fingerprint expert?"

"I did."

"That was Madison Seyler?"

"Yes, sir. We call her Maddi."

"Was this also on Friday afternoon?"

"Yes."

"Did you talk to the ballistics expert, Mr. Peralta?"

"Yes, on Friday afternoon."

"Did you or anyone else to your knowledge find a laptop computer that belonged to Esther Higgins?"

"No, sir."

"Did you or the techs find any blood on Ms. Higgins' clothes or on her body?"

"No, sir. When we got to the county detention center, a female deputy did a full body search of Ms. Higgins and took her clothes for the crime lab people."

"There was no blood or other evidence on Ms. Higgins' clothes that would indicate she had been involved in a murder. Blood, gunshot residue, that sort of thing. Right?"

"Right. But remember this was the day after we found the body. She probably wasn't wearing the same clothes."

"Did you check out all the clothes in her closet?"

"We did. It appeared that some of the clothes had been freshly washed."

"You would expect to find freshly washed clothes in most closets, wouldn't you?"

"I guess so."

"So the fact that Ms. Higgins had washed some clothes didn't mean anything to you."

"Not really. It was just an observation."

"I think you arrested Ms. Higgins about twenty-four hours after the body was found. Correct?"

"Yes, sir. I arrested her on Friday morning."

"Now, I want to get clear in my mind the evidence you had found by the time you arrested my client on Friday morning. You knew that a murder had been committed. You knew that Ms. Lathom had died from a gunshot to her back. At the time you arrested Ms. Higgins, you hadn't found anything in her house that would have led you to believe that she was in any way involved in the murder. You found no evidence in her house that a murder had occurred there, and you found no blood or gunshot residue on her clothes, either the ones she was wearing or the ones in her closet. And, you didn't follow up on the identity of the body when the medical examiner could find no record of her fingerprints."

"Right."

"And, at the time of the arrest, you did not know that Ms. Higgins owned a gun, or that the gun matched the one used in the murder or that her fingerprints were on the gun."

"That's correct," he said quietly.

"Detective Appelgate, would you speak up, please? The jury needs to hear your responses." It never hurts to point out to the jury that the witness is showing signs of unease at the questions.

"That's correct," he said, a little louder this time.

"And there was no evidence that Ms. Higgins had been in Paddock Square the night of the murder?"

"That's right."

"No evidence that she'd used her car to transport a body?"

"No, sir. We checked that."

"You never found the site of the murder, did you?"

"No, sir."

"Would it be fair to say that the murder could have occurred in any one of the seventy thousand or so houses in The Villages?"

"Yes, sir."

"Or, for that matter, at some place outside The Villages?"

"Yes, sir."

"Then I have to ask you, Deputy Appelgate, why in the world would you decide to arrest a retired schoolteacher with no previous criminal record and no physical evidence that she was involved in the crime, just on the word of Ruth Bergstrom?"

"Well, Counselor, her fingerprints were on the murder weapon, and it was found in her house."

My little trap had sprung. I knew the fingerprints would get into evidence when the lab techs testified, but by getting the deputy to blurt it out, I had a chance to make him look a bit disingenuous and further emphasize his overzealousness in making an arrest.

"At the time you arrested Esther Higgins, you didn't know anything about the fingerprints, did you?" I had dropped my voice into what I hoped was a menacing timbre.

"They were on the gun."

"Look at your notes, Detective. When did you learn about the fingerprints?"

He looked down at the notes, looked back at me, and said in a low tone, "Friday afternoon."

"I didn't hear you, Detective. You have to speak up." My questions were now coming rapid fire, pushing the witness.

"Friday afternoon," he said in a louder voice.

"And that's the same time that you learned about the gun found in the search of Esther's house?"

"Yes."

"So you couldn't have known about the gun or the fingerprints when you arrested Esther."

"That's right."

"Then let's get back to my earlier question. You arrested Esther Higgins on Friday morning based simply on the statement given you by Ruth Bergstrom. Right?"

"That was all we had to go on."

"Did you do any follow-up investigation after the arrest? For example, did you try to figure why Esther's fingerprints were the only ones on the gun?"

"No, sir."

"Did Esther threaten to kill Olivia Lathom to anyone other than Ruth Bergstrom?"

"Not that I'm aware of."

"And you didn't follow up to find out, did you?"

"No, sir."

"And you had to arrest somebody, didn't you? Lots of pressure coming down on your shoulders?"

"Not really. We had a lady, your client, threatening to kill Ms. Lathom and then Ms. Lathom turns up dead. That's pretty strong evidence."

"And if Ruth Bergstrom's statements turn out to be lies, what then?"

Meredith Evans was on her feet. "Objection, Your Honor."

"Overruled," the judge said. "Answer the question, Detective."

That was a close win. It was essentially a hypothetical question that only can be posed to a duly qualified expert witness. I was ready to argue that the detective was an expert in his field or he wouldn't be a detective, and if he wasn't an expert, he probably shouldn't be a detective. I didn't expect to win that argument, but I wanted at least to leave the idea with the jury that if I gave them plausible reasons why Esther's fingerprints were on the weapon and how somebody else had killed Olivia with Esther's gun, the state's whole case rode on the testimony of Ruth Bergstrom. If what she said proved to be untrue, an acquittal was in order. In the end, I planned to absolutely destroy Ruth Bergstrom.

The detective sat silently as if confused by the question. "You may answer," I said.

"Would you repeat the question?"

"Since the only evidence you had at the time you arrested my client for the murder of Olivia Lathom was the statement of Ruth Bergstrom, if her statements prove to be untrue, you would have had no cause to arrest my client."

"Correct."

"Nothing further," I said and resumed my seat.

Meredith rose and stood for a moment at counsel table looking over her notes. "Detective Appelgate, do you have any reason to believe that Ruth Bergstrom lied to you about the statements made by the defendant?"

"No, ma'am."

"Have you seen any evidence that contradicted what Ms. Bergstrom said?"

"No, ma'am."

"Have you talked to anyone who contradicted Ms. Bergstrom?"

"No, ma'am."

"Nothing further, Your Honor."

I rose. "Just a couple of questions, Your Honor."

"Restrict your question to any area brought out on redirect by Ms. Evans."

"Of course, Your Honor. Detective Appelgate, did you find any evidence that would corroborate the statements Ms. Bergstrom gave you, that is that Ms. Higgins either said she would kill Ms. Lathom or that she in fact did kill Ms. Lathom?"

"No, sir. Other than the fingerprints on the murder weapon."

"Which you weren't aware of when you decided this retired schoolteacher was a cold-blooded murderer. Right?"

"Yes."

"Did anybody else ever tell you they heard the statements Ms. Bergstrom reported or something similar from Ms. Higgins?"

"No, sir."

"Then, would it be fair to say that your whole case is based on the statement given you by Ms. Bergstrom?"

"Objection." Meredith had jumped to her feet, her voice resounding through the courtroom. "This isn't the detective's case. It's the state's case."

"Fair enough," I said. "I'll withdraw the question. I have nothing further of this witness." I had made my point and it was time for the afternoon break.

CHAPTER 44

MEREDITH WAS WAITING for me at the courtroom door. "You're a sneaky bastard," she said. "That last question was a doozy."

"I thought that'd get a rise out of you," I said, smiling. "But the shame is that Bergstrom's statement is about all you've got."

"Well, other than the murder weapon being owned by your client and having her fingerprints on it."

"There's that, but I think Esther will be able to explain it away. After all, whose fingerprints would you expect to find on the owner's gun?"

"The killer's maybe?" she asked. "I suspect you have something up your sleeve to show that Bergstrom is less than truthful."

"I might."

"Care to share it?" she asked.

"Sorry. It's work product. It's part of the stuff I told you early on that I wouldn't be able to disclose to you. Who're you putting up next?"

"Just technical people. The crime scene supervisor, the ME, the victim's traveling companion, ballistics. I was hoping to get finished with them this afternoon, but I didn't count on you being so long-winded. I think we'll go over into the morning. I'll call Ruth Bergstrom after lunch as my last witness."

"That sounds good to me."

* * *

After the break, Meredith called Peggy Keefe, the lady from Cincinnati who had been the victim's traveling companion. She was attractive, middle-aged, and well dressed. I'd talked with her by phone the evening before and knew what she was going to say on the witness stand. I always talk to the witnesses and never try to lead them into anything that's not the absolute truth as they know it. But I do need to be ready, know what their testimony is going to be, and be prepared to cross-examine them if need be.

Keefe's testimony went as expected. She told the jury how she came to be the victim's traveling companion, that on the night Olivia had been murdered, she told Keefe she was going to meet a friend for dinner, and that she didn't say if the friend was a man or woman.

"Did you ever see her again after she left the hotel to go to dinner with the friend?" Meredith asked.

"No."

"How did you find out about her death?"

"A couple of detectives showed up at my hotel room door at midmorning on Thursday and told me they'd found her body."

"Nothing further, Your Honor," Meredith said.

The prosecutor was just putting in the evidence she would need to build a timeline to show the jury the sequence of events. She could not use any facts in closing argument that weren't either admitted into evidence or stipulated to by me.

I stood. "Ms. Keefe, you've testified that Ms. Lathom did not tell you the name of her friend, but did she say anything to you about whether the friend was an old friend or somebody she had recently met?"

"She never said and I didn't have any reason to ask her about that kind of thing."

"Do you know what happened to the rental car that Ms. Lathom took to dinner that night?"

"No. One of my contacts at the publisher told me it was a good thing we had insurance, because the car had never been found, and the rental company wanted the publisher to pay for it."

"Did Ms. Lathom ever mention to you that she had a friend in the area before she told you she was going to dinner?"

"No. Well, at least if she did, I don't remember it and I think I would."

"Did you notice any interaction with Ms. Lathom and another person at any time that would make you think that person was the friend with whom she was going to have dinner?"

"Not really, but she did spend some time talking to a man at the Barnes & Noble store just before the signing."

"Had you ever seen the man before?"

"No."

"Did she mention him after the signing?"

"No."

"Did any law enforcement officer ever ask you about the man who was talking to Ms. Lathom?"

"No."

"So as far as you know, there was no follow-up on the man?"

"Objection." Meredith was on her feet. "Ms. Keefe couldn't possibly know that."

"I predicated that question on her personal knowledge, Your Honor."

"Overruled," the judge said. "You may answer, Ms. Keefe."

"Not that I'm aware of," Keefe said.

"Did anyone ever contact you about the man?"

"No, sir."

"No further questions, Your Honor."

"Ms. Evans?" Judge Gallagher asked.

"Nothing further, Your Honor."

"May the witness be excused?"

Both Meredith and I said, "Yes."

"Call your next witness," the judge said.

"The state calls Dr. Melissa Cooper."

The court deputy escorted a tall, attractive woman into the courtroom. She went straight to the witness stand, turned toward the clerk, and raised her hand to be sworn. As they say, this wasn't her first rodeo. I had met her when I took her deposition several weeks before. She was a meticulous and very experienced crime scene technician and had been a witness in many trials during her career.

Meredith stood. "State your name for the record, please."

"Melissa Cooper."

"And what is your occupation?"

"I'm chief of the Fifth Judicial Circuit forensics lab."

"What is your educational background?"

"Bachelor degree in biochemistry from Oglethorpe University, Masters in Forensic Science from Rollins College, and PhD in Forensic Science from the University of Central Florida."

"I'd offer this witness as an expert in forensic sciences, Your Honor."

"Voir Dire, Mr. Royal?"

The judge was offering me the opportunity to ask questions of the witness to attack her credibility as an expert before he ruled. If the court accepted her as an expert, she would be able to give opinion testimony on issues within the field of forensic science. I knew she testified regularly in this court and Judge Gallagher was not about to reject her as an expert today. Besides, she didn't seem to have any opinions that would hurt my client's case. "No, Your Honor," I said. "I'll stipulate to Dr. Cooper's expertise."

"Do you handle all the scenes where a crime has been committed in Sumter County, Dr. Cooper?" Meredith asked.

"Most of them, and all of them to some extent. Sometimes, we have to send evidence to the Florida Department of Law Enforcement lab in Orlando."

"When would you do that?"

"When there is evidence that is beyond our means, that we don't have the equipment or the expertise to investigate fully. Like DNA, for example."

"Do you lift and identify fingerprints in your lab?"

"Yes."

"Did your agency investigate the crime scene in the case of the murder of Olivia Lathom?"

"We were never able to determine where the crime scene was located. We did go over the place where the body was found with a fine-toothed comb."

"Where was that?"

"Paddock Square in Brownwood."

"Did you find any blood at the scene?"

"No."

"Did you find any other evidence in Paddock Square?"

"No. It was maybe the cleanest scene I've ever been to. But then it wasn't the crime scene."

"Did your lab receive a gun, specifically a twenty-two-caliber Smith and Wesson model 67 revolver, to test for fingerprints?"

"Yes. My fingerprint tech, Madison Seyler, took it in and examined it."

"Nothing further, Your Honor."

"Mr. Royal?" asked the judge.

"Thank you, Your Honor. I just have a few questions. Dr. Cooper, did your team do a full crime scene survey of Esther Higgins' house?"

"Yes."

"Did you specifically look for blood?"

"Yes."

"Why would you be looking for blood in her house?"

"The medical examiner had preliminarily found that she had been shot in the back with a small-caliber pistol. There wouldn't have been a lot of blood in the place where she was killed, but we expected to find some."

"Did you find any blood in Ms. Higgins' house?"

"No, sir."

"Could any blood have been cleaned up before you got there?"

"If it had been, we would still have found traces."

"How would you have found traces?"

"We spray a chemical called Luminol over an area. It will react with the iron in blood and, in a dark room, emit a blue glow. We used this procedure at many points in the house and garage and did not get a hit."

"Could somebody have cleaned up the blood and then keep the Luminol from working?"

"The only thing that would work to clean blood up to the extent that we couldn't find at least trace amounts of blood would be bleach. If bleach was used, the Luminol would react with the bleach and the area where the blood had been would light up with a blue glow."

"And that didn't happen in this case?"

"No, sir."

"Did you examine her car and her golf cart?"

"Yes. No blood in either."

"Did you use it on any of her clothes hanging in the closet?"

"We did. No blood."

"Would that be the case if she'd washed the clothes?"

"Even if they'd been washed several times, we'd find traces of the blood."

"As an expert in crime scene investigations, did you draw any conclusions as to whether Ms. Lathom was killed in Ms. Higgins' house?"

"It was my opinion that the victim was not killed in that house."

"Was the body transported in either of Ms. Higgins' vehicles?"

"No. Not in my opinion."

"No further questions, Your Honor."

"May the witness be excused?" Judge Gallagher asked.

"With the stipulation that she'll be available if we need her again," I said.

"Dr. Cooper's office is about two blocks from here," the judge said. "I think we can get her if we need her. He looked up at the clock. "I think it's that time of day. We'll be in recess until nine thirty tomorrow morning."

CHAPTER 45

I CALLED J.D. in Longboat during the afternoon break and asked her if she could get to Bushnell and meet with the Sumter County Sheriff the next afternoon. She didn't think it'd be a problem and said she'd talk to me that evening.

J.D. called while I was eating a take-out French dip sandwich and a Diet Coke from McCalisters in Brownwood and watching what passes for a news show on TV. "I'm all set with the meeting at three tomorrow afternoon," she said.

"Are you coming up tonight?"

"No, sweetie. I had a busy day and I'm beat. I've still got some paperwork to get done so I can take the next few days off. I'll see you tomorrow evening at Esther's. Do I need to stay undercover when I get up there?"

"Are you still a blond?"

She laughed. "So far. It's not growing out very fast."

"Then just be yourself. If anybody asks you about it, just tell the truth. I do think you should stay out of the courtroom until Thursday. It'll be too late then for any testimony to change because somebody recognizes you. And you need to see the results of all your hard work."

"Do you want me to open up to the sheriff on the evidence?"

"Completely. Tell him he can see the evidence firsthand for himself if he'll come sit in the courtroom starting with the session this afternoon."

"Okay. I'll go on to Esther's house after my meeting. I'll see you there."

* * *

Wednesday morning found me back in the courtroom, sitting at counsel table next to my client. I kept thinking about the beach, but duty was calling. Esther and I had met for a few minutes before we went into the courtroom. Her spirits were high, as they had been all through the trial. I thought it takes a special kind of person to stay positive when the weight of the state is bearing down on her, doing its best to put her in prison for life.

Judge Gallagher took the bench and said, "Who's up next, Ms. Evans?"

"Madison Seyler, Your Honor."

Ms. Seyler was a young woman with dark hair and a ready smile. I had met her when I took her deposition on the same day I'd taken Dr. Cooper's. I wasn't expecting any surprises. Meredith took her through her background, education, and training in the sometimes arcane discipline of fingerprint technology. "Can you tell us what you were asked to do in this case?" Meredith asked.

"I was given a pistol, a twenty-two-caliber Smith and Wesson model 67, to examine for fingerprints. I was also given a plastic bag with five complete bullets and one cartridge from a bullet that had been fired."

"Did you find any prints?"

"Yes."

"Tell the jury where you found them, please."

"I found a full set of fingerprints on the grip, or handle, of the pistol and partial prints on each of the six cartridges."

Meredith handed the witness the pistol, carefully sealed in a plastic bag. "Is this the gun on which you found the prints?"

"It looks like the one."

I stood. "Your Honor, Ms. Evans and I have stipulated that the pistol the witness is holding is indeed the murder weapon."

"Thank you, Mr. Royal," Meredith said and turned back to the witness. "Did you determine to whom the fingerprints belonged?"

"Yes. Esther Higgins."

"On both the grip on the pistol and the bullets?"

"Yes."

"How did you determine that?"

"I entered the prints into the Automated Fingerprint Identification System maintained by the FBI and we got a hit."

"Is that the program commonly called AFIS?"

"Yes."

"No further questions."

I stood. "Ms. Seyler, is there any way for you to determine how long my client's fingerprints had been on the bullet cartridges?"

"No, sir."

"So, they could have been there for years?"

"Yes, sir."

"And the prints on the pistol grip?"

"There is no way to tell how long they'd been there."

"No further questions, Your Honor," I said.

"Just a couple," Meredith said. "Ms. Seyler, did you find anybody else's prints on either the cartridges or the pistol grip?"

"No, ma'am."

"Nothing further, Your Honor."

"Call your next witness, Ms. Evans."

"Dr. Cassandra Wall."

A woman in her thirties entered and took the witness stand. She turned, faced the clerk, and raised her right hand to be sworn.

"State your name, please," Meredith said.

"Cassandra Wall."

"Your occupation?"

"I'm the medical examiner for the Fifth Judicial Circuit of Florida."

"What geographical area does that cover?"

"Five counties. Lake, Sumter, Marion, Hernando, and Citrus."

"You're a physician? An MD?"

"Yes."

"Board certified in any specialty?"

"Pathology and Forensic Medicine."

"As part of your duties as medical examiner, do you perform autopsies on murder victims?"

"Yes."

"Did you perform an autopsy on Olivia Lathom?"

"I did."

Meredith took the witness through the autopsy and her findings. "Did you arrive at a cause of death?"

"Yes. She died of a gunshot wound to her back. The bullet penetrated her heart and she died almost instantly."

"When you did the autopsy, did you find the bullet that killed her?"

"Yes. It was just inside her left chest wall. The velocity of the bullet was pretty well spent by the time it entered her back, but it had enough energy left to penetrate her heart."

"Thank you, Doctor. Nothing further, Your Honor."

"Mr. Royal?" the judge said.

"Dr. Wall," I said, "is part of your job the finding of cause of death?"

"Yes."

"And why do you need to do that?"

"I have to determine whether the death is natural or suicide or caused by somebody else. If caused by someone else, I have to make the determination if it's a homicide. And I have to be ready to testify in court about those issues."

"And you did that in this case?"

"Yes. The cause of death was definitely the gunshot wound in the victim's back."

"Were you able to determine how far the shooter was standing from Ms. Lathom when he or she fired the bullet into Ms. Lathom's back?"

"Several feet, at least."

"How did you determine that?"

"There were no powder burns on Ms. Lathom's clothes where the bullet penetrated the cloth. If the killer had been standing very close, the discharge of the weapon would have left powder burns."

"Do you have an opinion based on a reasonable degree of medical probability, absent any other facts, as to whether the fingerprints on the gun and the bullets point to the killer?"

"No. That is outside the purview of my examinations."

"Thank you, Dr. Wall. No further questions."

The next witness was Robert Peralta, the ballistics expert. Meredith took him through his education and experience, and qualified him as an expert in his field.

"Tell the jury what your job was as it relates to this case," Meredith said.

"I was asked to examine a bullet taken from the body of a woman identified as Olivia Lathom and determine if it came from a particular gun."

"Were you given the gun to test?"

"I was."

"Can you describe the gun?"

"It was a twenty-two-caliber Smith and Wesson model 67 revolver."

Meredith showed him the gun in the evidence bag. "Does this appear to be the gun you examined?"

"It does."

"Was the gun loaded when you received it?"

"No. The bullets had been extracted from the cylinder, but there were five rounds in a plastic evidence bag that I was told had been in the pistol when it was found by the police."

"Were you provided with a bullet that you understood to be the one that killed the victim in this case?"

"Yes."

Meredith held up the murder weapon. "Did you arrive at an opinion as to whether this pistol fired the bullet that killed Ms. Lathom?"

"Yes. That gun fired the bullet found in Ms. Lathom's body."

Meredith took him through the testing, how it was performed, and how he reached his conclusions. "No further questions, Your Honor," she said.

"No questions, Your Honor," I said.

Judge Gallagher looked at the clock and said, "It's near enough to noon that we can break for lunch. The court will be in recess until one thirty this afternoon.

* * *

We were just back from lunch when the court deputy told Meredith and me that the judge wanted to see us in chambers. "We've got a problem," he said as we entered his chambers. "One of the jurors got violently ill during lunch. He was taken to the hospital, but the emergency room doc over there tells us it's just something that he ate that disagreed with him. He should be ready to go in the morning, but we need to decide whether to seat one of the alternates or wait until morning to see if the juror is back."

"Which juror is it?" I asked.

"The prison guard."

Meredith and I looked at each other. We both wanted that man on the jury. She thought he would vote guilty, and I was pretty sure he would go for the acquittal. "Why don't we recess until in the morning," she said. "If he's not ready to go, we can seat the alternate."

"I agree," I said.

"Can you guys finish this by Friday if we take the afternoon off?"

"Yes," we said in unison.

"Okay. Let's let the jury know what's going on, and we'll call it a day."

I called J.D. and asked her to alert the sheriff to the fact that there would be no court that afternoon. She would tell the sheriff that the fireworks would begin on Thursday morning. I planned to spend some of the rest of the day getting ready for the big guns.

CHAPTER 46

ON THURSDAY, UNDER a sky bruised by dark clouds, I shared the morning drive to the courthouse with my fifth cup of coffee. J.D. had met with the sheriff the afternoon before and then spent the night with me. She had slept in while I was up early preparing for the day. I'm afraid I wasn't very good company the evening before, but J.D. understood. She would join me later at the courthouse.

I was jumpy from the caffeine I'd drunk while preparing for the day, and my mind was playing over the possibilities of the coming session in court, skipping quickly from one scenario to another. I knew that Ruth Bergstrom would be taking the stand. I had to somehow defuse the impact of her testimony. She would testify to the conversation she supposedly had where Esther threatened to kill Olivia Lathom. I knew that was a lie, and if she would lie under oath about the threat, I expected her to lie about other things, too. I just wasn't sure what else Meredith would want to elicit from her. I could only cross-examine on issues that the prosecutor brought up in her direct examination.

If I were Meredith, I think I'd put her on the stand and ask about whether she had given Esther's manuscript to Olivia, which she would deny, and then try to paint Esther as delusional enough to kill the object of her fantasy. I wouldn't go into anything else.

However, Meredith would know that I could call Ruth in my case as an adverse witness, which would give me the right to essentially cross-examine her by asking leading questions on any subject I decided to bring up as long as it was relevant to the issues we were facing in the trial. I would also be able to impeach her by questioning her veracity just as I would have on cross-exmination. I would not be restricted to the areas of enquiry the prosecutor had raised. On the other hand, if Meredith knew I had something that would reflect negatively on her case, she might bring it up herself. Such a maneuver would lessen the impact of my putting it into evidence.

It was all a matter of strategy, making decisions on how the flow of evidence should be managed, each lawyer knowing that there would be testimony that was inimical to his or her case and had to be dealt with. My ace in the hole, if in fact Meredith hadn't figured it out, was what I knew about Ruth, thanks to J.D. Meredith would have ferreted out some of the negative stuff and be prepared to rebut it, but, hopefully, I knew things that the prosecutor did not.

A light rain was falling by the time I got to the courthouse. I parked as close to the entrance as I could and moved quickly through the steady drizzle, my umbrella giving me a little protection. I cleared security and took the stairs to the courtroom on the second floor. Even a little exercise might relieve the anxiety brought about by a surfeit of caffeine.

I stopped in the restroom and used paper towels to dry off my trial bag and the wet umbrella. Meredith was walking toward the courtroom as I stepped back into the hallway. "Good morning, slick," she said.

"Slick?"

"Just like ole Billy Ray said. You're slick as a greased pig."

"Did I make you mad?"

"No. Actually I meant that as a compliment. You bobbed and weaved all over the evidence. I think you completely confused the jury."

"I thought you did a great job of getting everything you needed into evidence."

She snorted, a kind of truncated laugh she didn't mean to let out.

"Do you have any other witnesses besides Ruth Bergstrom this morning?" I asked.

"No. I'll put her up and rest as soon as you finish chewing on her."

"I'll be gentle," I promised.

Meredith laughed. "I've heard that before."

"Depending on how your direct goes, I might put her up first in my case."

"Okay. It'll save her a trip back to the courthouse."

We walked into the courtroom and took our seats. The court deputy told us that the prison guard on the jury had returned that morning so there would be no need to seat one of the alternates. I had a few notes to go over before we got started and, from the looks of it, so did Meredith. Spectators were slipping into their seats when the court deputy called the court to order. Everyone rose as Judge Gallagher entered the courtroom and took the bench. He waved us to our seats and asked, "Do counsel have any matters for my attention before we bring in the jury?"

We both stood and advised that we didn't. "Deputy," the judge said, "if you would be so kind as to bring in the jury, we'll get started." Meredith and I stayed on our feet while the jury filed into the box. When they were seated, we sat, and the judge greeted them and asked if they had anything for him before we got started. They all shook their heads, and the judge said, "Ms. Evans, call your first witness."

"The state will call Ruth Bergstrom," Meredith said.

The deputy went to the door and leaned into the hallway. He came back down the aisle followed by Ruth, who took the stand and was sworn by the deputy clerk of court.

Meredith took her through the preliminaries of name and place of residence. "Did you know Olivia Lathom?"

"Yes, she was my friend."

"How did she come to be your friend?"

"We worked together at a Fulton County Library branch in Atlanta for almost twenty years."

"Were you aware that Ms. Lathom was a writer?"

"I knew that she wrote and self-published two books and then hit it big with her third one."

"That was *Beholden*?"

"Yes."

"Did you know she was writing the book that was subsequently published as *Beholden*?"

"Only in the vaguest sense. My husband and I had retired and moved to The Villages, so I didn't see Liv regularly like I did when we worked together."

"But you knew she was writing a book?"

"She told me in phone conversations that she was writing, but she was always writing, so it didn't occur to me that she was working on a best seller."

"When did you find out about *Beholden*?"

"She called me one day to tell me she'd sold it to a publisher."

"Did she ever mention anything about how much she was paid for the book?"

"No. It didn't come up."

"Weren't you interested?"

"No, ma'am. It was none of my business."

"When did you first see the book?"

"About six months before it was published. She sent me an advanced reader's copy, one of those pre-publication books that go out to booksellers and critics."

"Did you see Ms. Lathom while she was visiting The Villages?"

"No. She called me about getting together, but I had already committed to taking a friend to the Orlando airport and I couldn't back out on short notice."

"Do you know whom she was supposed to have dinner with the night she was killed?"

"No. She didn't mention anything like that to me when we talked on the phone."

"Ms. Bergstrom, do you know Esther Higgins?"

"I do."

"How did you come to know Ms. Higgins?"

"We're in the same book club in The Villages."

"Do the members of that club ever read written works of other members? Sort of a critique group?"

"Yes. Regularly."

"Did Ms. Higgins ever give you a manuscript to read?"

"She did."

"Did you read it?"

"I read the first several chapters. It was awful."

"So you didn't think it was a publishable work."

"Not by a long shot."

"What did you do with the manuscript?"

"I gave it back to Ms. Higgins and told her I had been too busy to read it. I didn't want to hurt her feelings by telling her how bad it was."

"Did you ever give a copy of the manuscript to Olivia Lathom?"

"Of course not."

"Did Ms. Higgins ever accuse you of giving it to Ms. Lathom?"

"Yes. She told me I had given her book away and that the one Liv published was identical to the one Ms. Higgins had given to me."

"Was there any truth in her assertion?"

"Not a whit."

"When did this conversation take place?"

"A couple of weeks before Liv was coming to The Villages back in March."

"Did Esther Higgins say anything else about Ms. Lathom in that conversation?"

"Esther Higgins said she was going to kill Olivia Lathom for stealing her book."

"Did you think she would do it?"

"Not really. Frankly, I thought she was delusional, but I knew she had a gun. She'd shown it to our book club group a few days before."

"Nothing further, Your Honor," Meredith said.

"Just a couple of questions at this time, Ms. Bergstrom," I said. "When did my client give you a copy of her manuscript?"

"Just before Christmas a year ago. I remember that because several of our book club members were baking cookies for a Christmas party we were having."

"And when did you give it back to her?"

"A couple of weeks later. I don't remember the exact date."

"Thank you, Ms. Bergstrom." I turned to the judge. "Your Honor, I have Ms. Bergstrom under subpoena. I'll call her in my case."

"Ms. Bergstrom," the judge said, "you're excused for now, but you're still under subpoena and subject to recall. You are not to discuss the testimony you've given or that you will give with anyone during the duration of this trial. Someone will let you know when you're to return to this courtroom. Do you understand?"

"Yes, sir." She left the courtroom.

Meredith stood. "The state rests, Your Honor."

CHAPTER 47

Opening statements are tricky things. They give you the opportunity to tell the jury what you intend to prove during your case, to give the jurors a preview of the finished jigsaw puzzle. You want them to anticipate what's coming as you methodically introduce each piece of evidence so that at the conclusion of your case, the puzzle is complete and the jury has a clear picture to study as they deliberate.

The tricky part is making sure that you'll be able to prove everything you promise. If you've told the jury that you'll present certain evidence and then for some reason the testimony is ruled inadmissible, the jury will only know that you didn't deliver on your promise. You can bet the opposition will comment on that omission and your veracity will suffer. The jurors will be asking themselves if the lawyer can be trusted since he or she didn't do what he told them he would do in the opening statement. It can prove devastating to your case.

I rose with the usual trepidation to begin my opening statement. I had the advantage of knowing the state's case, but I had to be careful not to overstate my case. "Ladies and gentlemen," I said, "thank you for doing what is often a thankless, but nonetheless important, job. My client and I appreciate your attention during the course of this trial.

"The state has put on its case, and if I may say so, it's pretty thin. We have the testimony from the experts that a pistol owned by my client, Esther Higgins, was the murder weapon and that my client's fingerprints were the only ones on the gun. We do not dispute that, but we will show you why none of that points to Esther as the murderer. In fact, the evidence we will present will explain exactly how that happened.

"The only other evidence that links Esther to the murder of Olivia Lathom is the testimony of Ruth Bergstrom. You will see that Ms. Bergstrom lied to you, that my client never said that she'd kill Ms. Lathom. You'll also see that Ruth Bergstrom lied to you about the manuscript that became Olivia Lathom's book *Beholden*. In fact, the book was written by my client and the only way that manuscript could come into the possession of Olivia Lathom was through the good graces of Ms. Bergstrom, who stood to profit from its publication."

Short and to the point. I turned to the judge and said, "Your Honor, may I call my first witness?"

"Proceed."

"The defense will call Amber Marris," I said.

Amber took the witness stand and in answer to my questions testified as to her name and address.

"Are you employed?"

"I'm a bartender at the World of Beer restaurant in Brownwood in The Villages."

"Were you working on the evening of March 13th of this year?"

"I was."

"What time did you get off work?"

"I left the restaurant about one forty-five in the morning."

"That would be on the morning of March 14th?"

"Yes."

"Did you have anything unusual happen as you were leaving the restaurant?"

"Yes. A white van came shooting out of Paddock Square onto Brownwood Boulevard and almost hit my car as I turned onto West Torch Lake Drive."

"Which way was the van heading?"

"Toward Highway 44."

"How far from Paddock Square does the street intersect into Highway 44?"

"Less than a mile, I think."

"Can you describe the van?"

"Yes. It was a white Dodge Promaster City van."

"You're sure?"

"Yes. My husband and I had looked at one just like it at the Dodge dealer's the Saturday before. We were thinking about buying one."

"Did you get a look at the driver?"

"No, sir. It happened real fast."

"Were there any markings on the van? Graphics, that sort of thing?"

"No. It was plain white."

I showed her a picture of the van that Meredith and I had stipulated into evidence. "Did the van look similar to the one in this photo?"

"Identical."

"What did you do after the near collision with the van?"

"Nothing. I went home."

"So, you wouldn't have any idea about whether there was a body in the square at the time the van was leaving."

"That's correct."

"Thank you, Ms. Marris. I have no further questions."

"Ms. Evans?" the judge said.

"I'll be brief, Your Honor." She turned to the witness. "You don't have any idea if the van that almost hit you has any connection to the body that was found later that morning in the square, do you?"

"No, ma'am."

"And you can't identify the driver of the van?"

"I can't."

"Did you get a tag number on the van?"

"No."

"No further questions, Your Honor."

"Nothing further, Your Honor," I said. "May the witness be excused?"

"You're excused, Ms. Marris," the judge said. "It's almost lunchtime. Who's your next witness, Mr. Royal?"

"Lionel Steerman."

"Will he be short?"

"Afraid not, Your Honor."

"Okay, then. The court will be in recess until one o'clock."

CHAPTER 48

IN THE GUISE of Jade Conway, J.D. had announced her departure for Germany the day after I talked to Josh Hannah. Her divorce was final, her leave was up, and the Army needed her. We'd decided that since her job in The Villages was finished, she shouldn't stick around. If any of the witnesses put two and two together and decided that J.D. was not who she appeared to be, and that she and I were somehow connected, we might see a change in their testimony. It might be necessary for me to put J.D. on the witness stand to testify about her conversations with some of the witnesses if the witness lied, but that was the only way I would use her in the trial.

In the two weeks before the beginning of the trial, I was spending most of my time on Longboat Key. J.D. was back at work with the LBKPD, and Jock had returned to the murky world and the wars where he plied his deadly trade against the enemies of his country. J.D. had been stewing about Kelly Gilbert since their conversation at Sonny's in Lake Sumter Landing. That meeting had raised red flags, not the least of which was Kelly's excessive drinking.

On one of those evenings in mid-April, after J.D. had returned to Longboat, she and I were sitting in my living room enjoying the salt-scented breeze blowing through the open patio doors. A full moon was rising above the bay, its reflection on the dark water appearing as an errant moonbeam aimed directly at us. I was reading up on the rules of evidence and J.D. sat at my computer. I interrupted her. "Do you have that picture of the van driver taken by the security camera?"

"Sure." She tapped a few keys and said, "Here it is. You want me to print it?"

"No. You think your department geek is home?"

"I can call him. What do you need?"

"I'd like to send him that picture and ask him to Photoshop it. I've had a nagging feeling the last couple of days that I know that guy from somewhere. See if the geek can manipulate that picture by adding a full beard and a ball cap."

She had the picture within about ten minutes. I took a quick look and said, "I'll be damned. That's the guy who came after me in Darrell's Café a couple of weeks ago. That's got to be Buford Steerman, Chunk's brother, known as Biggun. Who the hell is the grandma, Sally Steerman?"

"You know, I went through the property records and didn't find anything on her in the three-county area. She didn't pop up on Google, either." She snapped her fingers. "I've got an idea." Her fingers flew over the keyboard. She'd stop periodically, stare at the monitor, and type some more. Ten minutes went by and she sat back and said, "Listen to this. I went into the Florida Department of Health's Bureau of Vital Statistics and found the marriage license of Kelly and David Gilbert. Guess what her name was before she married Mr. Gilbert."

"You got me. Smith?"

"According to this, her name was Sarah Kelly Steerman."

I sat up at that. "Steerman is not exactly a common name. Could she be Chunk's grandmother?"

"Maybe. Sally is often a diminutive for Sarah."

"Maybe we've found her," I said. "Is there any more information on her?"

"Just that she was born in Nashville, Georgia."

"That's near where one of my grandmothers lived. It's in Berrien County. Can you do a Google search on Sarah Steerman or maybe Kelly Steerman?"

"Sure." She turned back to the computer. After a few minutes, she said, "Nothing. She doesn't show up under either name."

"Didn't she tell you that Gilbert was her second marriage?"

"Yes. Her first husband died."

"If we assume that she lived the first part of her life in Nashville, she might have gotten married there. Let's check the Georgia records. Try the Georgia Department of Public Health website for marriages in Berrien County."

Five minutes later, she had the information. I called James Hurt in Cordele and asked if he knew anybody in Nashville who could help us. He did.

* * *

It was during the next week that everything started to come together, the little pieces of the puzzle falling into place. I spent a lot of time on the phone talking to people in two states, ferreting out the little odds and ends that hopefully would come together and eventually give a picture that would free Esther.

I coaxed Chunk Steerman into coming to Bushnell for the trial. I called him on his phone and asked if he was enjoying the barbeque at Fat Joe's. "How did you know I was here?" he'd asked.

"Chunk, you've got a very expensive monitor around your ankle."

"Oh, that."

"Yeah, that. Look, I need you to come to Bushnell for the trial."

"When?"

"Next week."

"Not sure I can make it."

"Look, Chunk. Here's the deal. You remember my friend from the truck stop? Jonathon?"

"Uh, yeah. The guy what sucker punched me."

"He's out in the parking lot at Fat Joe's. A quick phone call and he's going to be coming through the front door and hauling your ass out of there. He'll either bring you to Bushnell or he'll kill you. I wouldn't really care which, except that I need you to testify to some stuff. Either way, you're going to get badly hurt if he has to bring you down here."

"What stuff do I have to testify about?"

"We'll talk about that when you get here. In the meantime, my buddy will be keeping an eye on you. You make one false move, like trying to disappear or get rid of that ankle monitor, and he'll be on you like fur on a rabbit. You got that?"

"Yes, sir."

"I'll call you when it's time for you to get on the road. Don't screw with me, Chunk, or you'll end up in an unmarked grave."

A little coaxing often goes a long way.

* * *

The lunch break was over and we were ready to go. "State your name, please," I said to the man on the witness stand.

"Lionel Steerman. People call me Chunk."

"Your age?"

"Twenty-three."

"Do you have a brother?"

"Yeah. His name is Buford. We call him Biggun."

"Where do you live, Mr. Steerman?"

"Outside Camilla, Georgia."

"What do you do for a living?"

"I own a chicken farm. I raise and sell chickens."

"Do you know a woman named Sally Steerman?"

"Yes, sir. She's my grandma."

"Is she your natural grandmother?"

"What do you mean?"

"How are you related?"

"She's my daddy's mamma."

"Is your dad your natural father?"

"He adopted me and my brother after he married my mamma."

I saw Meredith rising to her feet out of the corner of my eye. "Objection, Your Honor. Relevance."

"Mr. Royal?" the judge asked. Meredith had let me follow this line of questions longer than I had expected.

"I'll tie all this up with the next couple of witnesses, Your Honor," I said.

"Be sure that you do. Overruled."

"Do your parents still live together?" I asked Chunk.

"No, sir. Mamma ran off with a truck driver when we were little. Our grandma helped my daddy raise us."

"That'd be Sally Steerman?"

"Yes, sir. We're real close."

"How'd you end up with a chicken farm?"

"My daddy came into some money and he bought a piece of land and gave me half and Biggun half. Biggun has a hog farm next door to me."

"Does your grandma go by a different name now?"

"Yes, sir. Well, sometimes."

"What is that name?"

"Kelly Gilbert. But to me and my brother she's still Sally Steerman."

"Mr. Steerman, I want you to think back to several weeks ago, the evening of March 13th, to be exact. Did you make a call to somebody and pretend to be an airline agent?"

"I don't think so."

"Maybe to tell somebody that her plane was delayed?"

"Oh, yeah. That was some kind of joke my grandma wanted to play on somebody. She called me at home and told me what she wanted me to say. She even sent me an email with the message and the phone number written down and told me she'd call me later that night and tell me when to make the call."

"Did you make that call?"

"Yes, sir. Some woman answered the phone."

"And you gave her the message?"

"Yes, sir."

"Do you remember the date of that call?"

"No, sir, but it was the same night Biggun left to come down to The Villages."

"Did you come with him?"

"No, sir. Not that time."

"Why did he come down here?"

"Objection, Your Honor." Meredith was on her feet. "Hearsay."

"Sustained."

"Mr. Steerman, do you have any knowledge independent of what your brother might have told you, as to the reason he came to The Villages that night?"

"No, sir."

"Did you ever ask anybody else about that visit? Like your grandmother?"

"No, sir."

"Let me show you a picture marked as Defense Exhibit A. Can you identify the person in this picture?"

"Yes, sir. That's a picture of Biggun."

"Your brother, Buford?"

"Yes, sir."

"Do you know where Buford is now?"

"No, sir. He left Camilla about a week ago. Ain't nobody seen hide nor hair of him since."

I introduced the photo of Biggun entering the Hillsborough gate in The Villages, the one taken by the security camera on the night of the murder, as Defense Exhibit one. I picked up the picture of the back of the van entering the gate and showed it to Chunk. "Look at Defense Exhibit B. Is that a photo of Biggun's van?"

"I can't tell from that picture if it's even a van."

"Look at the device covering the license plate. Have you ever seen anything like that?"

"Yes, sir. It looks like a gadget that Biggun uses to beat tolls. He hits a switch in the cab and down the little doohickey comes."

"Your Honor, I'd like to introduce Defense Exhibit B into evidence as Defense Exhibit two for the purpose of showing the device that covers the license plate."

"No objection, Your Honor," Meredith said. "We've stipulated that the pictures were taken on the night of the murder and at the gate to the Village of Hillsborough at Buena Vista Boulevard." She'd seen both the photos as part of the pretrial exhibit list I'd filed and she'd taken the deposition of the security supervisor who testified as to when and where the pictures were taken.

I showed Chunk the picture of the van that I had gotten from the local Dodge dealer and shown to Amber Marris. "Does this look like your brother Biggun's van?"

"It sure does."

"No further questions, Your Honor," I said.

"Ms. Evans?" the judge asked.

"No questions, Your Honor."

"Call your next witness, Mr. Royal."

"The defense calls Kelly Gilbert."

CHAPTER 49

A WEEK BEFORE the trial was scheduled to begin, I made the five-hour drive from Longboat Key to Nashville, Georgia, for a meeting with a lawyer named Bill Perry. James Hurt had told me that Perry had lived his whole life in Nashville and owned banks and practiced law there for almost fifty years. He knew everybody and knew where all their secrets were buried.

Perry was a pleasant man in his midseventies, tall and fit with a head of white hair. He welcomed me to his office and said, "James Hurt said you and he were law school classmates. He has a high opinion of you, and I told him I'd do whatever I could to help out. I understand you're looking into the background of Sally Steerman. May I ask in what connection?"

"She may be involved in a murder. I don't have any evidence that she did anything, but her name came up in my investigation in an odd way. Did you know she now goes by the name of Kelly Gilbert?"

"No, I didn't, but I did know that Kelly was her middle name. Her first name was Sarah, but everybody always called her Sally to differentiate her from her mother who was also named Sarah. Sally left here a few years back after her husband was killed."

"How did he die?"

"Car accident. He got T-boned by a big dump truck out on Highway129. The truck was coming out of a borrow pit area and didn't stop. Said he had brake problems, but I don't think anybody ever figured that one out. Anyway, Sally's husband died at the scene."

"How long did she stay in Nashville after he died?"

"About a year, I think. Maybe two. She got a pretty good settlement from the company that owned the dump truck, and she started seeing a lawyer from over in Adel named David Gilbert. They moved to Orlando and then he died of a heart attack."

"Did you know Sally well?"

"Pretty well. She worked as a waitress in the diner across the street for a long time. Started while she was in high school, I think. It was actually kind of sad. She could have been somebody."

"What do you mean?"

"She was Miss Berrien County back in the sixties. She sang opera music like an angel. She was a natural. She'd studied under one of the voice teachers over at Valdosta State while she was in high school and walked away with the talent contest in the Miss Georgia Pageant. She got screwed out of the crown by an unscrupulous judge, so she didn't get the scholarship money she needed to go to college. She came home and went back to work in the diner."

"Was the pageant fixed?" I asked.

"This one was. One of the judges, a man named John Peters, was having an affair with the eventual winner and he manipulated the vote so that Sally didn't even make the finals. Peters' girlfriend won."

"Are you sure about this?"

"Yes. Years after the pageant, Peters, who was a car dealer in Atlanta, was diagnosed with a terminal disease. He told me how he fixed the pageant and asked me to set up a trust fund for Sally's two boys. The money in the trust was more than enough to get them educated and set up in whatever they wanted to do after they graduated from college. He knew Sally wouldn't accept any money from him directly, but he also knew she couldn't turn down something that would benefit her sons."

"What happened to Sally's boys?"

"The youngest one is a doctor up in North Carolina and the older one is a drunk. He lives up in North Georgia somewhere."

"Did Sally ever find out about what happened with the pageant?"

"Yes. Peters went to see her and told her what he had done."

"How did Sally take it?"

"Surprisingly well. At first, she didn't seem at all bitter, but as the years wore on and she became estranged from her sons, her husband got killed, and she got older, she became more and more bitter. She once told me that her life had all gone to hell when she didn't win the pageant. She had become convinced that, had she won, none of the bad things would have happened to her later. Her life from the pageant forward just went downhill. Even the boys, whom she thought were the best things that ever happened to her, turned into disappointments. The doctor didn't want to have anything to do with her, and the other boy didn't even go to college. He pissed away, or drank away, I should say, all the trust money when he got it at age twenty-one. I just watched her fall apart over the years. I think the brightest spot in a lot of years was when she married David Gilbert and started a new life in Orlando. And then he died and the new life died with it."

"Do you remember who won the Miss Georgia Pageant that year?" I asked.

"No, but I've still got a couple of copies of the program from the pageant. I remember that the winner was from Atlanta, so she'll be in there."

Perry went to a file cabinet standing in the outer office and came back with the official program that had all the information of the contestants and pictures of each one. He thumbed through it for a few moments and then handed the program to me opened to a page. "That's the girl. Miss Atlanta Northside, Polly Norris." He turned a couple more pages and showed me another photograph. "That's Sally Steerman, but she was using her maiden name, Sarah Kyle."

"Can I get copies of those pictures?" I asked.

"Take the program," Perry said. "I've got a couple more in the cabinet."

* * *

I arrived back on the island feeling like the old horse that had been rode hard and put up wet. I was exhausted from the five-hour drive to Nashville and another five hours back. My day's nutrition consisted mostly of fast food and Diet Coke, plus coffee and the three donuts I'd had for breakfast while I drove north. I'd spent an hour or so with Bill Perry and turned right around and drove home. I called J.D. as I exited I-275 onto Highway 41 at Bradenton and asked her to order up some pizza and meet me at my house. I might as well continue my healthy eating routine.

The house was empty when I opened the front door. I shed my clothes and jumped into the shower. The hot spray felt good on the bunched muscles in my back, and I started to relax a little. It had been a productive trip, but ten hours behind the wheel was brutal. I didn't know how the long-haul truckers did it day after day.

As I was drying off, I heard the front door open and close, and the smell of pizza, diluted by the steam from the shower, wafted into the bathroom. I put on a pair of well-worn shorts and an old t-shirt bearing the faded logo of Moore's Stone Crab Restaurant and padded into the Kitchen. J.D. gave me a quick hug. "You look tired," she said. "Sit down and I'll dish up the pizza. You want a cold beer?"

I nodded, and sat, and marveled at my luck to have this beautiful woman to share my life with. We dug into the pizza, and I told her about my day. "Doesn't your department have one of those computer programs that will age a person's picture so that you can get a pretty good estimate of what he or she would look like many years in the future?"

"I'm pretty sure we do. Why?"

"Does it work the other way as well? I mean, could the program scan a picture of somebody today and get a pretty good likeness of what that person looked like forty years before?"

"I can ask, but why?" J.D. asked.

"I'm beginning to wonder if Olivia Lathom's murder had something to do with that Miss Georgia Pageant."

"How so?"

"Suppose Olivia had something to do with Sarah Kyle getting literally screwed out of the title. According to Bill Perry, over the years Sarah became very bitter about the whole thing. She might have been bitter enough to kill Olivia. And then we have her stepgrandson driving what appears to be a white van into Hillsborough Village on the night of the murder and driving out again at about the time that would have gotten him to Brownwood in time to almost run into Amber Marris. He's the same guy who accosted me in Darrell's Diner. Then, her other doofus stepgrandson, Chunk Steerman, tried to bean me with a sock full of quarters.

"Are you giving up on Ruth Bergstrom as the murderer?"

"I don't know. She had plenty of reason. We know she had to have given Esther's manuscript to Olivia, but I'm not sure I can prove it. Ruth is living on the edge of poverty and hates her husband. She needed money and probably expected to get a piece of Olivia's publishing money. Maybe Olivia stiffed her and really pissed her off."

"Enough to kill Olivia?" J.D. asked.

"Maybe. Ruth certainly seems to be a cold one. And we know she's been in trouble with the law before, including a stint in prison."

"But Kelly's the one who got Esther to show her the gun, possibly to make sure that Esther's prints were on it."

"Do you think we could call the geek again and see if he can run a recent picture of a person and see what she might have looked like forty years ago?"

The geek agreed to give it a try, and I pulled a publicity shot of Olivia Lathom from my file, scanned it, and emailed it to him. Thirty minutes later we got a picture of what purported to be a likeness of Olivia Lathom when she was in her twenties.

"J.D.," I said. "I don't want to let my suspicions prejudice this. Will you take the young Olivia's picture the geek sent us and compare it to the headshots of the contestants, chaperones, sponsors, and whoever else shows up in the program?"

I ate the last piece of pizza and watched J.D. match the picture of young Olivia to the shots in the pageant program. She would place the photo next to a headshot and move on. After about ten minutes, she looked at me and said, "I'll be damned. Look at this. An almost perfect match."

CHAPTER 50

"STATE YOUR NAME, please," I said after the witness had taken the stand.

"Kelly Gilbert."

"And you're also known as Sally Steerman?"

"I used to be."

"Can you tell me how you went from being Sally Steerman to being Kelly Gilbert?"

"My full name is Sarah Kelly Gilbert. I always went by Sally when I was a child, and when I married my first husband, I became Sally Steerman. After he died and I married my second husband, we started a new life in a new place and I thought it would be appropriate to start with a new first name as well as a new last name. I started using my middle name. Kelly. Not a big secret."

"But you didn't tell your friends here in The Villages that you were once known as Sally Steerman, did you?"

"It didn't seem important."

"Did you tell any of them that you were once known as Sarah Kyle?"

"No. Kyle was my maiden name. Nobody was writing my biography, so I didn't think it was important." She was getting a little testy, but I wasn't surprised. She'd called me when I'd had the trial subpoena served on her. To say she was nasty would have been like saying the New England Patriots are an adequate football team. I let her have her say that night on the phone and heard some words I hadn't heard since I got out of the Army. A lot of those words were slurred and now I wondered if she'd had a few drinks before she arrived at the courthouse.

"You were also once known as Miss Berrien County, weren't you?"

She seemed surprised and looked down at her lap before replying with a nod. "Ms. Gilbert," I said, "you have to answer verbally. The court reporter can't hear a nod."

"Yes. A long, long time ago."

"And you competed in the Miss Georgia pageant that year?"

"Yes."

"You didn't win, did you?"

"No."

"Are you related to Buford and Lionel Steerman?"

"Not by blood."

"I believe they're your stepgrandchildren."

"Yes."

"The adopted children of your eldest son?"

"Yes."

"They took your son's name when he adopted them?"

"Yes."

"Who is Polly Norris?" Sometimes when you can bring a question out of left field, it rattles the witness. I could see that this one hit home with Kelly, but it didn't rattle her. She made a face, a fleeting moue, as if she had suddenly sniffed an offensive odor.

"She was the girl that won the Miss Georgia crown the year I competed."

"Have you stayed in touch with her?"

"No."

"You were roommates at the pageant, were you not?"

"We were."

"But you never tried to contact her after the pageant?"

"No. I'd read about her appearing around the state as Miss Georgia, but we never got together again."

"Your testimony then is that you never in the years since the pageant have had any contact whatsoever with the woman you knew as Polly Norris?"

A shadow of a frown crossed her face. She shook her head and said, "No." My gut told me she had just committed perjury.

"Let me show you Defense Exhibit C for identification and ask if you can identify the person in the photo." I handed her a copy of a publicity photo of Olivia Lathom taken shortly before she died.

"Yes," Kelly said, "that's Olivia Lathom."

"Can you identify the person in Defense Exhibit D?" I handed her the picture of Olivia that our computer expert had regressed by forty years.

"No. I don't know her."

"How about this one, Defense Exhibit E? Do you know who that person is?" I showed her the picture that had been copied from the Miss Georgia Pageant program book.

"I don't know her, but she looks like the same person in the picture you just showed me. They're just dressed differently."

"You've never seen the person depicted in Exhibits D and E before?"

"Not to my knowledge."

"Ms. Gilbert, I want you to think back to the Miss Georgia Pageant you competed in and assume that the pictures of the younger woman, Exhibits D and E, are photos of a woman taken back then who was involved in the pageant. Would that refresh your recollection as to whether you know her?"

She looked at the pictures again. "No, sir. I don't know her."

"Thank you, Ms. Gilbert." I put the photo of Olivia into evidence as Defense Exhibit six and said, "Your Honor, may we approach the bench?"

Judge Gallagher waved us forward. Meredith and I and the court reporter crowded into the space in front of the judge. "Mr. Royal?" he asked.

"Your Honor, I have some film clips I'd like to have Ms. Gilbert authenticate for purposes of putting them in evidence, but I'd like to proffer them outside the presence of the jury."

He looked at Meredith. "Any objection to the proffer?"

"Are these clips listed on the evidence list?" she asked. The list is of all documents and other items we plan to offer into evidence. It has to be served on opposing counsel along with our witness list several weeks before trial.

"Yes," I said. "Number twenty-one. 'Certain film clips, videos, and other recordings in original form that will be made available to the state upon request.'"

"We were never provided with the recordings," Meredith said.

"They were originals, Your Honor. I didn't want to go to the expense of copying the clips if they weren't needed. I was ready to provide them to the state attorney's office for copying if needed. I did so. The state attorney's investigator, Mr. Bliden, and I met in his office and went over all the exhibits. He didn't see the need for copies of the clips I showed him."

Meredith looked at me. "You showed him the recordings you want us to look at now?"

"Yes."

"I'm going to kill that investigator," she said. "This is the first I've heard of these, but if Matt Royal says he showed them to Bliden, then he did. I don't object to the proffer, but I may object to the evidence."

"Thank you, Meredith," I said.

The judge gave the jury an instruction concerning his need to review some evidence outside their presence and sent them to the jury room. I signaled to the county's audiovisual technician in the back of the courtroom, and he wheeled in a table containing a large flat-screen TV and a compact disc player. I looked at the two discs and handed him one. "Will you play this one first, please?" I handed him a disc that had been recorded by a television station in Macon, Georgia. It contained an old film clip that had been digitized and put on the disc.

I turned to the witness stand. "Ms. Gilbert, I want you to watch this video."

I looked up at the judge. "Proceed," he said. The A-V guy hit a switch and some of the most beautiful music I'd ever heard filled the courtroom. It was a clip of a lovely young woman dressed in an evening gown singing Gilda's aria from Verdi's *Rigolleto*. Her performance was worthy of a headliner at La Scala in Milan or The Met in New York.

I looked at Kelly and saw tears running down her cheeks. I let the clip play out, and when it was over, I turned to the witness box and said softly, "Do you recognize that, Ms. Gilbert?"

She nodded as she tried to regain her composure. "Where did you get that?"

"WMAZ-TV in Macon. It was in their archives. It's you at the Miss Georgia Pageant, isn't it?"

"Yes," she said softly.

"It was beautiful, Ms. Gilbert. Now I want to show you another clip."

"Okay."

I turned to the A-V guy and asked him to play the second disc. A young woman in a majorette's costume was twirling a baton as she danced around the stage. When it was over, I turned back to the witness stand and asked, "Do you recognize that young woman?"

"Yes. That's Polly Norris."

"The woman who won the pageant?"

"Yes."

"That's my proffer, Your Honor," I said.

"I object, Your Honor," Meredith said. "Relevance."

"I will tie everything up, Your Honor."

"Your objection is overruled, Ms. Evans. Without prejudice. Bring the jury back in."

When the jury returned, we again went through the process of showing the videos and asking Kelly to identify them. When she had done so, I asked, "That was your talent at the Miss Georgia Pageant?"

"Yes."

"And the young woman twirling the baton, who was that?"

"Polly Norris."

"That's the woman who won and became Miss Georgia?"

"Yes."

"And she is the same woman as the one in the pictures identified as Defendant Exhibits D and E, isn't she?" I showed her the pictures.

"Yes, it would appear so."

"What made you decide to compete in the pageant in the first place?"

"The winner gets a good amount of scholarship money and that would have funded a college education for me."

"Were you able to go to college?"

"No. I went back to Nashville, Georgia, and went to work as a waitress in a diner."

"Were you bitter about being cheated out of the title?"

"What do you mean, cheated?"

"Do you remember John Peters?"

She visibly slumped in the witness chair, a look of surprise on her face. She was obviously taken aback by how deeply I had delved into her life. "Yes."

"He's the man who had a sexual affair with Polly Norris during the pageant?"

"Yes."

"And he's the man who lied to the other judges and told them that you were pregnant at the time of the pageant?"

"Yes."

"And that ruined your chances, didn't it?"

"Yes."

"And you found out about that because Mr. Peters showed up twenty years after the pageant and confessed to you what he'd done, right?"

"Yes."

"Were you bitter about him ruining your chances of winning and getting the scholarship money?"

"Not really."

"He funded a trust for your two sons, didn't he? An apology of sorts."

"Yes."

"And then your husband got killed when a dump truck ran a stop sign and hit him."

"Yes."

"And one of your sons, the older boy, spent all his trust money on drugs and alcohol and never went to college?"

"Yes."

"Your younger son is a successful physician in North Carolina and doesn't want to have anything to do with you?"

"Yes." By now her head was down and she was answering in a soft voice that matched the sympathetic tone of my questions.

"Your second husband died an untimely death from a heart attack a year or so ago?"

"Yes."

"And all the hard times resulted from your getting cheated out of the Miss Georgia title, right?"

"Who can say? Maybe. If I'd won, I think my life would have been set on a different course."

"And perhaps it wouldn't have been so full of disappointments?"

"Maybe."

"And this was all the result of Polly Norris having bought the title with sex?"

"Probably."

"When did you discover that Polly Norris had become Olivia Lathom?"

"I didn't know that."

"Did you suspect it?"

"No."

"Did you kill Olivia Lathom?"

"Of course not."

I didn't know the answer to that question before I asked it, but it could only have been either "yes" or "no." I didn't think any sane person would answer that question in the affirmative, so I really had nothing to lose. "Thank you, Ms. Gilbert. I have no further questions." I turned to the judge. "I'd like to introduce the recordings into evidence."

"No objection," Meredith said, "and I have no questions of this witness."

I had noticed that Meredith had not objected during my direct examination of Kelly, but then she had an objection on the record concerning the proffer. It must have appeared to Meredith that I had elicited no evidence from Kelly that was relevant to the murder and, therefore, there was nothing to cross-examine her about. I hadn't yet discerned her strategy, but I was pretty sure a lawyer as smart as she was not planning to go with the bare bones as she had done so far. Maybe Meredith had just made her first big mistake.

"Call your next witness, Mr. Royal."

"The defense calls Dr. Gary Burris."

CHAPTER 51

GARY BURRIS AND his wife, Debbie, were on the witness list I'd filed before the trial. For some reason, the state attorney's investigator had never contacted them. It may have been that their names on the witness list would have appeared just to be a couple of neighbors who would serve as character witnesses.

Gary took the stand and was sworn. I got the preliminary questions out of the way and then asked, "What is your profession?"

"I'm a professor of computer science at the University of Florida."

"What is your educational background?"

He told me about his degrees, including a doctorate in computer science.

"Your Honor," I said. "I'd like to offer Dr. Burris as an expert witness in computer science."

"Voir dire, Ms. Evans?"

"No voir dire, Your Honor, but I object to the witness appearing as an expert. I did not have an opportunity to depose him."

"Was Dr. Burris on the defense witness list?"

"Yes, sir, but apparently, my investigator never contacted him."

"The court will accept Dr. Burris as an expert witness in the area of computer science."

"Thank you, Your Honor," I said. "Dr. Burris, did you receive a laptop computer from me?"

"I did."

"What were you asked to do?"

"You asked me to examine the computer to determine the date that certain data was put into the computer."

"Which data was that?"

"Specifically, an MS Word document that was a book manuscript."

"Did you determine who owned that particular computer?"

"Yes. I examined it closely and found the owner's name throughout in online orders she made, emails she'd sent and received, and a number of other indicia that I can go into if you like."

I waved that off and asked, "Who did the computer belong to?"

"Esther Higgins."

"Was there more than one date concerning the manuscript?"

"A lot of them. It appeared that she worked on the book for several years and the dates in the computer corresponded to the dates she was writing."

"Were you able to determine when the manuscript was completed?"

"Yes. I concluded that the book was apparently finished when there was no evidence of further inputs."

"What was the date of the final entry?"

"November 12th of the year before last."

"Can these dates be manipulated, Dr. Burris, so that it would appear that a document was created on a date other than the date it was actually created?"

"Not without leaving an electronic trail, and I found no such thing. In my opinion, the book was finished on November 12th and nothing was added after that date."

"Dr. Burris, I'd like to turn to another subject. Take a look at these three pictures. I handed him the exhibits. "Did you at my request manipulate any of these pictures with a computer program?"

"Yes." He held one of the pictures up for the jury. "This is a computer-generated photograph."

"Tell me how that works, Dr. Burris."

He held up the publicity photo of Olivia and said, "I scanned this picture of Olivia Lathom into a computer program that will regress the age of the subject in the photo. In this case, I asked the computer to produce a picture of what Ms. Lathom would have looked like forty years before the present-day picture was taken."

"Is one of the other photos the one that the computer produced in response to your instructions?"

"Yes. This one." He held up a picture of a young woman.

"Do you recognize the picture the computer generated?"

"Yes. I've seen another picture of this young woman."

"Did you see it before you ran the computer program?"

"No. I saw it a few days later for the first time."

"Did you make any changes in your computer program based on what you saw on the later picture?"

"None."

"Do you have an opinion based upon a reasonable degree of probability as to whether the picture produced by the computer is of the same person as the woman in the third picture you have in your hand?"

"No question. It is the same person."

"Do you know where that picture came from?"

"Yes. It's a copy of a photo from a fortysomething-year-old Miss Georgia Pageant program book."

"Bear with me, Dr. Burris, but I have one more question because I want to make sure I understand your answer. Defense Exhibit three in evidence is a recent picture of Olivia Lathom."

"Yes."

"Defense Exhibit D for identification is the computer-generated picture of what Olivia Lathom looked like forty years ago."

"Yes."

"And the computer-generated picture matches the picture from the Miss Georgia Pageant program book."

"Yes."

"Your Honor, I'd like to mark this copy of the program book into evidence." I handed the program to the witness. "Dr. Burris, turn to page twenty-three in the program book and compare the picture generated by your computer to the picture on that page."

"It's the same young woman."

"Is the picture in the program the same one as the other picture I handed you?"

"Yes."

"Please tell the jury the name of the person depicted in the picture on page twenty-three of the Miss Georgia Pageant book."

"The name under the picture is Polly Norris."

"Do you have an opinion as to whether Polly Norris and Olivia Lathom are the same person?"

"No doubt about it. Polly Norris and Olivia Lathom are the same person."

"Thank you, Dr. Burris. Nothing further."

Meredith stood. "No questions, Your Honor, but I move to strike Dr. Burris' testimony on the grounds that it is not relevant to any part of this case."

"I'll tie this up with the next few witnesses, Your Honor," I said.

"Your motion is denied, Ms. Evans. Without prejudice."

That meant that she could renew the motion, but I thought she'd forego that after my next witness. "The defense will call Dr. Debbie Burris," I said.

When she had taken the witness stand, I said, "State your name and occupation, please."

"My name is Debbie Burris and I'm a professor of English at the University of Florida."

I took her through her qualifications including a PhD and her teaching assignments at the university including her emphasis on American literature. "Your Honor, I would offer Dr. Debbie Burris as an expert witness on the subject of American novels."

"Same objection, same grounds," Meredith said.

"Overruled."

"Are you related to Dr. Gary Burris?" I asked.

"Yes. He's my husband."

"Did you have an opportunity, at my request, to review a manuscript that Dr. Burris found in a computer belonging to Esther Higgins?"

"Yes."

"Did you compare it to a book titled *Beholden* published under the name of Olivia Lathom?"

"I did."

"Did you find any similarities?"

"For all intents and purposes, they're identical."

"Can you elaborate on that?"

"*Beholden* is comprised of approximately one hundred thousand words. So is Esther's manuscript. There is very little to distinguish one from the other. The book has some obvious editing differences from the manuscript, but that's all."

"Do you have an opinion as to whether the book *Beholden* is the finished, publishable version of Esther Higgins' manuscript?"

"Yes. There is no doubt that the book is the work of the author of the manuscript found in Esther Higgins' computer."

"Did you determine when Olivia Lathom submitted the manuscript of *Beholden* to her publisher?"

"Yes. The publisher received the manuscript from Ms. Lathom's agent on March 21st of last year."

"Assume, Dr. Burris, that Ms. Bergstrom testified that she was given the manuscript by my client a few days before Christmas the year before last. Assume further that your husband testified that the manuscript was completed more than a month before that. Added to your knowledge that the manuscript was submitted to the publisher about three months after Ms. Bergstrom received it, do you have an opinion as to whether the manuscript found on my client's computer was the one that was published as *Beholden*?"

"My opinion is that the manuscript and the book are one and the same."

"Thank you, Dr. Burris. No further questions."

"Ms. Evans?" the judge said.

"No questions, Your Honor, but I renew my motion to strike both experts."

"Overruled."

We took our afternoon fifteen-minute break and returned to the courtroom. "Call your next witness, Mr. Royal," the judge said.

"The defense calls Buford Steerman."

CHAPTER 52

Two days before Jock was called back to the wars, he drove to Camilla, Georgia, to have a talk with Buford Steerman. He arrived at Buford's property at dusk and found a double-wide trailer set on a concrete slab in the middle of a muddy field. A white van matching the one Amber Marris had seen in Brownwood was parked next to the trailer. Hogs roamed a nearby fenced area emitting a cacophony of snorts and squeals. A miasma of swine excrement hung heavy in the air. Jock took a picture of the van and a close-up of its license plate. He knocked on the front door.

A large man answered, a scowl on his face. "What do you want?"

"Are you Buford Steerman?"

"Yeah. What's it to you?"

Jock hit him in the solar plexus, that sweet spot just below the sternum, with a short powerful jab. As Steerman bent over in pain, Jock brought his knee up into the man's face, knocking him backward. He was off balance when Jock pushed him to the floor and sat on his chest, the muzzle of his nine-millimeter stuck in Buford's left nostril. "We need to talk," Jock said.

"Okay," Buford mumbled between gasps. "Who are you?"

Jock ignored the question. "If I let you up, will you behave?"

"Yes."

"Okay. Sit in that chair," Jock said, pointing. "If you make any kind of wrong move, it'll be your last one. Do you understand?"

Buford nodded. He was gasping for air, holding his stomach.

"Let me make myself clear," Jock said. "You are on borrowed time. Your life is about to end. The only way you have out of this predicament is to tell me the truth. Understand?"

"Yeah."

"And I'll know if you're lying, and you'll be dead in the next second. We clear?"

"Yeah."

"People call you Biggun, right?"

"Right."

When they were seated, Jock started the interrogation. He knew that Biggun had been driving what appeared to be a van through the Hillsborough Village gate on the evening of the Lathom murder and that was his starting point.

When he was finished, Jock said, "Biggun, you just won the right to live a bit longer, but there's another test coming up."

"What do you mean?"

"When my buddy Matt Royal calls you to come to Florida, you're going to get in your van immediately and head south. You got that?"

"Yeah."

"I've recorded what you've told me tonight, and when Mr. Royal puts you on the witness stand you're going to testify to it all. Right?"

"Right."

"Do you fully understand the price you'll pay if you don't do exactly as Royal tells you?"

"You'll kill me."

"Right. Do you believe me?"

"Yeah."

"Have a good evening, Mr. Steerman," Jock said as he walked out the way he'd come in.

* * *

The courtroom gallery had been partially full during a large portion of the trial, but it was an ever-changing cast of characters. I had learned a long time ago that trials brought out the retirees in small towns, probably because it was a cheap form of entertainment. Earlier in the day, I had noticed a man in his thirties wearing a suit and tie sitting near the back and taking notes. Curious, but I thought I might know just who he was.

Buford Steerman took the stand, bringing my attention back to where it belonged. "State your name for the record," I said.

"Buford Steerman."

"Are you the brother of Lionel Steerman?"

"Yes."

"He testified here that you had disappeared from Camilla about a week ago. Where have you been?"

"Here in Bushnell."

"Tell the jury how that came about."

"You called me and asked me to come down for the trial."

"Does your stepgrandmother live in The Villages?"

"Yes."

"What's her name?"

"Kelly Gilbert. It used to be Sally Steerman."

"Did you get a call from her back on March 13th of this year?"

"Yeah. She called me about nine o'clock in the evening and asked me to drive my van down to The Villages."

"Did she say why she wanted you here?"

"No. She just said she wanted me to pick up something heavy and take it back to Camilla."

"Did you come to your grandmother's house?"

"No. She told me to meet her at a friend's house."

"Did you know who lived in that house?"

"I do now."

"Who lived in that house?"

"A woman named Ruth Bergstrom and her husband, James McNeil."

"Was your grandmother at that house when you arrived?"

"Yes."

"Who else was there?"

"Mr. McNeil and Ms. Bergstrom."

"Anybody else?"

"No."

"Was this lady, Esther Higgins, there?" I asked, pointing toward my client.

"No."

"Did you ever hear her name in connection with the death of Ms. Lathom?"

"No."

"Did the people in the house have a package they wanted you to take back to Camilla?"

"Yes. The body of a woman. She was dead."

"Where was the body when you got there?"

"In the living room. She was laying partly on the sofa."

"Do you know if the body had been moved? Say, put on the sofa?"

"It didn't look like it. She was sort of splayed out there, half on and half off the sofa."

"Let me show you a picture, which has been identified as a photograph of Olivia Lathom. Was this the woman whose body you found in the home of Ruth Bergstrom and James McNeil?"

He looked at the picture. "Yes."

"What were you supposed to do with the body?"

"They wanted me to take it back to Camilla and bury it on my property."

"Do you know how Ms. Lathom was killed?"

"No."

"Did you see any weapons?"

"No."

"Did you ask how she died?"

"No."

"Weren't you curious?"

"Not especially."

"Did you do as they asked?"

"I tried."

"Tell the jury what you did."

"I put the body in my van and started out for Camilla."

"But you didn't get there."

"Yeah, I did. I went right home."

"With the body?"

"No. I ran into some trouble and had to dump her."

"What kind of trouble?"

"There was an accident on Buena Vista Boulevard. Or maybe it was a DUI checkpoint or something like that. Anyway, there were lots of cops and blue lights out there blocking the road. I sure as hell didn't want the cops finding a dead woman in my van. I took the first turn off Buena Vista and ended up in Brownwood. I had to get rid of the body, so I left it there."

"In Paddock Square?"

"Yeah."

"After the night you took the body to the square, did you get a call from somebody telling you to talk to me?"

"Yes."

"When did that call take place?"

"A couple of weeks later, I think."

"Who made the call?"

"I don't know."

"What did the caller say?"

"He told me that I had to get you off the case or my grandma would be in big trouble."

"Did you share that conversation with your brother, Lionel?"

"Yes."

"Did the caller say anything else?"

"He told me where you were staying in The Villages."

"Did you do anything in response to that phone call?"

"I went to talk to you."

"At Darrell's Diner?"

"Yes."

It's always a good idea to quit while you're ahead. "No further questions, Your Honor." Meredith had not objected to any of my questions. I thought maybe she had just figured that this other Steerman had nothing to add to his brother's testimony. Now she was faced with testimony from somebody who had been at the murder scene and testified that my client was not there.

Meredith stood. "Mr. Steerman, are you admitting here in open court that you committed the crime of accessory to murder after the fact, among others?"

"No, ma'am."

"Did you not know that what you did was a crime?"

"Never thought much about it."

"Mr. Royal never mentioned that to you?"

"No."

"I think you testified that you didn't know who killed Ms. Lathom."

"Yes."

"And you didn't inquire."

"No, ma'am."

"So you can't say whether Esther Higgins killed the lady or not, can you?"

"No."

"Did you notice a gunshot wound in the woman's back?"

He was quiet for a beat. "Maybe. There was a hole in her blouse with something red around it. Could've been blood, I guess. Probably the right size for a bullet hole, but I'm not sure."

"You testified that you had a conversation with Mr. Royal at Darrell's Diner. What was that all about?"

"I asked him to get off the case."

"What did he say?"

"He told me to go to hell and not ever bother him again."

"Did you? Bother him again?"

"No, ma'am."

"But you did talk to him just before this trial, didn't you?"

"Yeah."

"Did he tell you what to say?"

"He told me to tell the God's honest truth."

"Nothing further, Your Honor," she said. She hadn't shaken him. Home run for the defense team.

I rose. "No redirect, Your Honor."

"Call your next witness, Counselor."

"The defense calls James McNeil."

CHAPTER 53

THE PICTURE FROM the security video at Barnes & Noble had been the key to my next witness. When I had shown the photo taken from the video to Esther, she had identified the man as Ruth Bergstrom's husband, James McNeil. I didn't think his meeting with Olivia was by chance and I assumed he was discussing Ruth's cut of the book money for giving Olivia Esther's manuscript. Whatever the meeting was about, I probably wasn't going to get him to tell me anything, but he was a loose end, and I had to try and tie if off.

I knew from J.D.'s conversation with Ruth that James liked to play golf at the Glenview Country Club and played every day. On the Friday before the trial was to start on Monday, I called the pro shop and told the woman who answered that I was supposed to play with Mr. McNeil that day, but I couldn't get hold of him and I'd forgotten the tee time. She told me McNeil was scheduled to play at two p.m.

A few minutes before two, I watched four men approach the first tee. One of them matched the picture from Barnes & Noble. I approached him. "Mr. McNeil, my name is Matt Royal. We need to talk." His surprise and recognition of my name registered on his face.

"What do you think we have to talk about?" His tone was brusque, a man about to dismiss me.

"About the dead woman Biggun Steerman removed from your living room."

His face reddened, whether in anger or fear, I couldn't tell. "I don't know what you're talking about."

I lowered my voice, gave it a steely edge. "Mr. McNeil, you don't want to fuck with me. You know who I am. You can either talk to me in the restaurant over a couple of beers or we can do it at the Sumter County jail. I can have you arrested before you reach the second green."

He gave it up then, told his friends to go ahead without him, and followed me to a quiet corner in the bar. When we finished talking, the jigsaw puzzle was complete.

* * *

James McNeil took the stand and in answer to my questions identified himself. "Are you married to Ruth Bergstrom?"

"Yes."

"Do you know Kelly Gilbert?"

"Yes. She's a neighbor of ours."

"Do you know Buford Steerman, the one they call Biggun?"

"Yes."

"How do you know him?"

"I met him at my house on the night of March 13th."

"The night Olivia Lathom died?"

"Yes."

"Had you ever talked to Mr. Steerman before or after that night?"

"I called him a couple of weeks later."

"What did you say to him?"

"I told him that you were trying to railroad his grandmother, Kelly Gilbert, into a murder charge for the death of Olivia. I told him to have a talk with you, threaten you if necessary, and get you off this case."

"Did you identify yourself in that phone call?"

"No, sir. In fact, I was told to disguise my voice."

"Who told you to do that?"

"The same person who told me to make the call. Kelly Gilbert."

"Did you tell him how to find me?"

"Yes. I told him you were staying at your client's house."

"How did you know that?"

"Your client mentioned that to Kelly when she visited her in jail."

"I want you to turn your attention to the night Ms. Lathom was killed. Were you at the scene of her murder?"

"Yes."

"Where was that?"

"My house."

"Who killed her?"

He choked back a sob. "My wife."

"Ruth Bergstrom?"

"Yes."

"How did your wife kill Ms. Lathom?"

"Shot her in the back."

"Tell the jury what happened that night. How did it end up with Olivia Lathom dead?"

"It's not pretty," he said.

"Murder never is. Tell the jury what happened."

"Olivia and I were having an affair. It'd been going on for years when we all lived in Atlanta."

"Did your wife know about this?"

"I found out after Olivia's death that my wife suspected it."

"Why was Olivia at your house that night?"

"My wife was going to take a neighbor down to Orlando to the airport. She left our house about seven and I called Liv to let her know she could come over. I'd met with her briefly at the Barnes & Noble bookstore before her signing and had arranged it."

"Had there been any bad blood between your wife and Ms. Lathom before the night of her death?"

"Yes. My wife had given Liv a manuscript that had been written by your client, Esther Higgins. Liv used the manuscript to get a big book contract and had promised to share the proceeds with Ruth. She reneged on the deal and kept all the money. Ruth was livid about it."

"When did Ruth get back from Orlando?"

"She didn't go all the way there. Her friend got a call from the airline just as they were getting on the turnpike telling her that the flight was delayed until the next morning. They turned around and came home. Ruth showed up about eight o'clock."

"What did she find when she came home?"

"She found Liv and me in bed."

"Were you having sex?"

"Yes."

"Do you know that the medical examiner found no evidence of Ms. Lathom having sex just before her death?"

"I used a condom."

"What happened when Ruth caught you?"

"She grabbed a gun out of a kitchen cabinet and came into the bedroom. She was screaming that she was going to kill Liv."

"Did the gun belong to you?"

"No. I assumed it belonged to Kelly. She's the one who left it with Ruth. Said she had somebody's small child coming for a visit and she didn't want the gun around while the kid was there."

"What happened?"

"Liv tried to calm Ruth down. Ruth was screaming about the book money and being in bed with me. Liv told her that if they could just sit and talk they could get past all this. I remember her telling Ruth, 'You don't love James. You've told me that for years and that you two don't have a sex life.' She said she was sorry for the affair, but there was a lot of money left from the advance on the book.

She said she'd give Ruth half of it and she could leave me and start life over somewhere."

"Did Ruth calm down?"

"Yes, but she still had the gun. We got dressed and went into the living room, and I thought everything was okay. Ruth was walking behind Liv and still holding the gun on her. And all of a sudden, it was like something went off in Ruth's head. She hollered at Liv, called her a bitch, and pulled the trigger. Shot her in the back, and Liv fell forward onto the sofa."

"What did you do?"

"I got the hell out of there. I figured I'd be next. I ran down the street to Kelly's house to call the police. Kelly talked me out of it, and we went back to my house. Ruth was sitting in a chair, calm as a cucumber. Kelly kind of took over and called her grandson Buford to come get the body and take it back to Georgia and bury it. She said she'd take care of the gun. She stayed with us for several hours until her grandson arrived and we loaded the body into his van and he took off. We didn't know until the next day that the idiot had dropped the body off in Paddock Square."

"How did Olivia get to your house?"

"She drove."

"Where's the car she came in?"

"In my garage under a tarp."

"How did you come up with the story implicating Esther Higgins?"

"That was Kelly's idea. When she asked Ruth about the book, Ruth told her the story of copying Esther's manuscript and giving it to Liv and about the money Liv was supposed to pay her for it. Kelly told us the gun actually belonged to Esther and she would fix that so it pointed to Esther as the killer."

"Did you know that Kelly Gilbert arranged for her other grandson, Lionel, to call your neighbor and pretend to be from the airline and say that the flight had been canceled?"

"I didn't know that until you told me."

"Did you know that Kelly had been a contestant in the Miss Georgia Pageant forty years ago and was cheated out of the title by Olivia Lathom, whose name was then Polly Norris?"

"Not until you told me about it."

"Would it seem to you, knowing what you know now, that Kelly Gilbert orchestrated this whole thing? She had the gun ready for Ruth's use, she arranged for the phone call to ensure that Ruth got home in time to catch you in bed with Ms. Lathom, she arranged for the body to disappear, and she came up with the idea to frame my client, Esther Higgins."

"It does now."

"No further questions."

Meredith had made no objections and some of my questions were at least borderline improper. I was sure she must have something held in reserve that would attack James' credibility, perhaps destroy it. She rose. "Your Honor, may we address the court outside the presence of the jury?"

Judge Gallagher agreed and asked the court deputy to escort the jury out of the courtroom.

"Your Honor," Meredith said. "The gentleman in the suit in the back of the room is a Sumter County Deputy Sheriff, a detective. I'd like your permission for him to arrest Mr. McNeil and take him to jail. He's admitted to several crimes today. Charges will be forthcoming from my office."

"Detective," the judge said, "come do your duty."

"Your Honor, Mr. Royal," Meredith said. "I would like to explain to the court and to Mr. Royal what is going on."

"I'd be interested in that myself," the judge said. "Proceed."

"Yesterday, Mr. Royal's investigator met with Sheriff Cornett and told him about the evidence that would be produced today and invited the sheriff to come to court. He decided to send one of his detectives to sit here all day and watch what was going on. I didn't know anything about this until we took the afternoon break. I got a call from my boss who told me to make no objections to Mr. McNeil's testimony. In the words of the state attorney, I was to let him hang himself."

"He did that," the judge said. "What now?"

"I am instructed to dismiss all charges against Ms. Higgins with prejudice."

"That's your prerogative, Ms. Evans," the judge said. "You don't need my okay, but I would also caution you that jeopardy has attached, not that it'll make much difference, given your dismissal."

"I'm aware of that, Your Honor. I don't want there to be any question in the record."

The dismissal with prejudice meant that Esther was free. Once the jury was empaneled, jeopardy attached, which meant that by dismissing the case, if the state tried to bring it again, it would be barred by the US Constitutional prohibition against double jeopardy. In any case, the dismissal with prejudice would cover the issue as well. We had won.

The judge called the jury back into the box and advised them that the state had dismissed all claims against Esther Higgins and that she was free to go. He thanked them for their service and adjourned the court.

I had noticed that J.D. had slipped into the courtroom while I had Biggun on the stand. After the judge left the bench, she came through the rail and hugged her aunt and then her boyfriend, me. Esther had tears in her eyes as she joined us in a group hug. "Ah, Matt," she said. "You've given me my life back. How can I ever thank you?"

"Can I keep J.D.?" I asked.

"I don't see why not."

"That's all the thanks I need."

"You could make an honest woman out of her, you know."

"She has a standing offer. You can help convince her to take me up on it."

Esther laughed. "Higgins women are tough."

"They are, but they're worth it," I said and kissed Esther on the cheek and walked out of the courtroom arm in arm with the last two women of the Higgins clan.

CHAPTER 54

THERE WAS A short delay while Esther was checked out of the county jail and picked up her belongings. The sheriff had made sure the procedure went smoothly and quickly. Within a few minutes, J.D. and I were in my Explorer driving Esther to The Villages and home. J.D. had called ahead and her neighbors were holding an impromptu party in her driveway. Somebody had even stuck a plastic flamingo in the front yard.

Esther had hugged me and broken down in tears as Judge Gallagher adjourned the court. It was the first sign of distress I'd seen in her in the seven weeks she'd been in jail facing the possibility of a life sentence.

As we pulled into the driveway, my phone rang. The caller ID told me it was Meredith. I knew how it felt to lose a case and I hesitated to answer. I didn't want to say anything to this outstanding prosecutor that would leave her with the impression I was gloating. Finally, I decided it would be rude to ignore her. I answered.

"You glorious bastard," she said. "You owe me some whiskey."

"What's your poison?"

"Bourbon."

"Maker's Mark or Wild Turkey?"

"Ah, the good stuff. Either will do just fine."

"Why don't you come down to Longboat to drink it? You haven't met my girl J.D. yet, and she has a condo that you're welcome to use. She can bunk in with me."

"Is she the pretty blond who was in the courtroom today?"

"She is, except the blond is a disguise. She's a brunette and will be again as soon a her hair grows out."

"I won't even ask why she needs a disguise."

"Come on down and we'll fill you in. Maybe the boss will give you some time off. You sure as hell have been busy this week."

"I'd like to do that, Counselor. When would be a convenient time?"

"J.D. and I are going home tomorrow morning. You're welcome anytime after that."

"Thanks, buddy. I can sure do with some R & R."

"We'll be looking for you."

J.D. and Esther had gotten out of the car and joined the party. J.D. gave me a questioning look as I approached and I whispered, "That was Meredith. I invited her to Longboat and offered her your condo."

"That sounds like a good idea. Only, I'll have to sleep with you."

"And that's bad?"

"Nah. I can live with it for a few days, I guess."

The mob of neighbors shifted away from Esther and came over to congratulate me. There were hugs all around as I told them that J.D. had done all the legwork. She demurred, but the questions started to flow and we spent the rest of the evening giving them a blow-by-blow account of the investigation and the trial.

Toward the end of the evening, as the neighbors started to drift toward home, a car drove up in front of Esther's house. A man got out and walked toward me. It took me a minute to recognize him, but when I did, I detached myself and went to meet him. He gave me a bear hug, and said, "So Florida's best lawyer once more kicks some Sumter County ass."

"It always helps to have an innocent client," I said. "I've never tried a case up here without one."

"A little bit of luck never hurt anybody. Come on and introduce me to your girl."

I led him over to J.D. and said, "This is the woman I love, J. D. Duncan. J.D., this is an old friend. Jeff Carpenter."

"Dr. Jeff Carpenter?"

"Matt knew me better as the defendant Jeff Carpenter."

"Sheriff Cornett told me all about you and what you did for his daughter," J.D. said. "It really is a pleasure to meet you. Can I get you a drink?"

"No, thanks. I just came by to congratulate Matt. I've been following this case pretty closely, but I've stayed away. I didn't want to jinx your brilliant friend here."

"Thanks for coming by, Jeff," I said. "It means a lot."

"I can never repay you for what you did for me, my friend. Invite me to the wedding."

"As soon as she agrees to marry me, I'll let you know."

We slept in Esther's guest room that night, enjoyed the breakfast our hostess cooked, and said our good-byes. We stopped in Bushnell to get J.D.'s Camry and began our two-car convoy back to paradise.

CHAPTER 55

In May, Longboat Key turns into a somnolent little island peopled mostly by the year-rounders, the twenty-five hundred or so of us who make this tiny slice of paradise our permanent home. It is a quiet time, lodged between the end of the snowbird tourist season and the smaller onslaught of summer vacationers from the interior of Florida. Around the middle of the month, our annual scourge, humidity, envelops us and hangs around until mid-October. We handle it with the help of cool Gulf waters and air-conditioned bars and restaurants.

A week after the trial, Meredith Evans took me up on my invitation and came to visit for a couple of days. We didn't talk much about the trial, but we did drink a lot of good bourbon and told stories of our lives in courtrooms. Meredith and J.D. took to each other, as they say, and became friends.

As the month wore on, Meredith kept us up to date on the aftermath of the trial. Buford Steerman was the first to make a deal. He pleaded guilty to one count of moving a dead body and agreed to serve three years in prison in return for testifying against Ruth Bergstrom and Kelly Gilbert. His brother, Chunk, whose only crime was the assault on me, agreed to testify to what little he knew and I agreed not to press any charges. He was free to go back to his chicken farm.

James McNeil, Ruth Bergstrom's husband, was charged with being an accessory after the fact of murder because he did not report the crime. However, Sheriff Cornett and the state attorney, Meredith's boss, had a conversation with him the evening before I put him on the witness stand, and offered him a deal. If James would testify truthfully in Esther's trial and then plead guilty to the charge, the state would agree to a sentence of two years of probation. James would not go to jail.

Ruth pleaded guilty to second-degree murder and was sentenced to twenty-five years to life in prison. At her age, she'd probably never see the outside of the penitentiary. The charge of theft of Esther's manuscript was dropped in return for her admitting that she had stolen the book with the intention of splitting the royalties with Olivia Lathom. The admission would ensure that Esther would reach a settlement with the publishing company.

Kelly Gilbert, also known as Sally Steerman and before that as Sarah Kyle, walked out of the courtroom the day she testified and disappeared. She had not been found despite the nationwide search for her. Several calls a day came into the Sumter County Sheriff's Office reporting that Kelly had been seen in Miami, or Atlanta, or Columbia, South Carolina, or any number of small towns all over the country. The only trace of her was a letter she mailed to Esther from Atlanta. In it, Kelly apologized to Esther for causing her so much grief, but once she realized that Polly and Olivia were the same person, she had to do something. She admitted to her part in setting up the murder.

Kelly told Esther that shortly after Olivia Lathom's book was published, she was chatting with Ruth Bergstrom about the excitement generated by the book's success. Ruth was detailing her long association with Olivia and told Kelly that Olivia had once mentioned in passing that she had held the title of Miss Georgia. Ruth thought

Olivia was lying, but Kelly began to look into it. Given Olivia's age, Kelly assumed that she had been Miss Georgia within a one-to-three-year period before the pageant in which Kelly had competed as Sarah Kyle.

Her research turned up no trace of anybody named Olivia Lathom ever having won the Miss Georgia crown. However, the more she looked at photographs of Olivia, the more she became convinced that Olivia was in fact Polly Norris, the winner of the pageant that Kelly should have won. When she heard that Olivia was coming to The Villages, she set her plan in motion.

Kelly felt that her life had been ruined by the actions of Polly Norris at the Miss Georgia Pageant all those years before. As she grew older, her bitterness grew, and once she was on the trail of Olivia, she became certain that the two women were the same person. Olivia was Polly, and Polly was responsible for the shambles that the life of the young woman from Nashville, Georgia, had become. The irony of the situation was that Kelly could never have been sure that Olivia was Polly forty years later, although Gary Burris' magic computers did seem to confirm that fact.

Kelly wrote that she knew she was in trouble after she was cross-examined by me. She left town and found a hotel on the interstate near the Georgia line. She holed up and read everything she could about the trial. She was aware of James' testimony. Kelly was a very smart woman and had hidden her tracks well, but the testimony of James McNeil was damning. She was sure that Esther had put things together and was going to testify about the subterfuge Kelly used in getting Esther's prints on the gun, Kelly's access to Esther's house, and her knowledge of the times that the house would be empty while Esther was teaching reading at the elementary school. She knew the evidence of her guilt was piling up.

Kelly thought the elaborate preparations she'd made to hide her complicity in the murder would protect her. In the end, it didn't, and she fled. By the end of May, she was still a fugitive and the law enforcement agencies had intensified their efforts, so far to no avail.

The cops were still trying to find a trail that would lead to solving the mystery of who Polly Norris really was and where she came from and where Olivia had been in the years between the Miss Georgia Pageant and her marriage to Danny Lathom. That effort was petering out since it was not important to the murder investigation, but the whole mystery would probably join the lore that included questions about D.B. Cooper and other notable disappearances over the years.

The company that had published *Beholden* accepted that it had been defrauded by Olivia and paid Esther the same advance and agreed to the same contract they had had with Olivia. It was time for a second printing of the book, and the cover of this one had Esther's name on it.

It was all working out. Esther was happy, some of the bad guys were in jail, Kelly was on the run, and J.D. and I were enjoying the beach bum life to which we both aspired. And I once more vowed to never again set foot in a courtroom. Life was good on Longboat Key.

EPILOGUE

ON THE LAST day of May, the beach was virtually deserted. The snowbirds had gone home and it was too early for the summer visitors from the interior of Florida. J.D. and I had jogged four miles on the packed sand left by the ebb tide, and we were walking slowly as we approached the crosswalk over the dunes near the North Shore Road beach access.

It was only a little after seven in the morning and it was already hot and humid. I could feel the sweat seeping from my wide-open pores in a vain attempt to cool my body. My breath was coming a little harder than it had the year before and new aches had found their home in places that weren't used much while sitting in a courtroom.

I glanced at J.D. She was grinning at me. "What?" I asked.

"You look kind of worn out. Did I push you too hard?"

"That'll never happen, sweetcheeks."

She grabbed hold of my arm, leaned over, and kissed me on the cheek. "I think you should call Jeff Carpenter."

"Why? You think I need a doctor?"

"No. About the wedding."

"What wedding?"

"The one on June 6th."

"Who's getting married?"

"We are."

I stopped abruptly. I must have missed something. "We're getting married?"

"Yes. On June 6th."

"And this is the first I've heard about it?"

"We don't have to, you know."

"I didn't mean that. Why is this the first I've heard about it? June 6th is next week."

"I've just decided to accept your proposal. If you haven't changed your mind, that is."

"Never. It still stands. Tell me what's going on."

"My wise aunt Esther, who knows a thing or two, told me at the party the night the trial ended that sometimes the right man comes along, and although you know he's the one, for whatever reason you're afraid to commit. And so, the day arrives when he just walks away and you spend the rest of your life regretting your indecision, your weakness. She said that you're my right man.

"She's right, of course. Lately, I've been thinking more and more about what she said, and watching you today, breathing a little harder and showing signs of aches and pains you didn't have a year ago, I realized that you're getting older, and so am I. That blazing insight reminded me of that poem by Longfellow where he writes that 'time is fleeting' and that we should 'act in the living present.' I love you, you know, and I've decided to act."

"I'm glad you decided," I said. "But why the hurry?"

"A long time ago, I read somewhere that June 6th is the most propitious day of the year to get married. The oracles say that it's a day that ensnares lovers in a marriage that lasts a lifetime. Hopefully, the road ahead of us is fifty years long and I want us to walk every step of it together."

I stood for a moment on the hot sand, looking at my girl and thinking about life and death and love and the long road ahead. She smiled and my heart did a little jig. I nodded and pulled the sweaty phone from my pocket and called Jeff Carpenter.